A CITY FOR ST. FRANCIS

Books by Evelyn Wells

A CITY FOR ST. FRANCIS

NEFERTITI

THE GENTLE KINGDOM OF GIACOMO

JED BLAINE'S WOMAN

WHAT TO NAME THE BABY

THE FORTY NINERS (with Harry Peterson)

LIFE STARTS TODAY

MEN AT THEIR WORST (with Dr. Leo Stanley)

FREMONT OLDER, A BIOGRAPHY

CHAMPAGNE DAYS OF SAN FRANCISCO

A CITY FOR ST. FRANCIS

Evelyn Wells

DOUBLEDAY & COMPANY, INC.

GARDEN CITY, NEW YORK

1967

*With the exception of actual historical
personages, the characters are entirely
the product of the author's imagination
and have no relation to any person in real life.*

Library of Congress Catalog Card Number 67–13783
Copyright © 1967 by Evelyn Wells
All Rights Reserved
Printed in the United States of America
First Edition

Dedicated
to
LeBaron R. Barker, Jr.,
Who has been patient both as editor and friend.

ACKNOWLEDGMENTS

The story of the woman I have chosen to call Susana has haunted me ever since I encountered it in the unimpeachable records of Father Palou, the friend, fellow-worker, and biographer of Junípero Serra. He makes brief mention of Susana. He does not give her name or explain what happened to her after she was made infamous by the greatest scandal ever to rock Mexico City.

No other history mentions her. I have found no reference to her in archives so kindly opened to me in California and in Mexico. Her identity may be hidden someplace in family records in Mexico or Spain, but we have no reason to know this. Authorities on the social and moral codes of her era find it difficult to believe that such a woman ever existed. But we have the word of Palou.

Why did the historian-priest fail to report the rest of her story? The moral code of that time was severe, but pity was available, even then. Mexico's greatest woman poet, the angelically beautiful nun Inés de la Cruz, had written a century before Susana's time: "Who is more at fault with an erring passion, she who falls through entreaty, or he who entreats her to fall?"

In recognition of such compassion I have given Susana the chance for survival she may not have had, and joined her to that early group of pioneers who, several years after her recorded tragedy, followed the halting steps of Serra into the Spanish-American West.

None can say now that she was not on that historic migration. There were people from Mexico City in the Anza Second Expedition. Susana and her husband may have joined the group under other names.

As is true of pioneer groups, not all the Anza colonists were angels. The expedition was made up of a variety of ethnic and social beings. Some were of Spanish descent, others were Indian. The majority was of mixed heritage. Some were highly educated, and others were ignorant. Several were dons. The majority were poor in education, social advantages, and worldly goods. Together they made up a group of cheerful and indomitable pioneers.

Dress these original San Franciscans in modern clothing and place them today on Grant or Madison avenues, and no heads would turn. They were smaller in stature than most modern Americans, but so were most of the world's people at that time.

The major differences were in their manners, which were more courteous than ours, in their speech, which was more poetic and musical, and in the fierceness of their emotions, which lay close to the surface and could flare quickly to a lethal intensity. Honor was a word to write in blood, and love a word to be pronounced in tones that trembled. But they were gentle of manner and speech.

All that we know of Susana's life was lived in the great, sophisticated capital that was famed in her time as the Paris of the Americas. If her clothing is described as worn but costly, it is because it has been my privilege to handle the collection of magnificent garments in the Castle of Chapultepec which were created for the great ladies and gentlemen of Mexico City by the leading couturiers of eighteenth-century France.

Today's visitors to Mexico are attracted by its brilliant Indian overlay and likely to overlook the rich background of its imperial past. In old houses in Mexico and in colonial adobes in California may still be found carved furniture from Spain, painted furniture from France, and oil paintings, *bibelots*, jewelry, and sacred images brought from Europe centuries ago.

Much of the background of this book has been recalled out of my California upbringing and visits into Arizona and Mexico and friendships with schoolmates who were descended from Anza colonists. There are men and women in California who say, "My people came with Anza," with the same pride other Americans take in stating, "My ancestors came on the *Mayflower*."

With these young companions, I, the non-Catholic Yankee, often attended services in several of the old missions. On one adobe wall I remember seeing the imprint of a hand. I placed my own, which was then small, in the impression, and it exactly fitted, although the print was evidently that of an adult worker who had patted into shape the adobe bricks.

The argonauts from Mexico were a singing people, like the Forty-niners who in the next century would follow them west, and in recognition of both music-loving groups I have chosen to call by the old Spanish favorite name, Susana, the girl whose personal struggle for survival is played within the larger drama of the colonization of California. She is a fictional character as related to the Anza expedition. Don Angel, Gil José, and the Perea family are also figments of my imagination. All others mentioned in this book are part of California's history and, I hope, have been treated with the deep admiration and affection I have for many of their descendants.

I have not tried to reproduce the musical cadence of the speech of these people. For those unused to Spanish, it need only be remembered that the name of Gil José as pronounced by Susana would be heard as Heel Ho-zeh', Don Angel as Dohn Ahn'-hel, Felipe as Feh-lee'-peh, and Juan as Hwan.

To refresh my impressions of the Second Expedition, I read again Bolton's classic, *Anza's California Expeditions*, with its day-by-day accounts by Father Font and Captain Anza, and the lives of Padre Junípero Serra written by Agnes Repplier and by his friend Palou.

During years of California research I have had reason to be deeply grateful to the friendly and patient staffs of the California Society of Pioneers, the California Historical Society (these in San Francisco), the Bancroft Library in Berkeley, the Huntington Library in San Marino, the Suzallo Library at the University of Washington, and the public libraries of San Francisco, Seattle, and New York. I would like to offer special tribute to the understanding aid given me in Mexico City by the authorities in charge of the archives in the National Palace and in the National Museum of History in the Castle of Chapultepec.

My affection and gratitude go as always to Mrs. Fremont Older, whose devotion to California's past stimulated my own, and to her late husband, the San Francisco editor, Fremont Older, under whose editorial guidance I sought out and interviewed many then surviving from a vanished West, among them the last survivors of Forty-nine, and the last survivor of the tragic Donner Party; the families of such great Westerners as Carillo, Vallejo, Frémont, and others who contributed to my writings on such subjects as the dancer Lola Montez in her California days, the colorful bandit Joaquín Murietta, and Kit Carson.

My special thanks go to my friend John Dougherty, the dance authority and columnist, for aiding in a literal translation of the once popular music hall favorite "La Limonera."

I am deeply grateful to Carolynn Neumann, not only for her superb copying of a most difficult manuscript, but for suggestions and encouragement possible only from one who is the possessor of a B.A. degree and an intimate knowledge of California.

The perfect California setting in which much of this book was written was the former Huntington Hartford Foundation, in Pacific Palisades.

Evelyn Wells

August

CHAPTER ONE

[1]

Mexico is one of the world's oldest cities. At night the ancient capital rises out of the valley like a reflection carved out of the moon.

The moon moves over thousands of open courtyards to see its own ruffled face staring back from their fountains and wells. It molds into glittering fountains the elms and poplars lining the quiet streets, and the ornamental trees and shrubs in the Zócalo and Alameda and a hundred other parks and plazas. It slides over the silvered Zócalo and down the cathedral towers to the street, and then, as if feeling its way, touches the forbidding stone façade of a house a few doors north of the cathedral, on the Calle de Tacuba.

Tacuba is one of the oldest streets. The house too is very old. Its severe colonial front is broken by the tall arched entrance with the iron filigree gate, by narrow bandings of Moorish tiles framing the barred lower windows, and, at one second-story window, a decorative iron balcony overhanging the street.

The grilled entrance door is locked; open, it would admit the bulkiest carriage. In the stone vestibule a hanging oil lamp fails to relieve the cavelike gloom. Beyond, a once handsome courtyard lies open and defenseless to the moon.

Once, in this patio, a pretty dappled fawn played, and small lap dogs imported from France, and sleek, self-respecting cats. Once there were dignified jeweled peacocks, and singing birds in metal and willow cages. Then the courtyard was a cleanly place and fragrant with flowering trees and plants and shrubs.

But now the moonlight discovers colonnades pitted with age, and a fountain broken and almost dry. Fruits trees stand shriveled against the walls between pottery urns that hold the dried roots of dead plants. In one corner an ancient carriage sags under the row of turkeys a-roost on its top.

Little remains here to recall the once luxurious existence of a great family. Over the neglected courtyard and the dark building has settled the affliction of neglect that marks a house long unloved.

Suddenly from the house of the fowls comes an earsplitting crowing. The sound ricochets along the colonnades and up a stone staircase to the room where the balcony overhangs the Calle de Tacuba.

Sometimes, in a rift in the jungle, one glimpses far back in the darkness a single blazing tropical flower. The woman in the room is like that. Fashionably dressed, she sits in a tall carved chair with her smooth aristocratic head held stiffly against an embossed coat of arms. She seems to glow in the shadowy room, which is furnished with ornate French baroque—a carved bed draped with worn ruby velvet, a marquetry desk, an elaborate framed Venetian mirror, and a small primitive carving of the Virgin of Guadalupe.

In this splendid but tarnished setting the woman, as revealed by the moonlight penetrating the deep-set window, seems forlorn and very young. She is in her mid-twenties. Her simply cut gown and satin slippers have the look of France and her dark heavy hair is swept up fashionably in the strained, doll-like style popularized by Marie Antoinette (the gay and idolized model of all fashionable women in Europe and the Americas). The gold cross and broad wedding band are the only jewelry she wears. She sits with great eyes fixed on the scrollwork of the balcony with the rigid attentiveness of one who is afraid.

She has started to the cry of the cock, and now, settling back, hears from every part of the city the responsive crowing from other courtyards, the whisperings of waking birds, and the faint strum of a guitar. These are broken fragments of sound coaxed out of the sleeping city by the moon. The guitar music swells and is joined by those of a flute and violin, and out of the Zócalo and down the Calle de Tacuba staggers a little band of musicians, lamenting in minor undertones their lack of grace and loss of love. The woman's look follows them as they make their way toward the Alameda.

To such a woman, to be alone is to be afraid, and this one has known much loneliness. What does a woman think about when she dares not remember? Of the seal of warm lips and of heartbeat and a voice breaking with longing? Are these too evil to be cherished, when they are all she has left?

And for a moment the woman's face glows with tenderness and is inexpressibly beautiful, then the night is riven by the clangor of bells in the cathedral towers a few doors away, dolorous and terrifying.

She cannot escape and she cannot pray, for she is the Señora Susana María de la Luz Galván, the infamous young wife of that scion of Spanish nobility Don Angel Galván, and she will have reason to remember the passing of this midnight in the city of Mexico, in the year 1775.

[2]

On this second day of August now beginning, the first members of a group of American pilgrims known as the Anza colonists would bivouac with their tents and herds at the Presidio de San Miguel de Horcasitas, above San José de Pimas, in Sonora.

Susana knew nothing of these people. She only knew herself to be the saddest and loneliest woman in all Mexico, and as the clamor of bells faded on the outer rim of the city, she rose slowly and, with the movements of one in sleep, opened the Spanish commode and chose from the garments there an embroidered linen robe.

Under its scented folds she removed the tightly bodiced dress of heavy black silk, the undergarments of finely stitched lawn, the corselet, front-laced and whaleboned, the tiny black satin slippers, and the knee-high stockings of knitted white silk, inset with lace medallions.

Not once during this modest disrobing did she turn her back to the window.

It had grown quite dark in the room.

When dressed for sleep she reseated herself in the high-backed chair. Sitting with her bare feet off the tiled floor as a child might, she began removing the shell pins and combs from the elaborate coiffure. Her hands wove the thick waterfall of silky black into braids that almost touched the floor.

Then she sat motionless as before, with eyes fixed on the iron scroll that was almost invisible now outside the darkening window. So long and fearful had been the waiting that her expression did not change at the sound of a horse's weary stumbling up the Calle de Tacuba.

The wife of Don Angel knew that sound, and her body shrank to the imperious tattoo of a whip handle at the street gate, Tomito's bare feet scuffling over the courtyard, his surly query and a sharper answer, and the grating of a heavy iron door over stones. Still she waited, until spurs clattered along the upper corridor. Then she slipped soundlessly from the chair and into the great bed, where she lay huddled under the velvet cover with only part of her face showing and with eyes closed as if in sleep.

Don Angel made a great deal of noise coming into the room. He struck flint and set a dozen tapers flaring. Muted colors sprang out of the darkness, the ruby velvet of the bed, the lighter reds and golds of tapestries.

He was leaning over her, holding the candelabra so that thick drops of the tallow showered the velvet. She looked up at a man so tall his head seemed lost in shadow, and held in such a way it seemed out of proportion, as if a bird's head sat on the shoulders of a man. The candlelight accented this illusion by shadowing to an arch the curved nose set between deep lines, the gray unwavering eyes, and the jaw and forehead so narrow they seemed not to be fleshed, but carved of thinnest bone.

Many at first glance considered Don Angel one of the handsomest of men, for he carried his spare frame with the hauteur of one who thinks well of himself and his bearing and physique were of the kind often seen in antique Spanish portraits. But closer survey brought out detracting details, for the thin locks clung to a too narrow skull, the features were so colorless they seemed pinched from tallow, and the flint-sharp eyes were set too far back in their sockets to be capable of expressing tenderness. The frill of his linen shirt was yellowed with snuff and the skirted coat of yellow brocade and tight brown trousers were in such disarray that over Don Angel, as over his house, neglect showed like a spreading stain.

All this Susana noted, staring up at him like a witless child. "You have not slept, my heart?"

The gallant inquiry was almost playful. She made no answer, for there was never any answer. She lay pinned by the poniard look, waiting for the taunt or accusation, whichever it might be.

Instead, surprisingly, he sighed deeply and, turning, set the candles on the table with such violence that the flames leaped. Then, flinging himself into the tall chair, he stretched out his long legs and stared morosely into space.

"Damnation to this night," she heard him mutter.

She slipped without sound from the bed and knelt before him. She could turn her back to the window now that she was no longer alone. He did not seem to notice as she drew the spurred boots from the high-arched narrow feet and the silk knitted hose from the thin white shanks.

For a time both were silent and she remained on her knees, not knowing whether to speak or move.

The man was warm from riding, but she saw his long frame trembling as if with cold. Then from the tight thin lips came disjointed words.

"*Así*, it was to be expected. As if I knew . . . what more could happen to me? Vara by vara! Peso by peso! Stone by stone! Land and buildings and herds. Stolen, I say! Stolen."

He had lost at the cockfights again, she thought vaguely, for her mind could not accept problems beyond its understanding. How could a woman know how stone walls and tile roofs and wide pastures that had been held by a family for centuries slipped from a man's hands? Family fortunes did not melt overnight in Mexico. They grew with the years and the families grew and flourished.

She had learned to accept without judgment Don Angel's many misfortunes. Even in this house that had been her father's she had seen vanish, one by one, valuable furnishings that had been brought to America by ancestors from Castile. Nearly all the salons and bedrooms of this second story, the "family floor," had been emptied, and how often Susana had opened the velvet case to find dowry jewels missing. She had seen old family servants dismissed with no provision made for their futures, until only Quita and the lickspittle Tomito were left on the courtyard floor. She knew that Don Angel had been an impoverished grandee before their marriage and it was her dowry which had temporarily made him rich again. But all had slipped through his hands and the greater share had been lost long before the occurrence which he would never permit her to forget.

But, vara by vara, he had said. Stone by stone. The long hands gripping the thin knees were beaded with nervous sweat. This was a Don Angel she did not know.

Momentarily she forgot caution. "Don Angel, have there been robbers again at the hacienda?"

Her voice was low, as of one unused to speaking, but it served to draw the attention of the man.

"You may ask that, my wife. Yes, let us say—robbers again."

He sprang to his feet and glared down at her. Her eyes closed and her head bowed. Now it begins, she knew, always and ever this way. She tried to make herself invisible.

But the words drove down.

"You? To ask how possessions can be lost? You who opened my doors and threw all that was mine to the thieves? To question me—you who have cost me everything? What woman are you, to question! When from the beginning, from the first hour I saw you as a woman without pride or honor . . ."

(I was not that woman, my husband. I was a child. Have you forgotten the first time you came to this house, which was then my father's? I thought you taller than the cathedral towers and brighter than fire, so that I could not bear to look at you, and I ran and hid in Quita's arms. After you went away, my father told me you were pleased with me and thought I would be beautiful and he said you had spoken for me. And because my father was old and my mother had died, we were affianced, and it was you who put me into the Convent of Viscaines to wait until you came for me. And I was five years old. Ten years I waited, and they were happy years because many other girls in the school had also been placed there by their *novios*, until they were old enough to marry. When you thought me old enough you brought me back to this house, where of all I remembered only Quita remained; and the house was yours and I was yours—yet never yours, because by the time I became the woman you wanted you were no longer a man . . .)

"Look at me!" Don Angel saw her thoughts were not on his, and thrust his face down. "You are not listening! What are you plotting against me? What evil plans were you hatching when I came on you now in the dark?"

The only escape was in silence. She continued to kneel, white and remote in the clinging gown, with her head dragged down by the heavy braids.

"Tell me!" The tone became softer. "My orange flowerlet, my bride. Tell me, where was the beginning? In the cloisters? At the altar? In this house, where I first saw you playing with your hoop in the courtyard? Tell me, were you tainted then?"

She knew he was pointing to the terrifying open blackness of the window, where no moonlight showed, and the balcony was hidden.

"With a man of my own rank"—he was striding the floor now, striking his hands together, and she knew his rage was mounting to the familiar crisis—"that I might have understood—forgiven even—for such matters have been forgiven—yes, even in this city and in the proudest families! But pride has no meaning and honor has none, when a farm-raised brute is given preference, and why? Who can understand why?"

And he came back to her again, towering over her.

"I should have killed you then!" he was saying.

She sensed the beaklike thrusting of the head. She bent her own lower, mute in acceptance of the two moralities, one of which is for women and one for men. And by either of these, yes, she should have died at his hands. Then, there would have been an honorable burial worthy of the Galván crypt, with her dishonored body covered with jewels and flowers. He would have shown her mercy, dead; he could never show her living. And she knew he was pointing again to the night-black window overlooking the Calle de Tacuba.

"Yes, out there! Your body should have hung beside his, for the city to see. Tell me, are you never afraid? When you are alone, my wife, do you hear the creak of the riata on the balcony? Do you see him as you saw him that morning, when I dragged you to the balcony to make you watch his body swinging like carrion from the rail? And below in the street the people staring? Did he have eyes for you then? Think back, Susana! Or brazen as you are, have you forgotten?"

And, suddenly, the way an August storm can change over the

valley, his voice changed so completely, it was as if another man, not Don Angel, were speaking.

For he saw her body break with anguish, the hands go to her eyes and mouth, and only then, content, did he seem willing to release her, and spoke with no more than his usual querulousness.

"An end to this. Men will be here early tomorrow to assess our possessions. To think that even this house is lost!"

At the moment the enormity of his statement did not reach Susana, whose stiffly bowed body in the long gown went limp with relief now the volcano of wrath had ebbed, and she was quickly on her feet aiding Don Angel's impatient movements as he removed outer garments that were stained with dust and gave forth a tired smell of age. In the tight linen underclothing Don Angel appeared almost fleshless, and shriveled by exhaustion and his years. He was almost twice Susana's age and in the candle-light he looked older. Now that his anger was spent she need no longer fear him.

"To bed with you," he said peevishly. "Listen, it is almost morning."

From far across the city, over the canals, came the faint cries of the boatmen bringing the first produce to the opening markets.

She watched from the great bed as the narrow white figure strode to the window and closed it. Turning to the table, Don Angel cupped the candles and began blowing them out one by one. Over the last of the pointed flames she saw his face, un-fleshed by the light, and his eyes were those of a condemned man she had once seen facing the muskets against the walls of the palace. She waited. He was not without reason, when the anger ended.

"There is a still a way," he said at last. "There is always another risk to be taken by a man of courage. I have remembered . . ."

Was he speaking to himself? She listened, knowing he would tell what he willed.

"Yes! The king himself offers salvation to those who are very brave or very poor. Which am I? Both! So I will bow my knee and accept the royal pittance offered by King Carlos—I who have paid many times as much for a single bull!"

He glared at her over the dancing flames as if surprised to find her listening.

"You are startled, señora? Then look at me, Don Angel Galván, but no, not don, but emigrant. A simple colonist, and why not? My ancestors were conquistadors, and such blood as theirs made Mexico famed as the crown of Spain. Now another crown is to be added, and let me tell you, you who never heed what goes on in our world, that our monarch has eyes that see in every direction. He knows Mexico's danger, and is ordering our frontiers to be thrust farther north into the very jaws of Russia! Viceroy Bucareli has ordered, Captain Anza will lead the way, and the Russian bear will be forced to consider before it claws again at a Spanish frontier. It is decided. We are to colonize California."

The name dropped like a stone into her thoughts, for what meaning did it have for her? A threat, perhaps some sort of warning? But Don Angel warmed to his thoughts.

"Yes, I will sign with the group meeting at Horcasitas in Sonora. A great honor, to join an expedition such as Anza's. With such a captain setting up establishments on the frontier, then let Russia look our way! The bear will see everywhere the banners of Spain's lions . . .

"Do not look for luxuries, woman! It will be a long and trying journey and there are no inns beyond San Miguel de Allende. The way is without roads and settlements and there are pagans lying in wait to take our lives. For my part, I had rather see more guns carried to the frontier, instead of the cross. But credit the padre with wisdom though he is a priest, for it is he who has pointed out the Russian danger and persuaded our viceroy to convince the king that California must be colonized. In that empty land a man of my experience will be valued—a ranchero who can direct men in the matters every hacienda owner knows and can teach others. With my knowledge and the grant promised by King Carlos there can be another Galván hacienda and a greater fortune!"

Susana was only aware that Don Angel had made mention of a priest.

He was still boasting, ". . . the journey is in the nature of a pilgrimage, to build a settlement farthest north in California. It will be named in honor of St. Francis."

She was certain then.

"Don Angel," her voice was so low he scarcely heard, "must I go with you?"

She saw his expression change.

"Padre Junípero Serra has returned from California and the plan to colonize California is of his making. Surely you have not forgotten the good padre! By the Wounds, he will remember you! So you see, my wife, California is not the empty place you have thought it, for your fame will have gone before and will be waiting for you and he will be waiting."

So saying, he pursed his thin lips and blew out the candle but her eyes remained wide to the dark, seeing again the face of Padre Junípero Serra.

[3]

She had seen it the first time on the day, six years before, that ended life for Susana and made her the most notorious young woman in all Mexico.

They had been returning from noontime mass at the cathedral, she and the servant, Quita, and were making their way through the milling groups filling the Zócalo with sound and color. Holding small nosegays of pungent rosemary, mint, and veronica against their noses to fend off fever, they chatted together like birds set free.

Impossible not to feel hearts lighten, away from the gloom of the Galván house! Threading the great plaza, they exchanged swiftly murmured confidences with heads close, Quita's in the plain black *rebozo*, Susana's, with the high, shining coiffure draped in black lace. They seemed unaware they were not alone, and this was a pity, for around them in the clear light of noon the ancient streets raced with life.

By God's grace this space of freedom was theirs, and in the short walk to and from the cathedral mistress and maid could exchange confidences. While a *señora* of Susana's position was not supposed to stroll in the streets but should always be seen in her carriage, still she might, if demurely dressed, promenade the short distance to church with a duenna, and Quita was a dragon among duennas.

Susana walked in a rustle of full and fashionable black silk, and her face was glowing with life under the shadowing mantilla. In her secret happiness she saw little of the city's tumult sweeping around them, for she walked deep in love.

Only the babies held Susana's attention and the great eyes under the lace mantilla warmed with delight to each *niña* they passed.

Her voice trailed into tenderness as she bent over a tiny Indian baby sitting solemn and stiff as an idol on the stones by its vendor mother. Her hands moved like doves over the small dark head.

"Wickedness!" Quita murmured. "You should have a child. He might be kinder if you had a son—so proud he is of the family name."

A familiar dread knotted under Susana's heart, but she controlled herself with the skill of long practice and walked on.

The crowd seemed larger than usual and much of the human current was flowing out of the great plaza in one direction, which was toward the church of the College of San Fernando.

So reluctant were the two women to return to the dark gloom of the house on Tacuba that they found themselves following in the wake of the crowd, and it was Quita who said, recalling the gossip of the early morning markets, "These people are on their way to hear the little saint from Majorca who is a guest at the college. It would do our souls good to listen, *doña*. Surely Don Angel will not scold if we hear a sermon preached by the evangelist who is the talk of the city."

Susana permitted herself to be led to the plaza fronting the Franciscan college, where by this time a multitude had gathered. Women with heads covered, men with head bared, and nearly all with large cloth scapulars hung on backs and shoulders, were fingering rosary beads and crucifixes and muttering prayers, while all eyes were fixed in reverence on a small monk in a faded gray robe who stood on the church steps with his tonsured head bowed and his spectacled eyes closed in silent prayer.

With the nosegay pressed to her mouth to prevent any infection that might be rampant in such a crowded place, Susana studied the silent figure on the steps. The famed evangelist was such a little man, for all his vaunted greatness! She was not prepared for the shock of seeing the overly large head lift suddenly, revealing a pale and boyish countenance. Enormous eyes behind glasses seemed to flash across the plaza directly into her own. It was part of Serra's power that every person in the crowded square felt that burning gaze as a personal accusation. But it was Susana who shrank first before the flame.

The prayer she had been reciting mechanically died on her lips. She stared at the small figure that seemed to grow taller and more threatening and contain a supernatural power.

"Repent!" The Franciscan's sudden shout pierced the air. The cry seemed meant for her alone. The small sunburned hand of the monk leveled in the torn sleeve; over all that crowd it seemed to point only to her.

Of the many hundreds there, Padre Junípero Serra had looked first to Susana and read the markings on her soul. So it seemed to the terrified young wife of Don Angel.

"Can you look at me and not know your guilt?" Yes, the words were only for her and there was a threat in the strangely pitched voice. "Think then of having to carry your sin before the face of God! I am his humblest servant, but if I can look into your heart and see in it the devouring worm of evil, think of the hour when you must face the lightning in His eyes! Consider yourself as you lift your heart bursting with sin to the throne! Sin! Abomination! Evil! Call it by another name if you will, even dare to call it love, but you and I know the truth of it and the truth can never be hidden. You may have thought lightly of sin. You may have considered it the amusement of an hour or the night, to be forgotten by morning. But God will not let you forget! Never! Not during all the millions of years of suffering will you be allowed to forget . . ."

The voice was thunderous, coming from a man so small. The great eyes blazed. Susana swayed, scorched by the flame of the evangelist's words, of his look. That which had been beautiful was seared by evil. She did not know she was not alone in her panic and that many around her burst out in prolonged wailing. All who listened to Padre Junípero Serra fell under the spell of fear so great that each one seemed to be standing alone in a circle of hell-fire.

"Has your hand ever been burned by fire?" The little monk was crying over the wailing of the multitude. "Have you seared your fingers on a cook pot on the hearth? Then you know the suffering given by Brother Fire, our benefactor and our punisher. You know how fire can hurt! You pour olive oil over your burned fingers and perhaps in the morning the pain is gone. But the agony created by sin can never be eased and its burns can never be healed. No oil can comfort you in the everlasting flames of hell!" The Franciscan's voice lifted higher over the wave of moaning that rocked the plaza. The leveled finger was a sword pointing straight at Susana's heart.

"*Sí, siempre!* Forever! That is a word your thoughts cannot grasp because your mind is rotted by sin. Before you are condemned to face the everlasting fire you must think on that word—everlasting. You must repent! You must drive out sin! Remember the fire!"

"God have mercy on us," groaned the listeners.

"Remember the fire!" shouted Serra. "Look forward, O children lost to sin, to the hell yawning under your feet. Remember the fire! Your nails will curl into your feet and hands, your flesh will blacken and peel from your bones, your bones will be charred and your eyes and hair burst into flames. Who will hear your cries for mercy there, where even the ears of God are sealed? Who will pour water on the flames that devour you and will continue to devour you forever, while you die ten thousand deaths and still cannot die, you cannot perish, you cannot escape the flames, no, not through all the million years of hell!

"But now is not too late! Now is the hour of your salvation! Now is the final hour in which to beg for divine mercy and forgiveness and peace everlasting in heaven! Repent now, O sinful ones, now as I pray for you! Repent . . . repent . . . repent!"

The howled command pursued Susana as she fled through the wailing crowd followed by the terrified Quita. It continued to ring in her ears as she wept all day in the room overlooking Tacuba Street. Then she knew what must be done.

Not for the sake of her own soul, but for that of the lad she loved.

Because his eternal life was forfeit she could be strong. She could stand in the barred entrance to the street that night, seeing him dark and strong and beautiful in the shadow. Because she loved him she could make her words ring like iron. "You must not come to this house again. We must never see one another again."

He could not believe. To save him, she fought her tears and lied cruelly. "Go then because of the truth—I have tired of your love." Then she fled back into the dark house where before he had been welcomed, brought there from the country, in truth, by Don Angel himself after a day when he had watched them dancing together at the hacienda—mistress and vaquero dancing together as was the annual custom. Don Angel had apparently condoned an affair that began in mutual shyness and mounted to exquisite happiness. Susana, on her knees in her room, did not see the lad's lagging departure down Tacuba Street.

That night the old house was shaken to its foundations by one of the most violent earthquakes ever to visit Mexico City. The worst temblor of the century, it was said later. So that neither she nor Don Angel heard when the boy returned and climbed to the balcony and, tying his riata to the iron scrolls, hanged himself at the window of their room.

"Look to your lover now!" Don Angel's scream wakened Susana that morning, he having been torn from sleep by the steady moaning of the crowd that filled Tacuba, for apparently all the city had crowded into the street to see the body of the young man from the country who had died at his mistress's window. And all Mexico would know that this repentance and death were due to the powerful preachings of Serra, and the tragedy added to the fame of the evangelist from Majorca.

"Let all see you!" Don Angel, beside himself, shouted while dragging her to the window. And then, "Look down, harlot, and see what you have done to that which was a man!" She had looked and seen the dark and dearly loved head twisted against the rope. She heard the creak of the riata as the body she loved turned slowly, dreadfully, in the wind. But she did not hear Don Angel's continued imprecations or the long-drawn cry of horror the crowd gave at sight of her.

"Repent!" Serra had shouted. The terrible command had been for her alone, and she had repented, with knees worn harsh with remorse and eyes burned dry of tears, until all that remained of Susana on this August night in 1775 was a small still figure with hands folded over the white gown, dead but not dead, living but not quite alive.

Now the name of Serra had returned the past terrors and foretold others. There would be no more wondering. For Susana the expedition to California would be no ordinary pilgrimage but a march of doom, and at the end of the world the dread figure of Serra would be waiting like that of an avenging angel.

September

CHAPTER TWO

[1]

More than a month later a small, dejected figure might have been seen sitting on a dusty portmanteau surrounded by baskets, on a field skirting the northern pueblo of San Miguel de Horcasitas. It would have been difficult for anyone to recognize this Susana as the elegant young woman of Mexico City.

The smooth, rather childish features were gray with exhaustion and dust. The great eyes were shadowed with weariness under the wide-brimmed straw traveling hat that was tied with an ordinary black *rebozo*. Dust grayed the thick black woolen traveling cloak falling in folds from her throat to the worn leather slippers. She appeared now a tired young countrywoman, but the discerning eye might have noticed differences in the look of inexpressible sadness, the gracefulness of the exhausted body, the still-untouched softness of her hands.

Her weariness was understandable. In the past few weeks she and Don Angel had traveled more than a thousand miles to this rendezvous near what would be the northern border of Mexico. And Horcasitas was but the starting point for the Anza Second Expedition (also known as the San Francisco Expedition). From this place the colonists would set out on the actual pilgrimage of another thousand exhausting miles. Tired, thirsty, hungry, Susana stared dull-eyed at her surroundings.

Horcasitas lacked the charm of antiquity, having been founded only a quarter century before. Still it was not without importance, for it was the capital of Sonora and the home of the governor and above all, this September, it was the trysting place of the colonists preparing to set out for California under the leadership of Mexico's greatest military hero, Captain Juan Bautista de Anza.

Outside the town on the almost treeless plain was a temporary canvas village made up of several large army tents and a dozen or more smaller-sized field tents. These were the expeditionary tents, and in them the travelers would sleep like the soldiers of fortune they were.

Nearly one hundred men, women, and children of the Anza group were in the camp. With the exception of Susana, all on the field were occupied with a myriad of last-minute tasks. There was excitement in the air, born of the adventure ahead and the new possessions given by the king—more than any had ever owned before—to these families of soldiers and volunteers Anza had recruited in Sonora and Sinaloa.

Susana found little to interest her in her fellow-travelers, pledged to the colonizing of the newly found bay of San Francisco. All were strangers to her, and, if Don Angel had his way, all would remain strangers. Her incurious gaze went past the camp to the pueblo where in the sun-baked plaza facing the church two lines of soldiers were marching.

The tall, authoritative figure in the long leather military coat shouting drill orders to the marchers—could that be any other than Anza? A dim excitement penetrated Susana's weariness. Certainly a great deal was going on in this dusty border town! She turned to the scene around her as if aware of it for the first time.

The activity seemed to be centered on the stores of equipment and provisions heaped before every family tent. All had been chosen and purchased for the colonists by Anza after Antonio Maria Bucareli, the viceroy in Mexico City, had finally succeeded in wringing funds for these future San Franciscans out of the Spanish crown. "They must be newly outfitted from shoes to hair ribbons," Bucareli had impressed upon Anza, and Anza had purchased wisely and well. The truly splendid results were these materials and the herds grazing around the encampment under the watchful eyes of several dozen horsemen. Hundreds of horses, mules, and beef cattle were cropping the sweet new grass born of the early autumn rains; in fact, September had been chosen as the rendezvous month because of its good pasturage. And all these domestic animals, like the goods, were the property of the Anza colonists, given them in the name of their king, Carlos III of Spain.

Small wonder the mood in the encampment was of well-being and happiness! One might have thought these people were preparing to set out for a *marienda*—a picnic to be held a few miles away—instead of a dangerous, uncomfortable journey through a thousand empty miles.

The men jested as they sorted the new bridles and saddles and farming implements and blankets and muskets. The soft voices of women rose over the new kitchen wares and the bolts of bright cotton and gray linen chosen for them by Anza. The children wore bright new *camisas* as they ran between the tents with the dogs racing after them.

To the dispirited Susana these cheerful, hopeful people belonged to another world. Her head sank under the large hat, her shoulders drooped, and by one of those magic lantern changes that had made the past years bearable, she was no longer on this alien field. She was home, in the house on the Calle de Tacuba, and it was the last morning.

The old bulky carriage in the courtyard had been scrubbed outside and in by Tomito, and packed with the meager possessions Don Angel's creditors were permitting him to take from the old house.

"Woman!" came the peevish shout of Don Angel from the courtyard. "We leave! Now!"

She looked for the last time to the window and went down the stone steps to the place where the carriage and Don Angel and Tomito were waiting.

The door to the *cocina* was open, but Quita was not to be seen.

Don Angel was waiting with the sulky Tomito beside the overburdened carriage. In one of those bewildering reversals of mood that were impossible to anticipate or understand, Don Angel was almost amiable. He thrust a clenched hand toward Susana.

"Give these," he said, "to your friend in the kitchen. They will serve to keep the old cow from the abattoir."

With these careless words he provided life for Quita, who might otherwise have died of hunger in the streets as other aged

servants had been known to die after lifetimes of service. The
pearls from La Paz were Susana's and it did not occur to her to
question Don Angel's right to give them, since by law they belonged to his creditors. But her fears for Quita were over. That
afternoon Quita would ride one of the pack mules with the ore
train that left the plaza daily to return to the western mines.
Quita would live out her remaining years in modest comfort in
Taxco, the silver town in the mountains where she had been born.

Susana remembered nothing of the actual departure from the
old house that had been her only home. For as the carriage
lumbered out of the gloomy courtyard and into the brightness of
the city, with axles groaning and Tomito perched glum as an owl
in the driver's seat, Susana in imagination was still held in the
comfort of old arms as brittle as dry weeds.

They were late in starting, and the warm light rain of Mexico's
summer afternoons began as the heavy carriage dragged its way
under the hill of the Grasshopper. Reality returned swiftly and
painfully to Susana with a curt command from Don Angel.

"Look back, woman, and see for the last time the city you
have lost to me."

She looked through the dusty window and this moment she
would remember. Behind the moving carriage she saw the great
city of Mexico fall away into the receding plateau, and vanish
there with all its spires and towers, followed by the twin peaks
of the volcanoes that are the breasts of Mother Mexico. It was
as if the level floor of the valley rose, submerging forever the
great city.

El Camino Real was the finest highway in North America and
the pride of Mexico. To Susana it was harsh and endless, deeply
rutted, deep in dust, and crossed here and there by trails
broken by cattle herds and wild beasts. In places they met with
vast herds tended by incurious vaqueros, or a lone rider drew his
horse to the side of the road to make way for them. Several
times they met omnibuses laden with travelers from upper Sonora.

There was little conversation in the Galván carriage. The
mildewed upholstery and damaged springs were trials to the flesh
and spirit, and the two horses snorted continual protest at being
compelled to pull a vehicle intended to be drawn by four.

They were an oddly assorted pair. Major, a handsome black
gelding, was Don Angel's saddle horse and had never before been

forced into harness. He protested with every means he knew, balking, snapping his teeth, and attempting to fight his way free. Once when the cursing Tomito was trying to back him into position, he reared and, screaming, hammered with his hoofs on the carriage shaft as if it were some loathed enemy. Don Angel was unexpectedly lenient.

"A pity, old friend," he told the magnificent, shuddering creature. "You and I know what it is to be forced into labor beneath our dignity."

The companion in harness presented a curious contrast to the elegant Major. This was a small dusty brown mare, shaggy and squarely built, of the type known as a desert pony. Despite her small size, she did far more work than her temperamental harness mate. In her younger years she had pulled a solid-wheeled *carreta* at the Galván hacienda and had learned early that life held little for one born in peonage.

"You!" So Tomito spoke to her, or "Pig of a she horse." To such addresses she shook her hammer head with an air of boredom, not minding, apparently, that she had never been given a name.

It was heavy pulling through the thick dust. When, as sometimes happened, they reached a riverlet or spring, the two horses swelled their bellies with water.

There were nights when the Galván man and wife slept as best they could in the carriage, while Tomito lay rolled in his serape beside the road in a circle made by his riata, which he hoped would prevent attacks from snakes.

Tomito became more surly day by day and coughed a great deal. He was finding it difficult to breathe in the heavy atmosphere of the plains. Many Indians died in the lowlands after leaving the high pure air of Mexico City, and Tomito was Indian.

So it had gone with them for a thousand miles, until the Galván carriage came to a shuddering halt on the field at Horcasitas in Sonora that was the place of the Anza rendezvous.

"Speak to no person and let no hand touch our goods," Don Angel warned before driving off into the village with Tomito to attend to the sale of the carriage. Anza had forbidden vehicles. Only horses and mules could carry the colonists into roadless California.

Susana settled tiredly on the portmanteau with the baskets at her feet and watched without emotion the departure of the unwieldy vehicle with its faded gilt and crimson coat of arms on the doors. One hour went by and another. Susana rechecked the baskets, lingering over one containing the dried figs that were Don Angel's special luxury, to be shared with no one, certainly not with his wife.

Still she eyed them hungrily, for it was late afternoon and there had been no food since the bitter breakfast chocolate prepared by Tomito. The other baskets held only remains of withered vegetables and spoiled fruits, but she knew better than to touch the figs. Nor had she the courage to desert her post and investigate the encampment, where so much was going on.

Only a few of the people around Susana were idle. Before a nearby fire a young man lay with his head against the swollen lap of a young woman. Her *rebozo* shielded their heads, but his dark hands could be seen flashing among the wet leather strips he was skillfully braiding into a riata. Newly married beyond doubt, Susana decided, and preparing to set out together to found a family in a strange land. She sighed and turned her attention to a curiously assorted trio at the next fire.

There a woman squatted on a tule mat holding a small child against her knees. She was a thick short woman with hair that showed threads of gray, and in her many skirts and voluminous *rebozo* she looked round as a gourd. Across the fire was a young man—or was he older than he seemed?—who was also of rotund appearance and who was obviously her son. He lay against a bundle of cured hides, plucking the strings of a guitar that rested across his stomach, and half singing in an undertone as if making up both words and music. He was regarding Susana with an expression like that of a sleepy cat. She realized with a thrust of anxiety that he had been watching her for some time, probably since the departure of Don Angel.

To escape his attention, Susana stood up quickly and shook herself free of the bulky cloak. The movement only added to the interest being shown by the singer, perhaps by the grace of the movements made by the slim body or in the careless way she let the cloak fall as if expecting it to be caught by some watchful servant. For in another moment his song reached her and the words were clear:

> The little one, the lonely one,
> Rides by the tall grandee;
> I wonder why a lady joins
> Our humble company?

At this the woman scowled and her voice was like the snapping of twigs. "No mischief, my son. You make trouble enough with your doggerel, for yourself and for me."

Now another man approached, walking briskly and smiling, and Susana saw he was a Franciscan monk, sandaled and tonsured and wearing the gray robe of his order, and the white rope belt from which hung a crucifix. He came up to the woman and said in a pleasant voice that held undertones of sternness, "Love God, my daughter. And what is it you do to this little one?"

The woman scrambled to her feet, pulling up the child, and even Susana could see the small ears bore streaks of blood. But the little girl smiled like a cherub as the Franciscan touched her head.

The guitar was soundless.

"Little Father, I have only pierced her ears." The woman spoke too quickly. "With her parents' permission! Every *niña* must have the ears pierced, for what are ears to a woman without rings?"

"A maguey needle was used?"

"True. A sharp point from our good sister the maguey that gives us needles and thread and rope, and food for the stomachs of our cattle, and pulque for our own. . . ."

"Heed me!" The Franciscan did not rebuke her claim to kinship with the useful cactus because this woman was partly Indian, and Indians in common with St. Francis were given to claiming relationship with all that lived. So where a priest of another order might have scolded, this one did not. Also, Padre Font was experienced in the ways of voluble women and in the difficult art of keeping them to the subject at hand.

So he interrupted her. "Since you have done this, why does the child not weep?"

"Good little Father, why should she shed tears? I have

pierced the ears of many small girls and not one has wept. By
my soul, it is a skill."

"That I know," the friar answered with remarkable patience.
"I know much about you and what you do. I know you are
famed from Tacuba to San Blas as Tía María the herb woman,
and that you are the wife of Nicolás Perea the muleteer, and
mother to this Felipe, who is a shoemaker and a maker of music.
A *trovador!*" The Franciscan smiled unexpectedly. "I too am a
lover of music—you may know."

"We know," agreed the woman with what appeared to the
listening Susana to be sly amusement. "This son of mine, *ya! ya!*
A minstrel and idler. But a good shoemaker! He will be of
use in California. How often I tell this Felipe he must work
harder, but no, he must sing the hours *adios* and play games
with Gil José the soldier—"

"My concern is not with your Felipe and his friends," the
padre interrupted in a way that showed he was losing patience.
"My daughter, my concern is with you. I am told you know the
names and uses of every leaf and root and seed. Granted there
are many useful properties to be found in certain plants. But we
also know God has placed other herbs in the earth for His own
reasons that some medicine women have used for such abomina-
tions as love potions and fertility charms and even for the
termination of unborn life. Such a woman is likely to discover
the laws of the Church are just and severe."

"Good Father," the woman answered in a low voice, "it is
true that the cactus needle was dipped in the juice of a plant
that denies pain. To keep tears from the eyes of a little child,
tell me, can that be a sin against God?"

The child looked from the face of the woman to that of the
priest and put her finger in her mouth and smiled.

"I only say," observed the Franciscan, "that there are herb
women who use their knowledge for evil."

"By the soul of my mother who taught me, I am no such
woman," said Tía María, seemingly close to tears.

"See to it that you are not. Such a woman would have no
place in our expedition. We are going to a pagan land and carrying faith with us, not superstition. Faith, science, and culture are
the leading virtues of Spain. For centuries Mexico City has been
the center of these, and out of Mexico City Spanish culture has

spread all over the Spanish Americas. Now it is our privilege to carry it into heathen California."

Over the open, amiable countenance of Tía María there fell, like a dark curtain, a look as sullen and secretive as an idol's. Padre Font had often seen that look on Indian faces. It held centuries of stubborn pride and the determination to cling to ancient faiths and dignities even if threatened by death.

"The ways I know are also very old," the woman said proudly. All warmth was gone from her face and voice. "The mothers of my mother taught these things they knew long ago. Long ago, as they have told us, when Mexico City was Indian. When Mexico City was built by my people!"

"That I know, Daughter!" Padre Font was not to be caught in this trap, which had been set for him many times before by Indian converts. He would not argue the fact that Mexico City as built by the ancient Aztecs had probably been the most beautiful of all the world's cities, for it had housed many gods, but not the only and all-important god. He took refuge in a sternness that provided for no further argument. "What you were taught served your people long before white men came to America. But we live in an advanced century and a modern world. Your skill is admirable, but on this expedition it will not be needed. The Academy of Medicine in Mexico City is the world center of medical knowledge—its new school of surgery equals any in Europe—and its doctors have provided our good Captain Anza with a chest filled with the newest medicines and instructions for treating any who may fall ill on our way. A calamity we hope to fend off with our prayers!"

Then he smiled with great kindness and patted the child on her head and she ran off laughing to her own family, and he gave mother and son the sign of blessing and one last warning shake of the head.

"Let us love God," he said forgivingly, and then, impishly, to the herb woman, "In my country, which is Catalonia, the old women pinched the small ears against a cork. Then the lobes did not feel pain. That is also an old method. Try it. It works as well as your own."

The herb woman smiled with all resentment gone, and murmuring, again, "Let us love God," the priest turned Susana's way.

Susana lowered her head under the large hat in the hope of escaping notice. She had recognized the salutation (St. John's gentle greeting) which Padre Junípero Serra and his brother Franciscans had made famous from his native Majorca to California's bay of Monterey. It told her the friendly little priest was an emissary of Serra. If as simple a creature as the herb woman could fall under his suspicion, what part could the wife of Don Angel Galván have in a blessed pilgrimage?

So she sat as if invisible on the portmanteau until she heard the kindly words repeated over her head. "Love God! You are new to our company, little Daughter?"

Susana rose then and bowed with respect and dread, and the padre, seeing her distress, explained at some length that he was Fra Pedro Font, a Francisco missionary stationed at the mission of San José de Pimas, which was about fifty miles east of Hermosillo, and that he was to accompany the Anza Expedition as its chaplain. Because she still seemed too distraught to speak or even understand what he was saying, Father Font explained cheerfully that, while Captain Anza would attend to the colonists' physical security and needs on the long journey, he would look after their souls.

Susana was able to give him her name and explain that she was the wife of the colonist Angel Galván. It seemed to her that a change came over the friar as she pronounced the Galván name, but Padre Font gave no verbal hint of having heard it before or of having any knowledge of the infamous events in the Calle de Tacuba.

"You are from La Ciudad?" he asked, and wondered at her sudden pallor as she admitted sadly that, yes, she was from Mexico City. He had guessed that by her speech, with its almost Castilian softness, which was different from that spoken in other parts of Mexico. Shrewdly, without seeming to do so, the Franciscan studied the small figure in the countrified hat and gown; obviously a woman of good family, but curiously troubled.

Nor did she have the manner of a *pobladora*. Now if she were an officer's wife, instead of a colonist's . . . the wife of Anza carried herself with no greater dignity. But the look of dread was unmistakable. Father Font was trained in knowledge of the human frailties. He studied the small and perfect features, the clear ivory skin, the dark melancholy eyes, and the delicate hands, one weighted by the thick marriage band. The long earrings and cross too were of heaviest gold and the slender feet were shod in slippers worn but costly, as was apparent even to a Franciscan vowed to poverty. The slender shoulders seemed to carry an intolerable burden.

To put her at ease, Father Font chatted on, explaining that although he was Spanish born he also considered himself of Mexico City, having studied there in the College of San Fernando. But at this information, Susana's eyes widened in horror, seeing again the stone steps of the old church where the robed figure was standing, and the finger of accusation pointing . . . "Repent!"

Many times in the dim confessional Father Font had looked at the abject image of fear. But why was it here, in this place, on the eve of the sacred pilgrimage in the person of this attractive young woman?

He knew this was not the time to attempt understanding. Instead he spoke cheerfully.

"Try not to be heartsick for your city, little Daughter. You and your husband are fortunate to have arrived just in time, for all our Horcasitas group is here and anxious to set out. We would have left by now were it not for unpardonable delays." Father Font frowned, recalling the nature of these delays. "We will set out at any hour for Tubac, where the rest of our party is waiting. We hope to start from there on October fourth, which is the feast day of our blessed St. Francis."

Then he smiled with a gentleness that might have won her heart, but her eyes were on the dust at his sandaled feet. Father Font's legendary cheerfulness was being severely tested. Susana gave no sign of having heard. She was both grateful and relieved when he made the sign of blessing over her bowed head and walked briskly away.

[2]

Father Font, pursuing his sandaled way over the rain-greened earth, gave thought to the herb woman and her son and their sad little neighbor.

No matter how vehement her protests, Tía María's knowl-

edge of herbs put her under suspicion, for it is against nature not
to use wisdom once it is acquired.

The son's glibness of tongue and glint of eye might well be-
speak the mischief maker. There was always danger of hornet's
venom in as large and mixed a group as Anza's.

Most puzzling was the young woman Susana . . . the priest
frowned as he recalled their attempt at conversation.

Una niña perdida, thought the Franciscan, for in this active,
cheerful camp the unhappiness of Susana seemed that of a lost
child.

It was her lack of interest that puzzled, not her lack of knowledge, for even in this enlightened year 1775 little was known
about California. Father Font was considered one of the most
brilliant graduates of the College of San Fernando, but the California legend was not much clearer to him than to Susana.

California was the country everybody talked about and nobody
knew. For centuries men had argued—was it an island or group of
islands, a peninsula or a lost kingdom? Cortez, claiming it sight
unseen for Spain, had reported it on hearsay as being an island
populated only by women. Many still believed it to be the fabulous country ruled by Amazonian queens who lived in cities of
gold as described in the sixteenth-century novel by Ordóñez de
Montalvo—the book from which Cortez took its name. Even the
meaning of that name, California, was unknown.

Island, or fabled kingdom, Font thought with satisfaction, the
argument would soon be settled now that California was to be
explored and colonized. As a Christian country, it could be made
safe against enemy invasion. San Francisco was to be the most
northerly rampart set up by Spain in the long struggle to hold
California.

These colonists around him on the field were more than pioneers. They were crusaders, chosen to hurl Spain's challenge in
the teeth of her deadliest enemies.

Russia! The padre's lips drew down. Yes, that had been the
danger, ever since the discovery of America. The Russian bear,
she-wolf, she-monster, was slavering with lechery and greed.
Shocking reports concerning Catherine the Great had reached
even into the cloistered recesses of San Fernando. Catherine,
whose appetite for men and countries was insatiable, had pio-
neered the colonizing of Alaska and was now reportedly planning

to extend her colonies down the Pacific coast, making California a subsidiary territory of Russia.

France, too, licked greedy lips on the sidelines, and England never ceased to threaten. Father Font subdued un-Christian thoughts of Sir Francis Drake, "that British pirate," who while cruising the California coast in his *Golden Hind* had dared to lay claim to California in the name of Elizabeth, his so-called Virgin Queen! Not once in the past two centuries had Spain's California been safe, and now, in this most civilized eighteenth century, the danger was greater than ever before.

No wonder this was known as "the century of conflict!" France and England were not only locked together in a death struggle for world domination, but each was fighting within itself for survival. Why, even here in North America, in that odd little cluster of English colonies on the eastern coast, armed opposition was threatening the British crown! The reports that had reached Mexico City were incredible. One curious incident concerned bales of tea tossed into the harbor of a town called Boston. Father Font had heard of violent scenes at other places with harsh English names—Concord and Lexington and Bunker Hill. Certainly, worried the priest, walking faster, if England could not hold her own colonies she would covet Spain's, and as for Russia, the Russians always wanted anything and everything, and although they lived farther away than any other people on earth, somehow they always managed to seem dangerously close.

And whose voice had cried loudest against the danger? Father Font's pride soared, for it had been that of his beloved friend and spiritual leader Father Junípero Serra. Ever since Serra's arrival in Mexico in 1750 from his native Majorca the fiery evangelist had preached and pleaded that Spain's California coast be protected by colonization and its Indian population salvaged by baptism.

There were other, less publicized reasons for favoring the Anza project. Serra and Font and their brotherhood, being priests, were close to the hearts of the people. They knew that among the younger politicians of Mexico City there was developing a movement, impossible at present to pinpoint, urging Mexican independence from Mother Spain. Safety lay in the expansion of territories and power if the supremacy of imperial Spain was to hold.

Serra's powerful warnings and Anza's urgings had fired Bucareli, the Viceroy of Mexico, into pleading with the king for the defense of endangered California. Their combined arguments had at last been heeded in Madrid. Junípero Serra was now *padre presidente* of the fragile, newly founded chain of adobe missions set far apart in Alta California, inadequately guarded by their mud presidios since, to Serra's regret, the cross must always be protected by the sword.

Father Font recalled the triumphant day, only six years before, when on July 16, 1769, Serra had given his inaugural blessing to the cross of San Diego de Alcalá, (the first mission in the northern part of California). Now along the lonely California coast were other missions bearing the melodious names of saints—Font repeated them as if reciting his beads—San Diego de Alcalá, San Carlos Borromeo (on the Río de Carmelo near the presidio of Monterey), San Antonio de Padua, San Gabriel Arcángel, and lastly, San Luis Obispo, completed three years before, in 1772 (missions that Serra and Anza dreamed would in time become cities). Since then no new missions had been built in California, and the pressing need was to establish the one honoring Serra's patron saint, the gentle St. Francis of Assisi.

The hope of building of San Francisco was the shared dream of Serra and Anza. The two friends had fought together to break down the red-tape entanglements that Mexico City politicians had raised against further colonizing in California.

Father Font sighed. How many obstacles had been set in St. Francis's way! One marveled less at what had been accomplished in the past six years than that anything had been done at all. But who could doubt the power of prayer?

A trumpet sounded. Shading his eyes against the almost level rays of the lowering sun, Father Font looked to the plaza, where the soldiers were noisily breaking up from afternoon drill. Their plumed leader was shouting orders for dismissal. Font regarded with affection the tall figure of Anza. How different was this officer from other military leaders, particularly certain troublemakers stationed in California who had tormented Serra by hampering his efforts to convert the Indians!

Parfait knight sans reproach, so Font thought of Anza. Leader in peace as in battle, prince of pathfinders, and above all, Serra's friend. The Franciscan Font was vowed to poverty and to peace, but he felt only admiration for the heroic soldier who had succeeded in bringing together the colonists of the second expedition.

How varied they were, men and women, civilian and soldier, long-legged children and babes in arms! Father Font looked with affection at the darkly hopeful faces, noting the eagerness in the gentle voices and the air of pleasure and excitement permeating the camp, for word had spread, and not for the first time, that they were soon to be on their way. How courageous they were, he thought, how eager to turn westward (as had Cortez), riding horses descended from the mounts brought into the New World by the conquistadors. In the veins of many of these people ran the blood of those conquerors, while others were descended from the proud and brilliant Indian nations that had once owned Mexico; in the majority the blood of both had mingled in long-forgotten ways. In this venture for St. Francis peon and grandee would ride side by side.

To the compassionate priest, each was a mystery to be solved in time. Father Font resolved to trust to the length and trials of the journey to California to enable him to examine their souls.

[3]

Father Font had not underestimated the cleverness of Tía María. The herb woman was learned in ways of plants and the human heart, and she recognized despair when she saw it. She continued her preparations for the evening meal. For Father Font had turned in the entrance to his tent and was looking back across the field, and Tía María did not care to add to his obvious suspicions that she was a busybody.

Susana had lifted her head when the trumpet sounded, but lowered it again as if the great hat were too wearisome a burden. Under its protection she heard the cries of the dispersing soldiers and then the sudden musical patter of the late afternoon rain. She lifted her face to catch the drops on her dry lips, but the rain stopped as suddenly as it had started.

The patting sound continued.

She looked over to her neighbor. The herb woman was slapping lumps of wet corn meal between her capable hands and shaping them into the tortillas she was baking on a large iron pan set into the open fire.

Tía María saw Susana looking her way, and at that moment Father Font disappeared into his tent. At once she scrambled to her feet and bustled over to Susana, for she was kind of heart, and also, like her son, she was as curious as a monkey or a cat.

"You are alone?" she asked needlessly, and without waiting for an answer rushed on, "Our fire is yours if you will visit us, and the food is waiting . . . hungry and tired, yes, I can tell, and alone, and I too am alone with only my singing burro of a son. If you will join us since your father has left you . . . not your father?" She read Susana's dismay. "An uncle? Not a husband certainly?"

Her amazement was no tribute to the absent Don Angel.

"So, your husband. However that is, you have been left alone."

Somehow she had Susana off the trunk and was driving her ahead to her own camp with motherly flappings of the full skirt as if she were shooing a small, bewildered hen.

The son Felipe rose from his mat, only slightly embarrassed in meeting the stranger for whom he had made up the questionable couplet.

"My worthlessness of a son," so Tía María introduced him, beaming on him in a way that resembled the sun rising over a mesa.

His smile flashed white.

"Our home is yours." He spoke as politely as his mother, although theirs was no house but a tent piled around with goods and bundles of cowhide and provisions. There were also bags of seeds and bundles of herbs and saplings labeled with symbols of the herb woman's designing, since she could neither read nor write. Still the place was made homelike by the good smells coming from the iron and earthen pots in the fire, and the *petate* mats were spread in a most inviting way.

Susana murmured her thanks, liking the musician better at close range, where his curiosity melted into friendly interest. She settled on a tule mat before the fire and accepted a tortilla cooked to a fragrant gold and wrapped around hot baked pumpkin and meat cooked with beans and hot peppers. It was of such flavor as Susana had never tasted.

To offset the delicious sharpness of the food was the pleasure of water poured from a large red clay olla bedewed by evaporation. Due to the hours of thirst and to shyness Susana could not voice her appreciation, but she ate and drank with a childish greed, and her great eyes followed with awe Tía María's skillful movements with the pots and pans.

With Tía María, body and face and movements went in circles. Her many skirts cascaded in fluted lines around her active body so that in appearance she resembled a ripe squash. Her short hair swung around her round head as she talked. And she talked almost incessantly, with small feet and hands and *rebozo*-draped curves of breasts and belly moving in excited rhythm with her speech.

From the mother one looked to the son, thinking, so alike they were, here is one I have seen before! For the man was his mother in masculine shape, round in body and with a face that broke into a dark moon when he laughed. And he laughed a great deal of the time, when he was not singing. Happiness seemed to ooze from Felipe Perea and, like his mother, he took pleasure in all he saw and heard, and a great deal of this without too much thought he promptly made into song. His attentive eyes often contained a look of mischief that sometimes rode close to malice.

"If you will forgive me," he said, and, sinking to the ground again and striking the guitar, he swung it past an attentive ear to make certain the notes rang true. "I am composing a song," he explained, "to be sung as we set out on our journey, which is to say, if we ever set out on our journey."

"This son of mine," Tía María scolded while she beamed on the object of her disapproval, "lazy as a lizard on a warm rock and always patting that guitar, like one stroking a cat."

Felipe only smiled and said agreeably, "You must concede I make her purr, little Mother. But the *señora* should also be told I am useful in other ways. There will be a demand for my skill as a maker and mender of shoes on the rough way into California, where there are no roads."

Both mother and son pretended not to see as Susana drew her feet quickly under her long skirts to conceal the shabbiness of her slippers.

"*Perezoso!*" The mother was trying to rescue Susana from embarrassment. "Not in the least resembling his father, who is a man of few words and much energy, being a muleteer with the army and one of the best of men. Nicolás Perea is his name, and we are from Culiacán, in Sinaloa, where we lived many years in marriage and had many children. And of them some were taken by the Virgin, who loves children, to sit safely in her lap forever, and others are married and have children of their own. So we two old ones are setting out together with only this laziest of music makers to companion us in a strange land."

But there were sweetness and love in the scolding voice. Susana would soon learn that Tía María's natural affection often wore a disguise.

As for the son, Susana would discover that to Felipe Perea all things had only so much value, which was their capacity for being set to music. Always curious and amused, he could never be alone while his guitar was in his hands and he could be found under almost any circumstances plucking away at its strings.

Now under his breath he resumed the making of the song that foretold the impending *jornada* to Tubac, and the fearlessness of the Anza colonists, and how many there were and their intimate histories, and the names of these people and the names of their horses. This song, like nearly all Felipe's songs, would be forgotten as soon as it was sung.

All the time his sleepy feline eyes were fixed on Susana. It could be seen that Felipe's mind was as intent on their guest as it was on his saga of the Anza Second Expedition.

Meanwhile Tía María, that friendly one, bustled about plying Susana with good food and much information, which she was willing both to take and to give. Much that she was saying concerned her own occupation and family affairs. These Susana already knew from overhearing the herb woman's conversation with Father Font. Susana learned that while the Pereas had arrived only two days before, the names, personalities, and histories of every colonist in the camp were already well known to the herb woman, and so were those of most of the inhabitants of Horcasitas. Even as Tía María bustled and chattered she kept ears and eyes open to all that was going on about them.

The scene was as colorful as a country circus. The soldiers were leaving the plaza for their barracks in the village or to rejoin their families in camp. Among the groups leaving the village Susana saw no sign of Tomito or Don Angel.

It was almost possible to forget their existence in the comfortable presence of the herb woman and the son's muted music and the consolation of food and drink after hours of loneliness and thirst and hunger. Also the stone *metate* for grinding chile and corn and chocolate recalled to Susana the kitchen on Tacuba Street and the loved presence of Quita. So it came as a shock to have Tía María interrupt her own gossip with the abrupt demand: "And your name, and your husband's name?"

The query was so unexpected that before Susana knew she had stammered the answer.

"I am Susana María de la Luz, wife of Don Angel Galván."

"A don?" Now there was no kindness in the herb woman's voice, only a chilling suspicion. The guitar music stopped. "In truth a grandee! And the other man?"

"Our servant," whispered Susana.

"And the carriage? A large one." The woman who had been all friendliness was now colder than any stranger. "So. *Ricos!*"

"Not rich! We are very poor." Susana wrenched out the words, realizing how thoughtlessly she had disobeyed Don Angel's orders to speak to no one. If only she had not come to this fire, exposed herself to this relentless questioning . . .

"Poor? *Pobrecita!*" The herb woman touched Susana's *rebozo* as if recognizing the original cost of the travel-worn fabric. In her voice were centuries of helpless suspicion and hatred for the oppressors. "And where," the opaque eyes were all Indian now, and bleak as stone, "tell me, where have you lived out your years of poverty before joining our poor group being driven to the ends of earth?"

"La Ciudad," whispered Susana.

From the guitar came a brief dissonant chord.

"From Mexico itself!" The woman made no attempt to hide her resentment. "I have heard much of that great city. Is it true, all they tell of it?"

"I do not know what is said." Susana remained with the food halfway to her lips.

"Only that the roofs of the houses are of purest thick gold and inside the churches one cannot see for being blinded by the jewels and silver and gold. And that even the clothing worn by the saints is heavy with jewels." Then, angrily, "It must be true since your jewelry is not of the silver most of us wear, but gold.

Then your carriage with the crown on the door, and a husband who has no uniform but carries a sword, and a manservant. No, only one who is wealthy can be so poor . . . a rich woman!"

The scorn in her voice was like that in Don Angel's, hissing: "You—you have impoverished me!"

Tía María and her son saw the change in Susana's face.

"*Niña!*" the herb woman exclaimed. "What is it you see that frightens you? Dear girl, it is nothing, you are with friends . . ."

Susana became aware of mother and son regarding her with shocked concern.

Moved by the younger woman's despair, Tía María was suddenly all tenderness.

"Little one, you are white with hunger and no wonder, sitting those bad hours in the sun. Now eat your good food, for no more questions will be asked, and if they are, there is no need to answer. Nicolás Perea, who is my husband, tells me he is so silent because I talk for two."

Susana felt that the herb woman liked her and gradually the fear left her. She took another mouthful of the food and was again released to hunger, scraping the plate clean with the last folded tortilla as she had seen Quita do and somehow managing to convey to the remorseful Tía María her thanks for the supper and her inability to eat more.

But the voluble Tía María was off on other matters by this time, the people around her being the pages of a book she flipped to and fro, pausing to scan a few lines from each page. This family and that, she said, pointing to one tent, and then another, were known to her in Sinaloa and several like the Galváns were from Mexico City, where they had not known one another. But the majority were from this region of Sonora or from Sinaloa, and Tía María named them for Susana down to the smallest babe in arms.

While Tía María spoke at length of her neighbors, Susana listened with a dawning realization that she too was a colonist and her life would be shared with these people.

Tía María pointed to the next tent, where the young husband made no further pretense at braiding his riata but lay with his head in his young wife's lap with his face turned up to hers, and the girl's face over his wore a madonna look, and when the *rebozo* fell back one saw how great she was with child.

Tía María nodded toward the pregnant woman and said complacently, "That pod is about to burst! We will have a new colonist somewhere along the way, and there will be others." On her fingers she ticked off the women of the expedition who were to be mothers, and the months each had to wait.

"Dreadful!" said Susana, thinking of a birth beside a trail.

The herb woman asked sharply, "You have not been married long?"

"Many years," said Susana, and dropped her eyes as if the question, or the answer, were somehow shameful.

The herb woman studied her carefully and said no more.

Susana felt that with every minute she remained in this comfortable place she was adding to her betrayal of Don Angel. It was nearing twilight and the sun was dropping over the flat roofs of the village, and she shivered at the oncoming of night with its inevitable loneliness.

She said awkwardly, "I must leave you; I must watch our goods. One thousand thanks."

Her speech was stumbling. But Tía María's eyes grew warm with understanding and she spoke as if to a child.

"Now I have frightened you again with my questioning and after promising I would not. Ah, it does not matter. Who you are, where you are from, is of interest to me only because I like you. In this company most of us are beginning again, my husband and I out of poverty and you and your husband perhaps out of wealth or its loss, but either way, it is over for us all and the past, when we leave this place, will remain here. So sit with us and not alone, and be patient with me, for truly, I am clumsy and old and talk too much, but I want to be your friend, and we will have need of friends, for before us is a long journey, and when it ends we will all be strangers in a strange land."

Then she offered Susana the ripe peeled fruit of a cactus, urging, "Eat this. It cools the throat after chile."

Susana found the ruby-fleshed fruit refreshingly sweet after the peppery meat, and she ate it with a look trusting but timid. When she had finished she sat staring into the fire, and gave a long quavering sigh.

"You are tired," the woman said, watching.

Susana started as if from sleep.

"Yes," she admitted.

"It will soon be night and your husband will return. My husband will be here too, and Gil José." And Tía María added by way of explanation, "Our compadre Gil José, like ourselves, is from Culiacán. He has his meals with us and shares his soldier's rations, since he has no family. He is my son's friend of a lifetime, and ours. But unlike my worthless son, Gil José has done many things. Last year he traveled as far as California. That was with Captain Anza on the First Epedition . . . here he is now, the dear man."

Susana was bewildered, not understanding whether Tía María spoke now of the son or her husband or Anza or the unknown Gil José. The herb woman was looking out over the field where the herds were grazing, and happiness seemed to warm her like the last rays of the sun. "See, Susana, he has left the mules. Dear man, he will be hungry. . . ."

Tía María used Susana's name as simply as if they had always known one another, and Susana would soon learn this was the custom in the Anza group. Formality would be forgotten on this trek to the frontier, but politeness was retained. Susana saw a man approach who was short and muscular and evidently possessed of great physical strength. His mestizo features were badly scarred and the bridge of his nose was flat, a mutilation which Susana would learn had been caused by the hoof of a recalcitrant mule. He acknowledged his wife's bustling introduction to Susana courteously, but without speaking. His silence added to his air of restrained strength.

Father and son sat together beyond the fire opposite Susana, and for a time there was only the clash of iron spoons on pottery. The herb woman would not eat her own meal until the men had finished, nor was she content to let them eat in peace.

"What word of our leaving, my husband?" she demanded, but the quiet man only mopped at his plate with a tortilla and wriggled his broad shoulders.

"There is no talk of departure?" Tía María persisted, and when her husband again shrugged away all knowledge, she looked with frustration at Susana as if to show the helplessness of the normally curious when confronted by one who refuses to tell what he knows.

"There is talk," said the son, to tease his mother. "Is there not always, little Mother, where you are?"

At this the father lifted heavy lids to look sternly at his grown son, who subsided like a scolded child.

"Someone knows," said Tía María impatiently. "Someone close to our captain will have heard a rumor . . ."

"Rumor!" the father spoke for the first time. "Sometimes I look this rumor in the face and it is the face of my wife."

Tía María bent a thumb and forefinger together and waved them under her husband's nose.

"One pinch of pride I give myself! One only! Never have I been known to gossip."

"You know the uses of herbs," retorted the man. "Do you know of one that will stop the steady flapping of a tongue?"

"Better to speak much than never," retorted his wife smartly, while the son grinned at Susana, rolling up his eyes to signify that such badinage was to be expected in this family circle. But Susana was lost in wonder that a wife could speak so and no wrath show on either side; instead, the husband who seemed so silent and dour mellowed under the warming processes of food and fire and the unrelenting chatter of his wife.

"I speak when I have something to say," Tía María continued in the most virtuous of tones, "and I have this to say, which everyone in the expedition is saying, that all this confusion and delay is not to be blamed on our captain but on the wife of our captain, who clings to him and will not let him leave. A wish any wife can understand . . . but with so many people anxious to start it seems shameful to have Doña Ana shedding tears that are enough to wear down a heart of stone which our good Captain Anza does not have." Tía María noticed her husband had stopped eating and wound up with some haste, "For my part I know nothing, but that is what is being said in the tents."

The muleteer looked at his wife as if helplessness robbed him of speech. He had no gift for words.

So he said loudly, "While we eat, let there be peace." And there followed a dull interim of silence that could only be blamed on Nicolás Perea.

But Susana felt her heart open to the muleteer, who seemed a kindly person for all his surliness and was apparently willing to prevent the spread of gossip, and she wondered, "Might he not be more forgiving than the others, if the truth should ever, God protect me, become known?"

It had grown dark and cool on the plain and other fires began lighting the darkness. Susana moved restively on the tule mat, but she could not bring herself to leave the friendly warmth of the Pereas' fire.

Neither mother nor son could be silent for long. It was Felipe who said to his mother, "Gil José is late. When he comes, he may have something to tell us."

"That is true!" Tía María turned to Susana. "Our friend Gil José is very close to Captain Anza and he knows the Indian countries and California . . ."

"Gil José will tell you nothing," the father put in impatiently. "He is a veteran and respecter of military secrets, and also he knows California no better than we do, since he saw it only from this side of the Colorado, before he rode back to Tubac alone bringing messages for Captain Anza—"

"Blessed be the Virgin who protected him," Tía María interrupted piously. "He would have been better off with a wife to comfort him when he returned from that dangerous mission." Without raising her voice she continued, "This I am saying of you, Gil José, you need a woman of your own."

Tía María's voice had not changed, but its quality was different, holding affection but more formality than when speaking to her own men. Susana, looking up, saw the soldier standing in the firelight, burdened with the accouterments of the cuirassier—the musket case and sword—and wearing the red and blue military uniform and the sleeveless leather jacket, the *cuera*, made of seven layers of deerhide that could turn away arrows. Passing over the right shoulder was the military belt bearing the insignia of San Carlos de Monterey and on the leather helmet were the colors that marked the wearer as a member of the captain's guard.

Gil José looked down on Susana and his black eyes were those of a man confronted by a miracle.

There are openings in the land of Mexico where the earth falls away abruptly, and, looking down, one can see and hear the frightening turbulence of the underground rivers. Into these sacrificial pits maidens decked with jewels were hurled by priests of the long-ago people. Susana, staring up at Gil José, felt herself hurtling down into the vortex and heard in her ears the roar of the dark waters—but she was seated on the *petate* mat before the Perea fire and nothing in the night had changed.

The moment between them stretched into minutes, but there was no sound or movement other than the munching made by Gil José's horse, which grazed nearby.

The soldier and the young wife of Angel Galván were motionless. No one moved. It was as if all shared in this moment without understanding the torrents moving far beneath the surface of their lives.

Credit the herb woman Tía María, who, being closest to earth, was the first to hear the dangerous rushing of the underground waters.

[4]

It was Tía María who broke the spell by clucking at Gil José like an anxious hen.

"Seat yourself, my son's friend," she scolded. "Yours was a long hot afternoon's march in the plaza and you are in need of your supper."

Food was evidently far from the young soldier's mind, but he tore his eyes from Susana and in one dexterous movement divested himself of the heavy gun case and shoulder belt, then unbuckled the sword and thick deerhide jacket. Stripped of arms and cuirass, he looked less the soldier, but the arrogant head and the shoulders squared in the white cotton *camisa* were held with much the same assurance as that displayed by his leader, Anza. Gil José's buckskin boots came to his thighs and his dark cloth breeches were of becoming tightness.

He carried himself with an air of authority that marked all the members of Anza's guard. In fact all the male members of this expedition, military or civilian, were men of determination and substance. Each was being paid a peso a day by his king as well as food rations for himself and his family, and that had begun on the day of signing and would continue for two years. Each family had been given two mares and one mule with the fittings of bridles and packsaddles, as well as portmanteaus and clothing and bedding and all other materials needed for an adequate start on the land that would be given them in a new country. But a soldier received special advantages and possessions; he had his own carbine and sword and gun case and cartridge

box, his handsome uniform, and his spurs! This made a man
of modest wealth out of such a person as Gil José, who, like
the majority of Anza's people, had been born to poverty.

Here, Susana concluded, was a man!

Tía María found time for introductions while ladling food
from various pots for the newcomer. "This is Susana María,
who is newly arrived from Mexico City." And to Susana, "This
is our friend Gil José Terrez, who, like ourselves, is from Sinaloa."

Susana and the soldier acknowledged one another with formal
bendings of their heads, for speech at such a moment would
have been too great a risk. Nor did they look at one another
again for a time.

There was no need.

Imprinted on Gil José's heart were the delicate features of
one who had lived long indoors. As for Susana, even with lids
lowered she could see the sleek hips and wide shoulders, the
dark proud head and flashing long-lidded eyes that bespoke the
Aztec, for like the family Perea this man was both Spanish
and Indian.

"You will eat, Gil José!" Tía María began more by way of
command than invitation. She thrust a plate of savory food into
the soldier's hands. "You men who have no wives never eat
enough."

He had no woman, then. Susana withdrew into the secrecy of
herself and repeated his name over and over. Gil José Terrez.
A name as beautiful and strong as the man.

"Our rations are lavish, my friend's mother," Gil José was
saying. Evidently he would never be at a loss to stem the vocal
outpourings of Tía María. "Our captain is generous to his soldiers,
as you know."

"With his brandy!" sniffed the herb woman. "Do I know!"

"You are unjust," retorted Gil José cheerfully, and, balancing
his plate of food on one knee, he took a knife from its belt
sheath. It was a curious knife for a soldier to carry, and even
Susana could recognize it as a *puntilla*, which would be razor
sharp and used in the arena for killing bulls. She knew then,
due to certain lithe movements of hips and shoulders, that this
man had risked his life in plazas before turning soldier. The way
he handled the *puntilla* spoke of long training, for he sliced

the thick meat as if the knife were an extension of his arm and he had been born with it in hand. With its point he folded the meat neatly inside a tortilla and, eating, went on to say: "Forty tortillas a day to each soldier—is that not generous? You should know, since the sacks of ground corn given me I share with you, along with all other supplies provided by our good captain. And in return, little Aunt, I have the delight of your cooking and your company."

And Gil José added in lowered tones words Susana knew were intended for her:

"Still you are right, Tía María, and it is a sad thing to go alone into the village barracks every night and not into a comfortable family tent such as yours. But before long we will set out on our travels and then we will all be sleeping under canvas, soldiers and civilians alike."

The tenderness of his words was for Susana, but the meaning was something the herb woman could pounce upon like a coyote on a rabbit.

"You are saying, then, Gil José," she said quickly, "that the rumors are true and we may be leaving at any hour for Tubac?"

"My mother suspects you of knowing much you do not wish to tell," Felipe informed Gil José over his continued strumming. "I warn you, she is as skillful at drawing out information as she is at taking a sliver from a festered finger."

"Rumors again!" groaned the muleteer, who was still at his supper.

"Rumors fly around your head like bees to a hive, little Aunt," Gil José countered, permitting Tía María to place more food on his plate.

"Three times this week," Tía María almost shouted, "has your Captain Anza told us to be ready to start, and three times— delay, delay, delay! Tell me, Gil José, are those rumors?"

"It may be the weather that delays us. This is the time of the dust storms and hurricanes, and it is always bad to meet with gales and dust when we have so many people and cattle with us. Captain Anza is a brave man, and such a man does not take risks."

This gave Tía María her opportunity.

"We know the Apaches are on the warpath between this place

and Tubac, and that bands of those devils are raiding all over northern Sonora. Laugh if you will, it is true."

"It is always true." Gil José was suddenly the stern soldier. "The stretch between Horcasitas and Tubac has always been dangerous, ever since man remembers, but we are not holding back for that."

He looked furtively at Susana to see if this news frightened her, but she sat serenely with the bright color flaming in her cheeks, listening to all that was being said with deep attentiveness, especially when Gil José spoke. The talk of danger did not frighten her, for she had been well informed on the subject by Quita before leaving Mexico City.

For the Indian threat was at its peak in this fall of 1775. The entire southwest area was inflamed, and Apaches and Comanches were raiding the Spanish presidios scattered over the empty regions that in time would be Texas, New Mexico, and Arizona.

The Apache and Comanche tribes were hereditary enemies, and for centuries had warred against each other, raiding villages and kidnaping women. Now they had dropped civil warfare to hold their land against the invading white men. Fortunately, they had not joined forces. Even so, Spanish troops sent to protect the northern settlements were not always able to hold their own. The church of San Xavier del Bac had been burned. Other Spanish settlements in the areas that were to be Arizona and New Mexico, and beyond these, had been destroyed. Only recently the Apaches had attacked Santa Fe, a large pueblo containing some three thousand souls.

Even Susana knew that the Apaches were the most warlike of all the tribes. They were different from all other Indians. They were larger, stronger, more aggressive, and far more cruel. They rejoiced in combat and torture. They were the rulers of the western plains. The stretch of country between the small settlements of Horcasitas and Tubac and beyond, was Apache land, the most dangerous terrain in North America, and never so dangerous as now. Through this the Anza caravan must pass on its way to California.

"There is nothing to fear," Gil José was saying, to ease any fears Tía María's clamor might have aroused in Susana. He stole another look at the girl, but Susana was looking bright-eyed at the fire. "True, we will be crossing Apache country, but we will travel under heavy guard, and what harm can come to us under Captain Anza, who knows Apaches as no other white man knows them?"

"Oh, a great hero," agreed Tía María. She put her hands on her hips. "Why then was he not able to prevent what happened at this time last year?"

Susana looked at her hostess in surprise, for she knew nothing of an event of the preceding year, and Gil José, seeing her bewilderment, took up the story.

"That was not our captain's fault. It was in January, the cold month, just as we were about to leave Sonora for California. That was our First Expedition," he explained for Susana's benefit, "which we made to prove that we could make our way to California by way of the land. Just as we were to start a band of Apaches came down on us from the north, so that we were late in setting out . . ."

"Killing some of your men, stealing your horses," chimed in Tía María angrily, as if the event had taken place yesterday instead of in the year 1774. "Why did he not know—your Captain Anza?"

"For a very good reason." Now Gil José was indignant with Tía María, not only because she might frighten Susana but in defense of his respected commander. "He could not know of the raid in advance because he has no scouts among the Apaches. In every other tribe he has his allies, spies, if you call them that, and most tribes, as you well know, are his friends. Think the worst of the Apaches, but they are true to their own people, and they give ours no information. That is their strength. Their attacks always surprise. But our captain is more than a match for them, and we can trust to him to take us safely into California."

"We will never reach California alive," said Tía María, speaking cheerfully now her point was won. "Dear Mother of God, but we shall all be murdered, and left unburied on the desert with stakes driven through our hearts."

Gil José looked anxiously at Susana, but she was staring dreamily into the fire with a half-smile on her lips. She was thinking how foolish it would be to fear when guarded by such soldiers as Gil José.

"We must trust Captain Anza," repeated Gil José stoutly. "In spite of the raid last year, he made the First Expedition glorious, and this journey of ours will be an even greater victory because so many more of us are going and so much more will be done. And with Father Serra waiting for us in California, and guiding us toward him with his prayers, nothing can go wrong." At this the Perea family crossed themselves hopefully, for Gil José spoke with the confidence of a soldier, and then, looking again at Susana, Gil José saw the white fear on her face.

She shivered, despite the warmth of the fire. The dread name of Serra had struck her like a sudden cold wind.

Gil José was not a man of deep perception, but he was a soldier and had seen many faces masked with fear. He wondered why a young woman who had shown no anxiety at the talk of Apaches should show terror after that talk had ended. Surely the revered name of Serra, the gentle Franciscan, could not have aroused such dread.

He said reassuringly, "It will be the simplest of journeys. We are a large party, and after we pass the Apache country every Indian we meet will be our friend, for all Indians except Apaches are Captain Anza's friends. As for the lack of roads, have no fear. We have only to follow the North Star."

Then he turned to Tía María and said, "Now I have finished my good supper, and where is my wood?"

Tía María brought a piece of partially carved hard wood that Gil José proceeded to perfect with his *puntilla* into the ornate sort of wooden hand mill with scalloped wheels that is used for the frothing of chocolate. He gripped the blade far down toward its point and it was remarkable to see what minute carving he could make with the long knife.

"It is a *molinejo* our friend makes for me, since mine is worn away," Tía María explained to Susana, as if she and Gil José had never argued. "Gil José must always be working with his hands, unlike this son of mine, who idles his in music."

"I make very fine shoes," Felipe told Susana with good humor.

Tía María had noticed Susana's sadness and pallor, though her silence was no different from before. Not one word had Susana spoken since the arrival of Gil José. Nor had the herb woman missed the interest being shown Susana by Gil José. She wanted to forestall a problem developing under her eyes, and so she surprised everyone by turning suddenly to Susana and asking with studied carelessness,

"And your husband. Can he do useful things such as are done by our friend Gil José?"

Tía María did not need to look at the soldier to see the effect of her words. With a timid gesture, Susana drew the *rebozo* against her pale cheek, and only then Gil José saw the gold band on the slender finger.

"My husband is a ranchero," said Susana dully, for she could think of no other way to describe Don Angel.

"He is a don," Tía María explained unpleasantly to Gil José. "A rich man. He drives his own carriage and has a servant."

For the first time Gil José spoke directly to Susana.

"Then your husband will be a man of great importance in California. A ranch owner is skilled in many crafts, for to tell others how to serve he must first know how such things are done. So the hidalgo your husband must know how riatas are woven and wine is made and adobe bricks are mixed, and how olives and grapes are pressed into oil and wine, and how cattle are bred. And these are things he can teach us."

"So he has told me," agreed Susana, bewildered by Gil José's apparent approval of a man he did not know.

Gil José pursued savagely. "Before I became a soldier I was a vaquero on a hacienda near Mazatlán, and I know how a man such as your husband can make those beneath him obey!"

This Susana understood, and she could only look at Gil José in grief and bewilderment. The others too were silenced by his curious anger.

Felipe broke the tension with a cheerful shout, "*Viva el Vengador!*"

This was to a dog that had been drawn out of nowhere by the scent of their food. He was a stilt-legged tawny creature with an ingratiating air. Circling around the others, he chose the newcomer Susana. He pushed a long nose under her hand and waited with sad beseeching eyes.

"He is not ours," Felipe explained to Susana. "He belongs to no one in the camp and so he belongs to us all. Because he accepts food or blows with equal meekness, and resents nothing, we have named him the Avenger."

Tía María scolded the dog while tossing him the scrapings of the supper plates, and Vengador, seeing there was no more to be hoped for, gave Susana one last mournful look and melted into the darkness.

"He has chosen you," Tía María said laughing. "You have not seen the last of Vengador."

They were all smiling, and at her. There had been talk, but no true resentment. The thought came to Susana with the slow sweetness of *panocha* melting on the tongue, I am with friends!

She stretched out her hands to the fire with a child's gesture of delight, and Tía María, seeing the glow on the still sad young face, said gently, "Ay, he is kind to us, our Grandfather Fire."

At this moment Susana felt a hand on her shoulder like a bony claw and she saw the faces in the firelight change.

There was nothing in Don Angel's appearance to account for the curious miasma that seemed to emanate from his tall and bony frame, and to settle over the group around the fire, silencing them. Even the father felt it, and sat with head lowered like a man not knowing what could be said to this stranger who had appeared before them so suddenly out of the night.

[5]

Actually Don Angel was in one of his unusual charming moods, for he was pleased with the way he had handled the afternoon's negotiations. Three healthy horses, he informed the little group, had been given him in exchange for one old carriage that had certainly outlived its time. He apologized for having remained so long away, and thanked Tía María fulsomely for her hospitality to Susana.

"Ten thousand thanks for your kindness to my wife," he said, and lifted Tía María's dark hand to his lips and kissed it.

"It was nothing, Don Angel."

Susana recognized the quick displeasure of Don Angel. He was annoyed by the herb woman's use of the "Don."

"It is time to thank these good people and leave them, my wife. See, Tomito has started our fire."

Susana rose to her feet quickly and took Don Angel's offered arm. She looked frightened.

Gil José was regarding Don Angel under lowered brows.

"Did you think, sir," he asked dangerously, "we would let your wife come to harm?"

Your neglected wife, his tone said. Don Angel did not reply. His careless manner showed he preferred to remain master of the situation and not enter into argument. Instead he included the glowering Gil José in his flattering farewells. As the two Galváns walked away into the dark, Susana turned her head back with a murmured adios. It was a gesture the Pereas and Gil José found appealing. Tía María stood looking after the pair with one dark hand folded over the hand Don Angel had kissed, and her expression was inscrutable.

"A very great gentleman," she said at last.

"An old one," said her son, strumming some secret comment on his guitar. "What of the little one? *Estupida?*"

"No, she is not stupid," Tía María said slowly. "She walks with a secret in her heart. Some harm has been done to her."

Don Angel's hand tightened on Susana's arm as he hurried her over the dark field.

"You have lost no time," he said in a low voice. "After all my warnings, I am now known as a don to these people I have no wish to know! Did I not tell you I intended to travel simply as señor, a *poblador* among *pobladores?* No more of your betrayals! You are not to meet with those people again!"

They reached the fire, where Tomito was making a clumsy attempt at cooking tortillas intended for his own supper and Susana's, Don Angel having bathed, barbered, and dined in the village.

Don Angel's bad mood was temporary. He was too well pleased with the events of the day. He asked for a cup of the chocolate Tomito had prepared. Susana brought two cups from the portmanteau. They were from the old house and of finest French porcelain, but badly chipped, in holders of silver filigree. Susana thought of the goodness of the chocolate Tía María had served in thick pottery mugs.

Don Angel was still taken up with his own cleverness.

"After the carriage was off my hands," he was saying, "I

paid a courtesy call on Captain Anza, to thank him for approving my application, and I was well received by him and well liked, and given small glasses of good brandy in exchange for the political gossip I gave him from Mexico City." In another moment his mood changed again as he said arrogantly, "It is a solace to know this company contains at least one gentleman with whom I can converse as an equal. While my wife fraternizes with its lowest members!"

Susana was frozen under the attack, familiar, and still unexpected. Don Angel spewed out his drink.

"This chocolate? It is made of pigeon gall. And lumpy."

"I am not a cook," said Tomito with an astonishing show of spirit.

Don Angel gave him an ugly look. "That is true, and more insolence will leave you less than a man. Saddle my horse. I will find something fit to drink in the village."

Don Angel was obviously using this as an excuse to visit the popular cantina on the plaza. Its double doors were invitingly open and blaring forth a subdued roar of voices and guitars. The rest of the village was almost dark.

Tomito went off grumbling to the horses and Don Angel and Susana waited with nothing to say to each other. This was the moment the dog Vengador chose to materialize out of the night and come bounding up to Susana, wagging his long yellow whip of a tail in the friendliest way, and with a look of satisfaction on his clown's face as if to say he had looked for Susana and rejoiced at having found her again.

The very appearance of Vengador, as well as his familiarity, was an affront to the fastidious nature of Don Angel. But the dog had an affectionate nature, and believed in the principle that a friend once found is always a friend, and he frolicked happily around Susana, ignoring her timid attempts to drive him away.

"*Chucho!*" Don Angel said with contempt. "A cur's bastard. Or perhaps a coyote's."

This was unkind. Vengador's ribs stood out like the wickers of a bird cage, his thin coat showed the marks of boots, one eye was patched with black and the other red-rimmed, and the long limp tail hung down. Still there was sagacity in this bundle of bones and hide as he edged closer to Susana that showed he was a dog with an eye to the main chance.

"I will get rid of your friend," said Don Angel.

He took a tortilla from Tomito's plate and with it lifted a large ember from the fire. He folded the cake around the glowing coal and was about to toss it to the dog when Susana held his arm.

"No!" she cried in protest, so loudly that Gil José, thirty yards away, started up, but at a warning look from Tía María did nothing more.

Susana had never before raised her voice against Don Angel. Both were startled by her outburst. Whatever Don Angel thought, he did toss the tortilla on the fire and, Tomito bringing the saddled Major to him at that moment, he mounted and rode away, leaving instructions to Tomito to raise the tent against his homecoming.

Tomito's mutterings grew bolder as he saw Don Angel riding off to the village, a distance so short that any other man would have walked it in less time than it had taken to saddle Major. But Don Angel was of that breed of hidalgos who never took a step if it was possible to ride.

Susana was left with Tomito, whom she had never liked. He had been lickspittle and spy to Don Angel and the open enemy of Quita. His attitude toward Susana was unpleasantly insolent. Now they were away from the city and in frontier surroundings, Tomito's antipathy had widened to take in the man who had brought him to Horcasitas. Susana, listening against her will, was amazed to hear the servant's complaints being directed against Don Angel.

Susana tried not to listen. She had resumed her seat on the portmanteau with the dog settled at her feet. If Tomito would only be silent, then another voice might reach her from the Perea camp, the voice of Gil José!

But Tomito felt no need for silence.

"I tell you, Don Angel did not even give the man my name! What am I in this expedition? *Nada*, a nothing, a nobody, nameless! A servant, he said of me. With a word and at no cost to himself he might have named me *poblador!* Then I would have been a colonist, and fine goods and a mule and the promise of California lands would also have been mine. But no, by his silence he condemned me to the dust of slavery. In Mexico, in California, wherever I go with him, I am enslaved!"

His talk made Susana uneasy.

"You should raise the tent," she warned. "Don Angel may be back sooner than you think."

"Not he. There is much to drink in the cantina." Tomito's tone was both bitter and yearning, but he did go to the bundle of canvas that was the tent and start to unroll it. "Ah, but this is a bad thing he has done to me. It will not be forgotten. This is not the great city but the frontier, where one knows one is a man."

He began raising the tent, jerking it about in his anger.

Tomito had lost his wits, Susana decided, and glanced about uneasily, hoping the Perea family did not hear. She noticed Gil José had left. The Pereas had vanished into their own tent and their fire was dying. Sighing, she tried to turn her thoughts back to the problem in hand.

"You must not talk so, Tomito," she said with an attempt at authority she did not feel. "You will make a disturbance and our neighbors will complain about you to Don Angel. Then you will be beaten."

"You would complain of me?" the man demanded.

"I have never complained of you," she said so sadly that Tomito's insolence returned. He said with his ordinary surliness, "You would not dare."

She turned her back on the man and sat fondling the dog's head and thinking her own thoughts. The camp, like the town, had quieted, for nearly all the colonists were retiring early in the hope that Captain Anza would order departure in the morning. From the tents came the soft murmurs of family groups reciting the rosary. Only from the farthest and largest came a persistent tinkling. Father Font, who was the company astronomer as well as its diarist and chaplain, and had been out to make an official survey of the stars, was now rewarding his labors with an hour's music with his psaltery.

The arch of night grew darker and more vast, and against it the stars burned, ever larger and more clear. One shone more brightly than the others. It was set low in the north, over the flattened silhouette of the little town, and with sudden joy Susana recognized it. *Estrella del Norte!*

She remembered the words of Gil José, "We will follow the North Star."

Susana stroked the dog's head until his hide wrinkled with gratitude over his narrow skull, for whose hand had ever before stroked Vengador!

Vengador edged closer and lay very still, showing Susana that he was like some friendly person sitting there, not sharing but respecting her thoughts. She had forgotten the muttering unpleasantness that was Tomito.

But Tomito was infuriated by her refusal to listen, and he raised his voice again.

"Am I to be tethered here with you, like that dog, since I am considered no better than an animal? For what reason? To guard goods he does not value and a woman he does not love?"

It seemed to her beyond belief that Tomito would dare speak in such terms even in the absence of Don Angel.

"Leave me!" she ordered, amazing Tomito as well as herself. "You are not wanted. No harm can come to me here. I am surrounded by friends."

He gaped at her, eyes narrowing with suspicion.

"You will make trouble if I go and have me punished by Don Angel?"

"I will accept any punishment. As a favor, leave me in peace."

She did not look at Tomito again but watched the North Star. It was gleaming between the lower branches of a large oak, for it had not lifted far into the sky. Vengador growled softly, but Susana did not turn her head to see Tomito slinking away in the direction of the village. He would be entitled to what poor pleasures he might find there, she thought, for, mean as he was in spirit, he was one who had known little in his life except work.

[6]

She was watching the star when a strange thing happened. She realized she was not afraid!

To Susana the fact that she was at peace while alone in the dark seemed incredible. A long-lost sense of well-being came back through the many layers of emotional isolation in which she had long been wrapped. She fixed her eyes on the great star. Then, in one moment between seeing and not seeing, the star was gone.

Her eyes strained into the blackness. Surely there was a deeper darkness like a splotch of midnight, blotting out the place where it had been? Susana saw between the branches of the oak the silhouette of a head carved out of the night and held proudly. The shadow moved, the star shone again large and clear, and she knew him as if he had spoken, or his hand had touched her own. Still he stood silent under the oak, many yards away.

A horse whinnied nervously from across the field where the saddle animals were herded together for the night. Vengador pressed his long body closer to Susana and from his throat came a low whimper, as if he were moved by some unnatural fear.

What had the dog heard? He had not protested the presence of Gil José, who was known to him. Susana listened, but all that could be heard was a subdued ruffle of snorts and lowings coming from the horses tethered close at hand and the cattle herds farther away. The domestic beasts seemed to be conferring in some language made up of rumbling undertones. Whatever their meaning, they were understood by Vengador. The dog rose on his spindly legs, the meager coat stiffened along his spine, then his great mouth opened in a hideous cry of defiance, and he rushed off into the night.

His warning was heeded by all the other dogs in both camp and village, and orchestral howlings rose from half a hundred points. The summons brought men out of the tents, wearing only their shirts or struggling into pantaloons, but all carrying the guns given them by the king.

But what use are guns in the dark, where one may shoot a fellow colonist as easily as an enemy? Who was the enemy, and where? No time to wonder, for over the baying of the dogs and the bellowing of herds and the confused sounds of men running and shouting, in the village now as well as in the camp, an ominous drumming seemed to rise out of the very earth.

Hundreds of mounted raiders—or thousands—how many no one would ever know, were thundering over the Anza camp, riding down out of the north, and even Susana knew these

could only be the dread Apaches! In a screaming circle, "*Hu-eee!
Hu-eee!*" they raced between the pueblo and the camp, driving
the expeditionary herds ahead of them as they rode, while goods
and fires were scattered and tents went down. Susana heard
the hysteria of tethered horses as they snapped their riatas to
join in the flight, and the terrified lowing of cattle running
for their lives.

How flawlessly this raid was being carried out by the Apache
raiders! No other tribe was as skilled in pillage. Susana heard
the screaming circle of raiders growing smaller and nearer as the
Apaches' horses began narrowing in an adroit circle around the
terrified domestic animals and driving them in insane flight
through and past the camp.

The Galván tent was on the outer rim of the camp, since
the Galváns had been the last colonists to arrive. Susana was
in the direct path of the stampede.

She was on her feet. She was not afraid, for she had seen
the shadow materialize and become the man. She felt the safety
of muscular arms as she was held pressed against an oak by
Gil José.

Cattle streamed past them on each side. She felt their hot
breath as they hurtled by. Their horns knifed the air and one
tossing horn tore Susana's *rebozo* away. Still she was without
fear, although the earth seemed to heave and the oak shook
like a mast in a storm. At any moment death might knife the
two apart, but Susana felt only exultant awareness of the danger
that welded them together. Gil José's arms held her, and if both
died, what matter, since both died together! So in the heart
of the tumult, in air so thick with flying dust it was almost
impossible to breathe, and with glimpses, after the herds passed,
of naked, painted, screaming Apaches riding low along the necks
of their saddleless horses, even then Susana knew contentment
such as she had never expected to find again.

At last she heard the lunatic screams die away; the Apaches,
and their animal trophies, vanished over the dark plain, thundering northward.

The raid was over!

When Gil José spoke his voice was formal and almost cold.

"Ten thousand pardons, *señora*. There was no time to ask
your permission—"

Susana found herself laughing and the sound was as strange
to her as it was to Gil José.

"Pardon, man, for saving my life?"

But the soldier would accept no thanks, and could only mutter the conventional response that it was nothing, and their sense
of oneness was gone. Lamentation was rising on the field and
people began running to and from the village, and Gil José said
with concern that he must report at once to the barracks.

"I take you first to Tía María," he said, for the Galván tent
lay trampled in the dust, and then he added with sudden helpless anger, "You will be safe with her until your husband returns."

So it was with Tía María she watched through many hours
the renewing of the campfires that lighted dark angry faces as
the colonists conferred anxiously, trying to understand what had
happened and the harm done to them.

Anza came from the village, only partly dressed but clutching
his staff of power, and his soldiers gathered around him and
were joined by colonists including Don Angel, who walked
rather unsteadily out of the plaza leading Major. Anza sent
soldiers to aid the drovers in locating scattered beasts that might
not have been able to maintain the headlong pace set by the
raiders. The unhappy colonists collected their scattered goods and
tried to estimate how much harm had been done by the Apache
raid.

There was little sleep that night in the Anza camp.

By morning all knew the truth. Once more, as at this same
time in the preceding year, Apaches had driven away hundreds
of the horses and cattle belonging to an Anza company. Within
the space of an hour, the Apaches had succeeded in crippling
the resources of the San Francisco Expedition and the personal
fortunes of Don Angel Galván.

[7]

"Track down the hurricane!" The scornful cry was Anza's.
"Better that than try hunting our stolen herds. Let there be no
more talk of sending out posses. To chase Apaches is to stalk
the wind!"

His voice carried across the debris-littered field where the colonists had gathered to his early morning summons for a general meeting. Among them were many Horcasitas citizens, for during the weeks of the rendezvous strong friendships had developed between the camp and the pueblo.

Susana listened with eyes as wide as those of the children who, stumbling with drowsiness, had accompanied their parents to the meeting. She had been swept to it by Tía María and her son before Don Angel had been able to find a reason for her not attending. Now she found herself wedged in the heart of the crowd between Don Angel, who was clearly in a temper, and the excited Tía María, so that Susana had the uneasy sense of being trapped between a glacier and lava flow.

As a member of the elite guard Gil José was stationed behind Anza in the half-circle of mounted soldiers. Over their heads fluttered the red and gold banners of Spain. One glance flashed between the soldier and Susana; then both looked quickly away. Hastily Susana turned her head enough to get her first close look at the famous Anza. He might have served to portray the ideal image of Spain's vanished chivalry. Taller than most men were then, and made taller because of his plumed, high-crowned military hat, he sat his blooded horse, resting on one silver-trimmed stirrup the tall staff of his authority.

He was not a captain. His true title at this time was that of commandant, and his rank was that of colonel. Not even his soldiers addressed him by these titles. He was already Captain Anza to his admirers and to history. It was a title given him by the people of Mexico, not only because he was their greatest national hero, but in lasting respect for his father and grandfather, who as famous army captains had fought the Apaches along this Sonoran frontier.

The man Susana saw on this morning was forty years old, little younger, to her surprise, than Don Angel, but his appearance was that of a man much younger. His patrician features were curiously fierce and curiously gentle. His generous mouth was partly concealed by a mustache and goatee. He bore no visible scars, although more than half his life had been spent fighting Indians and he had once killed a famous chief in hand-to-hand contest. He was the foremost Spanish conqueror since Cortez.

His own claim to fame would not have been for his military prowess, but as a man of peace. His position as commandant gave him unlimited powers for good. It was his privilege to lead parties of exploration out of his Tubac headquarters, as well as parties of reprisal. These expeditions were to explore and map the Spanish territory and to meet with the people of the Southwest and assure them of his friendship. Between Tubac and the Colorado were more than fifty Indian tribes. Anza had met with each of their chiefs in turn, eaten and smoked and talked with them, and made of each a personal and trusted friend. Even more difficult, he saw to it that the treaties he signed with them, which they kept faithfully, were equally respected by his peers in Mexico City!

He was quick to punish and quick to forgive. Justice was dealt out equally to red man or white. Anza would punish one of his own soldiers as severely as he would an erring tribesman. It was this fairness that had conquered the tribes.

Only with the Apaches had he failed. The Comanches too remained enemies, but they were not as numerous or as dreaded as the Apaches. The friendly tribes gave Anza the same trust and affection he was given by his own soldiers, and, now, by the colonists he had brought together in the name of St. Francis. They listened with respect to Anza, for who could doubt words spoken by such a man? No one hearing his determined speech would have recognized the Anza who late in the preceding night had written in his diary the despairing words, "We have lost everything . . ."

"We have lost nothing!" he shouted now. "We have gained, for the enemy has done its worst and now they are gone. What if they have taken horses"—here he could not hide his bitterness—"granted, we have lost many. But we have not lost a single life, nor has one of our company been harmed, and look about on this damaged field and think what harm might have come to us had the Apaches chosen to take lives instead of beasts!"

He lifted his arm and leveled the lance of his authority, pointing to the endless bleak terrain to the north, incandescent now in the glow of the rising sun.

"That is their country. We will be in Apache territory before and after reaching Tubac, until we meet with the peaceful tribes, our friends on the Gila River. Until then we will not know a moment that is not dangerous. They will be around us and we will not see them, and they are prepared to swoop down on us as they did last night, without our expecting them, in numbers we have not been able to determine. We do know they are massing by the thousands between this place and the Gila. We know that this month of September has been decided upon by the Apaches as the month of crisis. They are planning a concerted attack on all Spanish establishments in a final attempt to reclaim the country they think is theirs. This we know. This raid is the beginning. We do not know when and where the next attack will come. We only know Apache power is massed in the north, to be launched against us somewhere, perhaps in the desert."

And still, in this hour of dawn on the Horcasitas field, the faces lifted to Anza's showed perfect trust. The San Franciscans gave no sign of fear. Their faith was in Anza, the conqueror, the pathfinder, and the peacemaker, to whom every mile of the way ahead was familiar ground. The men looked angrier, and the women more anxious, but no one interrupted.

"Last night was only a hint of what the Apaches can do. It was a trick—a typical Apache trick to show us how swiftly and skillfully they can strike. They were not out to kill, but to steal—to torment us." (Anza did not as yet know the attack had been two-pronged and that his Tubac presidio had also been raided. He did not know the full extent of the expedition's losses.) "Yes, we have lost much, but to an enemy we can respect as well as hate. There are no braver people than the Apaches. There are no more skillful horsemen on earth. There are no greater thieves, or more ruthless murderers. I know these people! The raid last night was to serve as an omen of what may happen to us if we carry out our plan to pass through their country on our way to California. But we are going! We can, we will, go through! We proved it could be done last year with the First Expedition when for the first time entry was made into California by land. Now we go to confirm that entry and establish a practical and permanent trade route that will last as long as the world endures. But that is not the main purpose of this Second Expedition. We serve not only commerce but God. We go to found a city for St. Francis in California, and by the power of our purpose and of our numbers we will pass through the Apache country unharmed. We will march through their country with stout hearts and what beasts they have left us, knowing that Apache trouble and other troubles will threaten us every step of the way. And whoever fears such danger, and would hold back, speak now!"

Susana looked at Don Angel but he did not move. No one spoke. All continued to look trustingly at the leader.

Anza smiled.

"I knew! You are people of my heart. And now too much time has been wasted and we must lose no more lamenting what has happened and what might have been and what may be. Let there be no more talk of sending out posses to recover our stolen horses. They are already in Apache hiding places where they will never be found. There is no time or money to seek out and buy others. We must set out for California with fewer and poorer horses than we hoped to take with us. They will be too heavily burdened for so long a journey and as we advance their forage will grow scantier and they will weaken. We must pamper them, for our survival depends on our horses. If need be we will go without water that they may drink. We will divide their burdens on our own shoulders. And men, women, and children must be willing to walk part of the way."

Again there were no objections, and Anza continued:

"I know you will not complain! You are pioneers! You faced catastrophe last night and did not show fear. You are brave people, and you will need your bravery, for we are setting out now on a journey that will be remembered for a thousand years. Padre Font and I have chosen the auspicious day for our departure. And so, make your farewells and be off to your packing, for we shall set out for Tubac on the feast day of our divine Prince Señor San Miguel!"

At this the colonists, who had been passive during Anza's talk of danger, started cries of consternation all over the field.

"Michaelmas?—only a few days away." And, "We shall never be ready on time," wailed Tía María, a lament taken up by other voices. For the camp around them was a tangle of wreckage. Goods were scattered and tents flattened under the trampling hoofs of the stampeding herds; truly it was a small miracle that

in all that ravaged canvas not a single life had been lost.
"Michaelmas is September twenty-ninth!" Tía María continued,
counting on her fingers. "Dear Mother, and so much to be done!"

But Anza gave no sign of hearing. "To California!" he shouted,
and he drew his sword and flashed the long blade in the
sun. "Follow the sword!"

Susana considered the challenge dreamily. "We will follow the
cross," Padre Font had promised. And she could hear Gil José,
"We follow the North Star!"

Her eyes lifted and met those of Gil José.

The colonists caught fire, for actually all were impatient of
the long delay at Horcasitas. So their shouts echoed Anza's,
"To California!" Only Susana and Don Angel were silent, Don
Angel because he was gnawed by a growing doubt of Anza's
project and ability, and Susana because she was accustomed to
silence. But a flash of awareness warmed her, seeing the excitement spreading over the field. For the first time she realized
fully that all these people were bound together in a common
destiny, and that she was one of them.

The great eyes warmed with sudden life, and Tía María at
her side noticed, for it was as if a child wakened to the
wonders of her surrounding world.

Not even Don Angel's dourness could lessen the enthusiasm
Susana shared at that moment with everyone.

None felt it more keenly than Father Font. This was the
moment he had pleaded for with Anza, and prayed for to God.
Now he took his place beside Anza, his cowled head coming
only to the captain's saddle, but his thin face ablaze with happiness. An oddly assorted pair of friends, these two, but each a
leader in his own right, and each possessed of great dignity.
For weeks the Franciscan had been urging Anza to start the
colonists on their way, and he had been openly critical of Doña
Ana as being responsible for her husband's delaying of the expedition, but now Font spoke from the fullness of his heart and
it held too much gratitude to refer to the night raid and suggest
to Anza, I told you so! Instead he praised the captain's decision
and the colonists' willingness to follow.

"Success is assured, my children," promised the padre joyously.
"It cannot be otherwise, for we have asked the Blessed Lady
of Guadalupe to serve as our patroness. [The Virgin of Guada-

lupe was the protectress of New Spain.] Captain Anza and I have held serious conference and requested the additional support of St. Michael, and for our own patron, St. Francis of the Portentous Wounds. We cannot fail, under the protection of three powerful saints!"

All cheered at this, and the padre lifted his hand.

"And now we must prepare to set out on an important journey with hearts and souls washed clean. In my tent which serves as your chapel, and in the village church, Masses asking support for our project will be said beginning this morning, and confessions will be heard into evening. I ask you all to purge your souls in preparation for our holy pilgrimage and to ensure its success with the power of your prayers. Mass will be said each morning in my tent, wherever we may be, and we will set out each morning to a hymn. And to those among you"—here the padre's face beamed like a seraph's—"who like the sound of music, I beg to announce that you will be welcome each evening in my tent where I shall offer the consolation of my psaltery."

At this a titter of amusement swept the assemblage, and those nearest Anza swore later that the captain was heard to groan under his breath, "By the Wounds, but I am a man tormented and cannot escape!"

Then Anza, lifting his staff to show that the meeting was ended, walked his horse toward the home of friends on the plaza where his wife was staying. He went slowly, this commander of legions, knowing that Doña Ana would know of his decision and meet with her beautiful face wet with tears and pleading that once more, for one week only, he would delay the start to Tubac. But his word was given and this time she must be told that not all her tears could delay again the San Francisco dream.

The colonists went their separate ways to their disordered camp sites and belated breakfasts. Don Angel stalked angrily at the head of his small group, with Tía María and her son in his wake, and Susana kept close to the herb woman like a kitten seeking warmth. Above all else now she dreaded being left alone with Don Angel, for she recognized the rage rising within him. His anger was against Anza, and for the loss in the raid of the horses for which he had traded his carriage, and the theft of the small mare. She knew the pattern of his anger. When Don Angel was angry, a victim must be found.

The blackness of his mood recalled that which she had temporarily forgotten. For her the blessed pilgrimage could only be
hellbound. Only Don Angel knew her true destination.

Padre Font had taken his stand before his tent and was industriously beating a pewter tankard with an iron spoon. This
was to summon the faithful to absolution before leaving. There
were moments when his cheerful features were distorted by
twinges of pain. He held it shameful that at this high interim of
departure he should be weakened by illness, and was determined
not to let it be shown to his flock or to Anza. Font had the
frail body and iron will that many missionaries possess. He was
always cheerful and hopeful. His joy at knowing the San Francisco
venture was to begin kept his thoughts from the pains and
aches his body suffered. Had not St. Francis, in whose footsteps
he followed decried the demands of "Brother Ass"?

Padre Font, having refused medicine in favor of prayer, gave
all his feeble strength to the pounding of the metal mug.

The mug was the personal property of Captain Anza. The
good father, having no chapel bell—bells for the California missions would be sent up from Mexico by sea—had assumed
proprietary rights in the tankard. Anza's dismay in having his
favorite drinking vessel put to this use had resulted in one more
of the small misunderstandings that came at times between the
two expeditionary leaders.

But the radiance did not leave Father Font's face, and he
was thinking, while pounding on his substitute gong, that it was
fortunate indeed for the San Francisco colonists that their
spiritual and military heads were not only leaders but friends. In
the larger matters he and Anza were in blissful agreement. This
was remarkable, as in the conquest of the Spanish West there
had always been controversy between the cross and the sword.
Certain military chiefs in California had made a point of attempting to undermine all Serra's attempts to civilize the natives.
But Anza, Font thought loyally, was not only a great military
leader, he was a very great Christian gentleman, a man of
culture and family devotion, and a respecter of all men created
by God. Yes, in Father Font's eyes the captain possessed only
good qualities, with a few minor flaws—the Franciscan thought
of the beautiful Doña Ana, whose power over her husband

eclipsed even Anza's desire for conquest. And then, most regrettable, was the fact that the great hero was tone deaf, and music of any kind was torment to his ears.

Father Font banged the metal mug and frowned. This was a strange problem to be found in so large a group, where nearly all were music lovers, and could carry tunes, and many had brought instruments of their own, like that lad Felipe Perea and his guitar—an instrument beloved in Spain since the twelfth century. As for the padre's, did it not have the indorsement of Holy Writ? "Praise ye the Lord with thy psaltery," was an order found in the Bible.

No wonder the colonists were amused. Anza had been unexpectedly unreasonable in his objections to the psaltery and the hours Father Font spent in practice in his tent. It was such a small and charming instrument, no larger than a zither, and the solace of Font's solitary hours. He had determined to take no heed of Anza's protests. Finally it was Anza who yielded. "It may amuse the Indians," he said, a bit sourly, and then added, "On the First Expedition we had with us a fiddle!"

"I have no time for chapel," said Tía María, trying to keep up with the long strides of Don Angel. "There is much to be done if we are to finish packing. Even my bags of seeds are scattered, though fortunately for us our tent was out of the path of the stampede."

"My mother will sift every grain of sand between this place and Tubac to recover her seeds," her son observed.

Don Angel did not speak.

"Actually, I do not see how we can be ready on the day our Captain has chosen," continued Tía María cheerfully.

"It is an impossible date," said Don Angel, speaking at last. "Everything expected of us is an impossibility. The entire project . . . I tell you, I have lost all faith in this expedition, and in the man Anza."

To this Susana said nothing. But the attack on Anza was too much for the herb woman to tolerate.

"You had best not let Gil José hear you say that," she said in a low voice, for the dispersing soldiers were joining their families and Gil José was coming up behind them, his horse following him with reins dangling.

"Am I to beg his pardon?" said Don Angel, so smoothly only Susana heard the ugly contempt under the words, coming from centuries of mastery, from Don Angel's kind of man to the sort of woman that was Tía María. The herb woman did not wholly understand, but she showed her dignity and her distrust.

It was in a chilly silence that the Galváns parted from the others at the Perea tent and went to their own, where Tomito, who had succeeded in reviving the trampled-out fire with flint and steel, was sulkily engaged in stirring a pot of thick and lumpy *atole.*

"And to crown these humiliations, there is that monster again," she heard Don Angel announce loudly, interrupting his list of grievances to hurl a clod in the direction of Vengador, who came bounding toward them with his long shape trembling and his jaws gaping with joy at finding Susana. The dog halted headlong, his clownish grin changing to a look of disbelief; then he made his way to a grass-coated hummock nearby. From that vantage point he could keep watch over the Galván camp and give reassuring flaps of his long tail whenever Susana glanced his way.

But Susana was roused to the dog's defense in a way she would never have dared twenty hours before. Was it the nearness of Gil José that gave such courage?

"He guarded us last night! He was the first to rouse the camp when the Indians came!"

"So?" Don Angel eyed Vengador with a little more favor, but the dog turned his head away. "Then he is not entirely worthless. Come to me, *perro.*"

But Vengador now knew all he cared to know of Don Angel. He continued to guard from a distance the Galván camp, clearly considering it his responsibility, and Susana his special charge. Susana knew how rapidly Don Angel's moods could change and it was best for Vengador that she pretended to ignore him. Don Angel turned suddenly on Tomito.

"And where were you last night while your master was being robbed?"

Tomito lifted his frowzy head and spoke boldly.

"No sooner did I see the Apaches than I took a blazing brand from the fire and rushed to the defense of the horses, and while I was trying to tear the riata of one horse from the

hands of a giant Indian his horse reared and struck me down
so that for a long time I lay unconscious . . ."

Tomito was not looking at Don Angel as he spoke, but
directly at Susana.

"She will uphold me in this. She saw the horse rear and strike."

The man's insolent eyes held hers and threatened. Susana
was caught by the memory of Tomito's tilma-draped form slinking into the shadows toward the plaza. Then he knew! Before
leaving, he had seen Gil José take up his watch over her!
Tomito had trapped her; if she did not tell Don Angel that his
servant had deserted the camp before the raid, Tomito would
not speak of the soldier who had stood guard under the oak.

Both men were watching her.

"Is this true?" Don Angel was asking menacingly. "Was this
man with you when the stampede began?"

She had never lied to Don Angel. But Gil José, innocently
eating his *atole* at the next fire—she could not expose him to
Don Angel's dangerous anger.

She said simply, "I was not alone."

It was not the lie direct. It served both Don Angel and
Tomito. The servant's look of triumph showed a venom she
knew she would have to deal with later.

Fortunately Don Angel's attention was distracted at this
point by the appearance of the husband of Tía María, who came
toward them without stopping at his own tent. The smile on
Perea's mutilated face made him almost handsome, for it showed
his pride in the fact that he was leading by a broken riata the
shaggy little mare that had helped the handsome Major pull
the Galván carriage all the way from Mexico City.

"*Hola*, my neighbor," Nicolás Perea shouted happily, "see what
we have found. Your little mare! I recognized her, when we
found her grazing a few miles from here. She could not keep
pace with the other stolen horses, and with a few others she
was left behind by the Apaches. She is yours, is she not?"

This was a great deal for the quiet muleteer to say at one
time.

Don Angel gave no sign of pleasure at seeing the small
mare. But the gelding Major lifted his head from his grazing
and whinnied in welcome, and the smaller horse answered; Major
at least was pleased to see his friend again.

"I had rather the three good horses I traded my carriage for had been found," said Don Angel.

The pleasure faded from the homely face of the muleteer. He looked shocked, as he had every right to be.

"This is a good small horse," he said in a puzzled way.

To this Don Angel retorted sullenly, "Do not think me ungrateful."

It was surly thanks for an act that had cost Nicolás Perea his night's sleep, but the muleteer spoke kindly to Susana before trudging away to his more hospitable fire.

For some time Susana had been aware of the clanging on the opposite side of the field where Padre Font was hammering on Anza's tankard. A few candidates for early Mass and confession had visited his large tent, but not as many as the good padre expected. The colonists were more interested in salvaging their scattered goods than in saving their souls. Don Angel did not observe Susana as she took from the portmanteau her scapular and rosary and a folded mantilla. Not until she placed the square of black lace on her head did he notice.

"And where are you going?"

"I promised the little father. Each morning he says Mass in his tent and he has asked that I be there."

"And this promise was made?"

"Yesterday, while you were in the village."

"What right had you to promise? How much can be done while my back is turned! I attend to the necessary details of business, and in that time you find friends to your liking and a priest to absolve you of such friendships, made against my express commands.

"My express commands!" Don Angel's voice rose. "Heed me now, woman, for the last time. You are not to be seen in chapel on this or any morning. I will not have you mewling your complaints against me to a man dressed in woman's clothing."

The old fear closed down over Susana. "I was not going to confession," she whispered.

"Nor to Mass," returned Don Angel sharply. "Nor to your friends—these people you have chosen across the way. Last night after the raid ended, and I returned here to find you again with them . . ."

He spat.

Susana said nothing. She dared not look at Tomito.

". . . and to find myself ruined," Don Angel wound up savagely. "You are with me because my conscience would not permit me to leave you, but God has not forgiven you, nor have I. So once more, I must regret my generous nature, now that all is lost. . . ."

The full extent of the expedition's losses would not be known for several days, when a messenger from the north arrived with word that on the same night of the Horcasitas raid a similar band of Apaches had swept down on Tubac and run off its herd of horses. In all, at least five hundred of the expedition's horses had been lost.

[8]

In the days that followed the Apache raid, there began a noticeable change in Susana. The shadow of tragedy that had followed her faded in the active setting of the Anza camp. She did not analyze the change. She only knew she was no longer acutely unhappy, and that her timidity in Don Angel's presence was lessening. She did not know if this was due to the encirclement of a hundred friendly neighbors or the fact that one of these was a soldier who did little to conceal his love for her. This attention was both a source of happiness and of anxiety, for a Don Angel angered could be dangerous. Fortunately, Anza kept his soldiers duty-ridden these last days before departure, and she saw little of Gil José.

She was drinking in the new experiences at Horcasitas with the avidity of a long-deprived child. She who had been without friends or social communication now had a friend of the most expansive order—the voluble Tía María.

The herb woman was responsible for Susana's new freedom. Don Angel spent most of his days and the greater part of the nights enjoying such worldly pursuits as the pueblo might provide. Tomito continued to present an armed truce and was unlikely to report Susana's strayings lest she report his to Don Angel. As a result, the Galván camp during these last days at Horcasitas was often left empty.

Susana had no housekeeping responsibilities. So when Tía María put in one of her frequent appearances, carrying large empty willow baskets, with the cheerful shout of "*Hola*, let us go!" Susana was glad to follow wherever the herb woman might lead.

For while Don Angel had expressly forbidden Susana to visit the herb woman, he had said nothing that would prevent her from going visiting with Tía María. This opened a way to evasion which Susana would never have attempted before meeting with the Pereas.

Tía María was a woman of boundless energies and many interests, all of which she was willing to share. The outings with the baskets were for the purpose of collecting replacements of vine roots and fruit saplings and other plants lost in the raid.

So the two would be off into the town, Vengador leading, carefully avoiding the plaza, where Don Angel might see them, with Tía María chatting incessantly and Susana listening.

They were made welcome in every *casa*, and passed from house to house and into the milpas. In these kitchen gardens Tía María was free to select plants and cuttings, and red and purple ears of the corn that was the staff of Mexican sustenance, and pods of chile seeds destined to renew their pungency in California earth. Returning to the camp, they would rest their burdened baskets in one tent or another so that Susana came to know many of the colonists by name. And the days of waiting went very fast.

Tía María had many friends. Susana was to wonder later why, with so large a choice of companions, the herb woman had chosen her, a silent creature of many sorrows, who had little to contribute to the interests that filled the lives of average women. The truth may have been as puzzling to Tía María.

At last it was the day before Michaelmas, which was the day chosen for departure. Each colonist wakened with the thought, Tomorrow we start for California, and still, so much is to be done!

The camp and the town were stirring long before the sharp summons of the bugle. Dawn quivered in the east when Gil José and several other soldiers raced their horses from tent to tent calling out the imperative demand: "Captain Anza's salutations and all is well! Prepare for the early start tomorrow!"

At the Galván tent Gil José received a surly nod from Don Angel for this courtesy and the privilege of a guarded glance at Susana, who did not raise her eyes.

Now that hours were counted instead of days, there was a great deal of rushing about and last-minute visiting and a great deal of work still to be done.

In an inexplicable burst of courage Susana found herself walking in the direction of the plaza with Vengador at her heels. Don Angel had forbidden her to attend Mass. But Don Angel had said nothing against a simple prayer voiced before an altar.

Even so, her daring smacked of mutiny, and Susana's cheeks were pale as she crossed the sloping plaza, where the earth had been beaten velvet-soft by the tramping of military boots.

The church was small and murky with incense and dimly lit with candles. Along the adobe walls were a few sacred paintings and images and painted stations of the cross. There was a scaffolding over the altar; the interior was undergoing repairs. There were no confessionals, but several priests sat on stools between the stations, while before them kneeling applicants waited their turns to confess.

Familiar faces were revealed to her in the dusk. The women were anxious for the morrow that would part them from all they had known. The men wore expressions of unusual reverence. These colonists were asking much of their favorite saints.

Over the candle flames and drifting incense and the murmured cadences of supplication Susana found herself listening to the sound of a voice.

Gil José was kneeling before the nearest confessor priest. The pale candlelight outlined his bowed body and shining head. She saw his lips move in words too softly pronounced for her understanding, but the murmur drove through her body like a knife. For the first time in years she was fiercely alive. This anguish that gnawed at the heart was jealousy! What sins was Gil José confessing that she had not shared? And with whom? What woman?

It was then that Gil José, looking up to receive the priest's hand on his head, saw the wild questioning in the great eyes under the shadowing mantilla.

Then nothing mattered but the need to escape, and somehow she was outside the church hurrying blindly toward the tents. It was inevitable that Gil José was beside her before she had crossed the plaza.

His voice trembled. "You have no words for me?"

She put out her hand in the immemorial gesture of dismissal. But the soft plea persisted. "When may we speak?"

"Never." She spoke so sadly he could not take offense. He stood watching her with his helmet pressed over his heart.

"That cannot be true." He was suddenly understanding and temperate; he had regained control. He was smiling. "We are *compañeros*, you and I. We are fellow colonists. How can we travel together more than a thousand miles and not speak?"

She left him without answering. But for a long time the sound of Gil José's voice remained with her, like a caress over the heart.

[9]

It was the day that would never arrive. It was early in the morning of September 29, which was the feast day of the powerful archangel San Miguel (St. Michael) and the day of departure for the Second Expedition.

Father Font sang the Michaelmas Mass honoring the saint in the open air. It was attended by the men in what time could be spared from their packing and the women between hasty preparations for breakfast.

Directly after Mass the camp burst into a frenzy of activity that would be duplicated, with only slightly less tension, every morning as these people prepared to travel.

The colonists followed the cheerful example set by Anza and his soldiers as tents were struck and animals mustered. Each man attended to his own and his wife's horses, saddling them and settling on their backs what burdens they must carry in addition to those human, while the muleteers caught the mules, urged them into line, and strapped on their packs.

Unfortunately, this long-awaited Michaelmas was from the beginning a day beset with problems.

This was not due to the colonists, who with the exception of

Don Angel were in the most cheerful and hopeful of moods. It was the fault of the mules.

The majority of the Anza colonists had been brought up among horses and were of the kind who might be called "horse people." Now that most of their horses were lost to the Apaches, many were left at the mercy of stubborn mules. Dozens of the mules had never been broken to pack or saddle. The greenest mule can recognize the touch of an unskilled hand, and it was regrettable that for the handling of the *recua* (pack train) of more than a hundred mules only a few men were capable of handling them with the special touch a mule requires. The leader of these was Nicolás Perea, who as a seasoned muleteer was in great demand. But not even this most capable man could be everywhere, and it was not long before the Horcasitas camp presented as great a shambles as it had after the Apache raid.

Susana stored her few possessions in the portmanteau and sat on it, keeping well out of the way of Don Angel's mounting anger at Tomito's awkward attempts to load the pack mule allotted to the Galváns, and watching the exciting drama around her. In turn she was eyed at a respectful distance by Vengador.

Everywhere on the field was being waged the unequal contest between man and beast. The voices of a hundred angry colonists and more than that number of equally indignant mules were joined in an uproar such as had probably never before been heard in Mexico. Added to this were the uneasy voices of the horses and cattle and dogs and domestic fowl, made nervous by the rebellion of the mules and the threat of the unknown.

Two men were needed to load a *mula de carga*, or pack mule. First the creature was blindfolded with a leather eyeshade. Then a sheepskin was laid over its back, and over this the *aparejo*, which was the thick leather pack saddle with its heavily packed bags. The saddle cloth was smoothed and the *cincha* (surcingle) of woven grass tightly drawn, since if the saddle were loose the beast's back would be rubbed raw.

All this the mules accepted with eyes rolling and ears laid well back, but once the packs were in place they brayed, reared, and broke free and were off over the plain, losing the contents of the saddlebags, and if possible their saddles, as they ran.

So many hours were lost hunting for the mules and their

missing packs, and men sent out to hunt them became lost and other men had to be sent for the missing men. The morning went by and it was midafternoon and the Anza Second Expedition was still not under way.

At last Perea and the other muleteers had succeeded in bringing about some sort of order. Runaway mules were returned, scattered goods found and repacked, and saddles were strapped once more on the still apprehensive beasts.

Slowly the cavalcade took on the ragged semblance of a line. A nervous expectancy swept the field where the people from the town had massed to watch the departure. Gil José and other soldiers were sent up and down the field to inspect the pack train, and upon their reporting that all was as well as could be expected, Anza sent them back again to cry out the order: "Saddles up!"

The horses that had been waiting many hours for this command moved into line with a dignity that put to shame the behavior of the bad-tempered mules. They accepted patiently the heavy saddles and pillions and the bladed Spanish bits that were cruel as iron traps in their sensitive mouths. Then they stood, as eager as their owners to be off.

Don Angel's handsome mount, the gelding Major, waited saddled and bridled with his fine coat rippling with excitement. He whinnied softly and pawed the earth. By contrast there stood beside him a study in humbleness, with hammer head sagging and tail a-droop. This was the small mare that had been rescued from the Apaches and which had fallen to Susana's lot. Like Susana, it preferred remaining on the Horcasitas field to setting out for grazing lands unknown.

The mare had shown mute resentment while being saddled by Tomito, and now stood with short legs planted far apart, in a manner reminiscent of the mules.

Since all around her were climbing into their saddles, and Don Angel had mounted, and Tomito, grasping the portmanteau she sat upon, showed his intention of loading it onto the mule, Susana stepped rather diffidently before the brown mare and took up the dangling reins.

"Now!" she said nervously to the creature, and again, "Now?"

It stared at her blank-eyed under a forelock that almost reached the length of its dusty nose. Certainly this was an unprepossessing steed! The mare was short and low, almost square in body, and had already started to grow the long coat against approaching winter. Braced and defiant, the mare stood, plainly daring Susana to mount.

Susana looked helplessly at Don Angel, but he was high above her, a tall man on a tall horse watching Anza for the departure signal. Tomito was busy lashing the trunk onto the nearest mule. She put her hands on the saddle horn and vaulted into the saddle, which as swiftly slipped over and under the belly of the mare. Half laughing and half crying with embarrassment, Susana rose from the dust between the hoofs of the motionless horse. Tomito caught the reins and stood over her, grinning. But Don Angel wheeled his horse while drawing his sword, and he belabored the poor beast that stood meekly with its hammer head between its knees, until a dark hand held back Don Angel's, and Gil José, who had pressed his horse between Major and the mare, was saying loudly:

"Mira, but that is no way to handle a horse that thinks it is a mule!"

"A mule or a goat?" demanded Don Angel angrily, but he saw the unreason of attacking an animal that could not be spared, so he sheathed his sword and his temper together. "But tell me, why could not this creature have been taken by the Apaches instead of my valuable horses? Why must I always be burdened by what is worthless!"

He speaks of me, thought Susana, frozen by the untidy side of the small horse. And she thought, Poor shaggy one. You and I . . . Her hand went to the hanging head that had bowed under the blunt edge of the sword. And Gil José, dropping from his horse to the ground to approach her, saw the fleeting look of tragedy on her white face, and having seen she was unharmed, he wondered, for he had not understood Don Angel.

He did know that this was not the time to add to Susana's problems, whatever they might be, by a show of emotion, so he addressed her as cheerfully as he might have spoken to Tía María.

"You are certain you are not hurt?" he demanded, and, being reassured, he turned to the mare. "Así, little horse, I know the kind you are. Or am I wrong? Is it this *cincha?*" He slipped his hand under the surcingle and waited, and as the mare sighed, releasing her breath, he spread his fingers, showing how loosely the saddle hung. Laughing, he drew the saddle back into place on the mare's back, speaking to the horse all the time in bantering tones. "Fortunately for the *señora* you are not a tall horse and she had not far to fall. Tell me, who saddled you?"

Tomito gave surly admission.

"My apologies for having such a beast," said Don Angel from his height. "And such a man."

Gil José did not answer Don Angel. He was rubbing the mare's dusty nose and ears and speaking to her in a confidential way.

"You must make up your mind, my friend, are you a horse or a toad? Remember, I am one who knows all your tricks, and I know what you are, and you are an air eater. Is this the way you are to treat a *señora* who will be kind to you, one you are fortunate to be permitted to carry . . ." For a moment Gil José faltered. "You see?" he explained to Susana, "the looseness of this *cincha?* Permit me to tighten it to make the saddle safe."

As he spoke the mare swelled her lungs with air, toadlike as Gil José had said, until her sides were like melons and the saddle was taut on her back.

"I know, my beauty. You do not like the tight girdle. But it is necessary for the safety of the *señora* and for you."

He held the girth's end in his hand and waited. The horse had to breathe at last. As its belly slackened, Gil José took advantage by jerking the girth tight. "It is a matter of patience," he told the mare. "We have all the time we need, you and I." Again and again he waited, and each time the mare was forced to breathe Gil José made the saddle a little tighter, until he shook its horn and the saddle did not move. "Now you see how a toad-horse must be treated," Gil José informed Tomito, and then, turning to Susana, "This must be done each time she is saddled, but once the saddle is set she will not hold it against you, because this is a good little horse and very wise. She is growing her long winter coat early because she knows this will be a long cold winter. These horses know things we do not know. And you will find her willing and strong and sure of foot.

For this is a desert horse that has been trained by Indians. As you see!"

He raised the hanging head with strong hands and parted the thick lips. The mouth of the mare fell open and Susana saw the cruel indentation where the tongue had almost been cut through. "That is the way Indians break horses, not to the bridle as we train ours, but by tying a rope around their tongues. The mark will last while she lives. She has been badly treated and is wise, and she will value your kindness."

"I thank you," said Susana.

"It is nothing," Gil José made the customary response, but both knew the importance of the casual words. And Gil José, to break the awkwardness, asked, "What is your horse's name?"

Susana looked up in doubt to Don Angel, but he did not seem interested. She turned to the quietly standing mare that had never been given a name, and shook her head.

"Every horse has a name. Mine is Fuego," he said, and Susana, observing the way the polished roan flanks glowed in the light from the lowering sun, could see that "fire" was a fitting name for the army-bred stallion. But the small mare? Susana shook her head, and Gil José smiled and stroked the dusty coat.

"You should call her Seda," he teased, and at this Susana burst into laughter, for no horse's coat had ever been more unlike silk. But she knew "Silk" would be her horse's name.

"Seda! I would have her shot," snorted Don Angel from his height, but neither paid attention. Gil José held the stirrup until Susana was in the saddle, then with a last intimate look shadowed by his helmet he rode away, leaving Susana to ponder all that had taken place, and patting Seda's mane because Gil José had said this was a good horse and she had decided Gil José knew horseflesh better than did Don Angel.

Now all the colonists were waiting, with readied horses or mules. Father Font was on foot. Like his superior, Father Serra, he was determined to walk all the way to California. The pilgrims formed a long, ragged line extending from the Horcasitas plaza onto the field. Susana waved in response to Tía María, whose group was ahead of the Galváns in the cavalcade. The Pereas' horses had vanished in the raid, and Tía María was mounted on a stout mule that was almost hidden under the herb woman's voluminous skirts and many sacks and baskets. Beside her was the musician son on a similar animal that was also heavily burdened.

It was then Anza lifted his staff high.

He shouted: "A *Tubac!*"

"To Tubac! Let's go!" Anza's order was echoed down the line.

The bugle sounded. Cries of "*Arre!*" began along the train. "For St. Francis!" shouted Father Font. Then the Franciscan, radiant of visage, tugging his mules into line beside Anza's mount at the head of the procession—spiritual and temporal heads leading the way—lifted his voice in the "*Olabado*," a hymn that had been sung for centuries in Mexico and Spain. All the company and their Horcasitas friends joined in the chanting, as the procession swung slowly into line and began crawling like some elongated reptile out of another age, away from the sun-baked adobe settlement and northward.

Dust rose in a heavy cloud over the procession, shot through with the red and gold colors of Spain. Anza rode ahead. On either side the mounted members of his guard fanned out as an advance shield. They served as dual protection, keeping watch over the line while maintaining an alert for any Apache sign.

After the soldiers rode the colonists, family by family, mounted on horses or on mules, and all chanting with Father Font the words of the "*Olabado*."

The pack train followed the riders, with the hard-working muleteers cracking their whips and trying to keep the mules in position, and the herds of free horses controlled by their vaqueros, and after these came the cattle herd with other mounted herdsmen holding the beasts together by racing from side to side.

So began the great pilgrimage, to song so exultant it sounded almost pagan. For these were a singing people, and their march began as it would end—with song. The villagers walked and sang with them, cheering them on their way, before falling back and waving their farewells as the massive expeditionary force moved slowly forward over the Sonoran plain. The sounds of grief could still be heard, but over all rose the sweet confident voices of men, women, and children in the hymn of thanksgiving.

Under the shadow of the wide-brimmed traveling hat Susana's lips moved without sound to the words of the *"Olabado"*:

"The glory of Thy sun overbrims
The vast theater of our world
Where all that exists
Is the work of Thy hands;
The growth of the flowers,
The greening of fields,
The fruiting of trees
With birds a-flash in the branches,
And the fish in their waters—
All these sing Thy name!"

She felt no trepidation as Seda waded with the longer-legged horses across the Río de San Miguel. It seemed appropriate that the fording of a shallow river named for St. Michael should bring his feast day to an end. For this Michaelmas was ending, never to be forgotten by the colonists, and now it was noticed that the mule train had fallen far behind in the dusk. The mules had grown lazy during their stay at Horcasitas and, remembering its green fields, had reconsidered their agreement to travel and turned back toward the good land they had left so short a time before.

The cavalcade halted on the northern side of the San Miguel, and listened to the far-off shouts of the baffled muleteers.

"We will camp here," decided Anza. "It is a good place to wait for the pack train."

The bugle rang on the heels of his order. Men and women slid from their saddles and began the work of unpacking the tents and bedding and cooking utensils they had packed with such travail so short a time before.

"At this rate," Don Angel grumbled, "we shall not reach California in ten years!"

The pilgrims had left Horcasitas at half-past four that afternoon. It was now five o'clock. They had traveled only a few miles. Susana was pleased with Don Angel's gloomy prophecy. She was enjoying the journey, dangerous though it might be. All the women were willing to rest after the exhausting departure from Horcasitas.

Each evening the routine was to be the same. The bugle call

ordering the halt might sound at sunset or whenever the caravan reached a source of water. No one dismounted until an officer rode the length of the procession with the company roster in hand calling out the names of the colonists to make certain none had fallen behind. When all were accounted for, the riders dismounted and preparations for the night began. The soldiers chopped down bushes and raised a brushwood wall into a circular barricade. Over this they spread their thick woolen military capes and *tilmas* and saddle blankets to cut the wind, for nights on the desert were always cold.

The tents were raised inside the brush fortress in a pattern that would always be the same, centering around the large one which was Anza's, so that on this first night, despite Don Angel's determination to avoid the Pereas, their tent was found next to his. And that was the way it would be, from this night on.

Don Angel blamed Susana.

"Did I not warn you, beg of you . . . ?" he would accuse again and again in the privacy of their tent.

But not in the loud, fierce tones he once had used! Canvas walls are thin, and, while Don Angel wanted none of his neighbors' friendship, neither did he desire their enmity.

But even their capacity for enjoyment was an affront to him.

Night came suddenly to the desert. After the firework display of sunset the dark came down as mysteriously as a mantilla dropped over the eyes. It was then, with supper over, that groups gathered for relaxation around the fires in the brushwood barricade, so that every evening would hold a sense of festival.

Of all the fires, the most welcoming was that of the Pereas, where the herb woman while completing her own domestic tasks maintained a lively interchange of gossip and information and amusement with all who came, to an accompaniment of guitar music by her son. If the talk became animated, Felipe played more loudly, and if it softened so did his music. At such times a sly smile might cross his sleepy features, for the talk then was of gossip, and even gossip in Felipe's mind could be fitted into song.

Susana found herself accepted as one of Tía María's group. She contributed nothing to these gatherings. She gave no sign of recognizing the looks of longing Gil José made no attempt to disguise. And always somewhere outside the bright circle waited her faithful attendant, Vengador.

Tía María said of Gil José, "He puts his heart in his hands." The soldier gave fierce concentration to whatever he might carve. No sooner was supper over than his knife was cleansed and honed and its needlelike point committed to shaping small wooden objects, not all of which were useful. As he worked his forehead furrowed with deep lines, bronze on bronze.

On this night he chose to make only toys. Children were in the firelit circle. Gil José carved tiny dogs and horses with jointed limbs, and saddles for the horses. He made a wonderful small *carreta* with solid wheels of the type that was used in harvest fields in Mexico. It was no larger than his hand.

"This is for Luis," he said, handing the cart to a three-year-old boy who thanked him in a voice that could not be heard. But the child's eyes sparkled with such pleasure that those around the fire smiled at the little boy (who was to become the famed Don Luis Peralta, founder of one of California's greatest pioneer families and grandee owner of the immense Contra Costa grant, across the bay from San Francisco, on which would rise in time the cities of Berkeley, Oakland, and Alameda). And for the devoted companion of little Luis, the tiny girl Loreto Alviso (the family name of Alviso would also leave its imprint on California) he carved a wooden doll with hands and arms that moved, and which he tossed into Tía María's lap to be dressed.

Susana lingered at the Perea fire against the expressed wishes— nay, orders—of Don Angel. She should leave, she knew. But she waited. She waited for the moment that always came, when someone asked, "Now from you, Felipe, a song?"

"What manner of song?" he might ask, flashing the whitest and broadest of smiles.

For Felipe knew hundreds of songs.

He once remarked lazily to Susana, "I like songs fantastic. Of life and death, and winter and springtime, and disgrace and maledictions, and of the birth and life of Jesus."

But he also knew the popular music hall songs of comedy and burlesque, and tender pastorals, and jolly children's songs about animals, and many, many hymns.

He knew love songs and could sing them in a way that opened

the coldest heart, and this seemed strange since, apart from his mother, Felipe showed tenderness toward no woman. His manner toward Susana was that of respect for his mother's friend; it was both solicitous and mischievous, and he often teased her out of her silences with some nonsensical ditty that brought out her shy, startled laughter.

Once he started singing, Felipe found it difficult to stop, and no one wanted him to stop. Each song recalled another and he lit them like torches one upon the other.

"You will sing yourself out of songs before we reach California," Gil José once told him, but Felipe only smiled his lazy smile and said there would always be songs. And for him this was true, for he sang not only the songs of others but those of his own making, which flew from his lips like birds leaving the nest that might never be heard again.

When he rested, and sat stroking the muted strings without singing, the storytelling would begin again.

Susana was to listen spellbound on these evenings to accounts both religious and pagan. She heard the legends, so familiar and always new, of the plumed serpent and of Tenoch and the eagle perched on a cactus devouring a serpent that marked the site on which was built the City of Mexico. She listened with awe to the often-told miracle of the appearance on the barren, wintry hillside near Mexico City of the Lady of Guadalupe, who in proof of her appearance filled the poor peon's *tilma* with roses in a month when no roses bloomed. She shuddered at terrible legends handed down through Andalusia and Castile, of monsters and ghosts and vengeance and thwarted love, and more recent truthful accounts of robberies and unfaithful wives in Mexico. And to these last Susana listened with a trembling heart, but never did anyone in this company speak of a love ending in suicide that had shocked all Mexico only a few years before.

To Susana most of the stories were pure magic, and the ecstasy of the approaching crux almost unbearable. She would be leaning forward with the expression of a child looking up at the gourd that is about to be struck open with its shower of small gifts. Always at such a moment it would seem, the harsh voice of Don Angel in his tent would come between Susana

and the climax of the tale. "Woman! The hour is late!" So
that many of the endings of these stories were forever lost to
Susana.

Don Angel, grumbling under his breath as he disrobed as
much as he considered necessary, fastened the tent flaps against
the night air and blew out the candle, leaving Susana to prepare
for the night as best she could in the dark.

"By the wounds of Jesus, but this army cot is hard as a tomb.
And that cat's concert next door, how can a man be expected to
sleep?"

She made no answer, but listened instead to the sound of a
guitar being struck and of laughter, and for one deep laugh
beyond all others.

Vengador was stretched before the tent entrance where he
would be every night, ready to give voice if danger threatened.
Insults and stones had failed to turn the good-natured beast from
his self-appointed post as Susana's guardian.

But Susana in the dark tent thought with gratitude of the
dog's presence, and of the song and laughter of the Pereas and
their friends. These raised a friendly wall between Susana and
the bitter diatribes of Don Angel. She moved quietly, sitting
on her narrow canvas cot to remove her slippers. The soles were
worn through and her feet were swollen and sore with the cactus
spines that lurked wherever one stepped in this country. Holding
her feet in her hands, she thought without resentment of the
thick white silk stockings and soft satin slippers left behind in
the armoire in Mexico City, and realized she soon must walk
unshod, like a peon's wife, with her feet hidden under the long
skirts.

She knew that when that happened Don Angel would not
notice, or care.

Not only the sentries were awake in the Anza camp. The two
leaders had duties that would last beyond midnight. Father Font
had concluded his evening concert in his tent, and now gathered
up the scientific articles necessary to the exploring of the natural
mysteries that were to be encountered in the outer night. Under
the stars that were as miraculous to him as to Susana he set up

trident and telescope and noted the changing positions in the great dark map of the southwestern sky.

Returning to his tent, he committed his findings to the solar map he would keep faithfully on the journey, and the day's events to the logbook which he would keep with equal care, for he was to become famed as the company's diarist. Making one notation, he frowned. Why, when every other item that might possibly be needed had been ordered, had no one thought to bring a compass? It was an oversight the padre found hard to forgive.

In Anza's large tent his army lantern would burn long after the other tents were dark. He, too, was writing in his leather-bound diary on the folding camp table that served him as a desk.

Having recorded the brief events of the first day of the march, Anza turned to the crudely drawn map pinned to his table. There were few markings on the parchment that showed the almost vacant area from old Mexico to the California coast. The commander's head bent intently over the inked lines. Two hundred miles lay between the presidio at Horcasitas and his presidio at Tubac. He placed a finger at the present camp site, Río de San Miguel, and moved it upward to the few marks on the map that showed the sites of Spanish settlements. Set far apart in those barren wastelands was the scatter of missions founded by Padre Kino in the preceding century, and their few presidios staffed inadequately with Spanish soldiers. Anza's finger traveled up to the cross that marked the site of his Tubac presidio and the minute ink drawing of the nearby mission of Tumacacori. The captain's eye lingered over Tubac. It was his headquarters, the presidio he served as commandant. The rest of the Anza company were waiting there.

The space that seemed so short under his hand was disputed territory. It was Apache land. One after another of the establishments indicated on the map were being systematically harassed by the enemy. This region through which Anza would lead his people was seemingly empty, but he knew that thousands of Apaches were camped on every side and every move made by the San Francisco Expedition would be followed.

Anza frowned over a portfolio of reports. Yes, this was the

worst of times for St. Francis's venture. Even now, in the night, this brushwood barricade was under observation.

The Indian threat was not the only danger. Anza traced the course of certain inked signs set farther apart on the map as the finger moved upward. The long distances between the water holes, lakes, and rivers held dangers even muskets could not combat. For lying in wait in the desert was the archenemy, thirst. Anza studied the moves ahead, from one water source to the next, with the concentration of a chess player. He knew how many miles his people could be expected to make in a day. He had charted out the time schedule to the hour, during the long wait at Horcasitas. And while he knew this country from Sonora to the sea, he did not know, for no man could, which water sources shown on the map were still active and which had gone dry. The summer had been long, and now the heat was excessive for September. A water source in the desert could be drained by the sun in a day.

Anza's high forehead creased with an anxiety no man who had ever traveled with him had been permitted to see. Then, with great deliberation, the goose-quill pen moved the brief way from one inked circle to the next. There! Tomorrow's march was decided, no longer than the writer's fingernail, but holding in its minute span all possibilities for success or failure. A slip of the Anza pen, an error in his calculations, might bring death to some of his charges, or to all.

No trace of the night's anxiety showed on Anza's patrician features the next morning. As was his habit when on the march, he was out of his tent by three, and working with his soldiers at the predawn tasks of feeding and grooming their horses.

The pattern set on this second day of the march would be followed on all subsequent days. The colonists had learned much from their troubled start the day before. Now matters went a little more smoothly, although an uneventful departure would never be achieved.

Susana wakened to the musical chanting of Father Font conducting early Mass in the open air, and murmured responses, and elsewhere in camp the soft whirring of the chocolate mills and the voices of busy pilgrims, joyous as migrating birds. These sounds drove away the residue of unhappiness left from the night and filled Susana with a sense of shared excitement that would strengthen in the days to come.

When Don Angel joined her for the morning porridge prepared by Tomito, his sight was bleared and his expression sullen as the servant's. But his gloom did not spoil Susana's pleasure in the drama around her.

Since the rule was to unpack as little as was needed at evening, the packing for departure became increasingly simplified. The mules seemed to have learned a lesson at Horcasitas, and on this second morning submitted with a little more grace to the heavy packsaddles. Everyone helped everyone else with the packing and saddling while the children raced about freely, and their mothers did not worry, for they were everyone's children and watched over by all.

The breaking up of camp was an enjoyable drama of which Susana was never to tire. And still, the routine was always the same. For her, the thrilling moment came when Anza's soldiers rode slowly for final inspection down the line and Gil José was invariably the first to reach Susana. This second morning he was greeted by the little mare he had named Seda, who rolled her eyes at him and snorted but no longer swelled her sides. With his head close to Susana's, Gil José slid his hand under the mare's girth to make certain it was taut. The moment for both was breathless, but neither spoke until Susana almost inaudibly murmured her thanks.

This morning all were in their saddles by nine. Then there was a brief delay as Anza, scanning the empty desert, conferred with his staff. The soldiers rode back down the line relaying the chief's order that placed a new responsibility on every man, woman, and child.

"'Ware Apaches today! Everyone keep watch!"

The children understood and their eyes grew large at a threat as unbelievable to them as tales of ghosts and monsters. Still they could comprehend danger, and the tiniest child would keep watch with its parents.

Once more the bugle sounded and before the signal faded the horses were stepping forward. Once more the cry rang down the length of the tremendous cavalcade, "To Tubac!" followed by the swelling sound of voices joining Father Font's in their favored hymn.

Eyes swept from one side of the plain to the other as the procession advanced. The bright-eyed children watched, and ears were strained for any suspicious sound.

On this first day and night on the way to Tubac, the pattern was set that would carry the pilgrims to California. Led by the tireless Anza, they would soon average from five to seven leagues a day. A day came when they traveled eight leagues, which was close to twenty miles.

With every mile the landscape grew more forbidding. The drab-colored plain was stained with patches of galleta grass and mesquite. There were a few late desert flowers. Slashing the harsh earth were rain-created barrancas, or gullies. Sand dunes were continuous, one lapping the other, and all topped with the rough desert grass. The eastern horizon was relieved by hills low and tawny as desert lions crouching under the sun. In this strange and lonely country the colonists would ride at times past clusters of huts fashioned of mud and branches surrounded by gardens where grew the small beans that were originally the wild Mexican lupine, and sweet potato plants, and pumpkin vines and corn. Shy Indians peered from the doors like prairie dogs at the mouths of burrows, but showed little astonishment at the passing of a tremendous cavalcade. The primitive settlements were far apart and very small.

Because there were so many members of the Anza company, and all were so closely knitted in purpose and in friendship, the starkness of this land did not impress them as much as its strangely compelling beauty. For it did hold beauty, with its strange flora and magical sunsets and pastel colors, and its vast silences. The mysterious land was theirs to conquer, and its very danger was a challenge to their well-ordered plan. The clean, sun-dry air filled their lungs, and their minds were filled with exhilaration for their great adventure and its brave beginning.

[10]

Two days on the march showed Don Angel there were advantages to having such neighbors as the Pereas. He was not bearing up well under arduous travel. ("Your man, he shows his years," Tía María observed to Susana.) Due to Don Angel's

ineptitude and Tomito's surliness the Galván tent was the last
to be raised at night and the last to be struck in the morning.
Without Felipe's good-natured assistance, the Galváns would
never have been ready to start. An offering of Tía María's savory
food in a pottery bowl aided in winning Don Angel's silence, if
not his amity. His opinions of these friendly people, expressed
privately to Susana, troubled her, and she would often wonder
if Tía María could be unaware of the many subtle ways in which
she and her family were snubbed by Don Angel.

If so, she gave no sign, but continued in her role of useful
and curious friend. Susana could brave Don Angel's scowl for
the privilege of riding beside Tía María, holding the small mare
Seda companionably close to Pancho, the herb woman's mule.

Tía María rode with sharp eyes raking the earth on every side
to see what might be growing that was new to her or familiar.
She was too active a person to remain hours at a time in the
saddle. The instant the caravan halted or slowed she slid from
Pancho's back in a meteor shower of full calico skirts, shouting
to Susana to follow. Then the two would lead their mounts
along the procession's edge that Tía María might hunt for
plants or seeds to add to her always increasing store. Anza had
stressed there must be no delays, but the herb woman was a
rapid walker despite her bulk, and by leading their animals at
riding pace the two women managed to keep abreast of the procession while gaining an intimate knowledge of this curious earth.

"By the miracles, but this plant I have not seen before," Tía
María would exclaim with a discoverer's delight, and root or
leaf or bulb would vanish into the *rebozo* she wore looped across
her broad bosom. But first she tasted whatever it might be.
Tía María was usually chewing something, a twig or lump of
pine resin or fragment of bark.

The riding was monotonous and the heat so intense that many
fell asleep as they rode, and jerked awake in time to save themselves from pitching from their saddles. The water scarcity was
not as yet an active menace, but the threat was growing. The
water sources were farther apart and many were drying. The
Apache danger was also growing. Every hour the expedition
penetrated more deeply into land the red monarchs were determined to hold. Anza warned the colonists not to let their

attention wander while riding, but to keep constant watch. His
soldiers, seasoned in Indian warfare, had no need to be told.

They were nearing the future border when the company was
alerted to the shrill pipings of a small boy. "Apaches! Apaches!"

Anza wheeled his horse and shouted in a calm voice, "Women
to the center!"

Instantly the line was broken, with the women's horses being
urged together and the male riders forming a protective outer
circle, in much the same fashion that prairie wagons would be
used to shield future argonauts on their way west. But before
the circle was formed it broke up again in laughter. The child
had seen over a dune a willow branch that from a distance
resembled an Indian plume.

But hearts had beaten faster for a moment, and all rode on
with a greater understanding of what might have been and still
might be.

That afternoon Tía María had word of a real calamity.

"Have you heard—our entire pack train has fallen behind and
is lost. Yes, all our mules, back there somewhere. And my poor
man with them, and no food. . . ."

Yes, it was true. The mules had once more reached a common
agreement and decided that travel was not to their advantage.
They had stubbornly resisted the long whips and the shouting
and had fallen so far behind that now the entire train was lost
somewhere in the rear. And lost with them were Nicolás Perea
and the other muleteers, to say nothing of hundreds of packs
stuffed with valuable goods.

At this moment Gil José chanced to ride past on one of his
frequent tours of inspection and was hailed by Tía María.

"What word of our mules, compadre? I was saying, my poor
man is lost with them and without his supper."

"He will be fortunate not to lose his scalp," grumbled Don
Angel before the soldier could answer. "The Apaches will be
sure to attack an unprotected train. Mismanagement, all along
our way."

"My poor man," mourned Tía María.

Gil José had halted willingly and the others also rested their
mounts. He did not speak to Don Angel but to Tía María. But
the black-lightning glance was for Susana.

"No word of the mules, little Aunt. But we are not deserting them or your man. The pack train has been reported some miles back and Captain Anza will order an early halt to permit it to catch up. We hope it reaches us before nightfall."

Gil José squinted at the western desert where a lowering sun promised another magnificent sunset which no one was in the mood to enjoy.

"Another unforgivable delay." Don Angel might have been speaking to himself.

Tía María saw the leather corselet over Gil José's chest lift with his resentment and spoke hurriedly.

"Another question, Gil José. During our traveling I have fallen out of touch with time. What day is this?"

Don Angel answered, "Since time means so little to our leader, why ask the day?"

Gil José forced himself to remember that, as a representative of Anza, he was to maintain authority and control. He fought to retain both, but his face was dark with resentment.

Tía María turned her full, innocent gaze on Gil José and reminded him that she had asked a question.

"The date, little Aunt?" Gil José regained control. "It is one of great importance. This is the final day of our starting, and now, we are on our way!"

There were exclamations! All agreed this was a day to be remembered, not only for the rebellion of the mules but because it had brought them so far from home.

The little group fell silent, pondering the importance of the exodus, and not realizing that the wasteland north of the future border they had entered on this September 30, 1775, was the very core of the Apache dominion.

There could be no lonelier place in the world than the site where the San Franciscans made camp that last night of September.

The land had changed with the crossing of the future border. It lay level and drab as dust, broken by dunes like waves that mounted in places into low hills, and by arroyos. These cleavages in the sandy earth could be dangerous. A horse and rider might shout for help after falling into one and not be heard. Or the arroyos might fill within a few minutes with a rush of water during the rainy season. Tía María told horrendous stories of travelers who had descended into these arroyos, perhaps for private reasons, and had been overtaken by flash floods and drowned. But at this time of the year the arroyos were dry.

The desert was not without greenery. The drabness was patched with clumps of galleta grass, and with such shrubs as paloverde and greasewood and mesquite and desert willow. On these the herds must rely for sustenance. Dominating this lower growth were the strangely shaped cacti—the spiky coral-tipped streamers of ocotillo, the stubby barrel cactus, and, most astonishing to city-bred Susana, the giant saguaro, stationed at intervals like monstrous sentinels with their arms stretched toward heaven.

This was the way the land would be for the pilgrims, desert stretching after desert, all the way into California.

In this desolation Susana remembered the gardens of Mexico City, lovingly tended, flourishing for centuries. The desert seemed to her inexpressibly bleak. With the others she watched the southern horizon, hoping at any moment to see the long-ears of the mule train bobbing against the sky. Then night came down, quickly and suddenly, and with it the cold, and still the mule train had not been sighted.

There was little song in the camp that night. The wives of the missing muleteers were sad, and all were anxious, and nearly all were in their beds but not asleep, listening with straining ear for the sound of the mule train bells. Many in the tents were still awake when midnight arrived. The month of September was over and the danger had not lessened; it was intensified.

October

CHAPTER THREE

[1]

Anza was the first one up the next morning. He stood a few minutes with his back to the dawn scanning the southern horizon for a sign of the missing mules. Seeing nothing, he turned north and swept the desert's rim with the intensity of an eagle. Only then did he rouse his guard. He was satisfied. He had brought the San Franciscans well over the Sonora border, and he had glimpsed no Apache sign.

He knew his enemies were not far away. Their failure to attack to date strengthened his hope that the size of his company was keeping them in hiding. He had other anxieties; for one, there was a chill in the morning air. October was the hinge month on the portals of winter.

This was the first day of October 1775, he remembered, and not an hour should be wasted. But there was no help for it, the caravan would have to wait until the mule train caught up. The roused camp attended the open air Mass, which Father Font was able to extend to a length of his choice, and still no orders were given. Anza saw no reason why tents should be struck or saddles packed until he was certain the mules were on their way.

The colonists were, of course, cheerful about the delay and regarded it as a holiday. The children were restless from the days perched on the rocking haunches of the riding animals. They were permitted to play outside the brush walls under the eyes of the soldiers standing guard. Susana wandered out in their wake, followed by Vengador.

Tía María came through the barricade exit dragging one of

the large willow baskets she and Susana had carried about Horcasitas while raiding the village gardens.

"Come with me," she coaxed. "My man is lost with his mules and my son sings as always, and your man sleeps as always." Tía María meant no offense. She was simply stating a known truth concerning Don Angel. "And when will we find a better time for filling a basket?"

"In this barren place?" Susana blinked against the copper sun.

"Barren?" snorted Tía María. "Permit me to show a city lady like yourself how barren this land can be."

Susana did not protest that the soles of her slippers had worn too thin for walking. She took a handle of the basket and stepped gingerly over sand so hot it seemed to scorch her feet. But she was accustomed to hiding hurt. Pride firmed her steps and kept her in pace with the hurrying Tía María.

With the dog loping in advance, the two women rounded the brush wall and came upon Gil José, who was standing guard duty with his musket on the ready and his eyes probing the horizon with such intensity that he started when they came up behind him.

"Good day to you," said Tía María formally, although she had only recently given this soldier his breakfast. "You watch for our mules?"

"For our mules and worse," Gil José did not mention the Apache danger by name. He stood stiffly as a wooden soldier, inwardly seething with the longing that affected him like an illness in the presence of Susana.

He said gruffly, "And you, *señoras*, are you not breaking the rule against leaving the camp?"

"The children are outside," Tía María reminded him smartly.

"They are being watched. They will not go beyond the sound of our voices."

"We will behave like the children, my friend Gil José. We will not permit ourselves to be captured by strange Indians."

The soldier, who could never outwit the herb woman in argument, contented himself with an ominous warning directed at Susana. "Then be most careful of the sun, *señora*. It is dangerous. There is a green leaf . . ."

"I know many leaves!" Tía María was annoyed, but Gil José was still speaking.

". . . which placed over your head prevents sunstroke. Even we who are soldiers wear the leaves under our helmets. And be careful where you step, for the day is growing warm, and in such weather the rattlesnakes may be rising."

Tía María had no more patience. "Are you speaking to one who has never seen a desert? I will make use of the leaves and as for the snakes, this is October and they are deep in sleep under the rocks." She pulled Susana forward with the basket, muttering imprecations against Gil José, whom she dearly loved. "As if I do not know ways to prevent sunstroke and snakebite! I who nursed children before that one was born!"

She was appeased by finding almost at once the shrub with the cool rubbery leaves which she placed under Susana's hat and her own *rebozo*. From another plant she stripped a handful of oily, malodorous leaves. "Crush these, and rub the oil on your ankles and face and hands," she ordered Susana, rubbing her own members. "They have an odor the mosquitoes cannot bear, and I see you are badly bitten."

Susana had not complained of the swarms of noisy mosquitoes that filled the tents by night and made sleep impossible unless one's body and head were concealed under blankets, which in turn prevented sleep. Tía María gathered supplies of the aromatic leaves to give to others.

They wandered on and Tía María maintained an incessant chatter while her sharp eyes raked earth and sky. She could read the veins of a leaf thirty feet away, but she was also on watch for danger. Any dune or broad-based cactus might hide a naked Apache. Nevertheless, Tía María became as lost in her surroundings as Susana did in her conversation, and neither realized how far they wandered.

Tía María's fund of information was inexhaustible. "That plant, Susana, do not touch! It raises welts on your flesh. Those ground berries are a pretty shade of purple but deadly to eat. This red vine is *venemo*—its leaves are so poisonous they will cause face and organs to swell. But—is this not strange?—a lotion made of the same leaves will cure its poison!"

They were wandering from one dune to the next, drawn on by the herb woman's curiosity. It seemed to Susana she was like someone being escorted around a garden by the person responsible for its growth, and, watching and listening, she learned about many of the desert flora, their usefulness, and names.

Wonder stirred in the mind of Susana. All the animals of the San Francisco Expedition were able to find sustenance in terrain that consisted mainly of dry sand. And here was Tía María with a large basket filled with gleanings that promised delectable provender. All this grew in a country she had thought ugly and barren. She looked about at the desert and saw it in muted colors as if miles of crystalline prisms had been entrapped by the sun. Each grain of sand seemed to burn with life. And although it was autumn, the monotone brownish green was shot through with unexpected color. For the first time she saw the desert. Flowers opened where no flowers should be, splashing the clear jade carvings of cacti with coral and yellow blooms, stippling the dry earth, and in places spurting geysers of color. There were small plants jeweled with blossoms and trees that tossed branches of gold and silver and purple bloom under a sky as hard and blue as turquoise.

Tía María was chuckling. "You thought this land barren, Susana?"

She had thought it empty of sound and life. During the walk with Tía María the desert revealed in its muted splendor flashings of life—brilliant ruby and sapphire birds, a gilded butterfly, an emerald lizard, a snake like a bright racing ribbon. All these were part of the desert. One had to look for them.

It was not the world Susana had known, with its architecture and carefully arranged gardens. It was no less beautiful because it was different.

The realization was a moment of miracle. Her eyes seemed newly opened, and speech long suppressed rose in her throat with the longing to communicate with the herb woman, who had helped in the unfolding. When she could speak it was on a subject unrelated to the present moment.

"Why is it you are making this journey to California?"

Her friend did not understand the importance of this question. She picked up the basket, answering lightly.

"In the way all wives are going. I follow my man."

It seemed to Susana the patient husband of the herb woman would more likely be led by his wife. But she persisted.

"Why is he going?"

"Why are other men going? For land. In Sonora nothing was ours. There was a bit of land too small and poor to grow corn. There was never enough of anything and no way of getting more. Now we have what has been given us by the king and promises of more in a new place where we will be given new lives. We will not be peons but landowners. In California we will be people of the land!"

How proudly the words rang. *Gente del pais!*

"And your son?" This was Susana who talked so freely?

"Our son?" The herb woman laughed. "That songbird does not care where he perches. He is happy wherever he sings. So he goes because we go, and his friends go, such as Gil José. As for Gil José, I do not know. A soldier is not a man of the land. For that one, it will depend on the woman he finds to share his bit of land, if it is land he will want when his soldiering ends. He is a man of much energy and will get what he wants."

Susana felt the fire creep from her throat to her heart. She had not intended to start a conversation about Gil José. But in this and later conversations with Tía María she found herself able to speak more freely. The long-closed lanes of communication opened. The need for speech, which is in its way the communication of love, was partially restored during these afternoon hours of discovery in the desert with Tía María.

Darkness fell swiftly over the land that was to be known as Arizona. In their barricade the pilgrims watched the overhead sky turn from flame to a bruised plum, and finally to impenetrable darkness. Bold stars appeared up in the abyss. In the camp were anxious conferrings and heavy hearts.

The mule train had now been missing for thirty-six hours.

Only Don Angel continued to sleep in his tent, heedless of the general anxiety because he had discovered that a brandy bottle held the cure for all annoyances.

Susana spent the evening with the Pereas. She had seen Tomito carry a plate of food into the Galván tent and emerge with it untouched and with his scowl more malignant than before. Certainly she would not be wanted there. And she was of use to Tía María. The two were paring the needle-set rinds from the cactus fruits they had gathered and filling small clay pots with hot jam. Cactus pulp boiled with brown sugar became a gelatinous candy to delight the palates of colonists young and old.

Tía María usually talked as much as she worked, but this night her thoughts were with her man, and her head kept turning toward the dark south where the mule train was wandering. Supper was eaten while the women continued their jam making, then Felipe played his guitar very softly but did not sing, and Gil José whittled on a strip of lacelike dry cholla, making of it a cane for a colonist who had been temporarily lamed in a fall from his horse.

Visitors came and went. Although little of interest was being said, Susana was for the first time able to take a small and timid part in the general conversation. But she never spoke first to Gil José, and when he addressed her she answered him without looking his way and in the shortest possible terms. Much of the talk centered around the afternoon walk in the desert and its variety of flowers and fruit.

"You should see this desert in the spring!" Gil José commented with a jealousy directed at Susana. "One cannot believe, to look at it now, how in springtime this land is covered with many flowers . . ." How he longed to describe for her the new leaves of the great cottonwoods in springtime, tipping with tender green the darker green, the rose froth of tamarisk, the piercing red tips of the ocotillo, and the incandescent wax tapers of the yucca. All these, and much more, Gil José longed to describe for Susana, but the words congealed in his throat. He was no poet, he was a soldier, so he could only repeat lamely, "Yes, the desert is a pretty place in March and in April," and feel unreasonable resentment of his friend Felipe, who would have been able to express this beauty in words and even, if he chose, put it into song.

Suddenly Felipe stilled his guitar.

"Do you hear them?" he shouted. And the campers listened, and all heard from far away the peevish brayings of the mules and the weary cries of their drovers. Fires were built up and food reheated as the mule train that had been lost so many hours advanced slowly out of the night to rejoin the Anza cavalcade.

Three days later, Father Font observed to his friend Anza: "I wish the day we wasted waiting for the mules were this day, that we might celebrate with extra Masses and extra prayers. Instead, a day of no importance was lost, while today is one of the most sacred in our calendar."

It was October fourth and the feast day of the expedition's patron, St. Francis. Certainly no day deserved more Masses and longer prayers. But the lagging mule train had enforced one more of the delays that were slowing the expedition's progress. Anza was sympathetic but firm.

"There will be time for longer Masses at Tubac," he assured the padre cheerfully, "and if we can get off to an early start today it will help make up for the time lost waiting for the mules."

The Franciscan yielded with like cheerfulness, although, as he had told Susana during their first meeting at Horcasitas, this fourth of October was the day he had hoped the completed San Francisco Expedition would set out from Tubac, and Tubac was still many miles away. Time being of the essence, Font was obliged to offer one of the earliest and briefest of Masses. But he could not resist a heartfelt personal message to St. Francis, begging their patron to understand why a lengthier celebration could not be offered on this day in which the gentle lover of all life had died.

Then, to his flock who waited with saddled mounts, impatient to start:

"St. Francis in paradise knows our love and our longing to set apart the day when nearly six hundred years ago he was welcomed into heaven. If there were time we would sing many Masses in his honor. But all our days are dedicated to him, and we are leaving now to continue in our purpose, which is to build a home for St. Francis on earth."

The San Franciscans kept this thought in their hearts as they moved along in the slow pace required by the mules toward Tubac, a journey which looked so brief on Anza's map, but which was proving to be arduous and long.

Trudging over the blinding sand, leading his burdened mules, Father Font spent the hours in communion with the saint on whose day the great procession was slowly advancing into the great desert.

October moved forward as slowly. The nights grew colder, but by day the sun was as relentless as before. The winds sharpened, and the desert grew drier. Water was rationed. Thirst grew, and the awareness of danger.

[2]

There was another incident on the way to Tubac. Several times the travelers glimpsed specimens of the wild cattle that were descended from herds brought into the Southwest in the preceding century by Spanish pioneers. Now as they rode toward the horizon there rose over it a grotesque mirage. It showed a large herd of such cattle. In the distance their bodies appeared to be no larger than those of ants, mounted on long stalklike legs that were seemingly several miles high. As the colonists rode nearer, the legs shrank earthward. The insectlike creatures enlarged into bulls, cows, and calves, cropping the coarse grass on the dunes. The illusion was created by the plateaus of hot glassy air over the mirrorlike sand.

The wild beasts lifted their heads and stared briefly. Then, perhaps because they had never before seen humans, they resumed their grazing.

Anza looked back at his followers. The hand of every male rider was on the riata over his saddle horn. The expression of each man burned with longing. These men of Mexico had learned to rope and throw as children. Anza had the same upbringing. He understood.

He said as if to himself, "We are making good time. A few hours will be no loss."

Father Font, trudging near the captain, overheard. "Our people do not need amusement. If there is time to waste it should be spent on extra Masses to protect their bodies and souls."

"I agree, little Father. They do not need amusement. But they thirst for it! Read the longing on their faces—you who see through to their hearts! And also," he appealed to Font's practical side, "consider the advantage economically! When these people signed with us we promised them a barbecue a day. We are not able to keep that promise because the Apaches cut into our supply of beef cattle. You know how these people have to content their stomachs with stewed jerky at the end of a hard day's riding. And they have not complained. They are good people, as you and I know, and a few hours given over to a hunt will not only provide some well-deserved amusement, but also help conserve our meat supply."

Father Font was convinced but thought it his duty to raise one more objection.

"Is it wise to loiter in this place where we know we are under enemy observation?"

Anza's haughty features relaxed in one of his rare grins.

"My revered friend, it is not only wise, it is excellent strategy! We will show the Apaches how Spaniards can enjoy sport in the teeth of danger."

Father Font smiled: "I yield!"

Anza swung his long body around in the high saddle. The stirring order was echoed along the line.

"Permission to kill!"

At once the excited horses were spurred forward. Shouting riders leaning over their pommels whirled over their heads the widening circles of rope. The herd burst apart like a pod casting seeds. The terrified wild cattle fled in every direction, throats bellowing, horns and tails high. The riders raced around them, blocking the stampede, rounding up the strays, keeping the cattle racing in a movement that gradually became circular and forced the agitated herd into a revolving core. A mushroom of whitish dust rose. Under it were glimpsed in flashes the melee of needle-horned plunging cattle, the well-trained but hysterical horses shrieking their excitement, and the crouched riders swinging their looped riatas.

The women left their saddles to watch. Their Madonna eyes grew round with excitement, for this was a *fiesta brava* they had never expected to see again. This was the sort of spectacle the privileged had seen on the great Mexican ranchos, which they had willingly ridden fifty or a hundred miles to see, and where greater daring and skill might be displayed than in the famed Plaza de Toros in Mexico City.

Even the very young knew the pattern of the ancient game being played before them on the desert. The rules were simple but inviolate. Susana knew them.

She felt the hot earth under her feet shake to the violence of

the hunt, and her heart quickened with the fearful pleasure
shared with those who watched and those who rode. Each woman
followed the movements of a single rider. For in this ancient
sport the struggle divided into the individual contests waged by
each man alone against his chosen beast.

The swift maneuvers Susana followed were not those of Don
Angel, but of Gil José.

The hunters circled the herd many times before making their
choice. Gil José chose for his victim a yearling bull, uncommonly
large and sleek as wild cattle go, but still young enough to
promise tenderness. The racing of the herd brought this animal
running along the outer rim of the herd. Instantly, Gil José's
Fuego darted into the herd and out, cutting the young bull
away. Fuego knew the rules of this game in which man and
horse worked in unison as well as did the rider who had
trained him. He raced beside the bull, preventing the terrified
beast from rejoining the herd. Gil José's body stiffened and
stretched over Fuego's neck as if his propulsion was sending
the rope forward. Gil José's riata flashed over the horse's head
in a circle that continued to widen, until it fell.

Susana's hand went to her heart. Gil José had not ridden
alone. In a sport each man played solo, intent on the victim of
his choice, Don Angel had been riding dangerously close to Gil
José.

There were cattle enough for all on the field. Why had Don
Angel chosen an animal so close to Gil José's, and cut it from
the herd at the same moment? In the confusion of the chase
Don Angel threw his riata just as Gil José flung his, and the two
racing bulls jostled together so that the noose flung by Don
Angel fell on the horns of the bull chosen by the soldier!

Through the curtain of dust Susana saw Gil José pitch forward onto the shoulders of the bull that had been brought to
a staggering halt. His hands were on the long pointed horns and
in one movement he lifted and flung away the noose that had
been thrown over his by Don Angel.

The riderless Fuego knew what next must be done. He backed
slowly, dropping the weight of his massive frame on his sleek
haunches. The leather riata linking his saddle horn to the horns
of the bull grew taut, aiding Gil José, who slid to the ground,
and, still gripping the animal's horns, began twisting them slowly.

The horse did not move now that the rope was taut, but stood watching rolling-eyed and whinnying with tension. Gil José's body twisted with that of the bull, which stood braced, gradually letting its neck bend under the agonizing pressure of Gil José's hands. Gil José tensed, toes on the earth, hands locked on the horns, body balanced over the horns, continuing to press down the great, dangerous head until it turned upward, almost facing the sky. The beast still fought the man, plunging from side to side in its attempt to free its horns and drive them into the face of Gil José, until the forelegs buckled and the bull went on its knees and the heavy body fell and turned on its side.

Susana had seen the look of disbelief on Don Angel's face. She heard the clucking of tongues as the women around her revealed their uneasiness.

Cries of *"Ole"* followed Don Angel off the field, but they were for Gil José. The don left with dignity, looping his riata in exact circles and returning it to the pommel of his saddle with a thoughtful expression on his aquiline features. His hooded eyes were veiled in a way Susana recognized.

She had always feared Don Angel, but never as much as in this moment when her dread was for Gil José. She knew Don Angel. He would not add a public display of temper to his humiliation. In the melee of the chase he and Gil José had become dominant contestants. All who watched had been able to see this was no ordinary hunt, but a struggle for power between two men whose enmity had been growing since their first meeting. As a former ranch owner Don Angel might have been expected to excel. In his younger days he had been one of Mexico's leading exponents in the roping and throwing of cattle. He had often boasted to Susana of his prowess. Why had he chosen as opponent a onetime vaquero who had learned to rope and throw on the western plains of Mexico?

Then she saw Gil José, straddling the neck of the fallen bull and holding ready the *puntilla*, the same knife that carved such delicate children's toys. The bull lay with eyes closed and sides heaving, awaiting the unknown. Gil José's was the stance of the gladiator, and his eyes hunted hers for approval. She smiled. What else could be done, when all were cheering Gil José? This was the moment of high victory, of death, for which all were waiting. It was Gil José's moment and—in her pounding heart she knew—her own.

In the next hour other animals were cut from the dwindling herd, roped and thrown and slaughtered, until a supply of meat was secured that would provide many a meal ahead. The ugly job of butchery was carried out under the hot sun by a squad of men. Most of the flesh was cut into strips to be dried into jerky by the sun. The young bull killed by Gil José and several smaller animals were left whole, skinned, cleansed, and seasoned for immediate celebration.

The hides were rubbed with salt and spread to dry in the sun. This was Felipe's responsibility. He would make shoes of the seasoned leather.

The butchers had chosen the leeward side for their work, but the clean air was befouled with the scent of the abattoir.

Other men dug pits and lined them with stones and scoured the desert for wood. When the pits held sufficient heat, the skinned beeves were set over the sunken beds of hot stones, then covered with wet hides and hot stones and sand. Many hours are needed to roast a whole beef underground.

Since the feasting would be late and should not be hurried, Anza ordered camp made for the night. The tents and barricade were raised. The rest of the long, hot afternoon was left open to leisure and hungry waiting.

Felipe had shared in the hunt, and a yearling of his had joined Gil José's on the coals, but its capture had been carried out with such lack of drama it had caused little excitement. He had shown much energy in throwing the fine young animal, and had taken part in its preparation, but this had not been done through choice but as part of the day's work, along with the curing of the hides. He had helped as always in the preparations for the night, setting up the family tent and assisting in the community task of raising the barricade. Now he lay before the tent with his guitar balanced on his stomach—the image of lethargy.

But Felipe was not idle. He was composing a ballad about two men who disliked each other and who, during a hunt, met with the misfortune of roping the same bull. How would the song end? Not even Felipe knew. He sang it under his breath so that his friend Gil José could not hear.

Gil José sat in matching idleness near Felipe. He held a length of cholla pith and the *puntilla* with which he had killed the great bullock that was now roasting in the earth. The tormenting odor of the roasting meat had driven away the scent of butchery and mouths were now watering with longing.

Gil José was not whittling. The fenzy of the chase had left him, and he was content to relax and watch the gradual appearance overhead of the tremendous stars. He and Felipe agreed that such stars as appeared nightly over this desert had never been seen in old Mexico—no, not even in the *tierra caliente*.

The men might rest while waiting for the opening of the pits, but the women were preparing tortillas and other foods to complement the roasting meats. Susana worked with Tía María, stealing timid glances from time to time in the direction of Gil José, but her uneasy thoughts were with Don Angel.

Her anxiety had not been quieted by the dignity with which Don Angel had left the field and its honors to Gil José, or his behavior since then. His manner had been exemplary. He congratulated Gil José before the entire company for his skill as a hunter and assisted in the preparation of the pits. He had directed Tomito in the raising of the Galván tent and then disappeared into it until the feasting should begin. Susana watched the tent with increasing dread, but it did not open. In spite of her anxiety, she felt a growing sense of respect for Don Angel. He had endured with icy dignity what to him must have been a supreme humiliation.

The hours of waiting became unendurable. Then from somewhere an open bottle was passed from hand to hand, and then another. Felipe and other musicians aided in filling the void of waiting with bursts of music. Before long all the cavalcade were joined in singing the old familiar songs of Mexico.

Captain Anza appeared at the door of his tent with Father Font. He regarded the celebrants with kindness.

"They have earned their fun," he told Father Font.

The Franciscan shook his tonsured head. He knew how easily merrymaking could get out of hand. Now no one was more eager than Father Font for the meat to appear.

But it was long after sundown before the first pit was opened.

As the rich, indescribable odor gushed out on the cooling air, groans of ecstasy burst from those who had been so long waiting.

The aroma penetrated the closed tent of Don Angel and brought him out to join the others, like them ravenous, but unlike them unsmiling. The colonists carried filled plates to their fires and formed companionable groups seated on the ground under the stars. They held their plates in their laps and ate from their fingers as barbecued meat should be eaten.

The Galváns sat with the Pereas, which was inevitable. It was also inevitable that Gil José should be eating with them and accepting compliments for the succulence of the feast of his providing. The meat was of exceptional tenderness and flavor, and Don Angel added elaborate congratulations to those he had previously offered Gil José. Susana, who knew him well, could see how difficult it was for Don Angel to maintain his air of debonair unconcern.

The great star that led them was high in the north before the feasters reached the point where not another mouthful could be eaten. Vengador and the other dogs were sharing a supplementary fiesta in the shadows with the discarded bones. The children fell asleep, curled up on the mats, but the adults were reluctant to have the celebration end.

"Sing to us," Tía María demanded of her son, who, having wiped his hands politely on a tuft of grass, had resumed the strumming of his guitar.

Felipe sang to the faces shining in the firelight another old favorite concerning the friendship of a dog for a cat and a game they played. As he sang, Susana's lips moved to the words that returned to her out of childhood and the old house on the Calle de Tacuba.

The others were puzzled by her entrancement, but Susana was remembering when life was without sadness and the house in Mexico City held laughter, and in the courtyard where the fountain played a young mother and the child Susana held hands and sang the nonsense song as they played the jumping game.

In the quiet that followed the song a chilling wind whipped the laced ocotillo branches of the encircling wall, and Don Angel jerked to his feet muttering of the early start and the need for sleep. He beckoned the reluctant Susana to her feet and stalked ahead to their tent.

"Pity her," said Tía María, to whom the night was still young. "She has need of cheerfulness, that little one who loves music."

"But she is not as sad as she was before," commented her son. "Have you not noticed, at times she smiles!"

"I have also noticed," said his mother rather crossly, for Tía María did not like to have it hinted that she might miss any item of interest, "that when she is seated she spreads her skirts to hide shoes that are almost worn through."

"It is no affair of yours, woman," said the father, who was content to rest his full stomach by lying on his back and observing the stars.

It was then they heard the terrifying scream in the Galván tent.

Susana's voice could be heard pleading for mercy. Then out of the tent's opening burst the servant Tomito, clutching his *tilma* over his shaggy head and howling as he ran.

Gil José had leaped to his feet but stood still. It was not Susana's life being threatened.

Tomito raced through the barricade's exit into the outer dark. The guard outside shouted, but Tomito did not stop. Only his cries ended abruptly, as if somewhere in the ink-black night he felt safe.

For a moment the stooped figure of Don Angel was seen in the tent's opening. He was holding his sword and glaring after the runner. Then he dropped the canvas. There was silence in the tent. Susana's figure was seen briefly shadowed on the canvas wall before the candle went out. The dim silhouette she presented would be long remembered by those watching. She had dropped down on the low military cot with her head lowered in the attitude of a woman lost to despair.

It was noticeable the next day that the men and women rode in separate groups. Opinions were being weighed as to Don Angel's attack, and the disturbing fact that Tomito had not been seen since running from the Galván tent.

There was much speculation as to Don Angel's reason for attacking the man.

Susana was surprised to find she was being shown special consideration. She had no intention of explaining to anyone the reasons behind the shocking scene in the tent, but after some skillful urging she confided certain facts to Tía María, and for some reason felt better after the telling. Tía María was not slow

in passing the information on to the other women, who told
their husbands, so that before the evening all the company knew
why Tomito had been driven into the night.

Don Angel, they learned, had entered the tent after the feast
carrying a candle lighted at the Galván fire, to find Tomito
crouched over the basket of dried figs where Don Angel kept
hidden his bottles of *aguardiente*. He was drinking when the
candlelight exposed him, and Don Angel began beating him
over the head with the flat of his sword. Only the thickness of
Tomito's shaggy hair saved his life.

For some curious reason, while the colonists agreed that
thievery in the expedition could not go unpunished, and Don
Angel was justified in his attack, their concern was more for the
missing Tomito than the abused Don Angel. The close watch
being kept for the Apaches was now divided with an equally
close watch for signs of water, and no man could survive long
in this dangerous region without food or water or a weapon of
any kind. Where had he found shelter, at nighttime in the desert;
where was he hiding now? Was he skulking on foot over the
blazing sand trying to keep the caravan in sight and himself
hidden?

The men agreed that when Tomito was found steps would be
taken to protect him from further reprisal by Don Angel.

There were reasons for this decision. Anza had given express
orders before setting out that no colonist was to bring any strong
drink of his own. Several, it was true, had smuggled into their
saddle packs a few bottles of pulque. But Don Angel's brandy was
better, as well as being contraband, and, even worse to men
and women who were sharing their all, he had never been known
to offer anyone a sip.

The majority of these people were of simple origin. They had
not been able to understand a colonist who brought with him
a servant, even such an unprepossessing one as Tomito.

As a result, little sympathy had been wasted this morning on
Don Angel when, for the first time, he had been forced to do
his own packing and saddling, and even less that evening, when
he struggled alone with the tent he had never been able to manage
even with Tomito's aid. He was rescued by the cheerful Felipe,
who took advantage of the situation to learn all his mother
might have missed concerning the disappearance of Tomito.

The joint efforts of Felipe and his mother failed to make understandable the mysterious extent of Don Angel's violence. Tomito's theft of a drink so strong he could surely have taken very little seemed trivial in contrast to the fury it had roused in Don Angel, who had obviously been ready to kill a man who had served him for years.

"I cannot understand why your man was so angry," Tía María observed that evening to Susana.

Susana could not explain, not even to Tía María. But she knew.

Don Angel's rage had not begun in the tent.

She had known, when Don Angel rode off the field at the height of the cattle hunt, that his fury against Gil José was close to the breaking point. With Don Angel resentment of any kind demanded a victim. Susana had borne the brunt many times of his anger resulting from matters of which she knew nothing.

Susana knew it was not Tomito who had been attacked, but Gil José. Tomito had merely served to divert them both from some nameless form of retribution.

Her thoughts went to the servant somewhere in the night and the desert. Try as she would, she felt little pity for Tomito. She felt only relief at being rid of the surly man who had known too much about Susana and Don Angel and who, as Don Angel's household spy, had for so many years been her enemy.

During the next day's travel Susana thought a great deal about Don Angel. She had never before thought critically of the man she had married or compared him with other men. Now as they rode she studied the hawk's profile set in unrelenting anger against the cobalt sky.

She listened to Don Angel, who talked a great deal in peevish undertones. She saw him, as if for the first time, among simple but valiant men who were engaged in a tremendous and dangerous undertaking and who could accept losses and discomfort and continue to make jokes and enjoy music and play games. Don Angel's complaints and ill temper made a poor showing against such men as Anza and Gil José and, yes, even the good-tempered, hard-working Felipe.

"Take your eyes from me!" The snarl was that of an animal about to attack. "Do you think I enjoy your idiot's stare?"

She rode on beside him in silence. She did not join the cheerful Tía María as on other days of riding. Her heart had no room for jollity; her probings had left it raw. She had at last dared to look deeply into the past and seen reflected there the future that must be hers.

[3]

They were nearing Tubac, winding northward in orderly fashion over terrain that became increasingly desolate. Anza did not urge haste on the riders. There was no need. The colonists rode at their maximum speed, which amounted at times to twenty miles in a day. This was an impressive rate considering the slow pace of the heavily burdened mules.

They were moving toward new dangers. October was the bad month on the desert—one of hurricanes and dust storms and drought.

There were times when Anza's soldiers raced the length of the caravan with the warning cry "*Huracán!*" Nothing could be done then but huddle down on the earth, well wrapped and shielded by one's horse or mule if the beast could be persuaded to lie or kneel, and remain there until the rush of wind-driven sand ended. But there was no defense against the restless sand, which harried them night and day. During the cold nights it sifted through the tightest-woven canvas and coated the bedding with thick layers of gritty dust.

By day it clouded the sky, driving through the air like silver rain. It gnawed the riders' lids and reddened their eyes and etched permanent lines in drying skin. Ears and throat, armpits and groin were invaded by sand. It was between their teeth and in their food and what water they found.

The men drew the *tilmas* over their heads and the women rode masked in their *rebozos*. Hooded like monks, they followed the endless way through the lunar waste that would be southern Arizona.

The disappearance of Tomito was discussed from time to time. Days followed the episode of the cattle hunt, and there was still no sign of the runaway. Perhaps Susana thought of him more often than the others, not only in dread of his being found, but with a growing awareness of what a man alone in the desert might be enduring. She thought of him in the misery of their hot, water-rationed days, when the clay and leather jugs were drained of water and no one knew when the next supply would be found. Not even Anza could be sure. Cross after cross on his map, once signifying water sources used by the First Expedition, were found to be dry patches on a dry desert.

Added torment to the travelers was the fact that they were apparently surrounded on all sides by water! On every horizon crystalline lakes sparkled where no lakes existed. Some were banked with trees and waving grasses. And while the colonists knew these were mirages, born of the burning sun that coated the distances with liquid glass, still they never stopped hoping that perhaps the tempting lake ahead might be real.

As for the low hills that kept appearing on every side, these might or might not be there, depending on the mood of the wizard sun.

The hills they reached early in the afternoon of October twelfth were actual. They were sandy and shrub-freckled and cast cool shadows soothing to bodies bruised by heat and the saddle. Anza led the way to an opening in them with the assurance of a man who knew the region. He had traversed it many times on journeys made between Mexico City and Tubac in behalf of the San Francisco project.

He stopped his horse at the entrance of the pass and lifted his hand. The colonists were bewildered. It was only one o'clock. They had never before stopped so early.

But Anza's order was emphatic. "Dismount. Prepare to camp for the night."

Tía María voiced the general bewilderment. "Why do we stop now, when none of us are tired? What is this place that is so important we must not go on?" Her son knew. He had been told of this by Gil José, who had traversed it with Anza. Its evil reputation lost nothing in Felipe's manner. He pointed dramatically at the narrow slot in the hills.

"That is Guambut!"

At that name Tía María's plump cheeks drained to tallow, and even Don Angel showed concern, for all Mexico had heard of the recent tragedies in the notorious El Paso del Guambut (near the future station of Casita). It was a favorite Apache ambush. The Indians lurked in these hills and had swooped down ,many times to rob and kill bands of travelers trapped in the narrow canyon.

"Now we will all be murdered," Tía María said as starkly as if a stone ax were already at her graying locks.

Susana looked from the pass to the crumpled hills. No feathered headdress showed. There was no thunder of hoofs or of shouting.

"It is empty," she said hopefully.

"They are there!" trumpeted Tía María. "It is a death trap!"

Her son nodded cheerfully. "Yes, by that name it is known. The murder pass! Guambut of death!"

Then, having succeeded in bringing drama into their day, he proceeded to comfort the two women.

"Do you think Captain Anza does not know what he is doing? He will have us rest this afternoon and night outside the pass to gain strength for the ride through it tomorrow."

"Where we will fight for our lives," moaned Tía María.

Susana saw that the mother and son were enjoying the taste of danger even though the danger was disturbingly close.

No fires were lighted that night and there was no singing. The barricade was built higher than usual and the guard was doubled. The colonists slept uneasily or not at all.

Susana was one who could not sleep. Her thoughts went to Tomito, who was somewhere in this dangerous night without protection. If a large, well-armed company had reason to fear the Apaches, what terrors might be his? She heard Gil José's voice in the night. It was a casual reminder, "All goes well!"

After a time she slept and almost at once, it seemed, was wakened by the lusty shout of Anza summoning his charges to action.

They obeyed quickly and with all the skill they possessed. Anza's summons had been made in his ordinary tone and gave no sign that this morning's start would be different from any other. The San Franciscans followed his example and chatted cheerfully as they saddled and packed, but with lowered voices, and eyes keeping careful watch on the range of hills.

Surrounded by his guard, at the entrance of the narrow canyon, Anza faced the serious, intent faces of those whose lives he was now to risk along with his own.

"I do not have to warn you to be cautious," he began. "Each

man must keep watch for himself. We must also take certain protective measures as a group. Our advance into Guambut will not be made in the ordinary way. As you follow me into the pass, crowd your mounts together. This massed display of numbers should discourage any plans for attack our enemies may have, and aid in our mutal protection if we are attacked.

"For your added protection, my men will not ride in advance with me, but with you. Now I ask the soldiers to take all the small children before them on their saddles, and if trouble comes, to guard them with their lives!"

At this his soldiers left him and rode through the procession collecting the smaller children before taking up their positions at regular intervals outside the line.

The mothers were understandably nervous, but they handed their children over without protest, knowing that to the Apaches a white scalp of any size was more precious than gold. None needed to be told that even if its life were spared death would be preferable for a white child to captivity among the Apaches.

Each soldier had a child before his saddle, and some held two or three.

They had not left Anza alone. Father Font was with him. Anza leaned from his saddle to speak wryly to his friend.

"My soldiers are so burdened that if we are attacked they will never be able to locate their guns."

Font smiled.

"The women will ride with greater courage if they feel their children are safe. You are a wise man, my friend."

"I am a soldier," said Anza, and signaled with his staff; no bugle would sound this morning. "Advance!" he called, so that those in front heard and set their mounts forward, and he and Font, turning together, the soldier mounted and the Franciscan on foot leading his mules, faced the narrow entrance to the pass.

All the riders moved, urging their mounts together shoulder to shoulder, head to tail. The horses scented the tension, and their flanks trembled and their nostrils drank in air and released it with soft, nervous snortings. All eyes were on Anza, who, riding a little ahead of Font, as if to offer protection for the monk, led the way into the pass.

Slowly, like a glacier formation, the expedition flowed forward. The soldiers' eyes raked the rim of the hills against the sky. Would the enemy pour down over these hills, or be waiting at the exit to bottle the cavalcade into the canyon? Anxiety was in every heart, but strongest in Anza's. He rode calmly, proudly, at the head of hundreds of living creatures. Let the hidden enemy see—and withhold! He rode as if this advance was no different from that of any other day.

Like the others, Susana watched the crest of the hills. Her expression was serene. At her side Tía María was calling on the saints, and on other deities whose names Susana had never heard but which she suspected were Indian. She was mildly puzzled by Tía María's anxiety. Tía María's mule was crowded against Seda's flank, and on Susana's other side rose the shining haunch of Don Angel's Major. On the other side of Tía María, between the two women and the hills, were Felipe and Gil José. The tremendous slow-moving company was a shield. Susana was not afraid.

Gil José held his two small favorites, the Peralta boy and the Alviso girl, before his military saddle. He was chattering nonsense to the children and both were laughing. Felipe was humming some sort of tune with his eyes on the hilltops. It seemed to Susana this was no different from other mornings, only all were riding more closely together.

El Paso del Guambut was not a long canyon. But it was hours before the slowly moving mass reached the opening that led into the open plain.

The San Franciscans poured out onto the desert after Anza with the sense of release other expatriates must have known in their escape from the Red Sea.

"God was guiding us," Padre Font wrote that night in his diary. But he did not fail to credit Anza for the military ruse that both leaders were certain had prevented an Apache attack. They knew what the others did not, that the Apaches had planned to ambush the company in the pass.

Anza credited the safe passage to the brave show of arms presented by his men.

They did not travel much farther that day. The tension had been great, and all were weary and thirsty when a small lake fringed with green appeared on the horizon. "One more mirage," the riders told one another, and would not let their hopes rise.

Then Anza turned in his saddle to wave and smile, and they knew the lake was real. The cattle scented water and galloped ahead of the line, and animals and humans together took heart. Camp was made in this place where were scattered a number of small lakes, and which was called Las Lagunas.

Father Font protested Anza's call for an early start the next day.

"We should celebrate our salvation with a thanksgiving service," he argued.

"We can keep thanksgiving in our hearts until we are a little safer than we are here, padre. We are still in serious danger. This is the veritable heart of Apache country, and any delay before we reach Tubac may have terrible consequences."

Father Font's heart was so filled with gratitude for their escape that he did not press the matter. He agreed that since haste was imperative Mass could be postponed until the longed-for arrival at Tubac. All were eager now to reach Anza's fortress in the desert where the remainder of the expedition was waiting.

Felipe, who had work of his own, had fallen into the habit of assisting Don Angel each morning and evening. Don Angel awaited his aid now as a matter of course.

Don Angel's attitude toward the Perea family had noticeably softened. He took pains to speak amiably, even gallantly, to Tía María. Susana could see the herb woman was not wholly won over to this new Don Angel. Tía María, she suspected, knew that his pattern of friendship was based not on liking but on need. If her son also suspected this, he gave no sign.

The two women returned to find Don Angel and Felipe deep in argument over the Galván portmanteau. The don wished it placed atop the mule's saddle pack as heretofore. Felipe insisted it was too heavy for the mule and should be dragged, as Indians dragged heavy burdens. Don Angel said that would ruin the appearance of a fine piece of luggage. Felipe, with a droll glance at the battered portmanteau, said such a fine article was beyond ruin. Don Angel shrugged his shoulders and turned away.

Felipe winked at his mother and Susana, picked up the portmanteau, and lashed it on the mule's pack.

Susana found herself laughing. She seemed to be seeing those around her with new eyes these days, and hearing them with new ears. She wanted to say then, I like you, Felipe! She might have done so if Don Angel had not been there.

The adobe mission of San José de Tumacacori rose out of the desert to meet the travelers before they reached Tubac. It was unlike any other Spanish church in the Southwest. It was domed and handsome; an important mission. The expedition halted briefly and left Father Font there to attend to certain churchly details relating to the expedition. He would join them within a day or so, he promised the pilgrims, at Tubac.

After that they hurried, putting spurs to the horses and using the argument of the long whips with the mules. They had left Las Lagunas at eight that morning and it was now past noon. The riders were seething with impatience. No matter how they urged their mounts, the entire caravan seemed in slow motion, so great was the longing to reach Tubac.

They had covered the first dangerous stretch of the long way to San Francisco Bay. But they had averaged a little more than twelve miles a day.

On this day they traveled more than twenty miles in the six hours of riding! For it was only two that afternoon, and the sun was still in full blaze overhead when Gil José left his place beside Anza and came racing toward them waving his helmet. His shout was exultant.

"Tubac!"

At first Susana saw nothing on the horizon but a shimmer of green resembling the lake mirages they had glimpsed so many times. But no, it was not a mirage. Ahead were cultivated fields of waving corn such as they had left behind in Mexico. Beyond the cornfields as they advanced rose the sturdy, thick walls of Anza's desert fortress, El Presidio de Tubac.

[4]

It was a triumph in itself to have reached Tubac, although the desert settlement turned out to be little more than a cluster of low mud buildings. There was a small church not unlike the one at Horcasitas, and the presidio, which was under Captain Anza's special command.

The welcome given the new arrivals by Tubac was far out of proportion to the size of the frontier outpost. The soldiers stationed there with their families hailed Anza as a father returned to his flock. The warmest greetings were given them by the other colonists, who for so many weeks had been waiting for them at Tubac under the command of Lieutenant José Joaquín Moraga, Anza's second-in-command.

There was no need for formal introductions. Before the travelers were out of their saddles they were friends with those who had waited and were eager to assist and welcome them with kisses and tears.

"As I said it would be, we are one big family!" Tía María was heard to exclaim many times. And this was true, and the way it would continue, and the friendships born of this meeting would last. The two groups formed a large, well-outfitted unit, bound by a loyalty as great as an actual blood relationship. First names were used, and such terms as "cousin" and "uncle," and this usage would persist through many generations in California, where descendants of Anza's colonists still retain their sense of kinship.

And still the augmented company was eager to leave, awaiting only the promised arrival of Father Font. The next lap of their pilgrimage would take them directly through the Apache-held country between Tubac and the Gila River.

As day after day went by, anxiety centered on Father Font. What could have happened to the Franciscan? No word came from Tumacacori. Everyone could see Anza was anxious for the safety of his friend. Much of the women's talk began centering on the mystery, and anxiety was expressed for the frail chaplain.

The visits in the presidio homes were enjoyable to Tía María and Susana, and still the two women invariably left them with the sense of escaping into a fresher and freer world. Dark walls were pleasant but confining to eyes grown accustomed to an unlimited sweep of sand and sky. After the brief weeks of outdoor living even Susana found the human scent of houses unpleasant to nostrils and lungs made sensitive by clean desert air spiced with the scents of mesquite and chaparral and sage.

"Will I ever be content to live within walls again?" Tía María once exclaimed to Susana as they were returning to the tents.

Susana saw no more of Gil José during the delay at Tubac than she had in the days of travel. Anza fumed as the week went by, and still no word came from the mission of Tumacacori. There could be no moving on without Father Font. Anza's annoyance showed in his shouted commands to his soldiers as he marched them around the hot, dusty plaza in the same exhausting routine they had followed in the plaza at Horcasitas. So the long, hot days of waiting that were so pleasurable for the women were even more exhausting for the soldiers than the days spent in the saddle, and any free time that might come to Gil José found him relaxing with Felipe at the Perea tent.

To Susana, even a wearied Gil José was too glowing a personality to be eyed with the frank interest she was beginning to show the others. The delay in setting out was a week's reprieve to her in which California seemed more remote than ever, and she could give full attention to the interesting people and events at Tubac.

Added freedom was hers after Don Angel's discovery on the sandy outskirts of the settlement of a small cantina with an adjoining cockpit. This served to make him consider Tubac a civilized community and accounted for much of his time, which left Susana with treasured afternoons and evenings to spend with the Pereas. For it was with the sociable Tía María, as if watching the reflections in a mirror, that Susana was learning the pleasure of meeting and knowing those with whom her life had been cast. Her interest in others expanded, and like a child entering the conscious world she began making friends. Her circle of attention advanced beyond the Pereas and Gil José. Her great eyes widened on each person she met, wondering with a child's passionate interest what their lives had been. She talked to all she met, but timidly, and the only one she could not speak with, and could seldom bring herself to look upon, was Gil José.

But he was always there, pressing his image between Susana and the others, intruding in her dreams. His campaign to attract her interest and draw her into conversation was as persistent as before and her determination to evade him was as strong. He could find no way to speak to her alone. Whenever he did have the fortune to meet with her, Tía María was always there.

Gil José had a healthy respect for the herb woman's temper. He could not risk the scene she was capable of making if he spoke to Susana in other than a comradely way. As for Susana, she was determined that a reasonable friendliness must serve Gil José, such as she gave Felipe. Their conversations remained brief and conventional. "Beautiful was your mother!" Gil José might remark, but both he and Susana knew the trite comment meant much more than an ordinary compliment.

During this delay at Tubac, Susana took trembling steps forward toward the recovery of a personality that had long been lost, or, rather, that had never been permitted to grow.

It began with conversation. Listening to the others, as she did with this new perception that was noticeably changing her from a sad, withdrawn creature into a charmingly responsive young woman, she had learned that one who listens should give in return. Questions were asked of her she once would not have dared answer. Now that Don Angel was intent on the amusements of the desert outskirts of Tubac and seemed to have forgotten his insistence on anonymity, Susana felt free to explain when asked that her husband was one who had come upon misfortune, and that it was to retrieve his future that the pair had joined the expedition to California. Little more needed to be added to this beyond the fact that the Galváns were from Mexico City. This always gave rise to an avalanche of questions concerning the fabulous city, for to all Mexicans their capital was a metropolis of a thousand wonders. Susana found herself recounting, lamely at first, to rapt audiences her memories of the physical aspects of the city and its life, and in a small way she became a celebrity.

The loss of Tomito changed life in many ways for the Galváns. Susana's attempts at cooking had brought little comment from Don Angel during the hurried days of travel that brought them to Tubac, for much of their food consisted of the boiled corn-meal mush called *atole*, tortillas, beef jerky, or beef broiled at a communal pit by the soldiers if time permitted. A minor catastrophe had been discovered shortly after setting out. Someone—no one ever knew who—had forgotten to pack the bean pots. They would have to do without the good frijoles that were as important to their cuisine as corn. But during these leisurely days at Tubac the women of the camp spent more time in cooking and produced more elaborate meals, and Don Angel, scenting the rich odors drifting from other campfires, knew that much was lacking at his own. His comments on Susana's attempts were harsher than his criticism had been of Tomito's cooking.

There was a day when Don Angel hurled the *atole* pot at the ever-hovering Vengador and refused to eat, and that afternoon Susana appeared at the fire where Tía María was preparing the tortilla dough for her family's supper while her men and Gil José waited, and asked with astonishing boldness: "Will you show me, please, what you are doing?"

The request pleased Tía María, who, had often heard Don Angel's complaints, and not without sympathy, much as she disliked the man.

"Watch, then." Tía María's hands slowed their movements to show when the grayish-yellow dough was kneaded to the right consistency, and how a lump was then patted and spun between supple palms. Susana watched attentively as the spinning disk became flatter and rounder, and fell without breaking onto the hot iron pan while another cake was shaping. She tried then, and her hands became more skillful until she too was making thin and round tortillas without their breaking, and suddenly she was laughing with pleasure at her own artistry, and Tía María and the others were laughing with her.

Tía María explained other matters to Susana, such as the herbs she had used in the stew, samples of which she gave to Susana, and the way the dried beef or mutton should be soaked before stewing, and how long these meats should be cooked and when rice or beans should be added. She gave advice to Susana most Mexican girls learn at their mother's knees, and Susana listened with head nodding and eyes glowing. She left to rejoin Don Angel and began at once to test her new skills at his fire.

That evening Don Angel was given a platter of the best food he had eaten since leaving Mexico City, and, smacking his thin lips as he scoured the plate with the last tortilla, he demanded, "Is it true you have cooked this?" When Susana admitted it was true, he looked at her sharply, and said: "It may be the hours you spent gossiping in my kitchen with that old woman were not all wasted."

Susana gave no credit to Tía María. It would only cause trouble.

Tía María inquired of Susana the next morning, "Your husband. Did he like the dinner?"

"He ate the food. He ate it all. He said nothing. No word of complaint for the first time, so I am grateful to you."

"It is nothing!" protested Tía María, but she knew a great deal had been done for Susana and there was a sly content in her look as if, in some undetectable fashion, she had succeeded in outwitting Don Angel.

During this stay at Tubac, Susana learned to speak and carry herself with new assurance.

She did not mind Don Angel's surliness and bad temper as she had before. His complaints meant increasingly little, while Tía María's good-natured praise for her efforts and the open admiration on the faces of Felipe and Gil José gave her such pleasure that she could close her ears and seal her eyes to Don Angel's carping.

Much of this new independence was owed to the fact that Tomito was still missing. When she remembered him, it was with the continued hope that he would never be found. Now only she and Gil José knew what had happened on the night of the Apache raid.

Don Angel did not at first realize that his power to torment Susana was weakening. His sarcasm and threats were as barbed as ever. She had never answered, and her continued silence did not betray her changed attitude.

Susana was no longer the meek young woman who had sat half a day in the sun at Horcasitas without drink or food, not stirring, because Don Angel had ordered her not to move.

While day followed day at Tubac, and the colonists enjoyed idleness and new friendships, Anza's temper was noticeably shortening. The weeks went by without the arrival of Father Font.

"I can't understand why he is staying so long at Tumacacori," the captain fumed to Lieutenant Moraga. "He knows how dangerous delay can be to us now." He had too much respect for Font to add his private opinion that the priest had little sense of the value of time.

Moraga hesitated. "He and his friends may have been waylaid. They are a very small party."

The faces of the military leaders grew grim as they pictured the robed figures toiling on foot over the endless sand.

It would not have eased Anza's anxiety to know that Font was not on his way. The Franciscan had fallen ill at the mission of Tumacacori and was lying there in a heavy fever, unable to walk or even ride his mule. Font's faith was as indomitable as that of his beloved leader Serra, but like Serra's, it was sheathed in a frail body. Faith was holding the gentle Franciscan to life now at Tumacacori, where he was being tended by the mission priests.

Anza had not thought of illness. He was afraid that Apaches had ambushed the priest's party. The commander discussed this and other fears with Moraga in the privacy of his office in the presidio.

Moraga was of an optimistic nature. He was certain all was well. The priests at the Tumacacori Mission had many Indian friends who would give warning if an Apache war party were in the neighborhood. The distance was short between that mission and Tubac, and surely if harm had come to them a scout would have arrived long before this with the evil news. Moraga was sure there was some logical reason for Father Font's delay.

Anza would not be cheered. This delay was endangering the success and the carefully laid plans of the San Francisco Expedition.

October was drawing to an end.

Winter was on its way to the Southwest. There were mornings when frost stiffened the rapier leaves in the cornfields. Anza knew from experience how cold winter can be on the desert. Most of his colonists had followed him out of a semitropical climate. Many were women and children and babies, and there were women ready to give birth.

Anza sent armed scouts out to search for the Franciscan's party and hoped for their arrival every hour. The delay that was so delightful to the rest of the people was one of torment for Anza.

It drew to an end and the company was still at Tubac. It was Sunday and the twenty-first of October before the first faint priestly halloo sounded over the desert.

[5]

Father Font showed the effects of his illness, but his meeting with his flock at Tubac was a radiant reunion. The San Franciscans had to divide the warmth of their welcome, for their chaplain was not alone. Two other Franciscan padres had traveled with him from the mission at Tumacacori. With them were three Indian servants and three Indian interpreters.

These two friars were famous throughout the Southwest and Mexico. They were the explorer-missionaries Father Francisco Garcés and Father Tomás Eixarch.

Both were missionaries after Font's own heart. They had traveled in remote and dangerous regions and made no enemies. Their religion was based on love for their faith and for mankind, and they treated the gentiles, as Serra's confreres spoke of the Indians, with the respect due them as children of God. As a result they traveled singly or together without guards and had never been molested. Their presence had served to protect Father Font. The San Franciscans were drawn at once to the two friars, and could not decide which was the more compelling, for both were gentle men with powerful personalities. They were great evangelists and had converted entire tribes. Much of the peace that prevailed in this region (in contrast to the enmity of the Apaches) was due to these Franciscans.

Father Eixarch was soft-spoken and thoughtful. He was no exhorter of the faith. He did not preach sermons brimming with threats of punishment and fire. He converted by example. He could sit with the braves for long hours without speaking, sharing their thoughts and tobacco, the way Indians liked to sit and commune with friends. He was stationed at Tumacacori.

Padre Garcés was a zealot, but a lovable one. He had penetrated to the loneliest regions in search of Indian souls. He had explored the Colorado and Gila rivers. He was the present minister of the Mission San Xavier del Bac near Tucson.

With Garcés was a figure who drew all eyes. This was the famed Indian guide Sebastián Taraval, a dark and princely man, devoted to the friar. All knew of Sebastián, who had guided Anza to California with the First Expedition.

These two priests would travel with the company as far as the Colorado River, where they planned to found a new mission. They would add prestige and protection to the Anza party on the dangerous stretch between Tubac and the great red river, where, like Anza, they had thousands of friends. They were not afraid of the Apaches. If captured, tortured, slain, their deaths would go as had their lives, to the glorification of their faith.

This conviction was shared by Father Font. The serene faces of the three Franciscans shamed any member of the Anza group who might have dreaded the next stretch of the way.

Father Font had his usual formula for celebrating the safe arrival and reunion. Mass was celebrated at once by the three priests, honoring the three patrons of the San Francisco Expedition, St. Francis, St. Michael, and the Lady of Guadalupe. No sooner was Mass ended than Anza made his announcement. "At last we are all together, and there is no time to waste. Be ready to start early tomorrow for San Xavier."

Font made a rapid amendment to the order.

"After Mass, children! Mass will be sung before we leave, and everyone must attend. Bring all your animals to be blessed."

There were the usual protests from the women and the declaration that they would never be ready, although actually for days everyone had been ready to set out at an hour's notice.

Early the next morning the presidio bugle roused those who were to leave and those who were permanently stationed at Tubac.

Preparations for departure went fairly smoothly in spite of the general excitement. The colonists had learned a great deal about the handling of mules since leaving Horcasitas.

How many were going to California? Father Font, always intrigued by the intrinsic value of numbers and even tempted to believe in their psychic powers, had spent some time figuring out the numbers of colonists and beasts and the estimated hours of march and dates of travel. The sum total promised well.

The assemblage filled the square and stretched from one end of Tubac to the other. The people were in three groups, united this morning for the first time.

The original division had come with Anza from the Horcasitas rendezvous. It consisted of one hundred and twenty men, women, and children.

The second group that had been waiting at Tubac under the

command of Lieutenant Moraga included Sergeant Pablo Grijalva and twenty-eight soldiers and their families. Of the sixty-
three members in this group, twenty-nine were women.

The third and final group were the three newly arrived Franciscans and their servants and guides.

All these, united, made up a grand total of two hundred and
thirty-five (or forty) souls. Of these, two hundred and seven
were to become settlers in California.

There were thirty families, possessed of one hundred and
fifteen children. Seventeen of these would become the founding
families of San Francisco.

There were also seven hard-worked muleteers, only one of
which, it had been discovered, was an adept at his profession;
three vaqueros; and now, with the addition of those from Tumacacori, five Indian interpreters, who were to introduce the emigrants to the friendly tribes between Tubac and the Río Colorado.

Of the thousand and more domestic beasts, four hundred and
fifty were riding horses and saddle mules. These were privately
owned by, or shared between, the colonists. The three pack trains
were made up of one hundred and forty mules heavily burdened
with baggage and provisions and munitions and tools and other
necessities needed to colonize a new world.

Anza's own pack train consisted of one hundred and twenty
mules carrying mess and baggage for himself and his guard. The
mules belonging to the priests were entrusted with their possessions and the secular material needful for spiritual care along
the way, for the mission Fathers Eixarch and Garcés planned
to establish on the Colorado, and for the church to be built for
San Francisco on the saint's own California bay.

Anza, looking over the processions of animals, and remembering with sorrow the five hundred horses, their finest, stolen by
the Apaches, was nevertheless able to make the proud appraisal:
"Never before has there been so well-outfitted a company—
no, not in the history of the world!"

The last blessing was given and the last prayer said. The
bugler sent his notes ringing over the fortress walls. It was the
signal of departure. Once more, although all was in readiness,
there was a certain amount of confusion as packs and saddles
were given final adjustment and strayed children accounted for.

Don Angel mounted Major and rode a little ahead. Gil José rode toward Susana to assist her. She had one foot in the stirrup of the little mare, Seda, when Tía María and her son came up. Both were smiling.

Felipe's guitar hung over his back, and his mule's bridle reins were looped over one arm. Something was concealed in a fold of his *tilma.*

"A gift. From the family Perea."

He handed Susana a pair of small, stout shoes.

She had noticed that between his bouts of work and of idleness in the past week, Felipe had been stitching and pounding with the tools of his shoemaking trade.

She put on the shoes at once, while the Pereas were touched by her childish delight. Don Angel had not noticed. The shoes were of calf's hide, well-seasoned and rubbed to such softness that they did not chafe the ankles. The soles were thick.

"I made the sides high so the cactus needles cannot harm you," Felipe explained, as happy in the success of his gift as was Susana.

"How did you know what size to make them?" she marveled.

The musician gave her a comical look. "Have I not eyes? I am a shoemaker, and your feet, they are not very big."

"They are strong shoes," said Tía María, proud of her son. "See, I know him to be useless, but he makes shoes that wear well."

"I thank you," Susana told Felipe, and the words were warm with pleasure for the gift that had been made for her.

"It is nothing," said Felipe grandly, and held her mare's stirrup before Gil José could dismount.

In the saddle Susana kept her eyes fixed on the stirrups. They did not hide the new shoes. She would gladly have walked in them all the way to the mission of San Xavier.

Gil José, looking down at Felipe, was scowling.

"I would have made her shoes," he said softly.

"The old man would not like that."

"He will not mind your having made them?"

"I—a musician? A singer? He knows I am alive only because I help him pack and unpack, which I do out of neighborly kindness toward his wife, and not for him. But for that, I am so far beneath him that I do not exist."

"You are right," agreed Gil José, who for once understood Don Angel's point of view. "No man can be jealous of a musician."

Once more it was departure, with the slow massed movement forward and tears from and for those who were to stay. This twenty-second day of October was truly the beginning of the great pilgrimage, for every heart held the magic knowledge that at last all were together and on their way. There were happy cries, "To San Xavier!" and Father Font's familiar challenge: "For St. Francis."

[6]

The riding was rough between Tubac and San Xavier. The early start had promised a fair distance to be covered that day. Then the usual troubles and a few unexpected ones began.

A child was reported lost, but was found asleep in a packsaddle after a half-hour search. A mule shed its pack and had to be argued into accepting responsibility. The worst handicap was the desert riding, which became increasingly difficult until it was not the mules, but the horses, that brought progress to a snail's pace.

There were areas covered with a thorny brush. The mules forced their burdens through the needled branches and came out unscathed. But the horses, only partly protected by saddle blankets, plunged through the brush as if breasting a sea of spines. The long thorns ripped at their heads and tender sides and through the cotton skirts of the women. "These bushes are known as the Thorns of the Crucifixion," Tía María explained, rubbing her sore thighs.

Men dismounted to lead the women's horses through the entanglement and spread their thick wool serapes or *tilmas* over their wives' knees.

Don Angel was ahead of Susana and did not notice when the short-legged Seda was trapped to her mane in the brush. Gil José was patrolling the line looking for trouble spots. He brought the floundering mare under control and, spreading his military serape over Susana's knees, rode ahead holding the thorn branches back before the mare.

The loan of a serape to another man's wife was too intimate a service to go unnoticed.

"Does the old one see?" Tía María asked her son in a low voice.

"He is not so old that he is blind. See his face? A storm cloud."

Don Angel was casting glowering looks over his shoulder, but he did not draw back, and Gil José did not relinquish his role as protector. As for Susana, she rode in bemused silence, for, having thanked Gil José in brief and almost inaudible terms, she was now nursing in her heart words whispered between them.

"Why do you turn from me when I care so deeply?"

Her answer came even more softly from the folds of the *rebozo* shielding her eyes from the sun. "I have told you. Because you must not."

That had been all, but the shared emotion left woman and soldier spent.

Riding beside Don Angel after the thorn areas were passed, she heard him remark in a biting way:

"Your choice of admirers does me honor! The first, a peon from my own ranch, and now, a poor soldier!"

No poorer than ourselves, Susana thought in defense of Gil José, and was relieved when days and nights went by and Don Angel did not refer to the matter again, although she knew better than to think he was forgetting.

The terrain became more arid, broken by sand dunes and the strange shapes of saguaro and barrel cactus. Color returned slowly to Susana's cheeks, and her thoughts, lulled with the monotonous riding, became sad and beautiful. She did not think of the land as ugly and the riding arduous. Her thoughts rode ahead with Gil José, whose helmet could be seen among the others in the Anza guard.

Don Angel rode with his chin on his chest; he had fallen asleep.

It was three-thirty in the afternoon and only fifteen miles had been covered, when a worried colonist by the name of José Vicente Felix left his place in the line to report to Anza that his wife was in the first throes of labor.

Anza gave the order to halt. He had his own tent, which was the largest, set up as a delivery room. The pilgrims were pleased to dismount, since it gave them a chance to stretch legs all but atrophied after the hours of riding through the thorn fields.

All watched, the women with concern and sympathy, as the pregnant woman walked unsteadily into the big tent assisted by her husband and followed by the members of her family. With them went several men, Gil José among them, who were the husband's friends. Anza entered last. He carried the medical bag given him in Mexico City.

Tía María pointed after Gil José.

"He goes to comfort the poor husband," she remarked sarcastically to those around her. "Why must men whose wives give birth have their friends with them, when it is the woman who needs courage?"

"Women are with her," Susana pointed out unexpectedly.

"Her own mother is with her, and other women of her family. I wish—" Tía María's wish was not expressed, but Susana knew its intent. Had not Father Font said the herb woman was famed on the border countries as midwife and *medica*? Why then?— but no woman could question Anza.

Neither Felipe nor Don Angel seemed to be listening, but each was observing the far horizon with looks curiously male. Felipe's usually smiling face had no expression, but Don Angel was plainly displeased, as if the delay were a personal affront.

Anza came from the big tent. Any examination he made had been brief, but he was seen speaking seriously to his staff. His orders went so quickly from lip to lip that the entire company knew them almost as soon as they were spoken.

"Prepare camp. We stay here tonight."

This order was received with dismay. They had traveled so short a distance from Tubac, and the day was still young! Even worse was their situation. It would have been difficult to imagine a more disagreeable camp site. The place was called La Canoa, since it was on a river of that name, and Anza had counted on it as a water source as was indicated on his map. But rain was late this year, and the Canoa's bed was dry and gritty with sun-backed sand. Nor was there for miles around a sign of water. Anza's next order, while calmly given, showed the travelers that their situation was serious.

"We will have to dig for water."

For the first time the colonists heard these words that would become more familiar, but never less ominous. Their first great danger had been the Apaches. Now as the drought worsened over what was later to be known as the Southwest they faced the threat of thirst. They had already experienced hints of how agonizing thirst could be. They had felt the water shortage since crossing the border, for they had no way of carrying water in the necessary quantities. There had been many days when each rider was rationed to a bottle each. When saliva ceased to flow over the drying tongue, and the throat and nostrils seemed lined with bitter dust, then they had sensed the terrifying panic born of thirst.

Now at La Canoa they tilted the clay and leather water containers and found them empty. The children sensed the situation and whimpered for water. The horses and cattle stopped in their tracks, their tongues hanging. Squads of grim-faced men with shovels set out under the protection of armed guards with orders to dig in any spots that showed water-marked depressions in the sand.

Anza returned to the birthing tent. He did not come out again. The boisterous jollity that usually accompanied the making of camp was missing as the men began raising the tents and barricades. Groups of women found reason from time to time to consult with Tía María. Although a recognized authority on birth, the herb woman knew no more concerning the present crisis than the others, but was willing to hazard an opinion.

"Our captain must have seen our poor little friend faces prolonged labor." Tía María was torn by an understandable resentment of Anza for ignoring her skill as a midwife and pity for a woman she longed to help. "It is a strange thing," she reminded her listeners, "that the Señora Felix should be one to keep us here for the night, since she has already given birth without difficulty to four children. This woman I know from Culiacán and I have been with her in these times, and I assure you, never before would she have delayed us by an hour. Our captain must be planning to give her many hours of rest after the birth. He is a kind man." This was said almost spitefully, then Tía María remarked in a thoughtful way, "or can she be taken so badly, this time, that she is not to be moved until tomorrow?"

There were murmured responses on every side from those in the group who were mothers, and none from Susana, who, never having seen or experienced the birth of a child, had nothing to offer but compassion. Anza remained in the tent, and the dreary speculation continued as to developments there and out on the desert where the groups of men continued what was apparently hopeless digging.

As the afternoon went by there began, outside the tight little canvas village surrounded by its brushwood fence, a tragic, persistent lowing. It was the cry of a thousand beasts for water— a noise that would sound in the pilgrims' ears through many subsequent days and nights. Adding to the creatures' misery was hunger. There was no forage at La Canoa.

The horses ate dry spikes of coarse grass and twigs they would not normally have touched. The vaqueros beat the cattle with loaded whips but could not prevent their devouring the thick branches of cholla that were rich in liquid but thickly coated with spines. Then the cattle lowed more piteously than before with mouths and tongues swollen by the needles.

The women working at their domestic tasks in whispering groups, heard cries forced out of the Anza tent that made those who had endured childbirth tremble with sympathy.

The wife of a soldier who had borne many children spoke.

"Never have I heard such crying! Women like our friend do not cry. She must be in torment. *Pobrecita!* There is medicine for such pain. You yourself, Tía María, gave me it when you cared for me at home with my first child. I was so afraid my knees locked together, and my jaws, but the medicine you told me was harmless put me to sleep, and when I woke my first-born, Manuel, was in my arms. . . ."

Tía María's heavy body sagged. "My cures are forbidden by Father Font. By the church. By the men of science in Mexico City. They forbid the use of any medicines but their own. They are wiser than my people, but what is evil in my cures I do not know."

The women echoed her despair with murmurs of sympathy and indignation, and one protested: "These cures are used by our people as long as is remembered, and only you among us, Tía María, know what they are."

For all knew Tía María was of the elect, entrusted with the secrets of medical wisdom handed down through the Indian generations, and that in her tent, in packets labeled with her markings, were narcotics of the kind that had eased generations of

Mexico's women through the agonies of difficult childbirth, and in the removal of tumors, and the setting of broken bones. Narcotics were used mainly by women and children. Men in pain seldom resorted to them; they were too proud.

"The men in Mexico City who make these laws, do they know how women suffer?" a woman of much courage asked.

"*Vaya!*" another observed, changing the dangerous trend of thought. "He goes to her, the little father. And the child is not yet born!" And all watched Father Font disappearing into the Anza tent, and there were murmurs of dismay, for since the padre had obviously not been brought to the tent for purposes of baptism—all knew he had been summoned to give spiritual aid to one racked beyond human endurance. They knew the seriousness of sending for a priest before a birth. A soul was endangered —was it woman or child?

The harsh, quavering cry came again. Tía María paced the sand. Her hands worked together. She spoke in a distracted way, appealing to the women around her, even to the inexperienced Susana.

"If this were a first birth!" Tía María repeated. "Never before did she cry out! Dear Mother in Paradise, let her womb open and release her from pain."

The others echoed the prayer, and some of the women went to their knees to beg for divine intercession in the agonizing delivery.

Then over the desert rang a halloo of victory, and men were seen holding up their shovels and shouting that water had been struck. The squads returned to camp with filled bottles and were received like heroes, but quietly. The opened pools were scented at once and stormed by the thirst-frantic cattle. The water was soon exhausted.

The cries inside the tent were coming weaker and closer together.

The women gave their families cold food prepared early that morning at Tubac, which already seemed far away and long ago. Since there was no water for cooking, no fires were built. A cold supper and a cold wind racing over the dry earth that filled the nostrils with gritty dust made for the most miserable evening the pilgrims had known.

There were no stories or songs. Not even Felipe could touch

a guitar string. An attempt at merriment would have been pro-
fanation. By the time night had blanketed the desert, nearly all
were in their army cots, but only a few could sleep.

In the Galván tent Don Angel groaned in some nightmare of
anxiety, present or past, but Susana stared wide-eyed into the
dark and could not close her ears to the woman who still cried
out from time to time.

The bleating of the still thirsty cattle and the quavering cry
of a far-off coyote joined the faint cries of the woman, like the
voices of ghosts, Susana thought.

She slipped out of the tent without waking Don Angel and
was joined at once by the friendly shadow that was Vengador.

Only Anza's tent, where the woman lay in childbirth, was
lighted. The others were dark, and there was only one small
fire in the camp. This was before the Perea tent. Tía María was
seated in its flickering light with her many skirts rising around her
like the petals of an enormous flower.

She was staring into the red heart of the coals with narrowed
eyes that seemed to be reading some ominous message. Susana
hesitated and almost turned back. This was a Tía María she did
not know. But the herb woman moved and called her name, and
Susana sat beside her strangely silent friend, and the dog settled
with a contented sigh at their feet.

Tía María leaned forward and stirred the contents of an iron
pot sunk in the coals.

"I make *atole*," she said in a dull voice. "When there is grief
I make *atole*. Almost always it is needed, and it gives work to my
hands."

A faint cry came from the birth tent. Tía María's heavy body
rocked in an age-old rhythm.

"She suffers."

"It may end soon," whispered Susana, knowing nothing of
such matters.

They spoke in low voices not to waken Don Angel or the Perea
men. But Tía María shook her head and her face was a fire-lighted
mask.

"Do you not feel it?" she asked in a dreadful voice.

At the words Vengador lifted his head and whimpered. Susana
shivered. For a moment her forehead seemed to be brushed by
wings.

"You are frightening me!" She moved closer to Tía María. But the herb woman's face was set like an idol's.

"Do not fear it!" Her voice was strained and high-pitched. "You have no reason to, nor have I. It is with us always. Never be afraid of it while you live, or even when your time comes to die."

Susana felt the power in her words so strongly she was certain she would never again be afraid of that which keeps watch with us all in the night.

A harsh, unfamiliar voice spoke over their heads.

"My captain asks for you, *señora*."

It was a changed Gil José speaking. His expression was hard and soldierly. By military brusqueness he tried to disguise his emotion. He addressed Tía María with the sternness of one who carries a serious message.

"*Señora*," he continued, "Captain Anza has need of you. It is," his face was pale, and he wiped his wet forehead with his hand, "it is a bad labor. It is asked that you come quickly."

Tía María bounded to her feet as if the summons had been expected.

"In this moment! You, Susana, bring the *atole*. I go for my bag."

"No!" The snapped order was also unlike Gil José. "My captain commands that you bring no herbs or preparations of your own, since the only ones to be used are already beside the bed of my friend's wife."

Tía María's indignation was majestic. "Am I not to be trusted? Does your captain suspect me of wanting to harm a poor woman who is already in such torment as is known only to women and to men being executed?"

Gil José's military crest lowered and he looked abjectly unhappy.

"Dear little Aunt, I am only the voice of our captain. He sends for you in great respect, because you are famed in midwifery and you may aid this woman whose mother and sisters do nothing but weep. They have cause for their tears."

Tía María showed deep concern. "If her mother weeps and is helpless, then it is indeed a bad labor. Dear man, we go with you."

Gil José took a lighted branch from the fire and led the way.

Tía María hurried after him, easy-footed as a panther despite her weight. Susana wrapped her hand in her *rebozo* and lifted the pot of corn gruel from the coals and followed Tía María, because the herb woman had given this order and it had not been remanded by Gil José.

The tent the three entered was murky with the light of oil lamps and candles, and seemed to Susana so crowded with people that her first reaction was relief that she had set the pot of steaming *atole* outside before entering.

Susana's shocked eyes went first to the woman on the cot.

She lay like one crucified, with lids closed and swollen and the mouth open like that of a plucked bird. Her heaving belly was upthrust under the blanket, and her head with its tangled braids moved weakly, constantly, from one side to the other. Her clenched hands held a rosary broken in her convulsions. Her cries were too weak now to be heard outside the tent.

Father Font stood at the cot's head. His eyes were closed in prayer and he was holding his crucifix over the woman.

The tall figure of Anza was bowed over the cot, no militant figure now, but the man of medicine, and baffled. He had discarded his long coat and sword, and his muscular arms and frilled linen shirt were splashed brightly with red. He looked relieved at the entrance of Tía María. Anza could ride all day in the sun without leaving his saddle, but this situation was almost beyond his endurance. His leather medical kit lay open at his feet, revealing the most modern scientific iron implements and jars and vials of medicines and ointments. Tía María's eyes flickered over these with professional appraisal as she took her place beside Anza.

Susana stopped inside the entrance beside a group of weeping women. Other women stood near Anza holding basins of the precious water and strips of white cotton and linen. The woman's mother sat on the dirt floor on the other side of the cot. Wrapped from head down in her long *rebozo*, she was a silent image of grief.

Gil José had rejoined the group of men who formed a close circle around the weeping husband. They were his friends, and there to give him support in this travail that was his woman's and therefore his own. The distracted husband turned from friend to friend, weeping now on one shoulder, then on the next.

In the silence two sounds could be heard—the murmured prayer of Father Font, and an ominous dripping. Tía María took a step forward.

"Sangre!" She spoke in an awful voice and pointed to the earth.

The face of the woman on the bed was candle-white. Face, arms, and hands were wrinkled as if drained.

"Ay, blood!" agreed Anza.

Susana sickened. The dirt floor under the cot was wet and glinted with a ruby glow. Anza spoke querulously. "How can one woman lose so much blood and live? Father Font approves your midwifery. Before God I ask your help for this woman."

Tía María stepped gingerly on the damp earth and looked down on the woman who lay unconscious with eyes closed and panting with each effort to draw breath. Blankets had been piled on her, but the clenched teeth chattered as if with cold.

Tía María pulled the blankets down. The men, excepting Anza, turned their faces away. The woman, fully dressed but with clothes loosened, lay on corn husks piled thickly to catch blood. The husks were soaked through and the dripping to the floor went on like the sound of the beetle that clicks out the moments before death.

"Captain Anza," Tía María asked carefully, "is there nothing in your medicine chest that will stop this?"

"There is no cure recognized by science," snapped Anza. He was at the breaking point. Tía María wisely said no more for the moment. But her mind and Susana's were with the trumpet-flowered datura they had gathered on the desert, waiting now with other simples in Tía María's stores.

The woman writhed in a brief, tired spasm of labor, and her cry was weak as a kitten's.

"Has everything been tried?" Tía María persisted. "A serpent's skin? A sword?"

"Oh, I know your superstitions," said Anza with surprising leniency. "A sword under the blanket to cut pain, or a rattlesnake skin to shed agony." He added, as if to himself, "There can be no harm in such things, and who knows what helps, if faith is there? Hand me my sword."

Someone gave Anza his sword, and he slid the long blade carefully under the woman. For a time all watched, and then a sound rose from the bed that was not a cry, but a grinding sound as of stones forced together, a sound given *in extremis* between locked lips and teeth. Tía María's hands went to the swollen abdomen with an understanding pressure that brought its living content leaping under her hands.

She said starkly, "This is very bad. The bottom is where the head should be."

"Do I not know?" demanded Anza. "How many hours have I been trying to bring this child into the position of birth! It is wedged as solidly into its mother as if it were part of her spine."

"More than the position is wrong, Captain. I have never seen a body so empty of blood, and still it pours from her—" Tía María pointed to their feet. "A root, my Captain, long used and harmless and long known to us—with your permission?"

Susana would never have believed Tía María could be reduced to such abject pleading. But Anza's expression was set in iron. Father Font's voice in prayer—had it for a moment grown louder?

"You may not!" The captain's voice was as cold as the look he gave the herb woman. "You are not here as a consultant, but as a midwife. How am I to know which treatments are on the banned list? With no offense to you, *señora*, I ask nothing but the knowledge in your hands which in matters like this are more skillful than mine."

Tía María did not answer, but her lower lip pushed out and her eyes slitted. Father Font's voice softened. "Pull!" Tía María commanded, gripping with blood-slicked hands the flailing hands of the woman. "If you hear me, dear one, pull against my strength." But the woman only twisted her trapped arms, and the convulsion ended. The swollen body sank and lay motionless.

Susana glanced around the ring of lamp-lighted faces to the sad, dark mask that was Gil José's, and she thought, If the father whose arms he holds were Gil José and I were the wife lying there, that is the way he would look, as that husband does now. We know so little of one another, but I know if I were dying that is the way he would suffer with me.

At this moment a faint cry came from the bed like a voice from another world. All heard it. All would remember.

"The child!" whispered Tía María. "This child cries out to be born!" And Anza answered. "Now I have heard this I have never heard before, for a child unborn asks for its own deliverance!"

The leader and the herb woman might have been alone in the tent.

"It must be done now, my Captain."

"At once. It cannot live long, now that it has cried out."

"The bad way?" Tía María's voice trembled. "Must it be the bad way?" And then, the herb woman was pleading. "Not the irons, dear Mother of all mothers, not the irons! They will kill mother and child!"

She shrank from the iron forceps Anza had taken from his medical bag. They were black and cold-looking and so large they might have been used in tending a fire.

"Science knows no other way. Nor do I." It could be seen that Anza was reluctant to use the cruel tongs. As he hesitated Tía María held before his face her small, strong, bloodied hands.

"The old way, señor! The kindest way!"

Anza dropped the forceps in the bag. He seemed relieved.

"Señora, I yield to you. Do what you must. Your hands are smaller than mine, and as I have said, more skilled. Now I will assist you; I will hold her hands."

He took firm grip on the twisting arms. The woman's body arched in agony. As the spasm ebbed Tía María did what had not been done before. She lifted the woman's clothing, and now even Anza's face turned away. Such private matters as an actual birth were usually carried out under the secrecy of coverings. Tía María made the sign of the cross over her own ample breast. "Forgive me, little friend, for what must be done," she whispered, and then to Anza, "I ask you, hold her well." Then with arms bared to her shoulders she bent down.

The women watched, but the man did not. Susana saw the small, capable hands slip gently into a stretched and spongy red mass where two protuberances glistening like pearls were the buttocks of the child. The legs were folded back under the hidden body like those of a trussed fowl. Tía María's forefingers wedged through the stretched membrane and under the minute hips. The heels of her hands massaged in cautious rhythm, urging the thighs back into the swollen birth canal through which they had fought their way through so many exhausting hours. The pulsing hands moved more deeply, until the tiny limbs burst out like unfolding twigs, and Tía María, hooking her fingers under knees no larger than her own knuckles, cautiously and relentlessly drew out a small, bloodied, birdlike creature that moved and whimpered in her gory hands. A gush of blood followed the deliverance, and the woman writhed and cried out in a voice terrifying in its weakness. Anza's hold remained steady on her arms. A crescendo of prayer filled the tent, and over the sound of her own voice Susana heard that the child born at last was a boy. Tía María held it up by its heels for all to see, and every heart grew warm with love for the insectlike creature with its disproportionately large head.

In that moment the woman on the bed lifted her disheveled head. With neck stretched upward and eyes opened she stared at the child, and her face was beautiful.

"She wakens!" The exultant whisper ran through the tent, but Tía María said nothing.

Anza severed the cord with his iron medical shears. It was knotted by Tía María. First, holding the squirming child, she turned to Susana, who was best known to her among the women. She handed over the newborn one as if bestowing a gift, saying only: "Do what is to be done."

Other women brought strips of clean cloth and a flask of oil, and Susana found without surprise that she did know what to do, although she had never before held so young a child. As she tended the tiny creature that was stained and sticky and whimpering in its helplessness, she reviewed the violent struggle this frail being had made for its life. Suddenly, unreasonably, her arms closed around the little cleansed and wrapped bundle, and she knew how deeply she loved and would always love this child.

Were all births miracles, she wondered? After the boy was cleansed and covered, she was not certain what she should do with him, and she carried him to his weeping father, who only looked at him once and wept so loudly his friends had to hold him upright. Even Gil José, whose hands gripped the man's arms, had no thought for anything now except the woman who had not moved since the last great struggle when the boy was born.

Susana moved back into the shadow, holding the child close in an instinctive effort to give it the body warmth it lacked. Padre Font, standing at the woman's head, moved his lips more rapidly in prayer. Anza and the herb woman were bent over the bed conferring in low voices. Tía María's fists sank into the depleted abdomen which she seemed to be kneading. The clothing massed around the woman's thighs were not stanching the flow of blood.

"Like a fountain!" Tía María said. And then, despairingly, "The afterbirth—it does not move!"

And all in the tent felt the silence that followed her words, and heard in it the slow dripping through the thick bedding to the earthen floor. The husband sobbed and covered his ears with his hands, for all knew the monotonous sounds were the advancing footsteps of death.

Quietly, Father Font left the tent.

Time ticked by. Anza said to no one in particular, "Pray God it will be over. One way or another, let it end."

As he spoke the body on the bed arched and strained.

Tía María pulled herself erect and faced Anza. Her stained hands clasped in a gesture of prayer.

"It may not be too late for her! The bleeding might be stopped . . . Captain, I promise by the Sorrows of Mary, the scrapings of wild grass seeds in warm water . . ."

"Little Mother," said Anza wearily and with great kindness, "I know your good heart and your wisdom and the cure you would use. But it is not my right to give permission. I am not the law. I only represent the law, and that I must do while I live."

Tía María was both meek and strangely defiant.

"A simple remedy, grown for us by our brother Corn, and every sort of seed grass, and used to save the lives of many women as far back as man remembers." Suddenly the usually placid woman turned virago. She turned on the men grouped against the wall. "I appeal to you all, to you, the husband of this woman; to you, Gil José. Uphold me! It is only a step to my tent, and the preparation that may save this dear life."

But the men only looked uneasily to Anza, whose iron mouth shaped refusal. "Enough of this. I must tell you, No! It is not on the prescribed list."

The herb woman's eyes glittered. "That is true! It is not accepted by your great doctors in Mexico City. But this is not the city. It is the desert. It is the world's end! And how can a growth from Corn be unlawful? Is Corn a sin, and do we ask forgiveness in the confessional for having eaten it? Why, then, is the eating of its grains a sin when they turn black for reasons we do not know? And if no sin, why should a law forbid its use? Who withholds it, and why, for this tormented soul whose children have need for her life?"

"I am a husband and father. I am not without pity." The commander's voice was unsteady. "But I took oath to use no medicines on this expedition that are not on the list. To uphold the oath . . ."

"I took no such oath," said Tía María fiercely.

". . . nor to suffer their usage," added Anza, as if she had not spoken.

Tía María knew the futility of argument. The use of the cures by Anza would almost be an act of treason. So two ancient medicines were refused on that night that had saved generations of Indian women from needless agony and even death. The datura (the common Jimson weed) was a powerful narcotic. The ergot, a fungus scraped from diseased wild or domestic grains, had been used by Indians for centuries to control hemorrhage and to contract the uterus after labor. (By the twentieth century ergot was to be used by reputable practitioners everywhere in the world.)

It is only fair to say that both Tía María and Anza knew the reason for the ban against these drugs. In inexpert or ruthless hands they could be lethal. The datura could bring on a sleep so deep it could only end in death. An overdose of ergot could paralyze veins and muscles and nerves. Drugs of this nature had been marketed for centuries, and not always for curative purposes, by herbalists who did not adhere to Tía María's strict ethical code.

As the two paused in helpless frustration, there was a sudden loud cry of grief from the husband of the dying woman, and all in the tent fell on their knees as an awe-inspiring procession entered. Father Font, a changed, unearthly presence, and the Fathers Eixarch and Garcés, came chanting and bringing with them the blessed candles and vessels pertaining to the mysterious rites of extreme unction. The candles flared on either side of the dying mother, whose eyes did not open again, and the weeping husband knelt by her side as the three fathers began the awe-inspiring relinquishment at the rim of eternity. The murmur of prayers that bring peace to the dead overcame the sounds of sobbing, and the pervasive fragrance of incense washed over the odors of birth and death. Susana, kneeling with the child in her arms and sensing through loneliness the presence of Gil José— for in this *extremis* every soul in this crowded place was alone— felt as if in her own body the will of the woman to live, and wondered if she did not know, dying, how bitterly her husband wept? And when the husband lifted and kissed the dying hands, did she not know?

It was late when Tía María glanced at Susana with a message she could not speak, but the girl read its meaning: *It is the hour God sends his angels!*

It was three in the morning. The child had been born at nine the night before. Tía María was the first to see that the mother had died.

Susana and Tía María were the last to leave a tent cleansed of birth and death. It was again the executive center of a great enterprise, with Anza and several of his staff, including Gil José, conferring at the map table as to the next line of advance, which Anza had not found time to outline in the preceding night.

The bloodied husks had been carried out and burned, the stained bedding folded to be washed when water was reached and clean sand coated the stained earth where the cot had stood. The widower had been led away to offer what comfort he could to his older children left motherless. Water had been spared for the washing of the ravaged body, and by the light of the blessed candles Tía María, with Susana's aid, had combed the long, tangled hair and dressed the woman in clothing she had worn years before as a bride, until she lay decently and at peace, with the rosary, broken in her struggle to survive, still clasped in the hands on her breast.

The two women paused outside the tent, breathing in the clean air under a sky that still held the bright streakings of dawn. Susana held the child folded into her *rebozo* in the way Indian mothers carry their children. The faces of both women were shadowed with weariness.

"Another hot day." Tía María turned her face upward, and Susana, following her attentive look, saw circling over the camp the sinister aerial wheels drawn by the wings of the zopilote— the black buzzards that are the messengers of death. "You knew, wise ones!" Tía María said reproachfully to the birds, and to

Vengador, who had waited the night through outside the tent for Susana, she added, "And you, foolish one, you also knew. Tell me, Susana, how can these creatures tell?"

But Susana could not explain why the dog had moaned in terror and flattened his long, trembling body against the earth when the canvas-sheathed body had been carried out of the tent.

They watched the sad little cortege leave the camp for the desert, moving northward. Four of Anza's soldiers were to escort the body and Father Garcés, who would accompany the dead woman to his own mission of San Xavier and attend to her burial in its pioneer graveyard.

Susana's thoughts followed the dead woman over the desert to a strange grave in a strange land and wondered which was her pity for, the woman or her children?

Anza stepped out of the tent. He was filled as always with boundless energy. He took the child from Susana, who gave it up with reluctance. "We will find a mother for this little one," he promised, looking down with affection on the small bundle that was not much larger than one of his hands. "One of my soldier's wives has a new child and will have milk." Then to Tía María, who had worked with him through the long night, "We have brought a fine new colonist into the world, you and I."

(This turned out to be true, for this child, first-born of the San Francisco Expedition and baptized by Father Eixarch, was to live long and become the patriarch of many generations of Californians.)

"It is still early," Anza continued, squinting at the sun. "We can still make an early start."

Then he left them, carrying the child, with many thanks for their aid during the birth, and Tía María, in spite of his courtesy, looked after him, as he made his way among the tents in search of the nursing mother, with what could only be described as a scowl.

"Men have no hearts!" Tía María's philosophical acceptance of the eternal verities vanished, and she mounted into one of her bewildering attacks of indignation. "Start! he tells us, as if she had not died! Because he never needs sleep, our captain, we are to set out at once as though this were a day like any other, without respect for a woman not buried. Oh, death is always an injustice and beyond all others to women! Of all living creatures, women suffer most, and they tell us it is because we have sinned. But can you tell me, Susana, do not men also sin, and are they made to suffer when a child is born?"

Susana was abashed at this unexpected turn.

"The poor husband wept," she said mildly.

"Wept?" The herb woman gave an unladylike snort. "A handful of regret for a good woman gone. Who will remember her in her grave in the wilderness?"

"We will all remember," said Gil José, coming behind them from the tent.

His eyes were red-rimmed from sharing the widower's grief, but they softened as he joined the two women standing together in the rays of the morning sun.

His pleasure in the meeting was brief. The harrowing experiences of the night, of having been refused permission to use the cures in which she believed, and not having dared to express her resentment to Anza for this denial, boiled into a volcano of wrath in Tía María that poured over Gil José.

"Now you have seen the end of your conniving!" She was standing on tiptoe, shouting into the astonished face of the soldier. "You men with your whisperings and promises and caressing hands! Yes, hang your head, for I cannot bear the sight of your face!"

"But I—I have made no promises!" The bewildered Gil José looked from Tía María to Susana without being quite certain what he had done to merit his friend's attack.

"Ho! Have you not? Never? Did you make no promises to the girl Palmita?"

The name sank like a stone into Susana's heart. Gil José saw her expression, and suddenly he was as angry as Tía María.

"Your son talks too much," he said coldly.

"All men talk, my son's friend, and it was you, Gil José, who told me of this girl when you returned last year to Culiacán after your first journey with Anza. You spoke of her beauty and her kindness. Yes, it was you who told me, Gil José."

"Then I talk too much," said Gil José, and the sorrow of his expression was reflected in Susana, and Tía María saw the harm she had done and at once wanted to make peace again.

"There now, I may have heard wrongly," she said, more gently. "You are a good lad, Gil José, as men go."

Her calm, orderly words fell like oil on hearts still bruised by the horrors of the night. The storm was over, but it left Susana with a question she had no right to put into words, although it was to haunt her nights and days, for who was Palmita?

The tireless Anza, having found a wet nurse for the child, ordered immediate departure for San Xavier.

He who never wearied, who could ride all day in the saddle without food or drink (and saw no reason why his soldiers should not do the same), would not permit further delay because death had passed.

The company was sad and sobered, and inclined to discuss the tragedy in little groups, so that they were slower in their packing, and it was two in the afternoon before the procession was at last on its way.

Voices were muted, and even the muleteers did not shout as loudly to their stubborn charges. Father Font followed the "*Olabado*" with a soft, chanted rosary for the dead, since they were following in the tracks of the funeral train.

Only three leagues were traveled that day.

But by the next morning cheerfulness had returned to the majority of the San Franciscans. Grief could not be permitted to paralyze a purpose as great as theirs. By dusk they had covered six leagues of forbidding desert, and sighted, far off against the blue-tinged Tucson Mountains, the low outlines of the small mission. Then even the weariest mules set their ears forward and moved faster, and at eight-thirty on this night of October twenty-fifth the long-drawn-out procession of Anza expeditionaries wound to a stop outside the adobe walls of Mission San Xavier de Bac.

[7]

The women in the company would have welcomed the chance to rest at San Xavier. They arrived in darkness and were warmly greeted by its administrator, Father Garcés, who had arrived ahead of the expedition with the body of the woman who had died. That night most of the pilgrims were too weary to respond to much more than the fact that water was plentiful at San Xavier, and some of them, saturating their thirsty bodies with this most blessed of drinks, found themselves with painfully distended stomachs and unable to sleep. But the next morning all were up early and, emerging from their tents, were eager to see at first hand the famous mission of which they had heard so much. They were met with Anza's announcement that the overnight stay was all that would be spent at the mission, and they were to prepare at once for the customary early start.

Father Font visited early among the tents, exhorting the pilgrims to take advantage of Mass being said in the mission— the last mission, he emphasized, they would see until they reached San Gabriel, in California. He urged everyone to make confession. "You are now," he kept repeating, "on the rim of the heathen world. Enter with souls washed clean, for we do not know what may happen to us there."

Three couples, all members of the expedition who had planned to marry in the projected mission of San Francisco, were married during Mass in San Xavier by Father Font.

Susana did not attend the Mass. She went alone to the new grave behind the low adobe walls of the mission where the body of the woman she had seen die in childbirth lay in consecrated earth. "Rest easily, little Mother," she whispered over the dry mound. "Your other children are well cared for and your baby thrives. Forgive me that I had no milk for your little one." And to herself she thought, Even in Paradise, a mother would want word of her children. When she returned to the front of the mission, she found a busy scene, for all the colonists were at their packing. No one noticed her as she slipped into the church. With its hand-carved crucifix and altar, its sacred paintings and stations of the cross on its walls, all made with crudity but profound sincerity by Indian converts, it was very like the one she had entered at Horcasitas.

She had one purpose. In hurried words she voiced her prayer, which was more of a sacrament. Tears blurred the memory of Gil José as she took solemn oath never again to be unfaithful to Don Angel. There, it was done! Gil José was safe, safe from her own increasing lightness of heart, and she would never break an oath, no matter how great the temptation, and temptation sharpened each time she saw the soldier. In the thousand-mile journey ahead, with no way to avoid him, an oath could be the only insurance against her own weakness.

It was not made on impulse. Somewhere in the emptiness was

a rival known only as Palmita. Susana could be certain she was a desert girl, since Gil José had spoken of her to Tía María after his return from the First Expedition. Gil José had once commented that some Indian women were beautiful. The girl Palmita was unknown, but not unknown to Susana was the jealousy her name aroused.

So Susana took her oath, and was about to leave the church when she went to her knees again with a hurried amendment, not to be unfaithful to Don Angel *while he lived!* It seemed to her the codicil was important, and she would not realize its implication until much later.

That morning they rode four leagues from Mission San Xavier and sighted the next and last Southwestern settlement. At a distance it resembled one of the prairie dog villages that dotted the plain, of the same color and texture of the land.

They reached it at eight-thirty. The colonists expected to pause there briefly and spend a full day in the saddle. But Anza had much to attend to at this forlorn hamlet. He gave an order: "Dismount, but do not unsaddle."

The San Franciscans surveyed the dreary stopping place without enthusiasm. It was an Indian rancheria serving as a temporary Spanish garrison. It gave no hint of an important future. But this early morning visit was its start to greatness, and Anza was immediately absorbed in the details of the transition, for he was arranging the transfer of his garrison at Tubac, which the expedition had recently visited, to this lonely outpost in the desert. The final arrangements were being made, and in a few months the move would be completed that would leave Tubac to become a deserted ruin, while the rancheria blossomed into a presidio that became the leading military headquarters of the Southwest, and, in time, the city of Tucson.

In an adobe hut Anza was facing problems more serious than his followers knew.

With him were four Indians. They were Pimas, of that friendly tribe whose home was on the Gila River, and the four were noted scouts and Anza's friends. He had sent them ahead to the Gila, the expedition's next objective, to explore and report on any possible routes to that river. They had been waiting his arrival.

Anza heard their report in silence. He studied his map.

The outlook was not good. To the Gila and beyond the Colorado stretched the formidable desert. The expedition would be in danger from the Apaches until it neared the Gila, with its friendly Indian villages. Then, nearing the Colorado, it would be welcomed and protected by Anza's friend Palma, chief of the Yumas and the most powerful Indian leader in the Southwest. But no one could protect the San Franciscans on the opening stretch from this place to the Gila.

There was another menace as grave as the Apache. In all the area ahead to the Gila there was no other river, no lake or spring or well, no water source of any kind. This had been a fall of little rain on the desert. Arroyos usually racing with water in October were dry. There were a few pools of stagnant water left in natural rock cisterns, the Indians said, but these were few and far apart and rapidly drying.

"Many will have dried since we left." Dark fingers pointed knowledgeably on the map.

Anza pondered. Two routes led across the desert. The Pimas had scouted both. There was no forage anywhere for cattle. They themselves had barely escaped although, as they pointed out, there had only been four of them, and all men, while Anza would be burdened with hundreds of people and animals and the added responsibility of many women and children.

"Bad." They shook their heads firmly. "Both ways are bad."

"Impossible?"

They answered as well as they could. "Almost."

Anza considered the lower route. It was the one over which he had hoped to lead his charges to California, for it cut straight over the desert to Palma's headquarters at the Yuma junction, where the Gila and Colorado joined. If only they could take that route! Not only time would be saved but also one hundred miles of dangerous travel.

His look questioned the scouts. Their frowns condemned the choice. His hand moved up to the northern route. It also ran in a straight line northwest to the Gila. If he could possibly get his people over that, then he could lead them down river to the junction—a one-hundred-mile trek. Still, they would have the river water to sustain them. If luck held, and they hurried . . .

It was a long chance, but the only one.

He asked the scouts, "Do you think we can get through?"

Maybe, was the best they could say. They had been born and reared on that desert, but they could not be sure.

But Anza's decision was made. He knew his charges; there could be no thought of turning back. They would take the upper route to the Gila in the hope that some of the pools would stay open until the rains began.

He spoke cheerfully. "We shall have to make a dash for it!"

It was late afternoon when Anza broke up the conference, thanking the scouts for their invaluable services and making them the customary gifts. He dismissed his staff. The soldiers were to inform the colonists that they were to remain overnight at the rancheria. He smiled giving this order, knowing how his charges welcomed delays by filling them with entertainment of their own making. To the last soldier to leave the room he spoke quietly.

"Ask the colonist Galván to come to me."

Don Angel was pleased to be summoned by the captain. He did not always approve of Anza's leadership but respected him for his reputation and aristocratic bearing. He entered the adobe with a jaunty greeting that died on his lips. Anza was pointing to a corner where lay what appeared to be a foul-smelling bundle of black wool.

"What is this?" Don Angel demanded peevishly.

Then he knew.

Tucson experienced jollity that evening such as the embryo settlement had never known. The colonists, having spent the day in idleness, were reluctant to turn into their tents. There was a great deal of singing and soft-voiced conversation.

It had become Susana's custom to open the tent flaps after Don Angel slept. Tonight she stood briefly in the opening, drawing in trembling breaths of the cool, clean air; then she joined the group at the Perea fire.

They had been speaking of the problems awaiting them in the morning when they would leave for the great desert. There was talk of the dangers, the water lack, and the Apaches, and Gil José was forced to admit that there were large Apache settlements very close. The conversation became so intense that Susana was drawn into it as never before, and she found herself addressing Tía María after Gil José spoke of the Apaches, and saying:

"That is true, and the Apaches are nearby. They have captured our man Tomito. They have killed him."

She could see that Gil José already knew of Tomito's death. But the others had not known, and Susana enjoyed a brief interim of importance pleasing to one who never before had been able to contribute to the general fund of information. Few of those present could recall the face of the dead man, and one asked, "Who was this Tomito?"

"You do not remember him?" Susana asked in dismay, for it seemed to her a sorrowful thing that a man could travel for weeks in their midst and not be remembered.

Every night, after this night, Susana slipped out of the Galván tent and joined her friends. No one told Don Angel of these meetings.

After the Perea family were left alone, Felipe spoke with amusement of the change in Susana.

"The little wife has become like a small parrot. Once she was silent. Now she is making up for all she has not spoken. Surely when she was silent she did not stop wondering and wanting to question, and some are such childish questions. Did you hear her asking, Are horses afraid of the moon? But when the old one is around she is silent. She does not speak when we are with Don Angel."

The mother smiled. "Yes, our little sleeper has wakened."

"She was not happy when she slept."

"No. But now she will suffer. I think she does not know that yet." The mother added in a lowered voice. "Nothing can stop Gil José, neither his suffering nor another's. We know this of him."

The father interrupted angrily. "I forbid such talk. Hear me?"

And for once the three Pereas were silent at the same time.

The talk in the camp that night of the nearing dangers had no sobering effect on the colonists. Only two men who heard were terrified. They were muleteers who had been hired by Anza. The two deserted that night after the camp and the small settlement slept. They slipped out of Tucson into the desert, turning southward toward home.

Anza was very angry the next morning when he learned the pair had absconded. Men who could manage mules were of vital importance to the expedition. Only one of the drovers, Perea, was an expert muleteer. The others, including the missing men, had gradually developed a certain amount of skill in the handling of their stubborn charges. The loss of two was a minor catastrophe.

Anza said they would start without attempting to catch the runaways, and that all water containers were to be filled—a reminder that should have sobered the colonists but did not. They left with irrepressible gaiety, calling out in merry challenge, "To the Gila," and chanting their thanksgiving hymn.

The great, empty desert before them had been crossed before. Armed companies had traversed it, made up solely of men. Now, for the first time, a mixed group would face its challenge. If successful, these would be the first white women and children to cross the great American desert.

Riding away from Tucson this morning in late October, they did not know they were the first of the Argonauts and the last of the conquistadors. They headed northward over a plain where dunes became hills that rose in turn to become the Tucson Mountains. They followed a winding course. Anza planned to lead them through dunes and canyons and mountain passes in the hope of finding hitherto unlocated water sources.

They looked back without regret to see the last flat roofs of the tiny settlement vanish over the dunes. The future Tucson was their last link with the Mexico they had known.

"Sing us that song you sang when we left the old country," Susana coaxed Felipe.

Susana was now able to chatter as freely with Felipe as with his mother. The three were together much of the time, and Felipe was a comfortable companion, helpful and jolly, and making jokes when he was not singing. Even Don Angel found Felipe amusing and liked him as well as he did anyone in the company.

But as with most of his compositions, Felipe had forgotten the ballad he had sung when they crossed the border. Instead, he lifted his face like a cherub's to the sky and sang of this new venture over the King's Highway into a world unknown. Words and music jolted as he rode, driving his heels into the flanks of his plodding beast. ("Why do you call your mule Cazador? Is he truly a hunter?" Susana once asked, and Felipe had answered, "No, but such a name is good for his self-esteem.")

Susana was taking in every aspect of the country with eyes fully opened to its wonders. Were there actually a thousand miles ahead of this bleak but strangely beautiful land? More saguaros were to be seen tipping the sky. Other cacti seemed to grow in curious shapes. Felipe told Susana that several men in the company who came from the west coast of Mexico and had hunted for pearls in the gulf had said the strangeness of the land around Tucson reminded them of the land that lies under sea water. Felipe was impressed by this information. He confided to Susana that one of his greatest longings was to see and hear the sea.

"Gil José has seen the Pacific near Mazatlán," he added, "but it did not mean to him what it would to me."

Susana could completely forget Don Angel while riding. She caught glimpses of the shy animals that lived on land where one would think no creature could stay alive. She saw them scurrying with fear before the earth-borne thunder of the cavalcade.

There were rabbits, some like long, loping streaks of tawny fur, and others midget and toylike, that could not cover a child's palm and would never grow larger. Sometimes a scurry of sound ebbed as a mother quail dragged a wing over the sand to simulate hurt and draw attention from her motionless brood huddled under the bushes, doing their best to be invisible against the protective coloration of dead leaves and sand.

There were the speaking ones whose voices Susana heard when the procession was not in motion. She was learning to distinguish the songs of many birds. The song of the wild doves was softer and sweeter than that of the pigeons of Mexico City. Her pulses quivered to a cougar's tormented laughter, or the warning yap of the small desert fox.

The prairie dogs were cunning as toys. They sat with dignity on the roofs of their burrows and returned Susana's stare with much the same interest. They barked back in chorus, at Felipe's whistle, then plunged headlong into their earth mounds.

Silent ones left their markings to be read. Susana learned from Felipe to distinguish the fronded spread of a wildcat's paw, the curved indentations of snakes, and the hieroglyphics that marked the majestic progress of one of the high-shelled desert turtles.

Even the smaller, stranger creatures no longer horrified Susana. She watched the ill-favored scorpion on his miniature march, and learned he was only angry when fear hooked his barbed tail forward. Who has died of a scorpion's sting? Tía María once asked. The herb woman had many arguments with her son on this subject, with neither giving way. They finally concluded that, while the scorpion might not be lethal, it was certainly one to avoid. The hairy tarantula was also suspect, but the children could not be made to believe this, and some made the great spiders into dubious pets and came to no harm. One pet tarantula, leashed around its bulging center with a red thread, was a small boy's companion.

But of all the desert's secret citizenry, one was most amusing to Susana. This was a veritable clown of a bird that seemed to appear out of nowhere to race madly ahead of the procession on stilted legs with its long, uptilted tail flying, like a crazy weathercock. It was pursued endlessly by Vengador and the other dogs, but they were never able to catch one, for the *gallo del chaparral* (road runner) was so fleet it could outdistance an animal. Felipe believed it a bad bird that ate the eggs and even the young of other birds. Tía María held it was a good bird because it ate insects and small snakes that would otherwise grow up to be poisonous. Susana, left with her choice of opinion, chose to think the road runner one of the best of birds because its appearance always made her laugh.

As she rode, eyes watchful under the wide-brimmed hat, her body moving to the comfortable progress of the broad-rumped Seda, there was only one small thought marring her contentment. Why had Gil José failed to appear during inspection time before leaving Tucson, to see as always that Seda's girth was taut?

Instead, that morning, when the soldiers detailed by Anza rode down the line on the last-minute inspection, a soldier known only by name to Susana rode up to the Galván group. As he approached, Seda, the small mare scented a stranger and forgot the lessons taught her with patient understanding by Gil José. Her ears flattened against her stubby head, her squat form swelled, and she became again the resentful toad-horse she had been at the beginning. And Susana, laughing but annoyed, was ashamed for Seda, and slid her own hand under the cinch while tightening it, and the soldier, seeing it taut, merely glanced at the bridles and girths of the other animals and left with nothing more to say beyond a warning to Don Angel that all were to

conserve the water in their leather bottles by drinking as little
as possible.

"As if we have not been told that ten thousand times," Don
Angel was heard to grumble as the soldier rode away, but Susana
had caught sight of Gil José. He was stationed on Fucgo at the
outer end of the guard line on Anza's right, which was a post
of additional danger and honor. Was this new position a form
of promotion for Gil José, she wondered?

Don Angel could have told Susana why Gil José had not ap-
peared on inspection duty that morning, and would not again.
Don Angel had not given Susana the details of his meeting with
Anza at Tucson.

Don Angel had no need to examine the object on the rough
table. "It is the *tilma* worn by that dog of a servant who ran
away."

"*Señor!*" Anza's tone held the clinking of ice. "He was a man!"

Don Angel bowed by way of apology. "May I ask how you
have this?"

"It was brought here by Pima scouts. They found the man
who wore it on the desert with a mesquite stake through his
heart. They buried what the vultures left. May his soul find the
mercy in purgatory he was not shown on earth."

"Apaches?"

"Apaches. Their way of killing those they capture."

Don Angel's expression was one Susana would have recognized.

"The man was a thief," he said coldly. "If ever a man deserved such a death, it was he. If I had caught him I would have
given him what the Apaches—"

"No more!" Captain Anza was now as angry as Don Angel.
"I have heard of your threats to punish the man if he had been
returned to you. I am in command of this expedition and I
dispense its justice. The man Tomito would have been given a
fair trial, and his punishment would have met with my orders!"

The frustration this rebuke roused in Don Angel demanded
outlet. His first thought was that Gil José had reported to Anza
his threats to punish Tomito. He knew Gil José disliked him as
heartily as he disliked Gil José.

The dark blood boiled into Don Angel's pale face, and since

he could not directly attack the company commander, he struck instead at Anza's greatest source of pride which was in his command, using as weapon a subject upon which he had been brooding. When he managed to speak, it was in a voice of silk, but his expression was malignant.

"It has been in my mind to speak to you of another matter, Captain Anza. One that has been a source of humiliation to me—yes, and of anxiety—for I am not a man who wishes to see trouble in a company commanded by a leader I respect as I do you. A small matter to others, perhaps, who are amused by it, but it is developing and will be worse if permitted to go on."

"Speak!" ordered Anza as Don Angel seemed to hesitate.

"There is one on your staff, sir, a soldier, who each morning inspects our riding gear before we leave. I make no formal complaint or challenge. The man is impetuous, and it may be my wife does not always keep her eyes lowered as she should. But as one man to another, I ask if such conduct unworthy of a soldier—"

"No more!" Anza struck the table with his fist. "You will not be annoyed again, Don Angel. I know the man you mean, and I promise you he will not ride inspection again."

Anza kept his word, although he had no liking for Don Angel. He removed Gil José from inspection detail to prevent scandal and to protect Gil José. Anza took a paternal interest in all his men, and Gil José was one of his most trusted. He did not mention to Gil José his reasons for advancing him, because Anza understood fondness for women, and he did not blame Gil José. He had noticed Susana the night the woman had died in childbirth when she had tended the child. He had thought her sympathetic in nature and quite beautiful. So he merely removed Gil José, as he thought, from temptation, not realizing that there would seldom be an evening along the way when Susana and the soldier would not meet in company with the Pereas and with veiled glances convey to each other their longing.

They saw one another after six o'clock that first evening out of Tucson when the expedition stopped on a plain facing the sierra. One of the Tucson Mountains was low and dark and extremely rugged, and Gil José pointed out that since it resembled a Negroid profile it was known by that name, La Frente Negra.

Night lowered over the mountains and desert, and the company were readying for their beds at eight o'clock, when there was a disturbance outside the palisade and six Indians from Tucson who were members of the friendly Pima tribe entered, bringing with them a roped captive. It was one of the muleteers who had deserted at Tucson.

Anza made the captors gifts of ribbons and beads and proceeded without benefit of trial to have the runaway flogged. Little sympathy was given the man, who had failed in the trust for which he had taken not only money but an oath to go with the company to California. He was given twelve lashes with a mule whip. His punishment stopped when Anza stepped forward, saying, "Mercy, in the king's name," and the people, with a sense of justice rendered, were able to turn into their tents for the night. The soldiers named this place Llano de Azotado (the plain where a criminal was beaten).

The next morning the travelers left the plain to enter a pass the soldiers also named Puerto del Azotado, after the plain of the day before, for they were joined in the pass by more Pimas from Tucson, who brought with them the second missing muleteer. He too was soundly beaten. To discourage any more running away by hired personnel he was given twenty-five blows, on Anza's orders.

Anza had chosen the pass as a protective measure, to avoid passing a nearby Apache village which he knew only too well, having attacked it many times on forays of reprisal. No move was made by the Apaches, and the company traveled the next day without disturbance and that afternoon made camp in the most beautiful place they had seen since the start of their journey.

And that day, which was a Saturday and promised such happiness, was to be one of the most critical of all Susana's days.

The camp was at one more of those places named Las Lagunitas for its cluster of fresh-water lagoons. These small lakes were a delightful surprise to the colonists and their animals who had suffered two days of waterless travel. They arrived late that afternoon, but early enough so that all might take pleasure in the water, knowing it would be many miles before they would enjoy it in such abundance again.

Anza set double guards. He was taking no chances of a surprise Apache attack. The colonists launched upon a carefree orgy of bathing and washing of bodies and hair, and the women attended to the neglected family laundry, using the soap bars brought by Anza or a stringy, soft soap made by Tía María and other women. There were various methods for soapmaking. Some boiled the bulbs of the wild amole (the soaproot), others pounded yucca roots to a foamy lather.

Susana sat in the sun drying her long hair and dreamily watching the children at play. The group she found most charming was presided over by Gil José. She was surprised and touched to see him in this protective role. He saw her watching and was at first abashed; then, leaving the children clamoring after him, he walked to Susana. For the first time they were alone together since the night at Horcasitas.

She came to her feet. Her lips were dry. She moistened them. "You are good to children." She could think of nothing else to say. It was the wrong thing.

"To my own, I would be most kind."

The emotion in his words touched her. She turned to go at once to Tía María and the others, but he moved lithely forward, blocking her way.

"Please hear me. I have wanted so much to speak. I never find you alone, to speak to you. And I must."

Her chin lowered to hide the trembling. "What is it you would say?"

It came in a cry of accusation. "Why did you marry him?" And then, when she did not answer, "If you were not his, belonging to him, then all I am, all I think and am and will be, would be yours."

Guilt knifed her. Gil José did not know that it was not Don Angel who stood between them, but a dead lad from the *tierra caliente*. Don Angel knew this, and Susana knew, but Gil José must not.

Gil José, whose emotions had been so long suppressed, was pouring out his heart.

"We can leave together. We need not belong with these people. We can live in the desert. Indians live safely in the desert. They have good lives and families, and they love each other. We can live as they live. I am part Indian, and I know. I can love and protect you, and that is my right and not the right of that monster. He is no husband. Yours is no marriage. Do you think I have not read the sadness in your eyes? And the love . . ."

His voice broke.

"Tonight, Susana? The guards are my friends. They will let us pass through the barrier."

Almost, in that moment of madness, she put her hand out to meet his, to say, "Yes, we will go!" But her hand remained by her side.

"I love you," she told him. There, it was said. "Now I have said that to you, and you have told it to me, and it must not be spoken again. Not by us ever again."

She wanted to tell him of the vow she had made at San Xavier. But she knew he would urge its breaking in terms she could not trust herself to withstand. She could not tell him of the deeper reason, of the flames waiting beyond death if she yielded.

"Why?" His cry was that of one damned. "If I am willing to leave my captain, to become a deserter for your sake, why will you not leave a man you do not love? And who it can be seen does not love you, or anyone?"

Her head lowered. She had to tell. She would give half the truth.

"I have taken a vow."

"Of chastity?"

She nodded. Let him think what he must. She could not meet the sickness in his eyes.

"Vows are broken, Susana. If they are bad they are worthless. This you have made is bad because it will murder our love. What is a vow but words—words that destroy? Break it, and we can have everything that is sweet and good together—love and children—our own home. Why should a few words rob us of these? Deprive us of life? Why did you make such a vow? When? Where?"

She told him, at Mission San Xavier.

"That was only two days ago!" Gil José's eyes were slits of fire. He was no longer the glowing and beautiful male. He was lowering, ugly with suspicion. "You made that knowing I loved and wanted you? You made it against me!"

"Yes. Against you."

She drew the damp locks of hair over her eyes to conceal her tears. The world was black and unfriendly, and she wanted to hide from it because it wore the face of Gil José. She did not hear him leave, but she would be haunted by the final voicing of his hatred:

"I will never forgive you!"

That evening the camp was still enjoying the pleasures of the oasis, but Gil José was so irascible that Tía María lost patience with him and complained to her son, "What is wrong with your friend? He is a man who has swallowed knives."

Joyousness was ended for Susana and Gil José, but both were obliged to attend, separately and sadly, the early Sunday Mass on the next morning, since Anza on the preceding night had announced that everyone had to attend. There was a rumor that a special announcement would be made by Father Font.

The last prayer died on the quiet morning air, and the worshipers rose to their feet to find the three priests and Captain Anza regarding the congregation as severely as if about to pronounce judgment. Anza's expression was colder than anyone present had seen, not even his own soldiers, who were watching him with something approaching apprehension. Only Gil José scowled into the sky as if nothing that could be said would concern him.

Anza took a step forward. He spoke carefully, letting every word drop as if weighted with iron.

"This is a proclamation," he began grimly. "Before we start this morning there must be complete understanding on a subject of great importance. If Our Lady continues to protect us, we will soon arrive at the Pima settlements on the Gila River. You know the Pimas are our most loyal friends in the Southwest. Last year, as you, my soldiers who were with me on the First Expedition remember, they welcomed us to their villages, to their homes, and their hearts.

"We learned then that the Pimas are innocents. They offered us all they possessed, even themselves. There are those among you who took advantage of their offers, who accepted Pima generosity to a degree I do not have to explain. I am warning you now, this is not to happen again. This time, Indian innocence is to be respected.

"Father Font, Father Garcés, Father Eixarch, and I have drawn up certain regulations. These new rules must be obeyed by every soldier and settler in our expedition."

Anza was now the threatening father.

"This I demand—that when we enter the Pima domain and later the Yuma country you are all to be on your best behavior. You will treat these Indians well and show them every kindness. You will set them the Christian example we hope they will respect and follow. These are courtesies every man and woman, yes, and even the children, among you must observe.

"There must be no stealing from the Indians. They do not hide their poor possessions from strangers, and to us, regarded as friends, they will offer all they possess. But to take from them will be thievery, and it will be severely punished.

"You are not to molest these people or harm them in any way.

"And to you, my soldiers, I give additional warning. Punishment will be given any person who may raise arms against any heathen except to defend his own life.

"I promise the severest punishment to any man who may violate Indian women. The temptations will be great. There is no need to seduce such women, for they offer themselves joyously as other women might offer a flower. But I pledge, adultery will be punished! You must steel yourself as soldiers to resist temptation and so conduct yourselves as to hold before these friendly people the majesty of our God and our king."

Anza stepped back, and Father Font took his place in earnest exhortation. Adultery was a sin, but the unmarried men of the expedition need not turn from the Indian women and continue to California to live in loneliness. No, for marriage was a solution recognized by church and law. He reminded the congregation that Padre Serra was urging the soldiers in California to marry their native sweethearts.

The effect of this pronouncement on Susana was one of jealous despair, for Father Font's advice was instantly linked to Gil José's reference to a girl named Palmita, and she was certain Palmita was somewhere in one of the tribal settlements ahead. Now that she, Susana, had finally ordered Gil José out of her life, it would be no fault but her own if he turned to an Indian girl.

The afternoon travel was brief, as hours go, but it was long in anxiety and thirst. After the Elysium of the lagoons the dryness of the terrain seemed more dreadful than before.

Susana rode with Don Angel, not wanting to submit to the curiosity Tía María would show, knowing something had gone wrong. The *rebozo* shielded her unhappiness.

The two horses at least were pleased with the arrangement. Major and Seda ambled along side by side, touching noses at times with gentle snorts that told their pleasure in being together. They did not look as strangely different as they had on leaving Mexico City. Don Angel had never been obliged to groom a horse, and Major, like the smaller horse, had grown the long coat needed against the desert cold. His fetlock shrouded his fine eyes and his mane and tail were tangled. His Arabian ancestry was concealed by the winter coat, and he looked like a larger Seda.

That evening water was doled out. Each traveler drank his measured share as a toast to the morrow, for Anza made a little speech, informing them that if they would settle down early for the night, and start early enough in the morning, then, if all went well, they might perhaps on the following day reach the Gila River.

The promise of water sent the pilgrims to bed like good children. Still, all were up at dawn the next morning, which was the thirtieth of October.

The riding was savage. The horses slogged through sand and brush. Clothing was torn and legs and hands were scratched.

But after a few miles of travel a change swept the cavalcade. The cattle lifted their heads and stretched their necks, and charged ahead with tails flying. The horses raised shrill voices and could not be held back. There was no wind, but over the arid desert their nostrils had caught a scent of water from the Gila River, which was still many miles away.

Sunset found the riders still in their saddles, heading almost due west into a sun like a fiery ball on the rim of the desert. The four scouts who had been sent ahead to inform the Pima tribes of the expedition's arrival had returned, and there were strangers with them, magnificent mounted figures boldly outlined against the sunset.

These were no ordinary Indians. They were the leading chiefs of the Pima nation. Anza spurred his horse forward to meet them. They were his friends. They had ridden out from their villages on the Gila to pay him honor. Anza accepted the traditional gift of beans that signified hospitality, and made a little speech of thanks. Another gift brought gasps from the colonists near enough to see.

It was two freshly severed scalps.

They were Apache scalps, the interpreters told Anza. They had been taken the day before from the heads of Apache warriors who had ventured into Pima territory. The Apaches were traditional enemies of the Pimas, who were unwarlike by nature but if molested could show rare talents for retaliation. Recently they had turned against the Apaches, who had persecuted the gentle, agricultural Pimas for centuries. Now any Apaches venturing into the Pima domain along the Gila met the fate of those whose bloodied scalps had been given to Anza.

As horrible as the trophies were, they served to lift the spirits of the San Franciscans. The scalps symbolized their freedom from the dread that had shadowed them all the way from Sonora. They felt safe for the first time since leaving Horcasitas. They had passed unharmed through the Apache territory, and from this place to San Gabriel, in California, the only tribes they would meet would be Anza's friends.

The chiefs remounted; Anza remounted, and shouted to the colonists that they were being taken to a source of water. The colonists cheered through dry throats and urged their horses forward, and the long procession moved swiftly through the rough country toward the river.

Four leagues farther and they were shown another Las Lagunitas, a group of lagoons lying close to the Gila. After the difficult struggle through the dusty desert the water-girdled oasis seemed beautiful. But they found conditions far from ideal. The pools were rimmed with salt. The water was brackish. The surrounding grass and bushes were gray with the alkaline deposit. The animals were thirsty and hungry, but they ate and drank with reluctance. The humans drank the water because their dehydrated bodies demanded it, but their stomachs retched. They could not wash their clothes or their hair.

"There will be illness from this water, you will see," Tía María warned.

Susana made no comment. Tía María looked at her sharply.

The girl looked dispirited and sad. For two days Gil José had ignored her. He had not spoken to her or looked her way.

Everyone else was enjoying the rest. They agreed that, in spite of the brackish content of the lagoons, water was water, and they had much to be grateful for. They had outdistanced the Apache danger. They had reached the Gila at last. Like Cortez, they were conquerors.

"Rest!" Anza told them the next morning. He beamed over the congregation gathered together for early Mass. "A day of relaxation will do us all good."

The suggestion was not wholly unselfish. Anza had an insatiable curiosity for the strange, the scientific, and the antique, as had Father Font. The two friends shared a common interest in North American history. Both had heard a great deal concerning the mysterious deserted ruin in the desert known as La Casa Grande de Moctezuma.

And the Casa Grande was only twenty miles away.

The first white men to enter Arizona, forty-seven years after Columbus reached America, had found Casa Grande abandoned. Those early Spanish explorers were aghast to discover standing alone in the immensity of the desert a shell of a building four stories high with walls of solid masonry four feet thick, and doors and windows open to the wind and sun.

Padre Kino, founding the first Arizona missions, visited the ruin in 1694, and reported it "equal to the finest church in Spain."

Father Garcés had been its third visitor. Now Font and Anza would pay Casa Grande its fourth visit, and they would be the last white men to see it until well into the next century.

The two leaders entered into a discussion with the four Pima scouts, who were curiously reticent concerning Casa Grande. They were devoted to both the captain and Father Font, but they would not lead the two to the Casa Grande.

"It belongs to the old people," they protested.

And when Anza persisted, asking, who were the old people, they answered in the Pima language that the old people had been the Hohokam, meaning "those who have gone before." No Indian had ever entered those broken walls or had taken one of the thousands of fine pottery dishes, red and white and blue and many unbroken (artifacts treasured later by antiquarians), that littered the desert around Casa Grande. "They belong to the dead," was all the Pimas would say. Anza argued they were not going to disturb but to observe, but nothing could persuade a Pima to go near the ruin that they believed was inhabited by the ghosts of the old people.

Finally Font and Anza rode off together without escort of any kind. Father Font had consented to ride his mule, and sat rather shakily in the saddle, for the bad water had affected him as it had many others in the company. After they left, an herb tea made by Tía María that was a centuries-old cure for nausea and diarrhea was dispensed in plentiful cupfuls from her fire, which, frankly, might not have been done if Father Font had been there. All who drank of the brew seemed to feel better, and as Tía María said, excusing herself for going even in this mild fashion against regulations, that anything was better than drinking the alkaline water. It may be that the boiling of the water helped the sufferers.

This afternoon Tía María did the talking. Susana was less animated than usual. She had a great deal on her mind. She forced herself not to run when Gil José appeared.

"So, friend, you are tired of my cooking?" This was unfair of Tía María, for Gil José was eating hungrily but with no sign of enjoyment.

He answered, but in words that shocked them.

"I shall miss your good food, little Aunt. It may be you will be kind and teach some of your cooking secrets to my wife."

The word fell like stones. Even the Perea father stopped, spoon in hand. Felipe was openmouthed as if about to burst into song, and the mother stared aghast at the box of mischief she had opened.

"You will marry, Gil José?" The glib Tía María was stammering.

"Father Font urges us, so, I will marry. A man who is not loved by the woman he loves will do well to marry the one who has waited."

This was Gil José in his most cruel mood, pointing the barb to Susana while avoiding looking at her. But Tía María leaned forward, gasping.

"Palmita? You will marry this Palmita? Who is she, then, and where is she waiting?"

The questions tumbled from Tía María's parted lips. She had forgotten Susana. Gil José gestured with his knife toward the west. "She is a girl of the desert."

"You may not recognize this Palmita." This was Felipe, who could also be cruel. "A year, is it not? She will have changed. There are Indian girls who age early, and their faces turn into pumpkins. You may not know her again when you look into her face."

"I will remember her body," retorted Gil José. "It is supple and brown like the seaweed that floats in the Pacific. Yes, her face may be forgotten, but her body I will remember."

"I thirst to see this girl who has won your heart," Tía María told Gil José.

"When you see her you will know her. She is beautiful. And when you see us together you will know she is not one to divide her love, to care for me and live with another. She will be no one else's. Only mine."

Blow after blow was being aimed at the defenseless Susana by Gil José, who had sworn to love her while life lasted. In their minds the two screamed against one another terrible, unforgivable things. But their faces were bloodless and impassive. Tía María looked from one to the other and said spitefully:

"You do not look happy for one who is to be married, Gil José."

The father turned to her, scowling, and Felipe said quickly, "Let us all sing!"

But Gil José returned to his dicing, and Susana filled a plate and carried it to Don Angel in his tent. He did not waken, and since Gil José was not there, she rejoined the Pereas. She could not bear to be alone.

Anza and Font returned at sunset, and they were awed and inspired by their visit to Casa Grande and its relics of the Hohokam. They brought samples of the pottery, and were eloquent concerning the wholesale vanishment of the people who had built Casa Grande. "A castle of mystery," they called it, and each had much to write of the ruins that night in their diaries.

The pilgrims would discuss the Casa Grande mystery for days, even years. They went to their cots shortly after the sunset faded, for Anza had stated they must make up for their day of leisure with an early morning start. It had been an absorbing day and with it October ended.

November

CHAPTER FOUR

[1]

The first day of November found the Southwest locked in the grip of winter. The morning was clear but very cold. The San Franciscans set out at nine-thirty from the place of the lakes with mixed emotions, reluctant to leave water but eager for their first glimpse of the Gila River.

The country was an extension of the desert they had been riding through, but the cold air stripped it of the shimmering illusion made by the heat of the sun. Now even the sun looked cold. The desert was the color of congealed smoke, shot through in places with clear flashes of color that were leaves turning and late autumn flowers, yellow and mauve and blue. The earth was so dry only lizards stirred, and clouds of dust continued to move with the procession as if the earth smoked despite the chilling cold.

The riders made a strange appearance. They wore *rebozos* or *tilmas* wrapped around their heads against the dust and cold, leaving only slits for their eyes. The children were wound in blankets like cocoons. The wind tearing down from the north cut through the thickest woolen wrappings. Many of the pilgrims were still weak with dysentery caused by the brackish water of the lakes. Still, most were light of heart because this was the first day of a month that promised a new beginning and because at any hour they would reach the Gila River.

So as they rode, they sang.

At one o'clock that afternoon they sighted the eastern bank.

At the sight of the sluggish river twisting like a snake through this gray land, weariness vanished and cheers burst from dusty throats, for to these people the Gila meant more than a goal achieved. It was the friend they had looked forward to meeting, for it would lead them down through the desert to its meeting place with the great Colorado, and on the other side of that junction was California.

Its water meant easement, too, to the thirst threatening their lives.

Beyond all, the river was the line of safety. No Apaches were tolerated in the region of the Gila.

Now the soldiers could ride at ease. Now the guards and night watches need no longer be doubled and on the ready. Women could walk with freedom outside the camps, and the children need no longer ride with sharp eyes on the watch.

Brush barricades were no longer raised at night unless to keep out the severe winter winds.

Anza had led them safely through a hundred dry, dangerous miles, past the threat of their copper-skinned enemies, and this was one more victory the San Franciscans shared with him. No one remembered the suffering now. The San Franciscans had other matters to divert their minds.

They were approaching a small lake near the Pima pueblo Uturibac (near modern Sacaton), which had been visited by the First Expedition in the preceding year, and even Anza was astonished by the reception waiting them there. He and Father Garcés had made friends then with the Pima tribe and it had looked forward for many months to his return. On the lake shore the Indians had reared a long pavilion of woven branches to serve as a reception salon, and this was crammed with such practical gifts as jugs of sweet water and firewood and vegetables and fruits. But the three friars found most touching the cross made of two tied branches which the Indians had raised at the entrance of the pavilion, symbolizing their reverence for the faith given them by their friend and teacher, Father Garcés.

One thousand Pimas came to welcome the travelers, advancing in two long lines, one of men and one of women, and all singing and dancing. Dark arms opened in welcome, dark faces glowed with affection for Anza and Father Garcés and the soldiers who had been with them in the preceding year, and for the others because they were Anza's friends. The Pimas showed their joy in the meeting as openly as children.

Susana's first thought was, Is Palmita among these?

Another glance and she was reassured. The Pima men were attractive, but the women were not. This may have been due to their bulging garments, which gave them the appearance of beetles when viewed from the rear. Their shapeless dresses were made of deerskin, and blankets draped over these covered their bodies from throat to heels. Their coarse black hair fell long and free and was cut in bangs across their low foreheads. No, none of these stocky dark women would be the desirable Palmita, whose body Gil José had described as being supple as kelp from the sea.

The Pima men were in dramatic contrast to their women. They too were very dark (the Pimas were among the darkest tribes of the Southwest) and their hair was worn long and brushed upward to form elaborate headdresses in imitation of the high-fashion coiffures popular in France and Spain. The hair seemed to be less combed than shaped; it formed masses like the nests of birds and held objects valued by their wearers, such as polished twigs, feathers, and bright yarns, and bits of shell and bone. The men wore brighter blankets than the women and hand-woven breeches.

But all these people, women, men, and children, shared one priceless asset—there was no resisting their smiles.

The Pimas were the first Indians the San Franciscans had met in such tremendous numbers, the first of the entire populations of settlements that would flock to meet them with no thought in their innocent minds but unadulterated joy.

Anza and the Franciscans were more formal in their greeting. They left their saddles, as did every member of the expedition down to the smallest child, and went forward on foot to meet their hosts. Manners on both sides were impeccable though simple. They came from the heart.

The Pima men danced forward, smiling and singing, and shook hands in turn with Anza. The Pima women followed and shook his hand. In gentle patois all murmured their pleasure in seeing him again.

Father Garcés was given a special greeting. On his lonely evangelizing sorties through the Gila country he had made this village one of his regular places of call. He addressed his Pima friends in their own language.

Anza presented each man with a twist of tobacco and each woman with a handful of beads as personal gifts from their Spanish king. He had bought in Mexico City, as gifts for the Indians, six boxes of green and yellow beads and many bolts of colored cloth and rolls of gay ribbon, and two bales of tobacco.

The Pimas showed their pleasure in the gifts and then rushed their guests off to the *enramada*. The pilgrims pleasured in clean water kept cool in pottery bowls and jugs, and in the fruits and vegetables. The soldiers made good use of the wood, starting the fires while camp was being made. The company's preparations for the night were amusingly hampered by the Pimas, who were inquisitive as children in all the travelers owned, used, or did. The smiling Indian women went from tent to tent, visiting one family after another, shaking hands over and over, exclaiming at the culinary ware and supper preparations, fondling the children, handling objects, touching the women's clothing and faces, and all the time exclaiming with delight and wonder.

Susana gave herself over to the Pimas' exuberance with a warmth that equaled theirs.

"Greet your friends, if you must, in the open," groaned Don Angel.

One had to admit the Pima scent was very strong.

Susana's attention was drawn to a great commotion on the field where hundreds of Pimas had surrounded Father Garcés and were clamoring to be shown "the pretty lady." At once, to please them, he brought out the banner that had become famous throughout the Southwest.

On one side was a brightly painted image of the Virgin with the Babe in her arms. The Indians moaned in awe at the beauty of the child and its lovely mother. They did not need to be told she represented all that was good on earth and in the sky. Father Garcés let them look their ecstatic fill. Then he whipped over the banner.

Wails of horror rose from the Indians. For the other side showed with crude realism a human creature writhing in the eternal flames of hell. What Indian did not know the pain that is given by fire?

This was the first time the San Franciscans had seen the

famous Father Garcés in his role as the evangelist extraordinary.
Father Font commented that Garcés was "the kind of man God
creates to be a missionary."

All this time more Pimas were arriving from other river villages.
Tía María made friends with many of the women and swept
Susana along with a group that took them to visit their own
village. Without knowing a word of Pima, Tía María managed
to convey her astonishment at all they were shown, the children
and primitive huts and the milpas (kitchen gardens) neatly
planted even in winter, and the fenced fields of cotton and
cereal grains that were watered by irrigation ditches leading from
the Gila River. Tía María was interested in the looms and sewing
articles, and the ways clothing and blankets were made of the
cotton these people raised and the wool shorn from their sheep.
(In most of the river tribes the weaving was done by men.)
Some of the Pima women had flocks of chickens, and Susana
and Tía María returned to the camp with their *rebozos* filled
with eggs.

The camp was noisier than before. Indians never tired of
dancing, and the Pimas had found the right dance companions.
The San Franciscans had suffered long boredom of the saddle
and delighted in this break in their monotonous days.

The Indians started the dancing in the two circles, one of
men and one of women, that widened in great swinging loops
of movement around the lake; then the leaders began steps that
were faster and more intricate, but the people from Mexico were
dancers all, and they followed the Pima choreography and even
added variety to the steps.

Susana sat watching with Don Angel and the Pereas. Gil José
joined them, but he had nothing to say. He watched Susana
furtively. The firelight flashed in her eyes—or was it excitement?—
and her hand was held to her mouth in the gesture of an
ecstatic child that feared at every drumbeat the dance would
end.

But it did not end. The dancers did not tire, nor did those
who watched. Gil José joined the dancers. Felipe had discarded
his guitar and seemed content to watch the weaving of moc-
casined feet. The rhythm was irresistible, and suddenly he was
on his feet and dancing in the circle of Indian men. His face
shone with their intensity and his nimble steps matched theirs.

In an unexpected movement, Susana was on her feet.

"We will dance!" she cried, pulling up Tía María, and they joined the laughing women and were soon following their nimble steps in a harvest dance that had been danced by generations of Indian women along the banks of the Gila.

It was late in the night before the Pimas departed in groups of hundreds for their villages. The bonfires sank to ashes and the camp on the lake was quiet. When Susana entered the dark Galván tent she found Don Angel was already in his cot. "Have you forgotten," he asked cruelly in the dark, "that tomorrow is the Day of the Dead?"

Yes, she had forgotten. The brief happiness of the dance died in her heart like a poisoned flower.

From the settlement on the river came a merry burst of drums. The Pimas were still deep in celebration.

"I shall never sleep with that noise," Don Angel grumbled, forgetting his vicious gloating of the moment before.

Susana took momentary pleasure in knowing that, while she could not sleep for dread of the morning, neither could Don Angel, for he would be kept awake by the voices of hundreds of singing Indians and their thumping feet. Was Gil José still with them, she wondered. If only she had not made the vow that held her captive beside Don Angel . . .

That thought could lead to evil and possible harm for Gil José, and she turned her mind from it firmly and was surprised to waken and find it was morning and that she had slept.

[2]

She woke in dread of the day and its meaning. Could this be the Day of the Dead—the day which had held a special terror for her since the suicide in the Calle de Tacuba? She saw no signs of mourning; she heard no sounds of lamentation. There was only the laughter of children and their amused parents.

The purveyor Vidal was surrounded by clamoring children. He was distributing candy which Anza had purchased for this day months before in Mexico City. The panocha shapes were those in which children of Mexico had long delighted on the Day of the Dead—candy coffins and skulls and serpents and eagles, all emblems of death.

But reverence was not forgotten. The three priests were celebrating nine Masses that day in honor of the dead.

Tía María came up to Susana. She had attended early Mass and was in a cheerful mood. "Padre Font put our hearts at ease with his sermon. He said, 'Remember the dead in happiness, for they are at peace.'"

Then she added, "How proud our dear dead ones must be, for surely they see where we are today and what we are doing. How can we grieve for them, since they know of us, and we are thinking of them?"

Susana pondered Father Font's message. Had the dead lad found peace? Or had his soul followed her here from the stone balcony of the window overlooking the street of Tacuba?

She tried to remember why she had so dreaded this day. When they were preparing to leave Mexico City, Don Angel had said to her, "We leave before the Day of the Dead. That should be balm to your heart, my Susana."

She thought her way back through her Days of the Dead.

She remembered the black-draped altars and the coffins. What had they meant to the others who knelt with her in the cathedral and the other churches where she spent the day in penance?

For others, the Day of the Dead did not end in the churches. In great, cheerful family groups they swarmed into the cemeteries, burdened with rich foods and flowers, to picnic amid the family tombs, with the comforting sense that their dead were near at hand and sharing with them the feasting. It had not been a day of mourning for others.

How, she dared ask herself now, had that difference been made between herself and others? Could all other deaths be guiltless?

Her untrained reasoning powers struggled with the problem. Who had condemned her to solitary grief on a day that was for others a feast day? The answer—by the edict of Don Angel. It was he who had told her that she could never be forgiven, nor could the lad be forgiven for having taken his life. By what right did Don Angel speak for God?

The intonation of the priests at the three altars reached her ears. "Let the dead be remembered."

She could be certain now that on this day, wherever he might be, the dead boy wished her well. He had loved her enough, as God knew, to wish that for her. One does not grieve on this day; one remembers. Susana would remember the boy again, one year from this day, wherever she might be. Now she said good-by to him with kindness, this morning near the Gila River, knowing that was the way it should be on the Day of the Dead.

Anza decided his people could do their remembering quite as well on horseback, and he ordered the march to continue. The bugle sounded, but it was almost noon before the procession finally started, with many of the children joining in the singing of the hymn still wearing their horrendous masks.

It was their most uncomfortable *jornada*, that day. The sharp-toothed November wind had the bite of winter. It drove gusts of sand between lips and eyelids and developed fine lines at the corners of eyes that would remain for life. So many of the horses were weakened by illness and hunger that they were given to stumbling, and there were minor accidents. Seda plodded on her serene way beside the nervous Major as if the catastrophes befalling other horses were none of her concern.

This day was one more of their many beginnings, for, having reached the Gila, they were now to make their way along its banks in a southerly direction, following the old Jesuit trail broken by the first Spanish evangelists. Facing them was another one-hundred-mile stretch across the arid Arizona desert.

It seemed strange to know they were headed again toward the old Mexico they had left with so much travail. Ahead, like the waves of a dead sea, went the lapping gray dunes of the desert. They merged in the distance with the gray sierra and rose into dark, massive peaks. Winter gave a reddish overcast to certain hills.

This was the true Indian desert, the dread *"tierra seca"* (dry land) with its monotonous gray relieved by the giant saguaro and paloverde. Scattered on the waste were piles of jagged rocks and in these lay the pools of bitter water on which their lives would depend. The scouts had mapped these pools for Anza, but there was no knowing how many would be dry by the time the company reached them.

And Susana, riding with new peace in her heart, looked out on this winter wasteland, when suddenly, out of the sands, it seemed, appeared an amazing procession. Advancing to meet them were some five hundred dancing and singing Indians in two lines, male and female, similar to those who had welcomed them to the Gila. These too were Pimas, joyous and affectionate in welcoming their friend Anza and his people.

And again Susana, once her heart had turned over, knew that these smiling people were not of the tribe of Palmita, for the women were no more beautiful than those she had seen before.

The Day of the Dead had begun with festival and would end with it. The tired travelers were no longer tired, and the dancing and singing continued until late in the night. Susana, drifting into sleep at last, after the Indians had returned to their huts and the pilgrims were tented for the night, wondered if the progress on and into California would continue to be a series of joyous welcomings from the peoples of the land.

[3]

Neither hardship nor pleasure served to delay the San Franciscans. The next morning, which was the third day of the month, they set out at an early hour in spite of their late celebration the night before. Anza never had to urge these people forward. Each morning Father Font's summons gave them new vitality. "To the Colorado!"

This morning the vitality died as one rider after another became ill. Sickening, they leaned from the saddles and had to be supported by relatives or friends. The procession fell silent, but Anza did not halt the march. His mouth was set in a grim line. The epidemic of nausea and dysentery was the result of drinking the bad water found in the desert's rock pools.

Nor did Father Font suggest resting, although he was one of the sick ones. His face was pinched with nausea. Then, as they rode, the heads of humans and animals lowered before the unexpected savage onslaught of the wind. It came whistling down the llano out of the north, driving blinding spirals of dust over the sand. "*Abajo!*" shouted Anza, and all left their saddles and crouched beside their beasts while the animals stood braced, tails to the wind, with eyes shut against the driving sand.

A roaring seemed to fill the air. Rain ladders formed in the sky. An eerie yellow light covered the desert and faded. Then with a rush the rains began. This was not the penetrating but gentle rain they had met before, but a relentless crashing down of solid sheets of water.

It was the savage winter rain of the desert. Anza had hoped to have his brood safely in California before it began.

They had traveled only two leagues that morning, but Anza knew that further effort was impossible. He gave the order to halt and make camp.

Raising the tents in the wind and rain was a struggle. More people fell ill. Warmth and clean water were needed, but there was neither. The soldiers cut wet brush and made fires inside the tents, not out of doors as before. They could not be large fires, but at least a small amount of cooking could be done. *Atole* was made for the sick people, and Tía María made pot after pot of her herb tea. The storm continued to lash the frail canvas shelters as if determined to drive them into the earth. The tightly woven canvas was not a complete defense against the rain. Those huddled within watched it crossing the canvas with wet lines and felt its spray stinging their faces. Smoke reddened their eyes.

From without came the incessant melancholy cries of the animals. It was their tragedy that in a world so wet they could find no dry places for resting or water to drink. There were a few shallow pools of bad water lying in grass gray with salt. The cattle, as always, sucked the wet sand, and had recourse to the lethal cactus. The people in the tents used the water that remained in their sacks for hot chocolate or tea.

Now the rains had begun, they continued until it seemed the skies must be exhausted of water, but no, the supply was endless, and the stoutest spirits quailed under the steady onslaught of wind and rain.

The next day, being November fourth, was the feast of St. Charles, the saint's day of their regent and patron, King Charles III. It was a day to be celebrated with feasting and relaxation.

Instead the pilgrims woke to a morning of terrible cold and continued downpour. More were ill, and the others were suffering from thirst and hunger and cold. The last of the water stored in the leather sacks was gone. The horses that had run away and drunk of the bad water were sicker than before. They were now three leagues from the Gila River.

They waited for Anza to give the word to dismantle the tents. But he did not speak.

Anza had seen the sick list swelling. Also one of the young wives was in labor. There could be no departure.

The pilgrims waited miserably in their smoke-filled tents. A fine way to keep the feast day of Carlos III! Anza understood. He could not let them spend the holiday in such misery. He ordered a pint of *aguardiente* distributed to each adult that they might drink a toast "in honor of our king."

After their long abstinence on the road the powerful brandy went like fire to the pilgrims' throats and brains. The gloom in the tents lifted. Song was raised, followed by loud laughter. There were some outbursts of rowdiness, and spurts of shouted anger.

Father Font left his tent for Anza's. His expression was grim and he looked, and was, ill. Soldiers stationed near the tent reported harsh words between the two.

In their case the age-old contest between the cross and the sword had been waived, but a residue of protest remained on either side. Font believed in spiritual exaltation, Anza in enjoying the good things of this world.

"This, of all days," Font protested, "should have been spent in Masses and prayers."

Anza's opinion was expressed as firmly. "These are good and brave people. They have suffered a great deal and without complaining. They have earned a little amusement . . ."

"A little immorality!" countered the friar.

There was a brief silence. The strain of the journey was beginning to tell even on its leaders. Both men sympathized with the problems of Serra in California, whose attempts to do good among the Indians were being consistently interfered with by the military. Neither Font nor Anza wanted conflict. But each was certain he was right and would not yield. In the quiet Font's jaws were heard to chatter.

"Little Father!" Instantly Anza was all compassion. "You must return to your bed."

Anza opened his medicine chest and found a prescription for Father Font, who had the ague and was high in fever. Font took the medicine and he did return to his bed. But he refused to lie down! Instead, sitting up, he drew from memory a fine sketch of the ruins of Casa Grande, inscribing it with the caption: "It all reduces itself to fables."

Anza visited Font and the other invalids, leaving each with the same message, "All will be well with us once we have crossed the Colorado." The promise raced through the camp—yes, all would be well once the dangerous river was crossed and they were safe in California. But the principal topic in the tents was the displeasure the two leaders had shown to one another, and for the first time. Loyalty was divided, but the majority sided with Anza, for all were enjoying the powerful brandy that warmed the marrow of bones congealed with cold.

The Pima guides showed the worst effects. They did not get boisterous, as did some of the other men. They became silent and sullen-browed, in a way that frightened the women.

"Indians should never drink," Tía María stated virtuously, evidently forgetful of her own Indian blood. "They cannot drink without getting drunk, and then they become very angry without knowing why and they beat their wives and fight with their friends, and the next morning they are sad and suffer from Indian dolor. Then they are ashamed and there are lamentations because they get more drunk than other people and suffer more afterward. No, Indians should never drink."

She drank her own cupful of brandy with gusto and no ill effects, accepting it as strong medicine that could defeat the penetrating cold. Susana sipped the fiery liquid more slowly. They stayed in the herb woman's tent to avoid the Indian guides who had been so amiable and soft-spoken, but who were now prowling the camp and might be dangerous.

Gil José came in at suppertime to bring word from Anza that Tía María's presence was requested in the tent where the woman was attempting to give birth. Susana went with her as an acolyte bearing the inevitable pot of *atole*. This time the corn gruel was not wasted, for the woman was young and in good health— she was, in fact, the girl-wife Susana had seen seated with her husband that afternoon the Galváns arrived at Horcasitas. Labor proceeded without difficulty and the baby was born early the next morning. But the child was premature, and through no fault of Anza's or Tía María's it was born dead. Tía María whispered mournful prayers as she unwound the looped cord from the wizened throat. Susana spooned thin gruel, heavily laced with brown sugar, between the trembling lips of the sad little mother. Nothing more could be done.

They returned to the Perea tent and stirred up another potful of *atole* to carry to Father Font, who was by this time shuddering with ague. Font was grateful. He remarked that not even Anza's chef could make as smooth a porridge.

He grew worse. The little mother who had delivered the stillborn child developed a high fever, and the postlabor pains did not lessen. Another woman was stricken with the effects of bad water, the miserable sickness marked by diarrhea and nausea and fever and chills. Then another woman sickened, and still another. Tía María and Susana did not rest. They patrolled the sick tents, doling out Anza's medicines and tea and bowls of *atole*.

Nicolás Perea returned to his tent shuddering with cold, and with bad news. Three of the horses that had drunk the bad water had died. Others were dying, and the hardier cattle were showing symptoms of the same sickness. Anza jotted down the lists of dying animals. It was doubtful if there would be enough horses left to carry the colonists! His list of invalids was growing too, and his medicine chest was always open. He cursed the bad water of this place and gave it a name that would endure, Laguna del Hospital. The lake was indeed an evil place, with its foul-smelling water and hovering mists. The cold was increasing. The rain lessened, but an icy drizzle continued to fall.

Anza ordered Gil José and several other soldiers to collect all the empty leather sacks so they could carry and fetch water from the Gila River. It was a miserably cold ride, for the river was almost ten miles away, but within a few hours they were back with dozens of the leather bottles filled with river water. The invalids drank and felt better. The childbearing pains that had continued to torment the little mother gradually stopped.

On November sixth Anza announced that, rain or no rain, they would set out again the next morning. They had lost three days at this miserable place. The pilgrims were willing to leave, as nothing could be worse than days and nights spent shivering in mildewing tents. As if in approval of Anza's decision, the morning of the seventh found the desert bathed in brilliant sunshine and as dry as it had been before the rains.

The travelers were finding the sudden shifts in climate bewildering. In one hour they would be deluged with rain and in the next panting for water.

It was one o'clock in the afternoon before the last rider was in the saddle, for many were weak with illness and unable to assist in the packing and saddling. The young mother was wrapped in blankets and held on horseback by her husband. Father Font was still shivering as he was lifted onto his saddle mule, being compelled by weakness to yield at last to Anza's pleadings that he give up his determination to walk to California.

The assemblage was ready at last, but it was not as trimly aligned as usual and its customary gaiety was lacking. Then, just as they were about to start, there was a hideous commotion on the field. Two of the horses began retching and thrashing about in the throes of colic. Nothing could be done to help them, and they died while their helpless owners watched. Meantime, three others started the spasmodic convulsions, and they were quickly unsaddled and turned loose. The San Franciscans left them on the desert to meet their miserable deaths, and set out in a subdued mood. Father Font's voice was too weak to be heard as he attempted to start the "*Olabado.*" It took all his strength to hold his frail body to the saddle.

The San Franciscans continued to follow the wavering line of the Gila in a southwesterly direction, meeting it and leaving it again. They were lonely travelers in a vast, uninhabited world.

The dry cutoffs between the river curves were danger zones, for the company was dependent then on the water secreted in the rocks. It was a remarkable fact that each time they became certain they could not travel another mile without water, water was found, and just in time.

Because of the water shortage they divided into two trains to thread a pass through the Maricopa Mountains. Late that afternoon the divisions struggled out of the canyon and rejoined on the desert, close by the river. Again, rising out of the desert to meet them, came another thousand dancing and singing Indians. These were Opas, a large Pima settlement straggling along the Gila's banks. The women wore short skirts of woven willow bark or deerskin and no jewelry, and they danced with a will.

The men made up for the nonornamental appearance of the women. Their dark bodies were streaked with black soot and red ocher and they wore elaborate collars and ear and nose ornaments made of beads. Some wore pantaloons woven of cotton grown in their own milpas. Anza was pleased to see some of the males wearing black blankets. He knew that wool was not a product of this village and the blankets were signs of trade, showing that the peace treaties he had set up in this region were still active.

The Opas advanced, murmuring soft greetings, and their smiles were beautiful with the innocence that at this time distinguished all the people of the Gila.

The San Franciscans made camp and the Opas went from tent to tent making friends and bringing gifts of baskets filled with wheat and corn and calabashes, and in turn Anza made them the customary gifts of tobacco and beads. The gourds pleased Tía María even more than the wheat and corn. While showing them to Gil José she commented rather spitefully:

"Your Palmita, is she like these women?"

The soldier answered coldly. "In her tribe there are no homely women."

"And when will we meet this paragon?"

"Soon."

Each time Palmita's name was mentioned Susana died a little. She knew the meeting was inevitable.

The San Franciscans were observing many differences in the Southwestern tribes as they made their slow progress toward the Colorado and the Indians continued to appear in swarms of two hundred, five hundred, and even thousands to greet their friend Anza and his company. Some were lighter of skin than others. Some were handsome and others actually ugly. But all were strong-bodied and gentle of spirit, and all were trusting.

[4]

Several hours after leaving the Opa settlement, Anza ordered the halt for the night. He could see that many of the riders were exhausted and all were miserable, for the cold rain had once more overtaken the procession. Theirs was a bad camp site in the mountains, in a place they called the Arroyo Seco (Dry Canyon). It was dry in spite of the rain, and there was no drinking water and no forage for the animals. Its only advantage lay in the encircling mountains that offered some protection against the wind.

By morning the drizzle had become a deluge. Two more colonists were ill. Tía María reported that the little mother's belly felt swollen and spongy, and horribly reminiscent of that of the mother who had died after leaving Tubac. Font's ague had worsened.

There was no thought of travel. The emigrants spent two miserable days and nights in the Arroyo Seco. The rain continued to fall.

On the eleventh the little mother and several other sick people seemed much better. Father Font was still weak, but he hid the fact from Anza and urged him not to hold up the march any longer.

They struggled forward at intervals the next few days. Whenever the rain abated they would ride. Humans and animals suffered agonies of thirst. They eventually passed through the Maricopa Mountains and struggled on again over the desert.

On the fourteenth they made camp in a place to be remembered, always with pleasure, for it was a natural spa in the desert known as Agua Caliente (Hot Water). Here the chill air was permeated by warmth generated by steaming pools of water so hot that eggs could be cooked in them, and around these pools were fields of fine new grass.

The Pimas knew the properties of their springs, which they considered medicinal, and stood about exclaiming with pleasure as the expeditionaries took turns bathing, family after family ("They have great need of it," Anza confided to his diary with paternal restraint).

They spent the entire day and the next at the springs, and the sick people soaked often in the hot water and felt much better, and the horses and cattle feasted on the good pasturage and grew noticeably stronger.

Susana wrung out the damp cotton articles, hers and Don Angel's, and spread them to dry on *fierro* branches. She sat by the spring to take pleasure in being warm and clean again. For her and the other women, the inability to keep clean had become the worst part of this journey to California. To be warm, to bathe, to have good water to drink and a modest supply of food were privileges they had never before recognized as being gifts

from God. Susana thought of this and much more as she sat
with her arms locked around her knees and waiting, dreamy-
eyed, for the wash to dry.

She wondered about Vengador, who was dabbing a paw in
and out of the bubbling spring, puzzled by its heat and the
rising stream. Certainly no creature had ever endured a harsher
life. It had left the dog with a permanently scarred eye and heel
marks like brands on his scrawny haunches. But joy of life
bubbled through that lanky frame, and Vengador was never at
a loss to find ways to amuse himself. Now, looking up into a
fierro tree, he saw a petticoat Susana had hung to dry waving
in the wind like a flag. In another second he had it in his jaws
and streaked away with it, in and out of the camp and among
the tents while she pursued him, calling and laughing with embarrassment and annoyance.

It was Felipe's whistled command that stopped the dog, for
Vengador stopped suddenly and returned to her, dropping the
cotton garment at her feet and looking up at her, wagging his
tail in the most ingratiating way.

"Why do you not beat him?" demanded Felipe, coming up
lazily after the dog, but Susana shook her head.

"How can I when I am laughing at him?" she retorted with
unusual sharpness, knowing she would neither beat Vengador
nor permit him to be beaten.

"That is true!" Felipe looked at the dog with new understanding. "In the theater we pay to hear laughter. But with
Vengador, one never has to pay."

And I, I am greedy for laughter, thought Susana. I have tasted
it on this journey and can never have enough. And much of it
has been owed to this Felipe. . . .

As if he heard her thoughts, Felipe grinned. "See, Vengador
and I are alike! We make you laugh."

In an impulse of pure friendliness she coaxed, "Sit with me
here."

They sat together beside the steaming pool in amiable companionship. No other man in the company could sit beside a
woman in such a way and not cause talk. But Felipe as a musician
was as he often said, the man invisible. He could take privileges
other men could not, and he asked questions no other man
dared ask.

"He is not a handsome dog," he remarked now.

"He is not ugly!" flashed Susana, with a violence that startled him.

"*Ajá*, so you can get angry! I thought you were made of milk and roses!"

They laughed together at this, and Felipe spoke kindly to Vengador, who was watching them with tongue lolling and clownish amusement in his intelligent eyes. Then the three sat contentedly watching the bubbles rising in the hot spring.

They set out at nine-thirty on the morning of November sixteenth, reluctant to leave the hospitable springs but still eager to reach the junction. Many were still ill, but the majority on the invalid list were feeling better. Father Font alone had not responded to the medicinal treatment of the springs. He was so weak he had to ride leaning over the horn of his saddle. He was worse than before but would not admit this to Anza, as he could not bear to delay departure by so much as another day.

They were held up for three days at the Cerro de San Pasqual (later Mohawk Peak) due to the birth of a fine boy who was named Diego Pasqual, and whose mother was left too ill by the ordeal to travel. She was not the only invalid, for the other sick ones, including Father Font, grew worse.

Anza was impressed by the success of Tía María's tea dispersings. He spoke to Father Font about the brew, stressing the fact that he considered its contents harmless and its effects good. Father Font realized his wretched illness was wrecking his health and also the progress of the project nearest to his heart, and he sent word to Tía María requesting that she favor him with a pot of her brewing. The herb woman was surprised and pleased and wasted no time, and within two days Father Font was completely well. He gave credit to the brew in his diary, describing how a woman in the company "gave me a potion."

The newest colonist, the small boy Diego Pasqual, was also thriving, and his mother was on her way to recovery. He was in her arms when she was assisted into her saddle on the cold and icy morning of November twenty-second. Father Font sang the "*Olabado*" as lustily as he had when the pilgrimage began, and he was still in an energetic mood at four-thirty that afternoon, when Anza gave the order to dismount and prepare to camp for the night at a place called the Cerro de Santa Cecilia (now Antelope Hill).

[5]

Deeply imbedded in the ethos of these people was the ability to face death without flinching. In the same vein they met their miseries. They joked as they followed the Gila's sandy course through tangled brush that ripped clothing and skin. Their animals had not these weapons of defense. In this barren land there was little food to give them courage. The hundred-mile trek down the Gila was their death march. The sensitive horses were the first to die. One after another staggered to its knees, and neither whip nor spur could make it rise again. The cattle at the rear of the procession broke singly from the herd with madness in their bulging eyes and raced back along the route over which they had just dragged their exhausted bodies. Not even riatas could pull them back into the procession. Some became trapped by their horns in the brush, and if the vaqueros did succeed in untangling them they charged their rescuers.

One by one the cattle perished, many of hunger, others of having eaten cactus. Their bodies were left to the coyotes and vultures, ballooned in death on the desert with stiff legs pointing to the sky.

This went on day after day, and when would the ending be, and where were Chief Palma and the Colorado? Where was the Promised Land?

Each morning the San Franciscans were slower in starting. Each morning more animals were found dead, and it took longer to bring together the weakened survivors and prepare them for the road.

Each day more people fell ill.

And still even the sick exchanged feeble jests that brought feeble laughter.

Anza's medicine chest was in constant use. But Father Font continued to get better, and his praise of Tía María's herb tea made the brew more popular than before.

Then on November twenty-fifth people's spirits were lifted

by a Yuma messenger from Palma, bringing greetings to Anza and word that the chief was preparing food and shelter and a warm welcome for the San Franciscans.

The message brought loud shouts of *"Ole!"* and cheers for Chief Palma, and misery was forgotten in the joy of knowing they were almost there! There was a great deal of rushing about by the women and searching of bags and bundles for hats and ribbons, for even the sick people wanted to look their best when presented to Anza's greatest Indian friend.

Don Angel watched with a sour face as Susana braided into her hair the red silk ribbons given her by the king. "Is it for savages you make yourself desirable, or for a cowboy turned soldier?" His sarcasm seemed senselessly cruel, since she and Gil José had not looked at one another for weeks.

"The Yuma Indians are Christians and our friends," she said sharply, and joined Tía María, who was pressing a half dozen of her petticoats on a flat rock, with a small pointed iron she had heated in the fire.

Father Font walked by and, seeing Susana, he asked a question that had long been on his mind.

"Why do I never see you at Mass, little Daughter?"

Tía María spoke for her.

"She is not permitted, Father. Her husband refuses permission."

"So?" The friar made no other comment.

But he expressed his opinion at Mass the next morning, and with astonishing violence. His flock had never seen Font in an angrier mood.

"What I am about to say," so he began his sermon, "is dedicated to certain husbands who are members of this expedition. Their names I shall not give. I leave to your conscience the question of their guilt or innocence. But these men are so jealous of their wives that they will not let them speak to anybody!

"They even prohibit their attending Mass!"

There were gasps from the women listeners and several husbands present without their wives turned noticeably red of face. Don Angel was not there. Tía María lost no time in reporting the attack to Don Angel and Susana, who were at breakfast.

"He named no names," she repeated, with an oblique glance

at Don Angel, "but he said he was very angry with these jealous
husbands."

Don Angel bowed to Tía María, holding his chocolate mug
from lips whitening with anger.

"My gratitude, *señora*, for bringing me word that I have been
publicly spitted from the pulpit by the good father. And thanks
to my wife for having arranged for my public humiliation."

Don Angel spoke with utmost courtesy.

"Father Font mentioned many husbands," stammered the
dismayed Tía María.

The herb woman seemed to be seeing the courtly Don Angel
for the first time and unable to grasp what she was seeing.
Susana could not bear the look of hurt on her friend's face. A
long-unused capacity for resentment flared against Don Angel.

"Tomorrow morning, my dear friend," she told Tía María, "I
will go with you to Mass, if you will permit me. And from tomorrow on, I shall attend."

This show of defiance surprised Susana as greatly as it did
Tía María and Don Angel, who said bitterly after Tía María left,
"I can expect no better of you. You are what you are."

Susana had given much thought of late to the time and place
where Palmita would enter their lives. The inevitable meeting
could not be far off. Gil José had traveled with Anza to the
Colorado only the year before. She only hoped her resentment of
Don Angel might give her courage to face the ordeal ahead of
meeting with the tribe she was certain was Palmita's.

Even if Susana had not guessed in advance that the girl
Palmita was of the Yuma tribe, she would have known in her
first glimpse of Chief Palma's people. They were the handsomest
and tallest Indians the San Franciscans had seen. In fact, the
travel-worn pilgrims suffered by comparison, for their appearance
had deteriorated in these last days of November.

The long-anticipated meeting took place at three in the afternoon of the twenty-seventh of November.

The travelers had fought their way all day along the Gila's
sandy bed and were now following it northward in a narrow pass
through the Gila Mountains. Riding toward them came thirty
mounted riders—but what riders! The foremost they knew at
once to be the famous Chief Palma. But those who rode with

him were equally formidable and magnificent. This was a procession of desert kings! And kings they were—the leaders Palma, chief of all the river tribes on both sides of the Colorado, and his brother known as Captain Pablo. The dignitaries with them represented all the tribes of the river region. They were tall, muscular, deep of chest, and powerful of limb. The fact they were almost entirely naked did not detract from their dignity. Their only garments were a blanket of cotton or black wool, or an animal pelt cape, flung back from the shoulders to reveal broad, brightly painted chests. Their bodies and faces were painted in designs of red and white and black, and their black hair was dressed high and stiffened with mud and pierced with feathers and other oddments, then sprinkled over with a silvery dust. (So elaborate were these headdresses that their wearers were often obliged to sleep sitting up.) Their ears were pierced, some with as many as five holes, and in these were the same oddments they wore in their hair. Some of the men wore nose ornaments of small white stones or bits of polished turquoise.

The Yuma braves were fearful in appearance. Actually they were peaceful agriculturalists, content with their good lives, but if lives and fields were threatened they could become the deadliest of warriors. They had been noble allies of Anza's in helping to keep the Apaches at bay. A Yuma brave on the warpath was a terrifying spectacle. Many a marauding Apache had turned his horse and fled before a painted Yuma, riding a horse bedecked and trained for battle, and carrying a war lance and club and quiver of arrows, and a bow as tall as himself.

No women were in this welcoming delegation. It was splendidly, magnificently all male.

The Indians halted and everyone left his saddle. Palma advanced to meet Anza. In one immense hand he carried a small basket. He put his arms around Anza, hugged him, then poured a handful of beans from the basket into Anza's hands. This was a symbol of hospitality. He kissed the hands of the priests. That was a sign of respect.

The two leaders spoke through interpreters. Absence of direct speech did not spoil their meeting. These two men understood one another. Their worlds would be riven by misunderstanding and injustice, but they would remain friends.

(All too soon, other Spanish colonists were to settle on the vast Yuma holdings and take possession of the fertile fields these Indians had tended for centuries, and bring misfortune to Palma's trusting people. But on this November afternoon there was no shadow on the friendliness between the white men and the bronze.)

The speeches and embraces took a great deal of the afternoon and it became too late to resume the march. The San Franciscans spent the night in the pass, and rose early the next morning for their first glimpse of the Colorado. There was one last crossing of the Gila before the junction could be reached, and then they had arrived! That barren desert on the other side was California.

They were too excited to notice that the land across the river was so like that they stood upon that one might have been a reflection of the other. The massive Indian gathering awaiting them was worthy of its splendid chief. Susana, scanning the multitude, knew that Gil José had spoken the truth and that among Palma's people there were no homely women, and many were beautiful.

The Yuma women were tall and supple of body. Like the men, they were athletic and good at games. They had their own horses and spent much of their time on horseback. Having been brought up on the Colorado, "half in and half out of the water," both men and women swam with the agility of eels.

Yes, all were beautiful, Susana decided with a sinking heart, and searched face after face among the women, wondering, Which is Palmita?

The bodies and faces of these women were brightly painted in red and white designs, but this did not spoil their beauty. Their scant costumes might have been designed to show their bodies at their best. These consisted only of two brief aprons, worn low on the hips to display their shapely thighs. The skirts were of deerskin, or more commonly, of the soft, inner lining of willow bark, and the pilgrims would note later the hundreds of willow trees lining the riverbanks that were dead or dying, having been stripped of their bark by the Yuma women for this purpose. They also wore small capes of the same material, but these, like the capes of the men, were merely hung about the shoulders and flung back, exposing breasts that had never known confinement. They did not wear their hair in the top-heavy coiffures the males displayed, but in a fashion delightfully childlike, cut in bangs across their foreheads, and the rest worn long and free and powdered with the same powdered blue clay the men used. Like the men, their ears were pierced, but not their noses, and they wore necklaces. Some wore strings of a green, metallic desert beetle (strikingly similar to the scarab jewelry of ancient Egypt), and others strings of beads that had been gifts from Anza on his first visit.

[6]

Susana found herself being swept along toward the open *enramadas* with the other colonists by the hospitable Yumas. She became separated from Don Angel and the Pereas and watched as Gil José pushed his way among their Yuma hosts, being welcomed on every side, for many of these people were known to him from his first visit with Anza.

He was obviously looking for one person. But there was no time for searching. The festivities were beginning.

The San Franciscans were ushered into the pavilions by Palma and his fellow dignitaries, where their beaming wives were waiting to serve the hungry pilgrims with a spread of such proportions as none had seen before, and, to top it all off, three thousand enormous ripe watermelons which the Yuma had gathered months before in late summer and preserved under dry sand against Anza's promised return.

The feasting was followed by music and games and laughter— this was indeed a *fiesta brava!*

Anza watched with a rare smile on his austere features. The Yuma was his favorite Indian tribe. Later he gathered with their leaders and presented his own serious problem to them. How was he to get his people, their animals and mountains of luggage, across a Colorado swollen with the snows of winter? The four soldiers who had scouted the territory across the river had returned to say the river was deeper than any Indian had known it before, and that crossing with so large a party would be impossible. They themselves, veterans of the desert, had returned across the Colorado at the risk of their lives.

Palma and the other chiefs agreed with the scouts.

"My friend Captain Anza," Palma began, speaking sorrowfully, for he knew Anza was troubled, "we who live on this river know the river. We know it is deeper now than your tallest horses. You have with you many women and children and heavy loads. You cannot get them across to the other side."

The other chiefs nodded their heavily coiffured heads. Palma spoke again.

"Dear friend, it cannot be done. You must not attempt so dangerous a crossing. You must all stay here with us."

Some time during this conference, Gil José slipped off to continue his search. Susana couldn't resist the temptation to follow him, and he was too intent upon his mission to notice. He walked past the huts of the river settlement and fields toward the river where the banks were thickly wooded with cottonwood and mimosa and willow. Evidently Gil José was heading for a place remembered. He reached the bank of the Colorado and halted abruptly at the sound of laughter, followed by a sudden splash. Someone had leaped from a hiding place under the willows into the icy torrent.

Susana stopped when Gil José stopped, looked where he looked, and saw the dripping seal-dark head and lovely, laughing face, and knew that it was Palmita. Gil José stepped quickly to the edge of the water and reached down. A dark, sinuous body flashed in the shallows with the ease of a water snake, turning gracefully in the water. The Indian girl had waited for him here in the place of their first rendezvous. Gil José gave his hands and she swung up beside him laughing, with her naked, beautiful body silvered over with water. But he held her at arm's length, devouring the beauty of this Nereid of the river. The red and white paint did not spoil the laughing young face, and the lithe, supple body with its rounded lines. Gil José was staring at her with that look of life Susana remembered, for once it had been for her. Then she saw the flame in him die.

Gil José took his hands from the girl. He was scowling at Palmita, at her breasts.

"What has been done to you? These have changed."

He pointed. The nipples on the high breasts were aureoled in violet against the brown. They were testimony even a man could recognize. The only flaws on Palmita's perfect body were the telltale rings. Gil José charged her brutally.

"You have had a child?"

She answered in the broken Spanish of his teaching. "A baby, yes. A boy child." She was still smiling. "Yours!"

His face darkened with shock, then paled.

"I would see this child now."

Then he pushed her away as her supple fingers laced in a gesture of strangulation.

"You killed it? Mine? You murdered my boy?" Gil José shouted. His hand went to his knife. The girl cowered before him. She had reason to be afraid. Then a resurgence of courage pulled her upright. She faced Gil José with dignity. "I have known no other man," she hissed, and turned and slipped away under the willows, graceful in her nakedness, a chief's daughter and fierce in her pride.

Susana had watched, unable to move. She saw Gil José bury his face in his hands in a gesture of bereavement, and she felt she could not bear the sharing of his tragedy, nor that of the Indian girl's. She turned and fled back toward the camp, and heard the sound of Gil José's spurs as he came running after her. It seemed the final horror that Gil José, the veteran soldier, was sobbing. He came up to her and walked beside her wiping away tears. When he spoke to her, his words were incoherent, pleading.

"Why did she listen? Her father, the chief, must have commanded her. To murder a child! Keep her from my sight while I am here! Tell her if I look on her face again I will kill her. Tell her . . . Susana," his cry became urgent, "Susana, tell me you forgive me?"

She could not answer. "Whom am I to forgive?" her heart asked sadly.

"Let me return alone," she told Gil José.

"Susana!" He wept her name. "It was you always. All the time I was planning to marry her, because Father Font said we men who are single should marry, it was you I remembered, not Palmita."

She tried to speak coldly to the man at her side.

"Then it is best that you forget us both, Gil José."

The Western Indians were innocents, as Font and Anza had warned. In the beginning the Indian women teased and petted

the strange soldiers with the abandonment of affectionate pup-
pies, but a soldier is a soldier, and grief followed wherever the
armed minions of Spain traveled among the Indian tribes. Months
after the first Spanish troops marched through the desert region,
the daughters of a proud and ancient civilization were forced by
tribal edict to strangle the half-white babies sired by the vanished
soldiers. The white man's seed was not wanted by the race-proud
Indians. A child showing signs of white blood was condemned to
death.

This was the start of the trouble that would result in the
slow breaking down of a content and independent people. Not
long after the Second Expedition passed, Indians would be sighted
riding over the desert whose horses wore as blankets the sweat-
stained velvet vestments of Spanish priests, murdered in reprisal
for the sins of Spanish soldiers. Even now, rebellion had begun
in California and reprisal would follow. They were to be part
of the heartbreaks of Serra. Five days after this fiesta at the
junction a priest was murdered in a massacre at the San Diego
Mission. "The Indians who killed him will be our enemies,"
Palma would promise.

The lists of "bad Indians" were growing in the West. They
did not regard themselves as molesters, but as avengers. Another
age might have considered them patriots, for they were willing
to kill, and to die, in defense of their homelands. This spirit
of revolt had not touched the Yuma and the Pima tribes.
Their trust was in Anza. But hatred was on the rise, and it
was shortly to play an important role in delaying the carefully
laid plans for the founding of the settlement for St. Francis.

For the present an Edenic spirit prevailed at the junction.
Only three people knew of Gil José's meeting with Palmita.
The Indian girl did not appear during the celebration that continued for the rest of the day. Gil José's haunted look followed
Susana, but she remained close to Tía María. She felt no exulta-
tion that the waiting was over and that Palmita had lost. She
needed now to rebuild her defenses against her own longings
and those of Gil José. She would not yield. She dared not.
She heard the other celebrants singing, she watched the dancing,
and her thoughts wrestled with the problem, repeating over and
over the vow she had taken at San Xavier.

Susana thought it fortunate that Gil José was given no time in which to nurse his grief. She saw him the next morning, which was the twenty-ninth of November, riding away toward the big river with Palma and Anza and a mixed company of their men.

Gil José was not to be blamed if his spirits lifted on the ride, for the day was crisp and clear and the mission important.

Anza had decided against all advice to try for the crossing of the Colorado.

They rode to the place where the First Expedition had crossed in 1774. Anza's scouts had forded the river in this place only a few days before. Now the river ran dark and dangerous with rain and melted snow. The scouts were right. The ford was impassable.

"Rafts?" Anza suggested. Palma shook his head. His braves were willing to swim in the river, no matter how cold, but they could not remain in the water long enough to steer heavily burdened rafts across the turbulent water.

"We would only be able to get one raft across a day," Palma protested. "A tilt, and all aboard would be lost. And your company is so large, it would take weeks to get all your people across."

"Then we will take weeks," said Anza, with the iron cast to his jaw his soldiers recognized.

Time was running out for Anza. Snow was threatening and delay could be dangerous. He studied the width of the swollen river.

"It cannot be crossed," warned Palma. Anza answered, "It must be."

Anza set the men to work cutting down trees to make log rafts. But he was not certain this was the only way.

"I am going to make one last search for a crossing place," he told Palma.

The chief remained with the wood choppers. Anza summoned Gil José and a Yuma guide and set out along the river.

They had ridden only half a mile up the wooded bank when they came to a place where the river was divided into three channels by inlands. The channels were wide but appeared passable. Each of the three men waded his horse across a channel to test the depth. The crossings were safely made.

The raft making was halted and the other men brought to the new site. For the rest of the day all swung their axes with Anza. It was late afternoon when they returned to the camp with their clothing torn and mudstained, to report a new road had been cut to an adequate fording place.

The camp and the village exploded with the excitement of learning that in the morning the San Franciscans would try to cross the Colorado.

[7]

By nine the next morning the San Franciscans and many of their Yuma friends were riding after Anza down the newly cleared road. It was the last day of November.

When they reached the ford, soldiers took the bridles of horses carrying the women and children to lead them across. Felipe saw Gil José turn toward Susana and with a deft movement he took Seda's bridle. It was an act of diplomacy on Felipe's part, for Don Angel was glowering from his high perch on Major.

All set out together, following Anza's plunging horse through the water. Each of the three channels was hundreds of yards wide. In depth they varied from three to six feet. A horse, slipping on the muddy floor of the river, could plunge itself and rider over both their heads. The horses footed their way through the swift water with great care. In some places they were forced to swim. As they neared the other shore they lunged forward frantically, again endangering their riders.

Ten soldiers had been stationed in a line below the fording place to serve as a protective barrier if a rider should be swept away. This precaution showed its worth almost at once, when a man holding a little girl in front of his saddle was thrown into the current. While the man floundered to shore the chain of soldiers rushed forward and caught up the child, passing her hand over hand to the opposite bank, which she reached drenched but squealing with amusement.

Susana had implicit trust in the sure-footed Seda with Felipe leading, but the little mare's short legs carried her out of her depth in several places, and Susana reached the other side with drenched skirts, as did most of the women.

The foodstuffs and other goods were unpacked and made into smaller packs and brought across in mule loads. Only one of the loads shipped water, and this unfortunately belonged to Father Font and contained the priestly vestments.

From the California shore Anza and the priests watched the last of the burdened animals flounder ashore. Long before the afternoon ended all of the families and nearly all of the herds were safely landed in California. The fording had taken three hours.

Anza's expression was inscrutable. The Second Expedition had crossed the great Colorado, and in winter, and without using a single raft! Anza had brought his people across the great southern desert, and now across this river, at the risk of their lives. Anza looked from one face to another and saw disappointment instead of triumph. The country was no different from that they had just left across the river.

"This is California?" Tía María complained. "And what were we promised, Gil José? We were told of blue water and green fields and flowers always in bloom. We were promised warmth, and roses . . ."

"We have also been promised snow, and very soon, little Mamma," put in Felipe, hoping impudence would distract his mother.

Tía María would not be diverted.

"We have been promised land. Beautiful land. Who wishes to own land where our feet slip on ice?"

The other women groaned agreement. Gil José spoke up. His temper had been at the breaking point since the meeting with Palmita. Still he did not like to see Tía María unhappy.

"Little Aunt, there will be no snow where we are going. This place is not our California. In ours, there will be sunshine, and roses."

Tía María had the last word.

"This is no different from Sonora."

It was true this lower section of California was identical to the land they had left on the other side of the Colorado. Soldiers like Gil José who had seen Anza's map would understand the resemblance. The San Franciscans had returned almost to the future Mexican border. They had left it by a route shaped like an arch from Tucson to the Gila, then marched down that river almost to the Sonoran line.

A pallid winter sunset found them camped a little farther down the Colorado and about a mile north of Palma's rancheria. This large settlement of clay and brush huts on the California shore was directly opposite the mouth of the Gila where it emptied into the larger river. It was surrounded by neat winter fields of yellowed cornstalks and the dead vines of the beans and squash and watermelons the colonists had so enjoyed at their welcoming feast.

That evening they dressed in their finest and rode along the riverbank to Palma's headquarters.

Anza had a great deal on his mind. He held a serious conference with the four soldiers he had sent ahead to explore this California side of the river in the hope that they could locate a better route than the one he had taken the year before. Their reports were disheartening. They had gone far into the California desert and found no water holes or forage of any kind.

Anza always wanted to meet danger head on and not wait for it. But this time there had to be a delay. Plans were to be carried out before leaving the junction.

He discussed with the three Franciscans and the Indian leaders the buildings to be erected in the next few days for Eixarch and Garcés, who were to remain there to establish the Southwest's newest mission. It would be built at the Yuma rancheria.

They discussed plans for the construction, the care and protection of the two fathers, and what provisions Anza should leave for them.

Palma promised to help in building the mission. "I am now a Spaniard," he said. He embraced Father Font, for whom all Yumas had developed deep affection. "And you—you are Yuma."

Again Palma pleaded that the colonists remain with his people.

"This will be a winter of winters," the chief warned Anza. "Never have we known this land to be so cold. And now is only the beginning."

Neither Font nor Anza could explain to their warmhearted friend's satisfaction that Francis of Assisi was not a saint to be kept waiting.

The tired pilgrims rode back to their own camp and much-needed sleep.

Anza's tent remained lighted. Alone, he pondered his newest and most dangerous crisis. He knew the next stretch of the way into the cold and lonely California desert would be more trying than any before. Many of his people were ill and all were weary, but he must ask more of them than ever.

Somehow, he must get them across the Mojave Desert to Mission San Gabriel!

Much had been accomplished on this day. The San Franciscans had crossed the Colorado. They were in California at last. They had met in conclave with the Indians, and all the talk between the delegates had been of peace, and means to maintain the peace.

Also, plans were under way for the new buildings at Palma's rancheria that were to be the nucleus of one more of Anza's dream cities. Did he see it, that last night of November, with tired eyes studying the worn map by lantern light, as the future city of Yuma?

December

CHAPTER FIVE

[1]

The days went fast at the junction. On the second of December the two cabins were finished. They were of raw lumber and smelled of the forest, but they were the start of the city of Yuma.

Anza announced departure for the following day. He set aside enough provisions to last the two priests through the winter. He planned to deliver the colonists to San Francisco Bay and return to Yuma in the spring, when he would take the two missionaries back with him to Tucson. He left them several horses, as Garcés planned to ride around the Colorado region converting other tribes and laying plans for the founding of more missions.

So it was farewell to the Yuma people on the great river, to Palma, to all that was strange at the junction but somehow friendly and familiar. Looking back, the San Franciscans saw to the last the two robed evangelists of Spain's newest desolate outpost in the desert, surrounded by dark Yuma faces, each one of which continued to smile.

"*Adios*, Brother Corn," Susana heard Tía María remark gently as they rode through the last of the Yuma fields, brown and crackling with winter. And when Susana smiled, Tía María reproved her. "Susana, this may be the last we shall see of Corn until we plant our own hillocks on St. Francis's bay. So say *adios* to Corn with his long arms and silken hair, because he is our brother and father and lover, and wherever he grows, our people are at home."

Susana murmured meekly, "*Adios*, Brother Corn!"

The dry rows rustled in answer. There is understanding between people of Indian blood and the spirit of the corn. The pagan in Tía María had spoken, not the pious Tía María who had interrupted her hymn singing to bid the maize good-by. Had not St. Francis professed kinship with all that grew? Like him, Tía María spoke with affection of "my sister the rose," "Grandfather Fire," "my brother the Corn."

The straggling procession, no longer magnificent in appearance, left the cultivated Yuma lands and pushed slowly into the desert, its riders advancing through dust and discomfort and cold, but fortunately unaware of a graver menace this land held for them. It was a slow and difficult advance toward the lake of Santa Olalla. They would follow the bottom lands of the Colorado in a southerly direction—it would seem to many they were turning backward, and they were—and dip briefly into the upper region of Baja California. It was actually a brief return into old Mexico.

It was the route Anza had taken the year before to Santa Olalla and the safest one he knew.

Upon leaving the Colorado River they had to fight their way through miles of an almost solid entanglement of thorny brush. As before, the spiked branches ripped through clothing to tender flesh and tore at the scrawny ribs of the animals. The riders struggled out of the bush at last and up the side of a hill. On the crest they halted in a long, exhausted line, and then burst into sudden excited cries.

"*Mira!* How beautiful!" They called to one another. This was the way they had known California would be! This was truly the *tierra linda*—"the beautiful land!"

Before and under them rolled the tremendous floor of the great valley (the Imperial). Like the land they had traveled before, it was desert, but, seen from their present elevation, it appeared as an Eden, untouched and primeval, tinted with winter green. To the north and northeast it was walled in by mountains that in their magnificence matched the beauty of the valley.

But after making their laborious descent onto the floor of the valley, the expanse that had appeared so beautiful from above turned into the same nightmare terrain they had crossed so painfully before reaching the Colorado. It was another desert, an extension of the southern deserts that joined California, link by sandy link, to old Mexico. The tender green that had enticed them from above was actually the familiar thorny thickets and the cacti the cattle continued to eat, though they died in the eating. Now the Joshua trees became dominant in the landscape, raising their clusters of green daggers. Why, Susana wondered, did nearly all the desert growth bear thorns or spikes? Even the sharp galleta grass cut the tongues of the cattle. The century plants lifted their clusters of cream blossoms from a base of clustered swords.

"How can it get colder?" the women wailed morning after morning.

But the cold increased and the menace of hunger and thirst became greater than ever before. There were added problems brought on by the deepening of winter as the caravan made its slow progress over the valley floor.

There was neither water nor wood nor grass. The cattle resumed their slow, sad process of dying.

The desert in winter was curiously silent. At times a coyote's quavering lament or the sharp yap of a fox might carry for miles over the clear cold air. But mostly the silence was oppressive, and even the muleteers harried their charges in lowered voices. Shouting required more energy than they could spare.

Much of the time the San Franciscans, muffled in their serapes and *tilmas*, rode in a silence as oppressive as that of the land. Even the simple exercise of riding was unpleasant after the days of rest and pleasure at Yuma.

Anza continued to set an example of determined cheerfulness. "All will be well when we reach Santa Olalla," he promised anew each morning, and in the pilgrims' minds the lake grew to enchanting proportions, an oasis of delight. "It is a fine, large lake," he repeated to give courage, while his own spirits sank as he remembered the sickening qualities of its water.

They made two stops during these days at the friendly Indian rancherias of San Pablo and Laguna Coxas. On the sixth of December they were dragging their way over the difficult terrain when who should overtake them, appearing over the horizon like an apparition, but Father Garcés! The explorer-evangelist had left Father Eixarch at the new Yuma Mission, busily making furniture and planting a garden, while Garcés set out to explore the mouth of the Colorado.

The San Franciscans welcomed Father Garcés as if they had been parted for many moons instead of several days. That day a flash of water was sighted over the dry valley floor that was not a mirage. It was the lake! Late that afternoon camp was made on the green-girdled lagoon of Santa Olalla.

It was a narrow strip of water running parallel with the Colorado River and banked with the familiar willow and other shrubs. There was a plentiful supply of tender winter grass.

On the bank, waiting their arrival, was a delegation of several hundred Indians.

These were Cajuenches, wearing short willow-bark skirts and friendly smiles like those of the Yumas, whom they greatly resembled. Spread on the grass by the water were their gifts for the travelers—baskets and bowls of corn and beans and *atole*, watermelons, calabashes, and fresh fish. Anza would report in his diary that three men caught more than a thousand fish in the channel in less than an hour.

Santa Olalla also abounded in quail that betrayed their presence by rushes in the willows, and were so unused to people they were easily caught.

The animals feasted on the fresh grass and lake water.

Anza gave presents of beads and tobacco to the Cajuenches, but he was in no mood for merrymaking. He observed what was happening to the cattle. The water of the lagoon was bitter, and the tender grass was coated with the gray alkaline deposit that blighted so much of the desert's growth. Watching, he saw one animal after another writhing in the throes of the sickness that always followed the drinking of bad water.

"We will rest here for two days and regain strength for ourselves and our animals," he told the pilgrims.

They were delighted to rest. They forgot the cold and the struggle ahead and the two days passed swiftly for those who were still well, for Anza allowed mugs of brandy to be distributed. The sick ones stayed thankfully in their tents and were brought hot tea and *atole* by Tía María and Susana. But their greatest craving was for the fresh melons, and Tía María permitted them to eat all they desired on the theory that the sweet juices might allay fever. Father Font shared in these attentions. He was again a very sick man.

On the morning of the third day Anza spoke to his pilgrims again.

"There are six springs at Santa Rosa," he promised. "To be sure, a barren stretch must be crossed before we reach them, but you have made many desert *jornadas*. And once we reach Santa Rosa, there will be water and forage and all will be well with us and with our beasts."

He had not outlined the situation so hopefully a half hour before, in consultation with his aides, Moraga and Grijalva.

"I need not tell you how bad the march will be. Even if we arrive safely, there cannot be enough water at Santa Rosa to save all our lives. Here is our only chance. . . ."

Now, to the assembled company, he outlined his survival plan.

The Second Expedition must split into three divisions. Anza's group, the first, including Father Font and twelve soldiers, and otherwise consisting mainly of women and children, since they were his chief responsibility, would set out on December ninth for Santa Rosa.

With them would go a large section of the pack mule train, part of the cattle herd, and a band of loose horses and mules.

The second division under the command of Sergeant Grijalva would follow the next day, which would be December tenth.

"On the same day," Anza continued, "the main cattle herd will leave, but later, with the unmarried soldiers and several vaqueros going along to protect the cattle." (At this Susana and Gil José exchanged glances they could not control, for, as one unmarried, he would be with the cattle train.) Anza continued, "They will not head for Santa Rosa, but will attempt a more direct route across the desert to San Sebastián, where if God pleases, we will all be reunited."

"The third division under Lieutenant Moraga will be the last to leave. It will start for Santa Rosa on the third day."

Then Anza summed up the situation. The three groups arriving at Santa Rosa on different days would give the springs time to refill. He did not need to explain to his listeners that if no water existed at Santa Rosa the only alternative would be death to most of the expeditionary force. The colonists listened in silence as he finished by saying, "My first group will conserve

what water may exist at Santa Rosa for the groups that will
follow. We can only pray that there will be water there, and
that you may follow us in safety. And now, no lamenting!
Our separation will be temporary and Santa Rosa is not too
far away."

He spoke with his usual assurance, but for the first time his
charges were unconvinced. The group had become as one large
family. The thought of parting frightened the women, for who
could tell what hardships they might suffer before all were together again, if ever they were reunited? The best that could
be said of the arrangement was that families would be kept
together. There was one exception, for the Perea father would
be in charge of the pack mules going with the cattle herd and
Gil José would be with him.

"The two men will be together," Tía María told Susana, and
this gave comfort to both, for differing reasons. "We will see
them again if God wills at San Sebastián."

[2]

They wakened on the ninth to stare with disbelieving eyes
at a world completely changed. Few of these people had seen
snow. Susana had glimpsed it on the distant peaks overhanging
Mexico City. But here, as far as they could see, the great valley
was an unblemished snow mirror. The mountains to the north
and east were newly peaked with white.

But Anza ordered his chosen group, the first division, to ready
for departure as calmly as if snow were to be seen every day.

First there was the pang of parting with Father Garcés, who
was leaving to explore and evangelize the lower regions of the
Colorado. The San Franciscans watched him disappear over the
snowy waste. (He would return to Yuma and meet his death
there at the hands of the Yumas, who until then had been the
friendliest of all the Southwestern tribes.)

Those of the other divisions who were to leave in an opposite
direction were listening to Anza's frank warning.

"I must tell you what to expect on this next *jornada*. Prepare
to travel fast and far. We must make what speed we can, for
our provisions are low and there will be no water or forage

until we reach Santa Rosa. Now fill your water bags for your own drinking and bring grass and corn for the horses, in the hope that they can carry us through."

The soldiers filled the leather bags with the bitter Santa Olalla water. Father Font balanced his with difficulty on his saddle horn, for he was still weak. The women helped gather the desert hay which was lashed in such great bales behind their saddles that the riders were almost hidden.

Then Anza's group sat waiting the bugle—a company of ragged scarecrows on horseback. Every wearable article they possessed was on their backs, and over these were wrapped their blankets, and still the desert gale cut through as if nothing were between it and their shrinking flesh. Susana looked as bulky as Tía María usually looked, while the size of Tía María was now beyond description. Through the mountain of woolens her eyes, lively and black, were all that showed of her.

The parting of the Perea family was dignified. They might have been separating for an hour, but, "The dear Mother of God will bring you back to us," Tía María told her husband quietly, and only the three Pereas knew the grief that was crushing their hearts.

Susana drew the blanket over her face to keep the cold from her nostrils. Through the opening she looked at Gil José, standing with those who would not leave until the following day, against a desolate depleted camp where the few remaining tents looked like white mounds in the snow. Flakes sifted white fragments against the black gloss of his hair as he stood with his helmet pressed to his heart. They did not voice their good-bys.

Around them were the movements and sounds of separation. It was the first dividing of the devoted company, and all knew that each group would meet with differing dangers.

Anza lifted his hand and the bugle rang. The members of the first division, mostly women and children, set out from the lake of Santa Olalla into the teeth of the storm, following Anza against savage winds and hurtling snow over the cold white floor of the valley.

Marching on their right as they advanced went the white peaks of the Sierra de San Gerónimo (The Cocopah Range). The Santa Rosa wells might have been a thousand miles beyond that wall of snow, so remote and wide seemed this cold white land. The valley floor was treacherous with snow, and the horses slipped and many riders fell. Each muffled rider had to trust his staggering horse to follow the one ahead.

The small mare Seda followed steadily the less certain steps of the tall Major. The mules bearing Tía María and Felipe plodded on either side. Susana noticed that Don Angel's hair, gray now as adobe, fell in long, thin strands over the blanket he had muffled around his ears. She remembered that Don Angel never complained except to her, and that he did his share in such arduous labor as gathering wood or digging for water. But he seemed to be losing strength, and his long body sagged in the saddle. Susana thought without caring too deeply that it was difficult for Don Angel to maintain the steady day-by-day pace set by Anza.

Susana pulled the blanket closer across her face to shut out the wind and the sight of Don Angel. She could trust the sure-footed Seda to keep their place in the procession.

What a jewel among mounts the little mare had proved to be! Seda showed her full worth on this *jornada*. Her small hoofs felt their way with assurance over rocks and slippery places.

Felipe once remarked that Seda never stumbled because she was closer to the ground than most horses and could see the prairie dog holes better. But Susana preferred to think it was the little mare's cleverness that kept them both from harm.

Seda was like Vengador, Susana thought, unbeautiful to the eye but valiant, and capable of intense devotion. But while Vengador's loyalty was entirely to Susana, Seda's was divided between Susana and her equine companion, Major.

Major was no longer magnificent. His sensitive skin with the full Arabian veins shuddered in the cold, for he had not grown the thick winter coat that protected the plebeian Seda. He had not been groomed since Tomito's disappearance, and there were ugly sores on his back and haunches. Don Angel could no longer take pride in Major, and the large but delicately boned horse could not be reconciled to the kicks and blows that now came his way. His tender mouth rejected the barbed iron Spanish bit thrust into it mornings by Don Angel. Once the tormented horse turned on Don Angel and bit his arm, and was beaten until Felipe interfered, tactfully explaining that under such pun-

ishment Major's heart might fail. Only this argument quieted
Don Angel. He had no wish to appear ridiculous on Seda or
the pack mule.

Anza continued to lead across the trackless valley with his
stern features naked to the wind. His keen glance penetrated
the light curtain of snow and recognized with satisfaction certain
landmarks that showed they were still following the route the
First Expedition had taken in the preceding year. He had the
manner of a man who knew exactly where he was going and
was impatient to be there.

Abruptly, the snow stopped falling. It melted quickly into the
earth, and the floor of the valley turned to slippery mud, as
dangerous to the travelers as ice. They had traveled only five
leagues from Santa Olalla when Anza gave the order to halt.

They camped on the naked floor of the valley, lashed by winds
sweeping down from the frozen peaks. There were neither water
nor wood at this site known as El Carrizal, and described by
Father Font as "a deadly place. . . ."

But Anza's practiced eye detected water signs. El Carrizal
(place of reeds) led him to suspect the presence of inactive
springs. He ordered out shovels, and the miracle happened—
enough water rose to the surface for those people and their
thirsty beasts and for the divisions to follow!

From this night on, until they reached the end of the desert,
the men of this division would be forced to dig for their daily
water supply.

The lack of firewood made for hardship. The travelers
crouched in their damp cold tents and chewed the unpleasant
salt meat that enhanced their thirst, so that they were grateful
that at least they had the blessing of water.

Anza started them off early the next morning. The day was
colder and the wind more savage. The San Franciscans rode with
heads lowered against the gale, and many of the women had
difficulty holding to their saddles.

The only green on the dry land was that of inedible desert
shrubbery and the lethal cacti that the cattle continued to eat.
The cattle resorted to the only pattern they knew, falling with
exhaustion or turning to race back along the trail. They could
not keep up with the procession.

"Let them go," Anza ordered the vaqueros. "The division following us will rescue them, if they are still alive."

The horses stumbled on, sickening of hunger and thirst and exhaustion. There were many barrancas in the dry earth. The horses could no longer leap the rain-carved ravines. They descended into them slowly and then fought their way up the other side.

The party camped again that night on the open valley floor exposed to the wind. Again there was no firewood or grass and no amount of digging brought water. The tired horses ate the last dry wisps of desert hay they had brought with them. Even Anza referred to this camp in his diary as "that dreadful place." But to his charges he spoke a few heartening words before seeing them into the dubious shelter of their tents.

"Colonists, we are now very close to Signal Mountain, which is not far from the wells of Santa Rosa. So far, you have done well. Do better tomorrow, and you will be well rewarded, for by tomorrow evening we should be very close, and we may even arrive at the wells!"

In Tía María's tent excited friends discussed the wells, magnifying them in their feverish imaginations into exotic oases, perhaps in a setting of palms. Might they be hot, Susana ventured, and Tía María was certain, yes, they would be warm medicinal springs such as they had so enjoyed at Aqua Caliente. But Susana did not want to remember what had happened at that place, and her thoughts went to Gil José, who would be setting out on this day with the cattle train from Santa Olalla, to follow in their wake.

She thought of him as she lay huddled under blankets in the icy Galván tent, hearing the groans of Don Angel as he turned and twisted on his narrow cot. His bones ached and only *aguardiente* could still his torment and his last bottle was empty.

The next day, the eleventh of December, would be remembered by the first division as the most dreadful of all their day's journeys, to be referred to as the "*jornada triste.*"

The keynote of its desperation sounded at three o'clock that morning, which found Anza up and dressed and by lamplight making a final study of the section of the map showing the way to the wells of Santa Rosa. He traced with his forefinger the trail he and his toughened soldiers had previously traversed from this present place to the wells. That group had been conditioned to living for days without food or water. Even so, they had almost failed. Their lives had been saved by the springs. Would the miracle work again?

Very early the next morning, Anza estimated the distance ahead, and wondered if his present group, mostly women and children weakened by privation, could possibly travel those miles and survive. To himself he admitted he was not sure.

A frigid-looking sun appeared over the snow peaks as if blown skyward by the driving wind. Anza selected three of his sturdiest soldiers to ride ahead to Santa Rosa and, if possible, open the filled-in wells. In a moment of compassion, he bade them go with God, knowing that their mission was one of life or death.

But the colonists were not to know the danger of their situation. When the sunrise bugle brought them, sleepy-eyed and shivering, from their tents, he spoke to them cheerfully, urging them to hurry their packing that they might be on their way. Inwardly, for Anza was a pious man, he was praying for strength to help them to survive.

At seven o'clock he had them all in their saddles and ready to leave.

He addressed them again as they sat their horses facing him, against the cold-looking sun, like a military leader sending his troops into battle.

"Colonists, if all goes well with us, if we can maintain our usual pace with no stopping, it is possible we may make the Santa Rosa wells today. It is only fourteen leagues—a day's journey. Then your ordeal will be over!"

The fourteen leagues he dismissed so lightly—that would be almost forty miles! On their best days, in the beginning, with well-nourished, healthy animals, the colonists had been proud to achieve between ten and twenty miles in a day.

Now their bony horses stood with hanging heads, and so many had died there were not enough to carry all the people. Some of the horses had to carry a soldier and his wife as well, or several children.

The saddle animals no longer fought against the loading of the packs. For one thing, they were too weak; for another, the provision supply had fallen so low that many of the saddle bags were empty. Into these were stuffed many of the smaller children, so cocoon-wrapped only bright eyes were showing.

As the cavalcade surged forward after Anza, Felipe's strong sweet voice rose with Father Font's in the summoning hymn. One by one the emigrants joined in, throats dry with thirst, lungs breathless against the cold.

The valley floor had dried overnight. An endless expanse of hardened mud was split with great cracks that trapped animal and human feet. Horses and men on foot stumbled and fell. But the procession did not halt. The saddles grew harder, and the women shifted their positions and sighed. For days they had been hungry and cold and weak with thirst, and many were ill. Had Anza forgotten that most of them were women and children?

Anza had not forgotten. He could not afford mercy.

For eleven hours of constant riding, unbroken by rest, the riders in Anza's division struggled over the floor of the valley.

At six that evening darkness dropped over the the desert as if the sky had collapsed. The horses stumbled on in the dusk past a mountain looming like a dark cloud (Signal Mountain, twelve miles northwest of Mexicali and the last peak of the Cocopah Range).

Then from the rear, where the depleted herd was dragging its way after the main caravan, came a burst of frantic lowing followed by the rumble of unsteady hoofs. The cattle had scented water! They raced past the riders in a mad stampede, and the exhausted horses were caught up in the excitement and staggered after, making what speed they could.

The cattle led the way into a dark gulch at the north end of the mountain, where the men Anza had sent ahead were making a desperate attempt to revive the dried-up wells of Santa Rosa.

So the San Franciscans reached the springs, almost unable to move with exhaustion, having traveled on this *jornada triste* fourteen terrible leagues.

[3]

The so-called wells of Santa Rosa consisted of six springs in a barren gulch. They had gone dry since saving the lives of Anza and his men in '74. The men sent ahead had dug all that day and succeeded in raising only a trickle of water. This meager supply the maddened cattle, stampeding into the arroyo, drank at once.

The San Franciscans had ridden all day with the dream of cool water trickling down their parched throats. They arrived in the dark gulch to find the water gone and the cattle sucking damp sand. No water remained for them or for their horses.

It was dark and cruelly cold in the gulch, and there were no trees and hence no wood for fires. But the most dangerous lack was water. If these people and their mounts were to live, the Santa Rosa wells would have to yield.

Anza ordered all men to the shovels.

All that freezing night they dug in relays, and Anza and even Father Font insisted upon doing their share. Fortunately a moon of frosty brilliance rose and they did not work in darkness.

One by one the six springs were opened. The sleepless pilgrims drank gratefully. The water rose so slowly and so far down that it had to be drawn up for the horses in tightly woven baskets. By two in the morning nearly all the saddle horses and mules had been watered, including those that had been first to drink and were thirsty again. Anza, renewing his digging after a brief sleep, ordered water for the cattle. They were frightened by the baskets and refused to drink. But in the night they found clumps of the tough galleta grass. The coarse forage served to keep them alive.

Long before dawn Anza sent a soldier on ahead to the Marsh of San Sebastián, where they hoped to meet the cattle herd, to see if water was more plentiful there. There was now enough water in these springs for his own first division but not enough to save the lives of the divisions that were following.

Whether conditions at San Sebastián were better or not, Anza would have to take his present group there and leave what waters might continue to rise at Santa Rosa for his people who were still on their way.

Anza was accustomed to suffering. But the condition of his colonists and their women and children, sunk in a misery they could hardly comprehend, unnerved him. The sick leaned on the stronger, unable to stand alone, and among them were several he had not expected to last through the night.

Calmly, with as much reassurance as he could summon, he told them the truth. They could not stay at Santa Rosa. They must set out directly for San Sebastián.

There was no reproach on the gaunt faces of his listeners. There was no murmur of disagreement. They saw that for the first time he showed the ravages of exhaustion.

Midafternoon found them crawling over the valley floor against a wind that had turned cold and hard as a granite wall, wondering if ever others had suffered so much, or if any other section of the world could be so ugly and evil. The earth had changed. It was now surfaced with hard clay pellets that turned under the hoofs of the horses.

Anza's hooded eyes raked the plain for familiar signs and found none. This was the route he had traveled before, but it had entirely changed. Only the "poor compass" Father Font had borrowed assured them they were keeping in the right direction. Font and Anza took turns riding back along the straggling line to encourage the riders and hold them to the course, no matter how difficult it was proving to be.

The San Franciscans did their best—still, only four leagues were traveled. Finally, Anza knew the riders were too dispirited to go on, and when a spot was reached where there was galleta grass for the cattle and brush for fires, he ordered an early camp. The women were grateful, although the exposed site was buffeted by the wind. This time the men's shovels could bring no water from the frozen earth.

The next morning Anza roused them early. Father Font sang Mass, the words crackling in his dry throat.

It was the thirteenth of December.

They set out, humped in their saddles against snow driven by a wind that increased in savagery. Anza led them on, hour after hour, toward the ever-darkening horizon and the deepening threat of the storm.

Late that afternoon a rider approached from the north. It was the soldier Anza had sent ahead to locate and report on the water supply at San Sebastián. What he had to say acted upon the despondent pilgrims like a healing draft, for water did await them at San Sebastián, and its promise set the riders more firmly in their saddles and drove their heels into the bony flanks of their mounts. The weary legs of the horses quickened as if the animals also understood the miraculous promise: Water ahead!

They pushed on, revived by Anza's shout that he had sighted the snow-crowned mountain he had been watching for. They hurried past the mountain, and came at last to the Marsh of San Sebastián on San Felipe Creek.

There was much at San Sebastián to rouse their gratitude. There was a small lake and a spring, and, as Susana had fancied, the waters of the spring were warm.

And there, praise to the Lady of Guadalupe, grew the blessed mesquite that would provide fodder for the beasts and wood for fires, and the water supply was apparently unlimited, and above all, this was the place of the great rendezvous, for it was here at San Sebastián, if anywhere, that the divisions of the Second Expedition would meet again.

The pilgrims drank slowly, warned by Anza to restore their dehydrated bodies cautiously with the life-restoring fluid from the earth, and in their exaltation they did not notice, as Anza did, that the marshy banks of the water sources were rimmed with salt. They had not yet escaped the threat of the desert.

Ahead lay more formidable mountains, blocking their way to the north. The camp site was sheltered by the mountain, but clouds from the north were moving down over them, dark and cold and threatening. The storm would break at any moment, and the paramount need was for fire. Even before the tents were raised men set out with axes into the snow-covered hills.

A few Indians appeared, but they were timid and poorly clad, and as the storm clouds neared they drifted away, returning, Anza surmised, to the nearby villages he remembered from his previous visit. They were of the mountain tribe of Cajuenches.

Long before the wood gathering ended, the rain came driving down, but all continued to work. Tía María straightened under a bundle of dry mesquite branches and looked dolefully to a southern horizon curtained in gray rain. "Where are our *compañeros?* And my poor man, where is he?" she asked.

Susana looked back over the empty expanse they had covered and echoed the lament in her own heart, for where was Gil José? The cattle herd, and also the Grijalva and Moraga divisions, consisting solely of men, should have arrived at San Sebastián by this time, if not before!

The tents were raised at last against the storm, and fires burned within. Crouched over them with eyes streaming from the acrid smoke, the women wrung out clothing and spread it to dry on brush racks. Their long, rain-soaked hair fell free as they cooked their poor dinners, tended their children, and welcomed with tenderness their men as they returned from long, exhausting hours of wood chopping.

[4]

During the night the violence of the storm stilled to an ominous quiet. The fires went out and the air in the tents became unpleasant with the odors of steaming wool still undried. Outside the lamentations of the cattle grew strangely muffled and weak.

The tired pilgrims slept.

They wakened to a world completely white. During the night the rain had turned to snow that was still being driven down on the plain by the fierce gales from the sierra. It was a blizzard without precedence in this region.

How could Grijalva and Moraga lead their divisions to San Sebastián in such a storm when in this place Anza's own men could not venture out to hunt firewood? How could weakened cattle survive?

Anza's was the only tent with a fire. The ailing Father Font shared its warmth and the captain's anxiety as Anza dispensed medicine and pored over his map, trying to determine where his lost men might be.

The snow kept falling as if it would never end, but Anza was always the optimist. He told his priestly friend the blizzard might be a blessing in disguise.

"The snow will melt and increase our water supply, and soon there will be enough for all in this group and our animals. The springs will be so full there may also be enough for the other divisions when they arrive. As soon as the snow stops, we will have wood for fires and forage for the cattle and horses. I think it best not to go on but to wait here for the others. Then we can all set out together for San Gabriel as we had planned."

Father Font looked doubtful. He had lost much of his strength and weight, but he grieved over every delay and would have set out willingly. Anza added quickly, "Staying here will give our women and children a much-needed rest and give our sick people a chance to recuperate."

When the snow lessened, every adult able to walk plowed through the drifts to hunt dead branches. Their reward was a brisk crackle of fires in the tents.

The strongest men carried their axes to the bases of the hills, where they cut down *fierro* trees. The horses ate the tenderer top leaves and the branches made excellent firewood.

Several cows had died during the night, and others were obviously dying. Anza had ruled that a cow or bullock dying of cold or starvation should be killed while still on its feet that it might provide the jerked beef that had become the expedition's daily fare.

The San Franciscans detested this beef jerky, and even Anza, who never complained about anything, confessed to his diary it was "almost unpalatable." It smelled worse than it tasted; it was stringy and tough and defied even the teeth of Tía María, which were strong as iron. But it was keeping them alive.

The men, Don Angel and Felipe among them, set about the work of butchering the dying cattle. The women prepared the jerky with expressions of disgust, for the meat had to be smoked in the tents and not out of doors as usual.

Susana and several other women worked with Tía María in the Perea tent, cutting into strips the bloody chunks of flesh the men brought them in dripping baskets, salting the strips with bitter gray salt they had gathered on the desert, and drying them slowly on brush racks before the fires. The greasy odor of smoking flesh was added to that of the damp woolens.

The men and women worked grimly at their separate tasks through the morning. It was midday when Anza's keen ears caught a faint, far-off *"Hola!"* from the south. All heard the second shout. Work stopped and the women came from the tents and gathered around Anza with red-stained hands and pounding hearts, certain that Moraga's group had found them at last. Instead, it was the cattle herd that had started the same day as the Grijalva group but had arrived first, having made a direct trek straight across the desert to San Sebastián.

The men in charge had not delayed their march by hunting water. Their food had given out and, like their beasts, they had been without water for four days!

The men were dreadful to look upon, but the Pereas and Susana were happier than they would have been made by the arrival of the missing divisions. Here were Gil José and three other soldiers and Nicolás Perea and the vaqueros. They were sunken of cheek and eye and almost powerless to move, but they were men of pride and would not be pitied. As they fell from their saddles no one stepped forward to help. Tía María stood holding the tent open that her man and Gil José might enter. Her round face was a golden moon of happiness.

Susana stared after the two men. Both walked with stiff knees and bent backs as if they were very old. Even Gil José entered the tent like an ancient. He looked in that moment older than Don Angel.

"Shall we help, my Mother?" She had not known Felipe was standing beside her. He spoke gently—was his compassion for her or for Gil José? The other survivors were being cared for by relatives or friends. She followed Felipe into the Pereas tent. There Tía María came into her own. She was at her best in a crisis, and her husband and Gil José were being tended as if they had returned from their graves, which was virtually true. The meat and clothing racks were pushed aside, and the two men given mats close to the fire. Tía María divided her time between them, preparing hot tea and bowls of steaming *atole*, giving loud praise to the Lady of Guadalupe that on this day there was fire. Susana assisted in the brewing of tea and stirring *atole*, while Felipe helped massage frozen ears and limbs back to life, a skill he had learned from his mother. Susana did not go near Gil José, whose eyes, sunk in dark pits, followed her. His aquiline features were a death mask, and his chin, always before clean-shaven, was concealed by a dark growth of beard.

When the two men had been cared for and were resting in utter exhaustion on their mats, the women learned that in this as in the other tents the work of meat processing must go on. Felipe returned to his work with the men who were cutting up the butchered cattle.

As the men worked they discussed the condition of the cattle newly arrived with Nicolás Perea and Gil José. This was the main body of the splendid Second Expedition herd, and it was a piteous spectacle. Many had died or been lost along the way. The survivors, on arriving, staggered en masse to the San Sebastián wells, and the combined efforts of the men had not been able to prevent them from drinking too much. Those that could not stop drinking would swell and die. But it was a strange thing that the equally weakened horses that had accompanied the herd did not rush to the spring, but went first to the clumps of grass. Several of the horses had died during the trek and those left were bags of bones, but they put hunger before thirst.

Anza surveyed the remnant of the herd and hid his despair. He told no one, but he was now convinced that both Moraga and Grijalva were lost in the storm.

[5]

The Perea tent was a cheerless scene for men newly rescued from death, Susana was thinking. The Perea father and Gil José did not seem to mind the smoke-filled place smelling of damp wool and bloody meat and unwashed bodies. From time to time Felipe or Don Angel brought baskets of fresh meat to Tía María or armfuls of brush for the fire. Several of the women who had been working with Tía María had come back to aid in the stripping and salting of the meat. Among them was the widow Feliciana.

Tía María tried to promote cheerful talk as she hung the bloody strips prepared by Susana and the other women on the brush racks. She asked no questions of the two men, and they were never to speak of the four dreadful days they had spent in the valley. Tía María did not want to hear of their sufferings. They had escaped. She was content. She enjoyed hearing of tragedies and dramas concerning people she did *not* know.

It was late afternoon and growing dark in the tent. The women worked on by firelight, their eyes red-rimmed with smoke. They were tiring and their hands moved more slowly among the meat strips.

Outside the wind grew stronger and colder. It battered the canvas walls that sagged with their weight of snow and forced its way under the tent sides until the reed mats rose like sails on the dirt floor.

The widow shivered. "Will this snow last through Christmas?"

Don Angel entered the tent carrying a basket of freshly cut

meat. For once Susana was relieved to see him, because she had been thinking of how much she wanted to put her arms around Gil José.

Don Angel's hands and leather coat were bloodstained and his features were drawn to a point with weariness and cold. He brought with him into the tent a shower of snow, which was still falling. As he placed the basket before Tía María he stared at Gil José, who continued to lie with his eyes closed as though dead. There was cruelty in Don Angel's expression that shocked Susana. It was not the look one human gives another who has suffered. And Gil José was still suffering; at times a leg or arm drew up in a spasm of pain as the blood slowly moved in stiffened veins and in those moments his face was a mask of pain. Tía María did not notice Don Angel's expression. She was looking with dismay at his filled basket.

"More meat to process? Our fire is going."

"You are out of wood?" Don Angel asked wearily.

"All is gone except that now burning. But my son Felipe will soon be here. . . ."

"Your son works with the last of the meat. I will go for wood."

At this Gil José opened his eyes with a look black with hatred for Don Angel, for he was stung by his own helplessness, and Tía María, although she no longer liked Don Angel, had the misfortune to protest.

"You must not go, Don Angel. I can see how tired you are, and my Felipe is young and strong."

No words could have served better to spur Don Angel into action.

"Dear *señora*, it is nothing. Be patient and I will return almost at once. I know of a dead cottonwood. Its lower limbs are dry and will make excellent firewood."

And he was gone, taking proud, determined steps out into the whirling snow.

Tía María stared after him in a puzzled way. "Sometimes I am inclined to think highly of your husband, Susana. Yes, there are times when I admire him very much. Then there are other times . . ."

Susana had no response to this. Gil José's eyes had closed again. The women went on with their work.

Felipe brought another basket of the cut beef. "The last!" he explained, a report that was good news to all. He drew a mat to the fire and sank down on it with a groan of pleasure. He turned a curious look on Susana.

"What is this with your husband? He has saddled his horse and is riding off into the hills with his ax on the saddle horn."

"He goes to bring us wood," Tía María explained before Susana could answer. "See, our fire is going."

"There is brush close by. Why did you ask such a service of the don, little Mama? He is not young, and should not be riding out into such cold."

"Silence, burro mouth," said his mother, cross because her conscience pricked her for sending Don Angel out into the storm.

[6]

By late evening the jerky making was over and only embers remained of the fire. Gil José came painfully to his feet. He thanked Tía María for her kindness and would not permit Felipe to assist him to the barracks tent. The widow Feliciana returned to her children and the other women to their families. Susana helped Tía María adjust the brush racks for the night. She was the last to leave. Felipe held open the tent flap before her and for a moment they stood looking into a night veiled in swirling white. The snow was still falling heavily. He said with a smile, "Your shadow is waiting and seems to be in difficulties."

Vengador was not a shadow. He was a long icicle of a dog, a congealed image of dog, the sort of dog Don Quixote would have owned. Long hours he had waited for Susana outside the Perea tent, and his haunches had frozen into the hardening snow. Felipe went into gales of good-natured laughter as he pried Vengador from his icy seat. The dog's pride was hurt, but he led the way stiff-leggedly into the Galván tent. Because he entered with her, Susana knew Don Angel was not inside.

The snow outside gave a luminous light to the interior and it took only a glance to see that the don's cot was empty.

"Sleep well!" Felipe called softly, outside.

She murmured conventional thanks for his having escorted her the few yards. She heard the clicking of dice in the barracks tent and decided Don Angel had found interest in a game with the soldiers. His absence relieved her as it always did; she could breathe and move about more freely with him gone.

But the air in the tent was so cold that breathing was painful.

Vengador scrambled into a space between her bed and the portmanteau where he could not be seen, and lay shivering in silence. It was too cold to disrobe. Susana wrapped herself in blankets stiff with cold and lay on her cot shuddering in much the same way as Vengador. Still the day had been long and heavy with work and she soon fell asleep.

She dreamed she was lying on her back on thick grass, looking up into a golden shower of mimosa. It was deep in summer and the air was heavy with garden fragrances, and in the branches over her head sounded a high-pitched humming. She stirred uneasily, knowing a great cloud of bees was swarming dangerously near, but she could not rise and run from the garden. The humming grew louder and more sinister, and she felt a touch, light and cold, on her hand, and jerked awake in panic. The humming came from Vengador, and was unlike any sound she had heard him make before. It was a high-pitched whimper that was almost human. The dog stood with his nose pressed to her hand, whining his ear-piercing warning.

An eerie light, brighter than before, pierced the canvas. Susana did not have to look at the other cot to know that Don Angel had not returned.

She went to the tent opening and stepped outside. She stared with disbelief upon a world that had turned to glass. The snow had stopped around midnight, and it was now nearly morning and all the desert as far as she could see had frozen to ice. The valley floor was sheathed in crystal. There was no moon, but under the stars every glassed twig stood out as clearly as if in daylight. The looming mountains were diamond pyramids. The night sparkled and the stars seemed to snap in the cold.

She stood in the tent's entrance, trembling in awareness of this pure beauty that was for her eyes alone, and which she knew she would never see again. For a moment she longed to waken and share it with the others. But the camp lay in profound silence. Vengador, silenced, trembled at her knee, sharing the miracle.

Then she knew the night was not completely silent. Around her rose the shuddering sighs of dying animals, muffled in the snow. She saw Major standing before the tent in snow to his belly, his head low under its weight of ice and his eyes frozen shut. He was still saddled and bridled. Don Angel would never have left him that way. The little mare Seda stood beside Major with her haunches pressed to his as if trying to warm his large frozen image back to life. Seda's eyes were also sealed in ice.

Vengador whined, ran a few paces toward the hills, turned back to Susana, and repeated his warning with his intelligent eyes pleading with her to follow.

She walked carefully to the next tent. The thin ice snapped under her shoes. "Tía María?" she whispered, but it was Felipe who heard and slipped out of the tent, pulling his *tilma* about him as he came. Then he saw their world crystallized, and his eyes grew wide with wonder.

Vengador renewed his argument, pleading with both to follow.

They conferred in whispers that crackled in the thin air. And when she told him, Felipe was certain he knew where they would find Don Angel.

"He went into the hills for wood."

"A dead cottonwood, he was saying . . ."

"Vengador knows."

"We must take Major. Shall I ask aid of Gil José?"

But Susana knew Don Angel would want no help from Gil José. Felipe rubbed the ice gently from the horse's lids. The unhappy Major opened eyes flooded with suffering. Seda, his friend, gave a distressed whinny and persisted in going with them. Their steps crackled on the ice as they followed Vengador into the hills. They passed the dead bodies of cattle, feet up, frozen into the hard snow. Major stumbled on the glassy surface. He was almost unable to walk. So it was the smaller, sturdier Seda who bore the burden when at last they found Don Angel at the base of the dead cottonwood with his ax fallen from his hands. Together Felipe and Susana lifted the long, cold body over the saddle and brought Don Angel, balanced like a log, to the Galván tent. Not until they laid him thickly blanketed on his bed did they know if Don Angel was living or dead.

They continued to speak in whispers, as if he could hear.

"Shall I go for my mother?"

"Please do not. And you, one million thanks, and you need your sleep."

It was dismissal. But Felipe did not leave until he had un-saddled Major and brought saddle and bridle into the tent. "You are certain you will not need me?"

She shook her head and Felipe left. Susana looked down at the unconscious man. Despite her brave words she had no idea what should be done for him. She recalled the unfeeling glance he had given Gil José when the soldier lay helpless by the Perea fire. She did need Felipe, but she knew Don Angel. She would spare him the humiliation of recovering and finding himself the victim of Felipe's good-natured pity.

Felipe returned while she was trying to decide what to do. He brought a small flask.

"This *aguardiente* I have been saving."

She thanked him, and in another moment Felipe was gone.

The fiery brandy ran from the locked mouth. A few drops were swallowed. Breathing became louder and more painful. Con-sciousness was returning in an agonizing way. The gray lips puffed with each dragging inhalation. Spasms racked Don Angel. He did not open his eyes, but she heard the tortured whisper.

"Hold me!"

She held him. The army cot sagged under their doubled weight. The chill of his body turned hers to ice. She felt her flesh freeze and the coldness of death enter her veins. Her white face over his wore the stricken look of the martyr.

Hours passed before she felt life flow again, slowly and pain-fully, into the long, spare body. Still she lay with him locked in what seemed the final coldness of death.

Vengador did not leave. He pressed his thin body close to Susana as if trying to share with her his own insufficient warmth. In much the same way, outside the tent, the little mare Seda stood pressed to the bony flanks of her companion, the larger and weaker Major. Both survived, while around them six cows and a mule slowly froze to death.

[7]

To Susana the night lasted forever. It was morning when she stepped to the entrance of the tent and looked dull-eyed on a world shorn of magic. The trees were no longer patterned in crystal but dripped melted ice. The freeze had ended and a light snow was falling; the morning was very cold. Susana shivered and turned back into the tent and stood looking down thoughtfully at the still comatose Don Angel. So Felipe found her when he came in with wood for a fire.

"The snow is not very heavy but the wind is strong," he said, and left, knowing she was in no mood for words.

The sounds of the rousing camp brought Don Angel out of his frozen lethargy. His eyes opened and his first look for Susana was one of unutterable hatred.

Felipe returned briefly with a bowl of hot *atole* made by Tía María. He left and Susana spooned the thin gruel between the cracked lips. The spoon wavered. Don Angel cursed—his first words—and struck the bowl from her hands.

Instantly Vengador was at her side with a growl swelling his throat. Don Angel cursed the dog weakly, then dropped his hand and turned his head away.

After this Vengador was to stay in the tent with Susana as if by right. If Don Angel objected, Susana could appease him with the reminder, "The dog saved your life." Her affection for the dog was openly expressed and Vengador changed in personality. His body was still lank as a bean pod, but that was no novelty in a starving camp where even the humans were showing their bones. Vengador carried himself with new pride. His head and tail no longer hung down.

The next morning a faint, snow-muffled call reached Anza's ears out of the snow-veiled south.

Every adult in the camp able to walk hurried to Anza. The wind was still heavy, but the snowfall had lightened and they were able to make out a cluster of dots creeping down the far-off southern hills.

The dots moved slowly down onto the white floor of the valley. They became recognizable as mounted men and a scattering of loose horses, cattle, and mules. Which group were these—Grijalva's or Moraga's? Fewer, certainly, than either had been when last seen. They moved with heart-stopping slowness, slipping and falling on the still icy crust, and it was seen that some of the horses sagged under the weight of two men. The riders rode humped-over and without movement, as if they were dead in the saddles.

Anza recognized catastrophe. His orders crackled.

"Everyone!—Collect every stick of wood to be found! Build fires outside the tents—build them high—"

Then with several of his men and extra horses he set out across the snow.

The group he brought into camp was not Moraga's. It was the division under the command of Sergeant Grijalva. It had been sent on the long route to San Sebastián; it should have been last to arrive.

Where, then, were Moraga and his men? The shocked Anza gave up all hope of seeing them alive again. Grijalva and the others were unshaven and haggard, their eyes were temporarily blinded; they were cartoon soldiers on skeleton mounts. The bridles hung on the saddle horns. These men could not move their hands or turn their heads. Every muscle in their bodies was paralyzed with cold. They had to be dragged from the saddles.

Anza had them placed before the open fires. He showed them the tenderness of a father. It took one soldier two hours to thaw out, lying wrapped in blankets between two fires.

Grijalva could hardly speak, but he managed to report to Anza. "We almost met death in the storm. With the help of St. Francis we escaped with our lives. But our poor animals—"

"Do not think of the beasts," Anza soothed him. But the loss was tragic, for only a few of the Grijalva cattle had survived, and five horses had died.

Now others were asking where were Moraga and his second division, which had now become the third and last? The query ran dolefully from lip to lip: "Shall we ever see our friends again?"

Anza made no attempt to quiet their fear. He confided to Father Font, "It may be that only your prayers can help Moraga now."

The Franciscan responded by summoning everyone to a special Mass to offer thanks for the saving of the Grijalva division and to ask special aid for Moraga and his men.

Father Font's voice astonished his listeners. It was stronger than it had been since he was stricken with the ague. He was obviously better. So was Grijalva, present among his rescued men. All the newly rescued had made an astonishing recovery.

The people left the chapel to find the cold increasing. No animals or men could survive long in such cold.

The next day was marked by irritation. It was discovered that many more horses were missing from the depleted herd. Anza at once suspected the miserable-appearing Cajuenches that had been lurking about the camp had driven the animals away during the night. This was verified when Indian and horse tracks were found together in the snow.

Sergeant Grijalva had apparently recovered completely and Anza sent him with a posse to follow the thieves to their nearby villages and if possible recover the stolen mounts. "Do not shoot unless they fire on you first," he warned. The men left early and did not return until after dark. They had investigated two rancherias, and nowhere had they sighted an Indian brave. But there were scowling squaws and the missing horses. No threats were given, but they brought back every stolen mount and were welcomed back to camp as if they had been gone for months.

Those in camp with Anza had spent an anxious day, alternating in watching the east for the posse and the southern hills for the missing third division. Watch fires burned through the night, but there was no sign of Moraga and his men.

The day following was the seventeenth of December. Anza could not bear the waiting. He was certain now that Moraga's group were trapped in snow somewhere and in desperate straits. He was convinced that Moraga's horses had died or been made useless. He chose twenty of the strongest horses and sent them in charge of two soldiers to rescue if possible the missing men. Again there was nothing to do but wait, and count the dead cattle, for more had frozen overnight.

Anza no longer hid his anxiety from his people. There was little activity. Father Font went from tent to tent visiting the ill, and those still suffering from exposure, and came in time to Don Angel, who remained in his bed, no longer in acute pain but complaining of numbness in his arm. Susana left them, grateful for a few free moments in the cold clean air. She returned to hear the Franciscan saying sternly, "Beware of a bitter heart, my Son."

Felipe came, bringing more *atole* made by his mother, and was received with uncommon friendliness by Don Angel. Susana had explained the way he had been saved, and Don Angel was obviously relieved to know his life was owed to Felipe and not to one he disliked as he did Gil José.

No one else came to the Galván tent. Don Angel's demands kept Susana at his side until midafternoon, when she ran outside, to the excited shoutings of "*Viva! Viva!* They are here!"

Once more black dots were moving slowly down the white slopes of the far-off hills, and it was only after hours of watching that those in camp welcomed with tears the members of the lost division, who were the last to arrive at San Sebastián. As Anza had guessed, they had suffered most. Fifteen of their saddle horses and mules had been left dead or dying in the snow; only six remained. Anza rushed first to assist Moraga, but his second-in-command stared at his chief with glazed eyes and could not hear the shouts of welcome—he had ridden with ears uncovered to the storm and was temporarily deaf!

Tía María and her aides were now skilled in the rehabilitation of men close to death. They gave the tenderest of care to Moraga and his men. Anza had no fear for their recovery.

He was agreeably surprised by the fact that the invalids in the company were much better. Now only five remained on the ailing list, and none of these was dangerously ill. Anza credited the general recovery to the watermelons the colonists had so enjoyed at Santa Olalla, for having purged the sick bodies of fever. Tía María commented rather tartly to Susana that their dosages of herb tea had certainly contributed.

Also the horses that had been afflicted by dysentery after drinking bad water were much better. Anza believed their rapid return to health was due to the rain which washed the bitter salt from their desert forage.

[8]

San Sebastián could provide only temporary shelter. Anza now had to force them on, away from the wells, and through the white wall of mountains blocking their way to the north. But he dreaded giving these hungry, weary people, only now reunited, the order to start again.

"Our people have earned a reward," he said to Father Font.

Font said nothing, knowing Anza would give them the only thing he had to offer—brandy.

The issue of *aguardiente* revived the colonists' spirits in an extraordinary way. Only a few hours before they had been sunk in exhaustion with many apparently on the verge of death. The sight of the small keg being passed around straightened spines and brought a glow into dull eyes.

Felipe, standing with a mug in hand, spoke for all.

"With this, we can celebrate! We can hold a fandango!"

The only opposing voice was Father Font's. He spoke to Anza.

"These people are exhausted. Many are still ill. And you know a fandango will keep them dancing and brawling all hours of the night. You know these people."

"I know them! I have limited their liquor allowance so they will not be able to drink to excess."

"But they need their sleep—"

"I know them!" Anza was losing patience. "No matter how late they dance, they will answer my early summons to march tomorrow morning."

Preparations for the evening's entertainment started. No colonist, no matter how weak or ill, intended to be left out. The rest of the afternoon was spent in collecting wood in the snow. Bonfires were built out of doors to permit dancing. As a matter of course Felipe found himself in charge of preparations, and in an inspired moment he sought out his friend Gil José.

"You remember the song of the lemon vendor?"

"Who of Mexico does not know '*La Limonera*'?" The two friends smiled with amused understanding. Gil José was still on sick leave, although his circulation had been restored and he suffered no permanent harm. He was seated cross-legged on his cot in the barracks tent carving a cholla staff for Father Font, who although much better was still finding it difficult to walk.

"Good! I would have you sing it tonight at the fandango."

Gil José was both startled and flattered.

"I! I am no singer!"

"You have the look of a man about town, as the song requires. And you need only act the courtier and speak the words."

"But it is a duet, for two people."

"To be certain. A man and a woman."

Gil José's skin turned dark. "And what woman?"

"I have considered the widow Feliciana." Felipe glanced slyly at his friend, his sleepy feline look holding the glint of mischief. "Do you not think her suitable? There is a gypsy in her body and in her laughter is the laughter of *gitanas*."

Gil José's suspicion relaxed in a lustful grin.

"How ably you describe her! Yes, I can see the widow Feliciana as the perfect one—the merry girl peddling her lemons. . . ."

"Then you approve my choice? And you are certain you are not still too weak to partner her in '*La Limonera*'?"

"I?" Gil José flexed chest and shoulders. "Your choice is excellent and I shall be proud to be her consort. As for my health, do not fear for that, for the widow Feliciana is one who could bring a dead man to life!"

The look they exchanged was one nearly all male members of the Second Expedition always assumed at mention of the widow.

The Señora Feliciana Arballo was the only widow in the San Francisco Expedition and its most popular member with the possible exception of Tía María. But where the herb woman was the image of the group mother, the widow represented all that was desirable in womanhood.

She was, like Susana, in her mid-twenties and the mother of two little daughters. She had not been a widow long and would not be one much longer, for she had joined the expedition as the fiancée of a soldier of Anza's who was to be stationed at the Presidio of Monterey.

Her beauty was more that of suggestion than actuality. Her walk held a rhythm that demanded close attention. In her were those curious indescribable genes that attract and magnetize.

Everyone in the camp, including those last rescued, forgot weariness, exhaustion, and even illness. All the conversation was of the fandango as the colonists stacked great hillocks of brush and branches for the fires.

"Father Font says we should not dance because we will be setting out early tomorrow."

"We can rest later. To think we will see the last of this place, where so much has happened!"

"I shall be glad to leave this San Sebastián. The fandango to-night—what better way of saying good-by to a place where we have suffered so much!"

"Ay, yes, the fandango!" Chapped lips lifted in anticipation. "But it must be a very quiet fiesta, or Father Font will be cross with us."

In the Perea tent Felipe rehearsed the widow and Gil José. Felipe, who had a thousand songs in the archives of his mind, had been able to recall all the lyrics of the lemon seller's song and to freshen them that afternoon in the memories of the widow and Gil José.

Suppers were hurried through and the excited colonists made attempts to improve personal appearances ravaged by recent suffering. As soon as darkness came the lavishly piled bonfires were lighted and the San Sebastián camp became an oasis in a white wilderness.

The celebrants sat on *petate* mats around the fires, warmed by the leaping flames and by the brandy, and gradually *tilmas* and *rebozos* were put aside and a sense of happiness brightened tired faces.

Felipe found time to visit the Galván tent. He was wearing his best coat and pantaloons and a broad red sash and his guitar was polished with tallow and hung with fresh ribbons. He brought a special invitation to Don Angel and Susana.

"I can promise you both an amusing evening. We have need of amusement."

Don Angel gave a dour refusal.

"I have not left this bed since my accident and shall not, until Captain Anza orders us to march."

"That will be early tomorrow. Captain Anza has ordered, but we—we have tonight!"

But Don Angel only sank lower under the blankets. He had complained of numbness in his right arm and Susana had made a sling from one of her *rebozos*.

"Man, can you not see I am helpless? And I suppose sleep will be made impossible."

"We will strive for silence," promised Felipe, as good-humoredly as ever, and turned to Susana, "And you, Doña Susana?"

She also refused and settled down to endure the hours of celebration alone with Don Angel. He was more demanding and unpleasant than before. Her body and her thoughts moved to the loudening music of the fandango.

There was the rustle of voluminous skirts, and Tía María backed into the tent holding a steaming pottery bowl. "My son tells me you fear not sleeping, Don Angel. Here is my herb tea with a strong flavoring of the good brandy given us by Captain Anza. It will promise you a full night of sleep."

Don Angel was unexpectedly amenable. He drank the tea and treated Tía María with courtesy he had not shown her since their first meeting. He even spoke gratefully.

"You have a tender heart," he informed the herb woman, and when she turned away, her smooth dark cheeks flushing with pleasure, only Susana saw the grimace of contempt that followed his words. He finished his drink, muttered a few vague general accusations, and closed his eyes. The two women talked in low voices.

"Now you can attend the dance."

"He may need me. I cannot leave him."

"Ha! But you can." Tía María shook out her full skirts in a gesture of triumph. "See, already, he sleeps."

"But he does not sleep well and wakes often. And if he should find me gone—"

"He will not waken." No one could have read Tía María's expression as she looked down on the slumbering Don Angel. "I promise you he will sleep for many hours. Quickly now, into your finest dress and mantilla."

"Tía María?" Susana fell silent. There was nothing to be gained by questioning Tía María. Whatever the brew she had brought, it would certainly be harmless and ensure a few hours of freedom. Felipe's music came temptingly through the canvas, and Susana's feet ached with the need to be dancing.

The two women left the tent like conspirators to find the music stopped and the dancers and musicians at rest on their mats sipping the strong drink from pottery mugs.

Susana joined the circle with Tía María, looking first to Gil José. He was on a mat, sipping his drink; their glances met discreetly. Then both looked to Felipe, who on this night had come into his own. Now Gil José was the lethargic one and Felipe, who usually gave a false impression of laziness, was the spirit of animation. Playing his own guitar and bursting at moments into song while conducting his little band of three other guitars, two Indian flutes, and a drum, he was the center of all eyes.

Surrounding the musicians were all members of the San Francisco Expedition with the exception of the three military leaders and Father Font and Don Angel. Even invalids had been brought out on their cots to fall under the rhythmic spell of Felipe's music. The others, their hunger-sunk eyes lighted with firelight and pleasure, clapped hands when Felipe willed, sang when he led them in song, danced to his orders. By his expressive shoulder movements he led as no shouted orders could, while his hands never left the strings, and as his mother and Susana arrived he began calling again for the dances, summoning one after another the fandango, the *jota*, *el sol*. When the dancers tired, the music poured on with everyone singing the old songs they all knew.

Susana did not dance. She sat with Tía María, who left her once to join in a lusty *jota* which she ended dancing solo with a tremendous flurry of skirts and *rebozo* that brought the audience to its feet in a frantic crescendo of *oles*.

Felipe waited until the applause had subsided, then stepped forward and held up his hand for silence.

"*Ahora!* With your permission, *compañeros*, a most special performance by two most popular in our company, the Señora Feliciana Arballo, assisted by the Señor Gil José Terrez, in that well-known duet—'*La Limonera*'!"

A shout of male approval, a tremolo of excited feminine laughter followed this announcement. Nearly all knew the duet concerning the gay young Spanish girl who sold lemons and oranges in the Prado of Madrid. It had been popular in the music halls of Spain and Mexico for ten years.

At last I shall hear all the words, Susana was thinking, edging forward on her mat in anticipation, for she had heard only the opening verse once in a theater in Mexico City. Don Angel, glowering, had led her out, why, she had not understood.

To the others, even the title titillated, for the song held several meanings, not all of which might be considered polite. It was a two-part song, sung by a man and woman and culminating in a suggestive bolero.

Felipe struck a chord that brought Feliciana and Gil José to their feet. The soldier was brave in his uniform. He carried a large bunch of winter-dry desert mimosa. Helmet cocked over the dark, ardent features, he approached his partner. His grin demanded and would not be denied. The widow retreated lightly, her smile provocative; an enticing and elusive Eve parrying his advance with the imaginary tray. Gil José pranced after her, offering the absurd bouquet, while the widow sang the opening words of the citrus seller's song:

> "I can't esteem men
> Who come courting with flowers
> And expect in return
> My invaluable hours.
> If they try for my love
> With a proffered bouquet
> I inform them at once
> I expect them to pay!"

With a profusion of skirts the widow gave a few steps of a coquettish cachucha, then, turning her back on Gil José, she addressed the audience:

> "I've lemons and oranges,
> Sirs, to be sold,
> They are juicy and plump
> And the color of gold.
> I sit with my wares
> In the Prado's cool shade—
> Ay! here comes a man
> With an eye for a maid!
>
> "How proudly he walks!
> A señor in a million!
> A man, do I say?
> Not a man but a stallion!
> I admit he excites,
> I can see what he offers,
> But still, to have me
> He must dig in his coffers!"

Her glances were more expressive than the words. Did they suggest lust and greed? Never mind, they were irresistible, and every line drew shouts of admiration from her listeners. Then, turning back to Gil José, the widow warned him:

> "Sweet words and sweet blossoms
> Mean little, I say,
> Unless they include
> A most generous pay!
> I'm a woman of business,
> Not known to be rash,
> So I'll take your bouquet, sir,
> If offered with cash!"

Tía María was clutching her sides against laughter, rocking her thick body against Susana like a doll-gourd set in motion by a child.

"Oh, I tell you, this Feliciana is an enchantress, a witch!" She kept repeating this, wiping the damp laughter from her eyes. Susana sat prim and angry beside her, doing her best to conceal her jealousy of the widow. Gil José, given completely over to his role, was irresistible as he moved in a narrowing circle around the woman. One could almost see the male crest rising under his helmet as he chanted in not unmusical terms the male response in which he had been coached by Felipe.

> "This charmer knows all.
> Every start, every ending,
> But how will she turn
> When I say I'm not spending?
> Gay, impossible she!
> Every move is capricious,
> It is easy to see
> Like her wares, she's delicious!

> "What she offers is tempting.
> One glance—I was sold—
> But still, to possess her
> Should I part with gold?
> For much as I long to
> Melt into her arms
> Shall I part with savings
> To purchase her charms?"

A stamp of heels, and Gil José turned away:

> "No, I shall not pay for
> Her samplings of honey
> For though I love Woman
> My true love is money!"

On this disdainful note Gil José tossed his bouquet at the feet of the enchantress. She kicked it away with like disdain, then facing one another with flashing smiles, and ignoring the frantic shouts from the audience of *"Otra vez!* Once more!" they flung their lithe bodies into a boisterous bolero with much stamping of heels and advancing and retreating by Gil José, and much flaunting of skirts and advancing and retreating by Feliciana. All this was to an incessant roar of approval from their fellow colonists.

Only when the bolero ended to a thunder of *"Oles!"* and Gil José and the widow had returned flushed with triumph to their places did Felipe start his orchestra into a quieter fandango. Married couples moved with clasped hands into the dancing space. But before the dance could begin all heard the scream, followed by a roar like that a bull gives when it charges into the arena. Anza came running from his tent, Font from his, in time to see the widow being dragged by her long hair out of the firelit circle by her enraged fiancé.

"I will teach you a song!" the soldier was bellowing. "Now sing, trollop! Sing!"

With each word he struck Feliciana with his fist.

The dancers stood paralyzed. The music stopped. Father Font turned angrily to Anza.

"Did I not warn you, Captain? Is not this what always happens when brandy is distributed?"

Anza strode over to the soldier who was holding the widow. The soldier was startled into lowering his fists. Font followed Anza.

"Do not interfere!" he begged. "This man is to marry this woman and he is only doing what is his right!"

Anza's jaw was set. "Not in my company. No woman in my charge may be beaten. I warn you, soldier, strike her again and

I will call a court-martial. To barracks with you! Cool your jealousy there!"

The fandango of course ended. The colonists went meekly to their tents, once more aware of their aches and general weariness. The weeping Feliciana left, surrounded by sympathetic women who were now forgiving her excessive charm. As for Gil José, he swaggered as he followed the jealous man to the barracks tent, and with reason. His success as an actor had restored much of the natural jauntiness that had been sapped by his recent ordeal in the storm.

Susana was not among the women who consoled the widow. She turned into her tent alone. Don Angel still slept.

There was praiseworthy attendance at Mass the next morning, for everyone was uneasily anxious to hear what Father Font would have to say concerning the preceding night. The friar trumpeted over the hanging heads of his abashed flock:

"Instead of holding such scandalous festivities in honor of the devil, you should have been on your knees thanking God for sparing all your lives, for bringing you all together again, for providing you with this shelter, and water, and food to save your lives and the lives of your children. . . ."

Tía María brought an account of the sermon to the Galván tent, where Susana was assisting Don Angel into his riding clothes, Anza having announced that in spite of sore feelings and sore heads the company must be ready to set out at a minute's notice.

"The little father is very angry with us." Tía María rolled her eyes in an expressive way. "But should we feel too badly? After all the misery we have endured the fandango was a welcome diversion, and permit me to ask, who was harmed?"

Don Angel cursed as Susana eased his sore arm into the sleeve of his leather coat, but he paid Tía María flattering attention.

"So I have missed this drama! He struck her, you say? Good! A balky woman and a balky mule should be whipped."

Tía María showed some indignation at this, but to her any audience was irresistible and she decribed the fandango in gaudy detail while Susana listened in dread lest Tía María reveal by a careless word that Susana had been present. But Tía María did not even mention Gil José's role in the melee.

"A pity you missed it, but then, you needed your sleep," she said kindly to Don Angel, and chuckled. "Father Font has made an amusing comment, I hear. He said, 'And to think I objected to the brandy, when who would think lemonade could cause such a disturbance!'"

Don Angel laughed heartily at this, and then winced with pain, and once more he and Tía María parted on the best of terms. Meanwhile the widow Feliciana was announcing to anyone willing to listen, and all were, that she would not marry her former *novio* were he to offer her all the pearls in the California gulf! Pearls the remorseful soldier had none, but he did offer tears and pleadings, and from these Feliciana Arballo turned with queenly scorn. Permit him to suffer; she would have none of him. There were other men in the world, she had reason to believe! There were other soldiers in this expedition! At this some of the wives tilted suspicious ears, but Feliciana instantly altered her statement with consummate tact, "And among these— some are still unmarried!"

The widow had won all hearts, including those of the most jealous wives. And as a result, this morning, everyone was on her side, even the men of the company, who although they held with Father Font that a man was authorized by divine right to chastise a flirtatious sweetheart, they were willing to make an exception in behalf of the widow. It was reported that bets were being taken in the barracks tent as to which member of the company the gay songstress of "*La Limonera*" would next turn to for consolation, and Susana learned that the betting was heavily in favor of Gil José.

"She will go to him, as she did in the dance," several women were heard to say. At this point the widow announced she was through with all men and intended to devote the rest of her life to her two little girls.

"Ho, that we shall see," scoffed the good-natured Tía María. "Shall we not, Susana!" And Susana agreed that the widow would not be solitary very long.

Anza disliked this kind of gossip. He put it grimly to Moraga, "I'll give them no time to cook up further mischief." Then he gave out word that there would be a bout of jerky making before the march began. There was no task the colonists hated as much. But the truth was two more cows had died in the bitterly cold night and five more were dying: these he ordered killed. All set to work, the men to the butchering and the women to slicing and smoking the meat.

Meantime Anza sent the remainder of the herd on ahead, with orders to the vaqueros to rest the weakened animals at intervals along the way. The colonists watched the staggering beasts go with mournful backward looks and piteous lowings; the poor creatures saw no reason for leaving the springs.

No sooner had the San Franciscans completed the jerky making and washed their hands and arms in the cold waters of San Sebastián than they heard the bugle summons, which had not sounded for almost a week.

The snow had stopped falling, but the world around them was still an unbroken sea of white as they began the work of tearing down a camp that had sheltered them for five days.

The final unpleasant task was that of gathering huge bundles of galleta grass. "Each beast must carry its own supply of food," Anza ordered. Once more they were to enter barren country. But this would be their final march through dreariness, he promised. The wasteland was nearing its end.

Anza lifted his staff over his head and the bugle sounded again. The long, untidy procession stirred. At that moment the sun that they had not seen in six days burst through the overcast sky. It was an omen that brought from the pilgrims a burst of cheering:

"*Ahora!* Now—to San Gabriel!"

[9]

They marched only "four dark leagues" that day but they reached the mouth of the Borrego Valley, which was the doorway leading out of the great desert into the sierra. It gave protection against the wind and, as Font noted in his diary, "There was some grass and no water."

There were trees, offering wood, and a few scanty fires were built and *atole* and chocolate prepared with water from the leather bottles filled at San Sebastián. But there was no music or laughter, and the hilarity of the fandango was a ghostly memory—could it have been only the night before? Already San Sebastián seemed far away and long ago.

Anza promised that on the next day there would be water. His map showed a spring ahead he remembered—the San Gregorio. Would it still be active?

The next morning led them from their camp site in the pass that linked the larger valley to the smaller Borrego Valley, and they found that the mountains they entered were not the frosted monoliths that had terrified them. They were lower and rose-tinted as if ledged with cinnabar, and no longer covered with snow. But the horses had been two days without water and like the cattle they continued to fall and to die.

"Many of us will arrive on foot at San Gabriel," Gil José was heard to say.

Felipe managed a smile. He had faith in his mule, which was as sturdy and uncomplaining as Susana's Seda. The mules were proving to be the most dependable of all the saddle beasts.

Anza, casting an eye back at the cattle, saw with dismay that they did not show the agitation they would had they scented water, for the cavalcade was approaching the San Gregorio spring. But he said nothing to his aides, and brought his thirsty procession to an early halt at only an hour past noon. The spring was there. The water was low and stagnant, green with algae and bitter with salt. Anza and his soldiers worked with their shovels, but no matter how deeply they dug, the water did not rise. Once more they must dig the night through.

The cattle did not arrive until well after dark, but there was no water for them. Again they munched on damp sand thrown up by the shovels.

In the morning Anza found three horses and five cows frozen to death and nearly all the rest of the herd missing. The cattle had stampeded during the night. He sent Sergeant Grijalva and another man back to hunt for the lost cattle and ordered an early march for the company, since no water remained in the San Gregorio spring. The sergeant chose Felipe to companion him in his search.

Susana watched Felipe ride away. Like everyone else, the musician had lost much weight, but this was disguised by his round and cheerful face. It seemed strange to see Felipe mounted on a horse instead of his mule and without his guitar.

Anza sent the remaining cattle on ahead that they might rest often along the way, and finally gave the order to march.

At nine that morning the pilgrims set out from San Gregorio and made their way into the mountains, threading the tortuous canyons. It was late afternoon when camp was made at a place called El Vado (a ford on Coyote Creek in Coyote Canyon). It was still light in the mountains, and the arrival of the expedition scared away several miserable-looking mountain Indians who were gathering seeds in the canyon and who fled, leaving some of their woven baskets and a rabbit skin cloak. The San Franciscans were interested in the baskets with their painfully gathered contents, but Anza would not permit them to be touched. "Their owners will return for them," he said.

The canyon was dry, but the men set to work at once with their shovels, and this time, oh, miracle in the wilderness, life-giving water rose slowly through the dry earth. There were some pasturage and firewood, so El Vado was not a bad place. The women set about their domestic tasks with renewed cheerfulness, aware of the terrified Indians who kept lurking about the camp, appearing from behind trees and rocks like ghosts. Finally one approached, and then another, then Anza called to them and offered handfuls of beads and tobacco and jerky, and these they accepted. Others came, and took gifts, but all remained fearful.

How different these Indians, the women said with pity, from those at Yuma and other prosperous Indian settlements they had visited on their trek through the Southwest and the lower section of Alta California!

Of the depleted herd of cattle Anza had sent ahead that morning, only seven arrived well after dark. Eleven cows had died on the way. Three of the vaqueros' horses and two other horses had been left behind to die. As for Sergeant Grijalva and Felipe, who had been sent to hunt the stampeded section of the herd—where were they? Anza sent two more soldiers back to the desert to hunt for them.

The water soon ceased to rise under the shovels, and there was not enough pasturage at El Vado to keep the horses alive. The canyon was a deathtrap. Anza moved the company on to another canyon, the Arroyo de Santa Catarina, where there was some pasturage and where water, dug for, eventually rose.

In this canyon the San Franciscans spent two dreadful days, suspended in anxiety, hunger, and cold, praying for the missing ones to appear.

Susana did her best to console Tía María, but finally they sat before the dead fire in miserable communion. They had given up all hope of seeing Felipe again, when the tent flap was pushed aside and Nicolás Perea came in. He was as excited as his calm nature permitted him to be, and he showed his exaltation in berating his wife, which he really did.

"Know this—our men are sighted! One I recognize far off as our son. And you have permitted the fire to die and no hot food or drink is ready, and hurry, woman, for they will need food and fire!" Then he was gone, and the two women with radiant faces raked the gray ashes for live coals with which they lighted twists of dried grass that served as tinder. A good fire was soon blazing in the tent and cooking pots filled before Tía María and Susana left to join the others who were watching the pass.

And at last, moving dots appeared in the mouth of the Santa Catarina Canyon, and yes, there was Grijalva, and there Felipe, and with them the two soldiers who had been sent in search of them, all showing the strain of the long search, but the cattle, where were they?

[10]

Anza drove them on without mercy the next morning, although those who had searched for the cattle were still worn in body. None had slept well, for the cold rain had poured down through the night. But when, that morning, the rain turned to a chill mist, Anza set them packing and marching up the arroyo to its source. They had gone only one league when the rain started again, heavier than before, and they were forced to stop and make camp at the spring of Santa Catarina (now Read's Springs). Nearby was an Indian village where there were about forty Indians but none of these ventured out, for, like all the natives of the sierra, they were timid people and fearful of white faces.

And again, all night, it rained.

The rain had stopped by morning, but the sky roofing the canyon was of an evil darkness. "We will march against the rain threat," Anza decided, and the damp and weary cavalcade dragged its way up a winding canyon trail for four exhausting leagues. Anza permitted them to make camp because the Señora Gertrudis Linares had begun the first pangs of labor.

"What a horror of a place in which to spend *la Nochebuena!*" gasped Tía María as she and Susana were carrying the requisite paraphernalia to the birth tent, where Anza with his medical kit was already attending the Señora Linares.

Susana had forgotten this was Christmas Eve. Like many others in the company she had lost track of time. Tía María was right in saying that a sadder setting could not have been found in which to celebrate the birthnight of the infant Jesus. The tents were set in the depths of a canyon. Overhead, dark and threatening, towered the wind-scoured peaks of the Sierra Madre. The canyon was dark and cold and its floor was piled with gigantic boulders.

But there, in this otherwise dry canyon, was a small spring which Anza had named Los Danzantes on his preceding journey, for which reason he had chosen this place for the night.

In the birth tent Anza and his two helpers did what they could to ease the labor spasms of the *señora*, who cried out at intervals, although she was one of the bravest of women. Those not directly concerned in the birth began their meager preparations for the holiest night of their year.

Anza left the tent between the pains and saw the brave effort his charges were making in building fires and trying to maintain a cheerful atmosphere. Again, over Father Font's protests, he issued *aguardiente*.

But first he called his soldiers together and spoke sternly. "I promise to punish severely any one of you found drunk outside of his own tent."

With the brandy the San Franciscans forgot the threatening mountains and the rain and their own cold and hunger. They built up their fires and Felipe and his musicians played that others might dance. Then, with everyone seated around the fires, they sang the old hymns of Christmas, including the *"Posada"* with its haunting refrain, "no room at the inn." It was not like any Christmas Eve any of them remembered, but for a few hours they could forget this.

Not all attended the revels. In the hospital tent Anza and Tía María and Susana, with the members of the Linares family, kept anxious watch through the tormented hours. And there, just before midnight, the ancient miracle was renewed before their eyes and Anza handed over to his two assistants a true Christmas child, a fine red-faced howling boy who was promptly baptized Salvador Ignacio Linares by Father Font.

And Anza, washing his hands in a bowl held by Tía María, commented with pride that this was his third successful delivery since leaving Sonora. For him, for the others who had helped in the delivery, and for the new mother and her family, this was a truly blessed eve.

The next day being Christmas, Anza announced there would be no traveling, due to the importance of the day and to give the little mother time to recover.

This was welcome news, for the canyon had filled with fog during the night. The sun was hidden in raw mist; tents, bedding, clothing, all were damp, and the canyon floor was coated with thin mud. But despite the wetness in the land and air, there was a lack of water, for the spring had yielded only enough for the pilgrims and there was none for the cattle. The fear grew that the beasts would stampede again, and then, close by, like a biblical discovery in the wilderness, a soldier happened upon one of the best of springs! Good grass hid it from view, and all hearts lightened to see the way the thirsty, starving beasts shared in a Christmas that was not turning out too badly after all.

There was wood, and fires were built high, and chapped hands reached to the warmth and chapped lips echoed Tía María's words of gratitude to Grandfather Fire. The rain held back, tents and clothing dried, and what if the Christmas dinners being prepared were of the inevitable stewed jerky? All the families were there. Incredibly no colonist had been lost since the mother had died in childbirth.

[11]

The day after Christmas was surprisingly fair, although still very cold. The new mother was weak but brave—she was willing to go on, she told Anza. They started out of the canyon, many of the men on foot, so few were the horses. As they climbed the steep, rocky trail winding over the ridges, one after another, the rains began again and turned to icy sleet. Anza feared the rain might injure the little mother, and as they came down into a rocky pass Anza ordered camp made.

While they were setting up their tents the wind turned to a gale and the rain to a violent storm, with all working frantically against the elements. They spent the rest of the day cowering in the wet tents, without fires or hot food, hearing the storm howling through the pass and knowing that at any moment the tents might go down.

They were confined to their uncomfortable quarters until the storm ended, which it did late that afternoon. They came out to find an ominous darkness closing down over the pass. There was an eerie silence in the air and a sense of dread and waiting.

The dog Vengador crawled to Susana's feet and crouched there, with his coarse hair rising in ridges along his spine. Looking up into her face, he lifted his voice in the strange falsetto whine with which he had heralded the Apache raid and the accident to Don Angel.

"What is it the dog fears?" Don Angel asked nervously. As he spoke the floor of the canyon heaved and its trees bowed down to the trembling earth. A cosmic convulsion hurled men, women, children, and animals to the ground, left there, without will or strength of their own.

The women crawled to their men and were held by them. The children whimpered and clung, and families held together as shock after shock ravaged the San Carlos Pass.

Only Susana of the women was alone, staring wildly at Don Angel, who had been thrown to his side and was clinging with his good hand to a guy rope of the tent, which was lifting and falling like a live thing.

When the earth ceased to move, she heard Gil José's voice. He had run to her, staggering over the heaving ground, ignoring Don Angel and the others. His low words were only for her. "My heart's love, are you harmed?" No, she was not harmed, nor was Don Angel, nor the Pereas, nor any of the others, picking themselves out of the mud now, talking of the quake in shaking voices.

The shock was over. Then Felipe's countenance, round and anxious, was between Gil José and Susana, and Felipe was asking. "Is all well with you, Susana? Do not be afraid. It is only an earthquake."

They woke the next morning to find the pass sheathed in ice. In the night a freeze had followed the rain. But shortly before ten the pilgrims were on the march again, winding up the slippery pass and over rocky ledges made more slippery by ice. Once more Susana had reason to bless the small, sure hoofs of Seda, which clung to granite like those of a mountain goat.

Gil José dropped back beside his friend Felipe.

"I see you continue to assist the don mornings."

"I give aid out of no consideration for him, I promise you. For the little wife."

"That is good. She needs help, and since I am forbidden to go near them," Gil José's grimace was ugly, "you serve in my place. Serve her well."

"To the best of my poor ability," was Felipe's bland reply.

His friend gave him a look sharp with suspicion.

"Do not forget, while serving, it is I she loves."

"She has told you that?" Felipe's thick brows were comical arches.

"Certainly!"

"Recently?"

Gil José hesitated only a moment. "Yes."

Felipe leaned forward to assist his mule on its upward climb over a rock ledge and his face was hidden from Gil José. It bore a curious smile. He knew Gil José was his friend, but he also knew that men do not always tell the truth in matters concerning women, not even to one another.

The uphill riding was tiring and precarious, but they traveled six leagues on this twenty-seventh day of December. Then, at two-thirty that afternoon, the cavalcade came to a halt in the exit, leading away from the last peaks of the Sierra Madre. There in the mouth of the Cañada de San Patricio the travel-stained and weary pilgrims looked out and into a new, and different world.

Before them lay California as they had known it would be. They were spellbound by the beauty of this land they glimpsed. Valley after valley lay carpeted in green. To the east the mountains they were leaving sank down into the gentler crests of the Sierra Nevada, tipped, far overhead and far away, with harmless snow.

After the hundreds of miles of barren desert, after the frozen passes in the dark Sierra Madre, this magic scene opened before them as their true, their Promised Land.

Susan's eyes sought Tía María's in confirmation of such beauty and saw sorrow cross the broad kind face like a drawn *rebozo*. Did she, and other older women, grieve for a land as quiet as this, and as beautiful, left forever?

The strong voice of Anza broke the spell. "Only a little more courage, *compadres!* We are very close now to San Gabriel."

They had forgotten the mission. The sound of its name gave them new courage, and those fortunate enough to have mounts took up the reins again, and those on foot moved on, taking longer strides than before down the treacherous trail.

But the Sierra Madre had not released its hold on the pilgrims, and their tantalizing glimpse of Eden vanished. The mountains closed in again on either side, blotting out their view of the green valleys. They slogged their way through Bautista Canyon, which had turned into a sea of mud. Here again the mountains towered over them, massive and threatening and heavily covered with snow, and under the riders yawned dark canyons.

Bed rest was imperative for the new mother, so the San Franciscans were forced to camp in that dread place (near San Patricio), walled in by the ghostly white peaks. The night was one of intense cold, and the next morning the little mother had fever. Several others were ill.

"We will stay here today," said Anza, although it was not a setting conducive to rest. He sent the remaining cattle and the weaker horses on ahead for several leagues to lighten the next day's trek for them. After a conference with the purveyor, Vidal, concerning the company's depleted food supplies, Anza sent three soldiers on ahead to San Gabriel.

These men were to report to Father Antonio Paterno, the father-missionary, in charge of the mission, that he, Anza, was on his way with a large party. Would the friar please send horses, since many of Anza's people were on foot? Also, Anza asked that the father send word on to the commandant at Monterey, Don Fernando Rivera y Moncada, asking Rivera to send badly needed provisions to San Gabriel that Anza's people might have food when they reached there. Anza further asked that more provisions should be waiting for his group when they reached Monterey and that Rivera would expedite there the continuance of their trek on to San Francisco.

Rivera was expected to aid them in the founding of the settlement for St. Francis.

It was a great deal for Anza to ask of Governor Rivera, a man he did not know, but behind Anza was the authority of the viceroy.

The colonists saw the three messengers depart and knew the nature of their mission. This did much to encourage their belief that they were actually nearing the Mission San Gabriel.

The next day they rode, the little mother being better, with the dream before their eyes of Spanish civilization awaiting them in this wilderness, and this helped to sustain bodies doubled over in the saddles against the knives of the wind. They were moving down the Bautista Canyon, which was threaded by the Río de San José, a river that Anza vowed "we crossed two hundred times." It was rough and tortuous going.

No reply came from the mission. Nor did word come the next day, nor the next, in which they continued the descent through the valley. Anza was driving them now as if they were soldiers on forced march. The cattle herd had fallen far behind. And still no word came from San Gabriel.

[12]

Each day's *jornada* was more difficult than the one before. Now it was the thirty-first day of December, the last day of the year 1775, which was the most important of all their lives. They thought of this during the hours of forced marching, as Anza led them past the base of a mountain (Mount Rudolph) and then for more than seven hours through a narrow pass that gradually widened and became the valley of Santa Ana.

Weary as they were, they saw at once this valley was no illusion. After all the barren miles of desert and the dark mountain passes, their eyes feasted on the rich green of level pasture lands, patched in places by the soft carpetings of yellow and pink and mauve and blue that were California wild flowers.

Tía María's senses were keener than most. She was the avid observer, taster, and sniffer. She had enjoyed all scents along this pilgrimage, no matter how strange, and it was now, as they moved on over the plain, that she lifted her face into the wind and declared she smelled roses!

Those riding near her teased Tía María. Roses in December? But Tía María insisted she was right, and the procession moved on for another mile and then all saw and scented the spread of pink against the green, and yes, there they were, their first California roses, the small and spicy wild flowers, known as "*rosas de Castilla*," that had so delighted Father Serra on his first trip into California. To him, and to these weary people, they offered the fragrance of Spain.

The women of the Anza expedition had carried in their veins for centuries a love for roses, and now they were in tears again, but these were happy tears. The soldiers were off their horses and slashing into the fragrant spiny bushes with their swords, and bringing the rose sprays to the women, who filled their arms with them and buried radiant faces in their sweetness.

"Did I not promise you roses in California?" said Gil José to Tía María, slashing through spiny branches to cram her plump arms with the flowers that were small and not in their freshest bloom. "Here are your roses, and we are only a few days past Christmas!"

Tía María understood Gil José's touch of arrogance. She had scolded him without mercy for his promise of roses in California. No one enjoyed their sweetness more than Tía María, but her practical nature shoved aside the sentimental and she was presently off her mule and calling Susana to assist her as she walked beside the caravan among the roses filling a small basket with the coral-colored hips. These she collected, eating many as she did, and encouraged the others to eat them, and soon all were nibbling their sweet powdery pulp and saving others, which Tía María said could be made into a health-giving broth.

Slowly, the San Franciscans made their way across the Santa Ana Valley to its river, known to Anza as the Río de Señora Santa Ana (now the San Gabriel River).

The mission was very close to them now, on the north side of the Santa Ana, but the pilgrims were no longer certain of their welcome there. Anza concealed the fact that he was torn between anxiety and anger. What had become of the messengers he had sent to the mission? Why had Father Paterno sent none of the aid the pilgrims so desperately needed—particularly horses and food.

The main cattle herd was still far behind and a bridge used by the first expedition was washed away. The Santa Ana was a swollen torrent. It was too late in the day to attempt crossing. Anza chose their camp site on the southern bank, placating the disappointed pilgrims by assuring them that San Gabriel was only a few miles away on the other side of the river and could be reached early the next morning.

(This camp was on the west side of Mount Rubidoux, not far from an Indian village known then by the Chinese-sounding name of Yang Na, which would become in time the city of Los Angeles.)

January 1776

CHAPTER SIX

[1]

Early in the morning of the new year, Anza rode along the high banks of the Santa Ana, looking for the bridge of brush and logs on which he and his men had crossed in '74. It had washed away and the river was high in winter flood.

Nor could he gain access to the river. The banks were grown over with blackberry and willow.

He returned to rouse his men. "We must cut a road to the river and restore the bridge."

Hours later the company joined Anza and his soldiers on the riverbank. A rough road had been cleared down to the water, which was now spanned by two cottonwood logs. The women recoiled in horror from the makeshift bridge. Under the slippery logs the floodwaters raced, dangerous with uprooted trees and other debris. This was their most frightening fording since the Colorado. No animal, and certainly no human, could fall in that torrent and live.

Anza was encouraging. "Only a few steps to the other bank. From there, it will be an easy ride to San Gabriel. . . ."

The magic name helped to steady their courage.

Riding across would be too dangerous. The soldiers walked first over the shining logs to show it could be done, then returned to assist the women. The male civilians edged across one by one, among them Don Angel. From the other bank he waited glowering under the willows, clutching his useless arm. The soldiers led the women over and carried the children. When it was Susana's turn the nearest soldier was Gil José. For the first time in many weeks their hands touched and clung in fierce understanding. But their faces remained impassive.

Susana did not see the floodwaters lashing the bridge. Gil José's hold was steady and strong. Still when she reached the north bank she sank to her knees, as did the majority of the women, who gave prayers of thanksgiving for having safely crossed. Tía María, led over the logs by the purveyor, Vidal, made a comic performance of the ordeal; still she was relieved as any to reach safety. The widow Feliciana turned a haughty shoulder to her former fiancé's offered hand, and crossed with a graceful flaunting of skirts, but keeping a firm hold on the hand of another soldier, to whom, all noticed, she had paid flattering attention since the night of the fandango.

After the last colonist had crossed, the soldiers carried over the cargo and perishable goods. Then began the difficult task of getting the animals over the logs. Some of the horses, terrified, had to be led over blindfolded. One slipped and rolled away, screaming to its death in the flood. The cattle that had caught up again with the company were driven across with frenzied bellowing.

It was two o'clock that New Year's afternoon before the last animal crossed the Santa Ana. The San Franciscans were accustomed to disappointment and delay, so they accepted without grumbling Anza's decision to camp there for the night. They had only crossed from one bank to the other, but the effort had tired everyone.

He sent the weary cattle on ahead that they might be nearer San Gabriel when the march was resumed the next day.

Anza's followers had learned there was a practical reason for his every order. In this case they understood the delay before the tents were up, when three horsemen, driving a band of horses, were sighted galloping down from the north. These were the three soldiers Anza had sent ahead to get help from San Gabriel. They brought seventeen well-nourished mounts that made the expedition's look like nags ridden by Don Quixote. But Anza noted the riders' saddlebags lay flat, and read gloom on their faces.

The mission fathers were sending no provisions to the Anza expedition. Nor had they forwarded Anza's request for aid to Governor Rivera at Monterey. Instead, they themselves had sent word to the governor asking that he give aid and protection to San Gabriel!

The San Franciscans had arrived in California as it was bursting into the flames of a race war.

The revolt had started early in the preceding November (as the San Franciscans had been wending their arduous way across the freezing southern desert). Indian protest against Spanish occupation began at Father Serra's first establishment in Alta California, the six-year-old mission of San Diego de Alcalá. At a time when many of its guard were away assisting in the founding of a new mission, that of nearby San Juan Capistrano, one thousand renegade Indians armed with war clubs, crept in silence out of the woods and fell upon San Diego, howling, looting, burning, slaying. They killed the mission's blacksmith and carpenter and wounded every soldier of the remaining guard. They stole the church's vestments and statues, burned the chapel, and even melted down the mission bells.

Father Luis Jayme walked out into the shrieking mob. He pleaded in Serra's words, "*Amar a Dios, hijos!*—My sons, let us love God!" The Indians ripped off his Franciscan robe and with their war clubs beat the priest into a bloody pulp.

Mission San Diego was wiped out. Its handful of remaining occupants were in barricade awaiting a second attack. All work had stopped at Capistrano, where the soldiers had rushed back to defend what was left of San Diego. The revolt had spread and every Christian settlement in California was in danger. The once-friendly California Indians, so loved by Father Serra, and hitherto noted for gentleness, had turned overnight into a nation of murderers, and no one knew where they would strike next. Serra himself had almost died under Indian arrows. His mission on the Carmel River was now reported under threat. As for San Gabriel, surrounded by Indian villages, an attack was expected there at any hour.

Summed up, Father Paterno's message was to the effect that San Gabriel had no help of any kind for the San Franciscans, and certainly none could be expected from Governor Rivera. Father Paterno's advice was clear: "Go back! Take your San Franciscans and get out of California!"

Anza did not hide the danger from the colonists. The more

they discussed the setback, the more absurd it seemed that they who had outdistanced the dread desert, Apaches, illness, mountains, floods, ice storms, and even an earthquake should now be stopped in their tracks by a revolution!

No one asked, Shall we turn back as advised? The thought did not cross their minds, nor Father Font's, nor Anza's. They had come too far to retreat. And even if Mission San Gabriel was under threat, the vision of it still dazzled, and they were now temptingly close. Any danger waiting there was better than turning back, or staying encamped on this valley floor to become the possible prey of marauding Indians.

That night a double guard stood watch in pounding rain over the camp on the Santa Ana. The pilgrims were heavyhearted in their damp tents, and only Don Angel had other matters on his mind.

"I saw him look at you when he led you over the bridge. Your hands touched. What did you say to him? No, do not lie, your lips moved! If only I were not cursed with this bad arm! What does he know of swordplay? One thrust, and he would be carrion!" Her thoughts kept pace with his mutterings, thinking, if Don Angel did harm to Gil José, she herself would find some way to avenge him.

But Don Angel changed his attack:

"Why do you refuse him, my dove? You know what he wants of you and you of him. All in the company know. It is on your faces when you meet. You gave yourself once to one of his level. Why not to him?"

She would not attempt argument. His attack was one more injustice to stay hidden and fester with the others. When he knew she would not speak he concluded bitterly, "Yield, my wife! It is my advice! Then you will be richer in sins to confess when you meet Father Serra."

Only then did he know triumph, hearing her shuddering gasp in the dark.

[2]

Rain threatened the next morning, but Anza said they would start nevertheless for San Gabriel. The order was welcomed by the colonists, who had set their hearts on reaching the mission, even if, as seemed likely, they would find it under siege or burned to the ground.

Anza sent two soldiers ahead with a written message to inform Father Paterno that the Anza party was on its way and might be expected at the mission on the following day (the march was not turning out to be the easy one he had promised), and that since the party consisted mainly of women and children, he hoped the friar would send him warning should San Gabriel be attacked in the meantime so that he, Anza, might protect his followers.

The San Franciscans, knowing nothing of this grim request, set out cheerfully from the Santa Ana River.

They rode in the same defensive formation that had brought them safely through the Apache domain, with women and children in the center, soldiers fanned out on either side, and every eye on the alert. They rode slowly, wary of Indian ambush. Their vision was presently limited by a dark curtain of heavy rain that changed to a heavier downfall of mingled rain and snow. As before, the pilgrims rode soaked to their skins. Because the tree-less plain offered no wood for fires, Anza marched them on through six miserable hours without a break.

That night the guards again stood watch until dawn. The fires were inside the tents, which were always damp now and smelling of smoke and mildew. Around midnight the storm quieted. Then, into the tents drifted the scent of rain-washed wild roses.

[3]

Next morning they rode six slow leagues through a renewed storm and the mountains, threading a canyon awash with mud before meeting again with the river. Fortunately they reached it at a place where the floodwaters were low and the horses were able to wade across. It was growing dark when the horses floundered up its muddy bank to a level meeting place of the two canyons.

Here Anza sat his horse dismayed, for on this spot the original San Gabriel Mission had stood when he visited it in '74.

It was now five miles to the north, but the mud was deep and Anza did not want the expedition to arrive at an endangered mission in the dark. The disappointed colonists made camp on the riverbank.

[4]

Nothing could have held them back the next morning. This was the day they would reach San Gabriel. The women were up in a wet and clammy dawn, ransacking their luggage for such poor finery as remained to them. Dressed in their best, they left the canyon early and rode for two hours, drenched with rain.

They came to a well-traveled road (a rudimentary stretch of El Camino Real). It was deep in mud and almost impassable, but they followed it gratefully because it was the King's Highway and the passageway into Spanish California.

It led them over the level floor of a rich and beautiful valley.

Father Font was deeply impressed by his first glimpse of the San Gabriel country. "A land of plenty!" So he described it.

His farmer's eye calculated its natural advantages. The primeval land, dark and rich, cried out for cultivation. There was the San Gabriel River offering the benison of water, and many live oaks, promising wood both for housing and for fires.

As the San Franciscans advanced, the wild growth by the road gave place to cultivated fields watered by irrigation ditches running from the San Gabriel River. Cottonwood, alder, and live oaks yielded to grain fields, stubbled gray now with winter, young fruit trees in orderly rows, and staked rows of well-tended vines.

They were nearing the settlement. The hungry travelers observed herds of fat cattle, thick-pelted sheep, pens of fat hogs, and flocks of chickens. Their imaginations soared with each forward step. These too shall be ours, they gloated, when we build the place named San Francisco!

Then over the tilled fields rose to meet them the low-thatched roofs of San Gabriel Arcángel.

The mission did not match the magnificence of their fevered imaginations. It was a pioneer settlement of rough one-story buildings of adobe or oak logs roofed with willow and tule.

There was a church, very small, and a long wooden barracks for the soldiers of the mission guard, and another long wooden building that housed the mission fathers and also served as a granary and storage shed.

Adjoining the settlement was a large village of tule huts. In these were hiding at their approach, the travelers would learn, five hundred Indian converts. The San Gabriel neophytes did not live in dormitories, as they did at other California missions, but in their own rancheria. If trouble came to San Gabriel, it would start in this and other neighboring villages where the Indians had previously been docile.

But the San Diego Indians had also been friendly, until the revolt.

Advancing down the road to meet them came the father-minister of the mission, Father Antonio Paterno. But his robed presence was overshadowed by one who strode at his side. Anza knew this could only be that bird of ill omen Don Fernando Rivera y Moncada, formally known as Governor Rivera.

Anza had expected the governor to be awaiting his arrival at Monterey, but hid his concern at finding the governor at San Gabriel, and with no apparent intention of offering the newcomers either assistance or welcome.

Rivera was of an excitable temperament. He was heavily bearded. Hands and beard waggled as Rivera plunged without the usual amenities into the problems at hand.

He had left Monterey on the preceding afternoon, he informed Anza, having received word that a new uprising was expected at San Diego. He had set out with a dozen Monterey soldiers to stop the rebellion. Then, reaching San Gabriel, and learning that the renowned Indian fighter Anza was on his way to the mission, he had remained there overnight to meet Captain Anza, the most famed of all famous men in the two Americas, Spain's greatest conqueror since Cortez. . . .

Anza interrupted the flattering outpour.

"These people are the San Franciscans, Your Excellency, and they are very hungry and very tired."

Father Paterno offered a few welcoming words, although he seemed deeply shocked by the appearance of two hundred starveling visitors and their skeleton beasts.

The weary, bedraggled pilgrims dismounted. They had reached, at last, the objective of their long struggle. This was San Gabriel!

The mission had been founded in 1771 under the protection of a small garrison sent there by the viceroy. The inevitable misunderstanding began at once between its missionaries and the armed forces. Father Serra, at the Carmel Mission, was horrified to learn that members of San Gabriel's garrison were pursuing Indian women into their villages, where they lassoed and then raped them.

"Soldiers make trouble always," groaned the father of missions.

One San Gabriel Indian dared to protest his wife's violation. He was shot and killed, and his head ornamented a pole before the stockade. The Indian population was roused and planned to annihilate the soldiers. The priests could control neither the soldiers nor the natives, and more soldiers had to be rushed to the new mission to protect the soldiers protecting San Gabriel.

"If I had been there I would have closed the mission," was Serra's angry comment.

The San Franciscans, knowing none of these unsavory details, were basking in the glow of their arrival at Mission San Gabriel. Rivera obviously resented them, but Father Paterno and the other priests concealed their dismay and joined with the garrison to make the emissaries of St. Francis welcome. A fiesta was prepared such as the starving travelers had never hoped to see again.

Mouths watered and eyes bulged at the spectacle of a large ox and several whole sheep barbecued, bread made of corn grown in the mission fields, golden butter and cheeses from the mission cattle, and fresh vegetables from the mission milpas.

To the San Franciscans, who had endured hunger and thirst over such a long period of time, this lonely settlement in the wilderness was indeed a garden of plenty. Even Anza was amazed by all that had been accomplished there since his first visit. It had been a poor mission then, beset with many problems, and he and Father Garcés had doubted its ability to survive.

Now, following the feast, he and Father Font were shown over the mission holdings by Father Paterno and the other priests. The tour was somewhat marred by Governor Rivera, who had attached himself to Anza and was buzzing away about the San Diego situation with the persistence of a horsefly.

Ostensibly the following day was to be devoted to the relaxation for which the travelers had been longing.

But as the hours went by the colonists grew uneasy. Why was their captain spending the morning in his tent with Governor Rivera?

It was a tense conference between the two commandants. Anza and Rivera would never be able to understand one another. Anza was open of expression and speech, and as for Rivera, who could tell what a man so heavily bearded was thinking? Rivera talked in a spate of language, like a waterfall.

Rivera had opened the conversation by recounting Anza's prowess as the leading Indian fighter of the Northern Hemisphere. Rivera did not respect Anza the peacemaker, but Anza the avenger.

"I was on my way with my men to squash the resurrection at San Diego when I learned you were on your way, Captain Anza." Rivera repeated, "I had reason to wait for you." The governor poured San Gabriel wine with a lavishness that would have dismayed Father Paterno.

"You honor me." Anza was cautious of both words and wine.

"Not at all! Sufficient honor can never be paid the great Captain Anza, not in all the centuries! His place is with lions! Truly you have been sent here just in time. Not only San Diego, but all California is in danger. If the Indian rebellion is allowed to spread, it will end Spanish supremacy in California. Our establishments will be razed, and we will all be murdered. I tell you, my honored friend, we must nip this revolution in the bud, punish the San Diego leaders, avenge, chastise, draw blood for blood. We and our soldiers must do this."

We? thought Anza uneasily. He had led many a reprisal party against Apaches, but never in hatred. He was dedicated to justice. He did not like Rivera's attitude.

"We are on a peaceful mission," he parried, adding, to give his position strength, "I am commissioned to lead these people on to Monterey and from there to San Francisco. To interrupt their plans now would not be just, for they have suffered much and bravely. They expect to go on."

"Ah, but they cannot!" Teeth glittered through the hairy growth in an unpleasant grin. "You cannot possibly take your company, with so many women and children and your exhausted horses over the road from this place to Monterey. I rode it yesterday with stout men and strong horses, and we had great difficulty getting through. The highway is a river of mud. This is the height of the rainy season in California, and your expedition cannot possibly get through to the coast."

Rivera continued fiercely:

"Can you put the wishes of these peons above the need of vengeance? Would you let the murderers of a priest go unpunished? Have you no respect for the needs of Father Serra?"

"San Francisco is his greatest wish, and mine." Anza knew argument was hopeless. But he bore down with the greatest authority he could summon. "The responsibility of the founding of San Francisco has been entrusted to me by the Viceroy Bucareli."

Rivera lifted his thick chest. "In California," he announced arrogantly, "I represent the Viceroy!"

It was checkmate.

With these words a temporary stop was put to the founding of San Francisco. Rivera was right. He represented the crown in California. Anza's authority was limited to the San Francisco Expedition. He would have to yield to Rivera's demand.

He asked wearily, "How many Indians took part in the San Diego rebellion?"

"Six hundred to a thousand. Reports differ."

"And how many soldiers are with you?"

"You have seen. Twelve only."

"And you expect . . . ?"

"Your co-operation!" shouted Rivera. "You and your men must march with me to San Diego!"

"And—the San Francisco mission?"

"It must wait. After the rebellion is over and the last Indian renegade punished, and the rainy season ends, then will be time enough to think of a new mission. Meantime we must protect the already established missions, and not plan any new."

"But what of my colonists?"

"They must stay here at San Gabriel." Rivera waved a careless hand in dismissal of the San Franciscans. "Father Paterno will care for them. Now let us plan. We will take your mule train and all the provisions in the San Gabriel storerooms. Father Paterno will gladly donate supplies to the rescue of San Diego."

"Are my colonists to be left here without food? They are already on starvation rations. And my mules are weak—they cannot possibly survive the long way to San Diego."

Rivera would not listen. "Your people must sacrifice. Captain Anza, you have been sent to me by God."

Anza had no alternative. He would have to leave his helpless
San Franciscans and dash off with Rivera to the rescue of San
Diego. According to Rivera, the reprisal would take little time,
and, once San Diego was saved, he would turn all his gubernatorial powers over to the cause of San Francisco.

It was Anza's unpleasant duty to inform Father Font of this
change of plans, and also to tell the hard-working San Gabriel
priests that they were to be burdened for the present with two
hundred unwanted charges.

"How long?" asked the unhappy Father Paterno.

Anza could not say. "I will try for a swift and sure campaign.
I cannot leave my colonists for too long a time."

What might happen to them at San Gabriel he did not permit
himself to think.

Father Font asked sadly, "What will become of them?"

"They must remain here until I return."

"Until we return," corrected Father Font gently.

"Dear little Father, you must not think of making the long
journey! There is only mud between this place and San Diego . . ."

"My place is with you, Captain Anza."

Anza only said, "I will be grateful for your prayers in the
south."

Then both leaders fell silent, wondering with heavy hearts
when, if ever, St. Francis' city would be built.

Anza ordered Moraga to command the company in his absence.
He could not have made a better choice. He carried out the
distasteful task of choosing seventeen of his twenty soldiers to
ride south with him on Rivera's campaign of vengeance.

Among the chosen was Gil José.

[5]

The next day was the sixth of January.

Under ordinary circumstances, this was one of the happiest
of feast days, for it was the day of the Three Wise Kings
(Epiphany).

At San Gabriel the day was observed without elation. The
San Franciscans found it difficult to render thanks with full

hearts, for they had been informed of Rivera's plan. There was sadness in knowing their ranks must again be divided, for who could say how long, and for such a dangerous purpose.

The next day, Sunday, began with tears for the women and anxiety for the men. The reprisal party was to leave at noon. Again Susana and Tía María shared bereavement, for Nicolás Peréa was to go in charge of the mules.

So it was an unhappy departure, with the priests trying not to resent the presence of the colonists; the colonists grieving for the loss of Anza and his soldiers, and all trying to mask their resentment of Rivera as the instigator of the tragedy.

No Indians appeared. They seemed to know Rivera was their enemy, and stayed hidden, peering through crevices in their tule huts.

Father Font, still showing the effects of long illness, looked as unhappy as the San Gabriel priests as he was assisted to his saddle. It would take strong prayer to rid this friendly priest of his resentment for Governor Rivera.

After the avenging party vanished through the misted mouth of the valley, the Indians began appearing from their tule huts, some timidly, others in a defiant mood. The colonists regarded them nervously. Tía María called greetings to several, but was not answered. She commented with doubt. "They seem to have good faces."

"They hate us," Felipe spoke cheerfully.

They are afraid, thought Susana.

Tía María continued, "When I think how friendly the Yumas were, and the other tribes in the south! They had so little, but they gave us everything, and all we met were our friends. These are not friendly people."

"Ah, but they were," said Felipe. "I am told until recently they seemed friendly enough."

"Then how have they changed in so short a time?"

But all listening knew the answer. That man Rivera! He had drawn a line of hate in California between red man and white.

The deserted colonists might have lapsed into careless ways if it had not been for their new leader. Moraga was as stern a martinet as Anza. He kept the handful of soldiers left to him in readiness for defense of the mission and the colonists, and chided the latter for their idleness. "Is there no work for your hands?"

So they filled their days with small tasks, mostly in the way of repairs, for the rigors of travel had left their possessions either threadbare or damaged. The men mended saddles and bridles and tents, polished leather, and cleaned muskets. The women washed and mended clothing. Felipe took time from his guitar playing to re-sole shoes worn in desert sand, including Susana's.

"I will make you a pair of slippers for dancing when we are settled at San Francisco," he once promised, and she gave him a mournful smile, knowing that when this pilgrimage ended the wife of Don Angel would not dance again.

All this was work the colonists could carry out in their tents by the encina fires. The weather continued to be a dispiriting mixture of mist and rain. Don Angel made little effort toward refurbishing his damaged gear. He spent a great deal of time lying on his cot, staring into space.

The San Franciscans kept their hands occupied, but their minds remained gloomy. The delay at San Gabriel seemed unjust to people who had traveled so strenuously and far.

Then, soon after Anza left, Father Paterno took their purveyor on a tour of the mission storerooms. He did not have to explain the situation to Vidal. The empty bins spoke of famine. Rivera had all but emptied the granary and other storage places.

"But you prepared a feast for us!" stammered the shocked purveyor.

The priest explained sadly, "We gave you all we had. We exhausted our supplies to welcome you. Now we can only depend on our future. Our crops are promising, but until they yield we have no way of getting more food."

Vidal carried the dreadful news to Moraga.

This was a crisis, and in it Moraga showed for the first time the ability that was to make him an outstanding leader in early California. He told the colonists he was putting them on half rations.

They did not protest. They trusted Moraga. First, he had been chosen for them by Anza, and, secondly, he was, like most of them, a native of Sinaloa.

Among the San Franciscans, Susana was among the least miserable. She was grateful for any postponement that kept distance between herself and Father Serra. Also she welcomed invitations from Tía María, who, weather permitting, was as eager as Susana to escape from canvas walls.

She often said to Susana: "Bring your basket. We will find something to fill it."

They carried willow hampers as they set out over the sodden valley, passing the rancheria.

"Hola!" Tía María shouted cheerfully to the few Indians in view, but not even a child smiled back. "They will speak, the next time," she promised, undismayed. "Then we will not be strange to them."

To the herb woman, who had found provender in the desert, the lush valley was an inexhaustible larder. The baskets filled with plump white mushrooms born of the rains, and roots that could be cooked or eaten raw, wild celery and onions, and parsnips, and one root that tasted partly like a potato and partly like a turnip. There were cress and wild lettuce and tender dock leaves and dandelion and other greens for salad.

There were small, wild peas that, when dried and ground, supplemented their reduced allowance of corn meal, and the roots of cattails, which, when boiled, tasted like rice; this tule dish had been eaten for centuries by North American Indians.

There were grapes that had dried into raisins on the wild vines, and dried blackberries and rose hips, and of these they made sauces and jam. There were heavy-headed thistles to boil and eat as salad (forerunner of the artichoke).

There were wild herbs to be used for seasoning.

"No wonder these Indians do not plant gardens," Tía María observed to her son. "All this California is a garden."

"They are too lazy." Felipe, the image of inertia, was lying on his back strumming the guitar balanced on his stomach.

"They are good people," snapped his mother, just as Susana opened her mouth to make the same indignant protest.

"I mean to say, they are too wise," amended the musician. "Why should anyone work in a country where food falls from the trees, swims into nets, and flies into one's hand? I could live in content in this valley."

Ah, and I, dreamed Susana, but Tía María was speaking.

"Do not become too content, my Son. Remember, we are to build a place named San Francisco."

Each time she and Susana walked past the Indian village, the people seemed less antagonistic. No human could remain suspicious of Tía María. A few days more and she, with Susana in her wake, was being regarded by the Indians in the friendliest way.

These San Gabriel converts of the Beneme and Jeniguechi tribes were small and dark and rather flat-featured, with sparkling white teeth revealed in radiant smiles once their aloofness ended. Father Serra had seen them first wearing brief cloaks of rabbit or otter. Now they wore cotton dresses or trousers, mission style.

They clung to their original decorations, being heavily painted and some of the men tattooed. Men and women alike wore handsome necklaces, the most valued being teeth of the sperm whale from the Pacific, and all wore in their ears circles of abalone shell trimmed with hawk feathers, and, around their throats, leis of wild flowers.

The children were shy and especially appealing. "Precious creatures!" Father Serra had exclaimed, seeing them first at San Gabriel. They held equal enchantment for Susana and Tía María.

Friendships developed between the two friends and the Indian women. Before long some of the latter were joining Tía María and Susana on their provender-hunting forays, learning much and teaching in return. The two were offered, and approved, native delicacies. They were given round loaves of Indian bread, made of acorns leached in water, ground in stone mortars, and baked between hot stones. The bread was gray and heavy but had a pleasantly nutty taste.

The acorn crop in the valley was valued by the Indians as well as by the mission's herd of pigs, which fattened on them winter long.

Susana flinched momentarily before one delicacy. Forced by courtesy to taste the roasted grasshoppers, she found them delicious and not unlike the small sun-dried shrimp brought overland from the Gulf of Mexico and relished in Mexico City.

The gathering and preparation of food filled many cheerful

hours for the two friends. Other women colonists became interested and foraged for their families. Moraga was pleased that
his charges had found such pleasant ways of helping to fill their
empty larders.

He marveled, too, that with such anxiety as was theirs his
charges could continue to enjoy their endless conversations and
singing and listening to music.

Tía María was learning a great deal about Indian troubles in
California. She was asked into the tule huts, where the women
came to confide in her their fears and resentments. She reported
to her fellow colonists the injustices responsible for the revolt of
a once gay and friendly people.

Tía María became a bridge of understanding between the mission and the rancheria. She may have been responsible for the
fact that days and then weeks went by at San Gabriel and no
hint of rebellion showed in the Indian villages.

Moraga was worried about the soldiers, not the three married
ones left him by Anza, but the eight members on the San
Gabriel guard.

The bachelors of San Gabriel, Moraga could see, had appetites
roused by the women from Mexico they made no effort to control.
The widow Feliciana was a major target, with the little Galván
wife a close second. Having learned that her man was an invalid
and disliked, the soldiers were bold in addressing Susana and
murmured soft endearments in low voices as she walked between
the tents on one errand or another.

Moraga was relieved to see that each time this happened there
would appear between Susana and the admirer a good-natured
and smiling shield, the musician Felipe Perea.

Neither Moraga nor Susana knew Felipe was upholding a
promise made to his friend Gil José before that soldier left for
San Diego with Anza.

"Guard Susana," the soldier had pleaded. "For me."

Felipe lifted expressive brows. "I had thought your interest
was drawn toward the widow Feliciana."

"I have but one interest." Gil José became dangerously gentle.
"Your little plot did not work, my friend. I know you partnered
me with the widow for love of me, to turn my thoughts from
the little wife of the Galván. Let me tell you, you failed! There

is only one woman in my life, and it is death for me to leave her in this place where an attack is almost certain, and not be able to protect her—Felipe, friend of all my years, I leave Susana in your hands!"

Felipe had answered solemnly, "I will guard her with my life."

So it was that during this tense interval at San Gabriel that Susana Galván and Felipe Perea were often seen together. Tía María would come upon Susana laughing at some joke of Felipe's or listening raptly to one of his songs, and her eyes might narrow. Tía María shared Moraga's opinion that idleness made for mischief, but what tasks could she set for her son in such endless rain?

[6]

No word came from San Diego, and the San Franciscans, stranded at San Gabriel, summoned what courage was theirs and prepared for the celebration of St. Anthony's day, which would be on January seventeenth. On this day the blessing of the saint was open to all domestic creatures.

It was noticeable that, while the San Franciscans were growing leaner on their half rations, their animals had improved on the rich, wild pasture of San Gabriel. Seda's belly no longer hung like a deflated sack, and even Major bore some resemblance to the fine horse he had been. But his once sleek coat was still rough with ragged growth and desert soil, and Seda's hung in ragged hanks to her knees. Felipe combed away the tangled growth and polished the coats of both horses.

He did not overlook Vengador. With his shoemaker's tools he made for the dog a wide leather collar studded with copper rivets, and a rawhide leash.

On the Sunday morning that was St. Anthony's, a vast assemblege of animals gathered in the plaza before the church. Hundreds belonged to the mission and the expedition, while others were brought from the tule village by their Indian owners. The cattle and loose horses were driven along by their vaqueros. How few remained to be consecrated! the colonists murmured to one another, but without sadness, for the day of St. Anthony was the blessed time when man and beast walked as equals under the effulgence of heaven.

Susana patted Vengador's head when they had passed the priests.

"No! my brave one. You are under the protection of St. Anthony, and even he will not harm a dog that has been blessed."

Vengador flailed his whip of tail, understanding that "he" meant Don Angel.

Of late, if Don Angel raised his voice even slightly to Susana, the hairy crest along the dog's spine rose and he growled. Several times the man had threatened to run the dog through with his sword.

Romance sparked this otherwise somber January.

The delightful Señora María Feliciana Arballo de Gutiérrez wearied of her widowhood.

This did not astonish Tía María, who was chatting with a group of women including Susana when approached by the widow. Feliciana's shining head was held high, and her eyes flashed.

"Así! Tía María! You are my friend and the first to know I am wearied of this journey that never ends and of being criticized for trying to cheer others and beaten for singing a popular song!"

Tía María drew herself to her full height. "Have I spoken criticism?"

"Not you, Tía María. Now those who are my friends will wish me well. I am not going on with you when you leave San Gabriel, if that miracle ever takes place. I am to marry and remain here. My husband to be is Juan Francisco López, who is stationed at this mission, as you all know. We will live together in happiness here at Mission San Gabriel."

The wedding was a quiet one. Feliciana had caused enough excitement at the fandango. After the ceremony in the little church there was no food to spare for a wedding feast. However, the event would leave its mark on California history.

The charm and vitality of Feliciana Arballo, now López, would carry through the rest of the eighteenth century and on to this present day. Her descendants were and are exceptional. The women were noted for their beauty and their brilliant marriages. Among the men would be two California governors, a world-famous architect, and two delightful actor cousins, the late William Gaxton and Leo Carrillo.

[7]

Other months of the pilgrimage had seemed endless, but January at San Gabriel was lasting forever. The San Franciscans were certain they would never again be warm and dry and have enough to eat. They were never free of the dread of an Indian attack. The village continued to keep the peace, but there were nearby rancherias where the Indians were less trustworthy.

When there were rifts in the rain, the San Franciscans peered anxiously over the stubble fields to the misty southern horizon, knowing there was no hope of the Anza party returning so soon, but praying for a messenger to let them know what was happening at San Diego. The mythical messenger became the emblem of their hope, and Susana found herself dreaming that it would be one special soldier who would come galloping out of the mists toward San Gabriel.

Moraga was a devoted guardian, but he had no way of protecting his charges from misery and threatening danger. He faced the final seriousness of their situation during a second tour of the mission storerooms with Father Paterno. Vidal accompanied them.

The father-administrator pointed to bin after empty bin.

"You can see, I cannot continue to feed your people."

"But you agreed to support them!" Moraga was shocked. "Rivera assured Captain Anza provisions would be left here for us!"

The priest shook his head. "You can see for yourselves that was not done. I have deprived mission people to feed yours. Now I will continue to give your colonists their half rations for eight more days. After that, there will be no more food for them."

Moraga did not argue. He summoned the male San Franciscans and gave them the evil news. The men were outraged. Moraga calmed them. He spoke as sternly as Anza.

"Our women and children shall not starve to death. I am

sending word to Captain Anza at San Diego. We need him more than Rivera does, and when he reads my report, no matter how serious the Indian troubles there, he will return here at once and lead us to Monterey."

The colonists watched the five soldiers carrying the message to Anza disappear in the southern mists. It would take the riders at least four days to cover the muddy miles to San Diego. At least four more days must pass before a reply would come to their cry for help.

Now nothing could be done but to count the days and wait.

February

CHAPTER SEVEN

[1]

At San Diego, Anza was carrying out Rivera's campaign of reprisal, but his concern was growing for the helpless hostages he had left at San Gabriel.

This did not interfere with his methodical squashing of the rebellion. The swifter the campaign, the sooner he would be free to return to his San Franciscans.

Day after day, despite heavy rains, he and his command raided Indian rancherias in the vicinity. Each time a few rebel leaders were rounded up. They were taken to the smoldering ruins of the once thriving settlement and flogged into confessions at the whipping post in the plaza. Fifty lashes were given each Indian. One was thrashed so severely he died.

The rebellion was over in a week. The San Diego Indians were thoroughly cowed. Anza wanted to stop the campaign and return to his colonists. He was worried about them although he had no idea how serious matters were with the deserted ones. Anza knew Rivera had commandeered nearly all San Gabriel's food supply for the San Diego campaign. He had seen the almost depleted bins. Now he knew the sacrifice had been useless; San Diego's storage rooms had not been burned in the uprising and were amply filled. So at the week's end Anza spoke frankly to Governor Rivera.

"Your Excellency, the spine of the revolt is broken. There will be no more trouble here, and I must return to my colonists."

Rivera had commandeered an unburned cabin for his gubernatorial headquarters. Here, before a pine table burdened with papers, he was in his element. Seated, bristling with importance, he put a pompous end to Anza's plea.

"Reprisal has only begun, Captain Anza. Now we are reaching to the roots of the rebellion. I am convinced those Indians we have punished to date were only cat's-paws. Now we must uncover the true criminals. Charge with your soldiers into every village for a hundred miles around. Take the testimony of every Indian still alive. Sift every clue they give to its source. Only then will we have the complete truth."

"But that will take months!" protested Anza.

"Then we will take months!"

"But my duty to the colonists—"

"Your duty is here!" Rivera was shouting now, verging onto one of the hysterical attacks with which Anza had become dismayingly familiar. "Would you desert your post, Captain Anza? Would you desert me? Now, when we are nearing the truth of the massacre?"

The scenes were repeated daily through the second week. Anza was as stubborn of purpose as Rivera. He held back his temper. His respect for the governor lessened as his anxiety for his colonists grew.

The discussions always ended with Anza being ordered out to harass another village, to threaten and question in an endless investigation that pleased Rivera but that Anza could see was leading nowhere. He began to fear too that the campaign, if continued, would defeat its own purpose; it might foment a new revolt that would endanger every Spanish settlement in California.

Font was sharing Anza's unhappiness at San Diego. Rivera had let the friar see that his respect for the priesthood was no higher than for the San Francisco colonists. Font knew of the running feud the governor had carried on with Father Serra, whose control over the Indians had been based on gentleness.

Both Font and Anza had reached the conclusion that Rivera's craving for Indian blood could never be sated. Anza conferred with the Franciscan, but his final decision was made alone. The king himself had ordered the colonization of California! The San Francisco project was authorized by the crown! A showdown was inevitable between himself and Rivera.

The day Anza chose was as depressing as the confrontation it-self. The third day of February brought the heaviest downpour of the season to San Diego. The plaza was a lake of mud, and in it the bloodstained whipping post was being washed clean. The charred ruins of the church stank in the rain. Anza slogged his way through the mud to Rivera's headquarters. His mind re-hearsed the arguments he would bring against Rivera's stubborn-ness: "You must continue without my soldiers. I am returning with them to San Gabriel."

This time he would listen to no arguments.

Before the blackened ruin of the church his men stood beside their saddled horses, awaiting the day's orders, and watched his progress with sullen looks.

They were a despondent group. Their army cloaks of wool tightly woven to shed rain were stained by months of travel, and any parts of their once handsome red and blue uniforms that showed were faded by months of alternating rain and sun. The hip-high boots were coated with mud. Their expressions were resentful. To a man, they hated the governor.

Among the surliest faces was that of Gil José. He was think-ing of Susana. Certainly she and the others were hungry, since all the expeditionary supplies were here at San Diego. Gil José's fist clenched on his musket as he thought of the clear ivory cheeks thinned with hunger.

Then his expression tensed. He raised his gun to point north, and gave a great shout, "Viva!"

Five riders appeared through the mist. Anza stopped with his hand on the rawhide latch of Rivera's door. Yes, these were his men! Only an emergency could have brought them from San Gabriel.

Father Font came from his tent. The riders were surrounded by their excited fellow soldiers. The report from Moraga was handed to Anza, and he read it aloud to his men.

He did not curb their fury when they learned of the hunger and humiliation their families were facing.

"Take us back, Captain, now!"

Anza gave a grim nod to his men's pleadings. The message from Moraga drove the iron into a mind already sure.

"We are going!" he told his men, and went his interrupted way to the showdown with Rivera.

The governor was fussing with the papers on his littered desk. He lifted his eyes to Anza, who said in a voice that defied answer: "I am returning at once to San Gabriel with my men. We are taking our provisions and our mules with us."

Until that moment Rivera had been in command. Anza saw dismay and pressed his advantage.

"From San Gabriel, I am taking my people on to Monterey as planned. Rain or no rain, we are going! There is no danger of an uprising at Father Serra's mission. The colonists will be safe there while Father Font and I go on to San Francisco Bay and explore its area and choose the sites for the buildings. I hope when we are ready to build that you will help us found San Francisco, as has been planned by Viceroy Bucareli."

Riveria was at a loss. He was in command of California, but Anza was the most adored man in Mexico and a close friend of the viceroy's.

"Go if you must," he finally told Anza. "But your soldiers must stay here to protect me. For I am not going back to San Gabriel with you, and certainly not to Monterey. Nor will I help you build San Francisco. I shall not take part in the founding of a new California settlement while those already in my charge are under threat." Rivera had the foresight to add, "Unless, to be certain, new orders come from the viceroy."

Their argument continued, politely enough on the surface. The impatient soldiers waited for the conference to end. When if did, it left neither leader victorious. Anza might leave with the mule train and provisions from the San Diego stores, but he could take only seven of his soldiers. Rivera insisted that the remaining ten must stay with him at San Diego until ten San Gabriel soldiers took their places.

These were the only terms the governor would accept. Anza gave him no chance to change his mind. He rushed riders off to Moraga to let the San Franciscans know that supplies were on their way, and that he and Father Font and seven of their men would follow as quickly as horses could travel. Anza wrote Moraga that, allowing for the incessant rain and the muddy road, he and his party would arrive at San Gabriel no later than the twelfth day of February. The colonists should be ready to start with him at once for Monterey.

While this was being written and dispatched, a usually

phlegmatic Nicolás Perea was joyously overseeing the filling of the mule train's saddlebags with corn and beans from the San Diego stores.

It was Anza's unpleasant task to select seven of his seventeen soldiers to return to San Gabriel. It may have been by an oversight that Gil José was chosen, since he was not a family man. Or, Anza may have been moved by the passionate longing on the strong, dark face.

Rivera glared at the messengers when they set out, at the laden mule train when it departed with the provisions he had protested Anza's taking, and lastly, at Anza's party as it left San Diego in blinding rain. The breach between Anza and Rivera was complete. It would never be healed. The San Francisco project was Anza's strongest motivation; it was anathema to Rivera. St. Francis had a powerful enemy in the Governor of California.

[2]

The San Franciscans were a volatile group that could make magical transitions from gloom to ecstasy. At San Gabriel they had reached the nadir of despair. Then Anza's messengers arrived from San Diego with Anza's message:

"I am on my way!"

Who thought of hunger then?

The women started packing, knowing the foolishness of the move but ecstatic at the prospect of escaping from San Gabriel. That night Moraga ordered a chain of watch fires set across the valley. But Anza did not return, and the morning of the twelfth day dawned, blessedly rainless, fair and clear.

Everyone was out early, hoping to catch the first glimpse of the Anza party. Few had slept, and faces were pinched with weariness and hunger, but all were cheerful. Susana stood watching beside Tía María and drinking in great draughts of the morning air freshened by the night of rain.

Felipe joined them. He had tended a watch fire through the night and was weary and smudged. His bloodshot eyes raked the horizon but caught no movement.

Their watch was as anxiously shared by the priests and soldiers attached to San Gabriel. Anza's return meant liberation to them also, for he had promised to take their unwanted guests on to Monterey.

Don Angel remained in his tent. He slept much of the time these days.

Felipe said abruptly, "What has gone wrong for Vidal?"

The purveyor came running from the commissary building, where he kept stored the meager remains of their expeditionary supplies. He left the door of the long shed standing open. Father Paterno and Moraga hurried to him, and the three searched the shed with growing consternation. The storage rooms were empty. On the barren floor were scattered a few strands of tobacco, broken bits of chocolate, and a handful of glass beads. Boxes and bales and casks had been emptied; their contents were gone. The rooms had been looted during the night when most of the expeditionary males had been in the fields tending the fires.

The stolen goods were important to the San Francisco project. They had been intended as gifts to any Indians who might share in its building.

Father Paterno demanded a complete investigation, which was energetically carried out by Moraga. Every tent and building was searched, and every adult questioned.

The wife of an Anza soldier provided the first clue. Moraga had been certain the scattered bits of chocolate were indicative. Several times before they had found such evidence of the chocolate boxes being raided.

Now the woman timidly admitted to having been offered chocolate by a soldier whose offerings and advances she had rebuffed. Who was the soldier? Neither Father Paterno nor Moraga was surprised when she named a man attached to the mission garrison.

A prompt roll call was given the San Gabriel soldiers. One did not answer when his name was called. It was the soldier she had named. He had deserted during the night, taking with him, investigation revealed, several of Anza's muleteers and a servant, with all the loot they could carry—property belonging both to the expedition and to the mission.

"Tally the horses," ordered Moraga, suspecting the worst.

A rapid count revealed that twenty-five of the San Franciscans' best saddle animals had been stolen (twenty-three horses and two mules). Only the poorest mounts remained.

The deserters had left an unmistakable trail on the muddy road going south. Moraga studied the hoof marks drying in the sun.

"They are miles away by this time. They will be heading for Mexico on our swiftest horses, and we will have to follow with the worst. But if we let them reach Sonora we will never see them again. Time is of the essence." He turned to the shocked company. "I will need ten men. Who will volunteer?"

Soldiers and civilians stepped forward, among them Don Angel, who had been drawn from his tent by the commotion. He cradled his damaged arm in his left hand, but he held it high. Moraga overlooked him, and Felipe, in choosing his ten. All were Anza soldiers and family men.

There was delay while the strongest of the poor remaining horses were chosen, but at last the posse was ready to start. Moraga looked over the group of colonists.

"I am asking you a question," he charged them earnestly. "This posse will be returning as you know along the trail we took coming here. We may even go all the way back to Mexico! Are there any among you who have tired of the San Francisco project and would like to return home? If so, speak now, and go with us. It may be the last chance you will ever have to see Mexico again."

He looked from face to face—men, women, and children. No one spoke until Felipe answered for all, and his grin was infectious.

"Why should we turn back when we are almost there? Do you want us to miss our first sight of the Pacific?"

At this there was a relieved burst of laughter, for everyone at San Gabriel had heard of Felipe's obsession with the sea. Moraga's sternness relaxed.

"Thank you," was all he said, and was off with his ten avengers on their wretched horses on the long trail back.

The San Franciscans remaining at San Gabriel were now in the charge of Sergeant Grijalva, with nothing to do for the rest of the day but watch the southern horizon and pray for the posse's safety and for Anza's return.

That night the men rebuilt their chain of watch fires.

"By the twelfth, at the latest." So Anza had pledged his return. That night the fires blazed again across the wide valley, and morning came and brought no further sign from Anza.

[3]

Still, the morning was their most beautiful at San Gabriel. The valley seemed to hold its breath in the sun, enraptured by its own beauty. The fields were square emeralds, and the sky a polished blue.

The little brown mare was made restless by the seasonal change.

Susana rode Seda out onto the fields followed by the faithful Vengador. She dismounted, tethered Seda, and sat in the sunshine on a large boulder, overlooking the valley.

Suddenly she heard the distant shouts and the echoing cries from the mission as people poured out of the buildings and tents of San Gabriel. She saw the Indians come silently from their huts. Then all were hurrying down the mud-dry road to welcome the Anza riders, who came on with heart-stopping slowness, no larger at first than ants, and then resolved into the recognizable figures all had longed to see. But how few they were: how disappointed some of the wives would be! Susana recognized the captain and the bowed figure of Father Font, and, yes, among the reduced ranks of riders, that was surely the stalwart figure of Gil José! There was Nicolás Perea with the mules—how happy Tía María would be—and the mules bore full panniers promising an end to the hunger. Susana's thoughts were warm with the happiness of Tía María and her cheeks hot with the thought of Gil José. But she clung to her perch on the rock.

The long body of Vengador shuddered against her. A low, savage growling rose to the falsetto warning he had given the night Don Angel had almost frozen to death in the hills. The coarse yellow hair was high along his spine, and his long neck swelled with sound—was it of anger or fear?

The dog stood balanced, looking wild-eyed down the side of the boulder.

Susana looked down and felt her body shrivel.

At the same moment, Seda gave a terrified scream and lunged to her rope's end under the tree. She, too, had scented the primordial enemy.

Of what followed, Susana would only remember the terror. Even before the sibilant hissing started, she knew what it was.

The rattlesnakes rose like a tide against the smoke-stained side of the rock. She saw the blunted heads lifting and the forked flickering of tongues; she saw the hooked menace of the fangs and the inhuman staring of serpent eyes.

The terrible heads were coming closer, lifting on their coiling body loops, driving upward to strike. They were less than a yard below the stout shoes made by Felipe.

How many snakes were there? One dozen? Two? They slid their dreadful lengths endlessly from under the rocks. Susana could not move.

Through clenched teeth she whispered: "Vengador!"

Instantly, the dog sprang downward. Vengador's long jaws snapped from side to side, killing and killing but never enough. He killed until he felt his own life going, then he ran shrieking away from the rock, from Susana and all that he had trusted and loved. Snakes clung to his flanks, one to his lips, and he paused in flight to tear them from him, and, rocking his great head to and fro, snap their spines. He left a trail of them dying on the earth as he vanished into a clump of live oaks, and Susana did not see him reappear.

She would never be able to tell anyone fully of Vengador's leap onto the fetid gray mass, and the way it boiled up over and around the dog, and the striking of the projectilelike heads.

Then she looked down and saw that many snakes were still whole and active, and these, hissing and lifting, were recommencing their ascent up the side of the rock. One larger rattler wound upon itself and uncoiled, shooting up like a spring. Its fangs almost touched the sole of her shoe. She could not move her foot. The snake fell back, and others followed, advancing steadily.

How had she come to her feet? She was standing, balanced on the ridge of the boulder, staring down blindly into the hissing tide that continued to rise, upward, closer, very close now, under her feet.

Gil José did not dismount when the reprisal party arrived in the plaza. He was haggard and spent from the long ride from San Diego and muddied from head to foot, but his only thought was for Susana. He leaned from his saddle to speak briefly to his friend Felipe. Then he wheeled his horse in the direction of

Felipe's pointing hand and set out alone, hoping to first see Susana apart from the others.

Susana did not hear the sound of Fuego's nearing hoofs. Her senses were numbed. She did not see Gil José as he brought Fuego under the sycamore where Seda was tethered, and flung himself to the ground. He raced with clattering spurs for the rock and drew his sword as he ran. He waded into the mass of rattlers, slashing to and fro with his sword, while the snakes struck time after time against his thigh-high leather boots. But although he killed over a dozen still others came from under the rock, toward Susana.

Gil José sprang back and sheathed his sword. He stood, braced, with feet apart and arms open.

"Leap, Susana! Over their heads—to me!"

It was a soldier's command, shouted in the voice Anza used when ordering attack. Susana obeyed automatically. She who had been immobilized by fear moved, clutched her skirts, clenched her body, and sprang forward. Gil José staggered under the impact of breaking her fall. Then they were running hand in hand to the protection of the tree where they had left the horses, at a safe distance from the snake-infested rock.

Only, no horses were under the tree.

They stood panting, holding to one another, fighting for breath. Gil José spoke first.

"My horse is gone! And yours! It is not like Fuego to run away!"

Susana could see that Gil José was angry with the stallion he had trained as a colt to stand waiting for him, no matter how long. She thought it best to explain.

"Fuego is not at fault. My little mare enticed him. It is her time." She put it as delicately as she could.

Gil José understood. He was still holding Susana.

"Animals!" he cried. "Even they have chosen one another! They will return to the camp satisfied. They are wiser than we, Susana. Why did you not run away with me when I pleaded with you in the desert? We might have had these months together in happiness in some place secret and safe, and without the misery I have endured, having you near, but held apart from me, and I in torment. Night after night I have dreamed of holding you in my arms, as I do now, but each night you slept in another man's tent . . ."

His voice broke.

"Why did you marry him, Susana? By what right does Don Angel stay alive? A man ill and old, and still able to terrify you —even now at his name you are trembling. Do not fear him, my heart's love! I too have a sword. I will go to him and defy him to hold you!"

"You must not speak to Don Angel," she said with all the sternness she could command. "He is a man you cannot understand. *Mira*, even now he urges me to go to you! Because he wishes that, we must be more careful than ever before."

"How can you know that?" Gil José spoke fiercely.

But she could never explain Don Angel's reasoning to anyone, and certainly not to Gil José. She expected the wicked suggestion would cool his ardor, but her words added tinder to the flame.

"So! With his permission? As he wills it, then! As he gives you to me!"

The great-branched sycamore was a pavilion over their heads. Its branches curtained sight and sound of the settlement. As both had longed to be, she as strongly as he, they were alone in secrecy. Lips and bodies fused in fire.

Then her lips shaped the anguished "No!"

He did not hear her. Exultant and not to be denied, body and mouth held hers. "You and I!" The words were flame against her lips. "Together, *siempre*, forever."

The furnace opened again and was sucking her in. Once more Susana held a man's life in her arms. More than a life, a soul! One she could condemn for all eternity. She had to place a door between herself and Gil José that could never be opened. For his safety, not hers. She never loved him more than in that moment when, pressing him from her, she began speaking of the boy who had died at the balcony.

After the first words she had no need to hold him away.

He heard her through.

After she stopped speaking, they stood separate, frozen.

Now that Gil José knew her to be a woman damned, he could understand the fear she had always shown on hearing the blessed name of Serra, and why she had looked forward with such obvious dread to the journey's end, which was so ardently desired by the other San Franciscans. All this Gil José now saw clearly, and the shock was as great as if a worshiped image had turned to filth before his eyes. Then he sighed, so deeply his body shuddered.

"So you were that woman!"

Her head bowed. Would it ever lift again?

"We heard of you in Sinaloa. We did not know your name. We were told that night of his dying a great earthquake struck Mexico City, and the streets split open, and hundreds of citizens fell into the fissures and were never seen again. We were told rivers of red lava flowed from the mountains above your city and formed a flaming cross miles high in the snow. This we were told of you in San Felipe de Sinaloa . . ."

"There was no fiery cross." She spoke dully, not in self-defense, but in behalf of a truth that no longer mattered.

". . . And that all who pass your house still make the sign against evil, in fear of the soul of the hanged and she who lived there."

"Of that, I do not know."

"So you were that woman!" Repetition strengthened understanding. "She who was infamous from Acapulco to Vera Cruz. The most notorious woman, so they spoke of you, in all Mexico.

"You have evaded me. You need not do that again. I will never try to touch you again, or speak your name. If I can avoid it I shall not again look your way."

His anguish gathered upon itself and exploded in hatred.

"*Puta!*"

She accepted the word. Don Angel had often called her whore.

Gil José flung himself from Susana and started the long way back to the mission. She followed, keeping pace to the clanking of the iron rowels of his heavy Spanish spurs.

Don Angel saw them returning, and so dim had become his vision he seemed to see them walking closely together, although actually they were yards apart. He stood in his tent entrance glowering at their approach with a suspicion that, ironically, was no longer justified.

Tía María called out to them in her joy at having her man Nicolás Perea home. The San Franciscans were clustered in an excited group around Anza, who was hollow-eyed and mud-splashed but somehow magnificent, and Father Font, whose weary face was transformed with love at seeing his deserted flock and their soldiers together again.

Still there was evil news to give and receive from both sides. There was wailing among those families whose men had been forced to remain at San Diego with Governor Rivera. Then Anza had to learn of the theft of their best horses and provisions, and how Moraga had left San Gabriel in search of the thieves.

Anza trusted Moraga. He commented with pride, "He will catch those renegades if he has to chase them all the way to the Colorado! I had thought to start with all of you at once for Monterey. But now? We had best wait until we have word from Moraga. Perhaps we will hear from him in the morning. We should not start without him."

With food simmering again in the pots, the conversation among the colonists became more hopeful. Even those wives whose men were still separated from the company felt braver, now that Anza was back.

Felipe was interested in Susana and Gil José. He watched the soldier stalk grimly off to the barracks and Susana slip into her own tent under the grim observance of Don Angel. After she vanished, her face remained with Felipe as he had seen it first, and now again, the mournful and beautiful face of the sleep-walker.

Don Angel delayed his interrogation until the colonists and the mission people were in their beds. Then the attack began in the darkened Galván tent.

"Where did you go with the soldier? What did you do with him that brought you skulking back to camp with the look of a sated bitch?"

She was weary to death of Don Angel's accusations and of Don Angel.

"Be at ease, my husband," she said. "You have no need to attack Gil José Terrez. You may stop your efforts to urge me into his arms. He will not look my way again." The words dragged their way through pain. She said, "I have told him."

There was the sound of violent movement. Don Angel had

left his bed. He struck flint into tinder. She closed her eyes against the sudden light of the candle. Opening them, she saw him leaning over her, the light casting an aura around his head. She shifted her body and sat upright with bare feet on the cold earth floor, looking up calmly into the protruding eyes.

"You told him?" he whispered.

She answered calmly, "I have told him everything."

He clutched his throat with his good hand.

"Tell me, all you have told him."

Then, when she finished speaking:

"And now, once more, you have betrayed me. The soldier will tell everyone!"

"He will speak to no one of you or of me. He has told me, he will never speak my name again."

The hand holding the candle struck like a hawk's claw. Flame and the hand struck her cheek together. Once more the tent was in darkness.

She lay quietly with her hand to her bruised face. She felt emptied, hopeless, but defiant, for by closing the door on Gil José she had ended Don Angel's power to harm him.

All the unhappiness in her life, all the miseries of the long journey, seemed to congeal in this tent she was condemned to share with Don Angel.

After a time she missed a presence in the dark, and wondered why Vengador had not returned.

In the outer darkness Felipe Perea moved quietly away from the Galván tent. He had not intended to listen with his head pressed to the canvas and his mouth agape with the shock of all he heard. He had been playing cards in the soldiers' barracks to cheer up his friend Gil José, who had been in a black mood since his return to the camp with the Galván wife. Then, passing the Galván tent, he had heard the don's voice raised in anger.

Felipe had learned so much concerning Susana he thought it his right to know all. Now he understood the sadness of Susana. He remembered having heard in Sinaloa of the tragedy in Mexico City (as had Gil José). So she was that woman! thought Felipe, as Gil José had before him, and then, a moment later, the thought came, she was no more than a child!

So Felipe's first reaction was pity.

As he walked softly toward his own tent, the pity extended
to his friend Gil José, for the grief his friend must be enduring,
having loved so deeply and learned so much! But there, Gil
José was an army man and would not suffer overly long from
heartbreak. Even now, Felipe was certain, Gil José was sleeping
the sleep of the tired soldier. But Susana, would she rest on
this night? Felipe's smooth features twisted with compassion in
the dark.

A shadow loomed beside his.

"So it is a listener at canvas walls I have for a son? A
peeper through tent flaps? Mother of God, that this should be
given me!" His mother continued in an eager whisper, "What
is it you have heard?"

And then, sharply, "No, do not tell me. What concerns my
friend Susana I have no wish to know."

"Nor do I wish to tell you," Felipe answered so sadly that
a flash of understanding went between them in the dark. "It
was long ago and should be forgotten."

His mother pressed his arm. "You are right, my Son. Never
stir old graves. That which lies within may still be alive."

He lay with his arms crossed under his head, staring up into
the darkness of the Perea tent. Had such a drama ever before
been tossed into the hands of a troubadour? Felipe's fingers
twitched with longing for the strings that would translate the
melody forming against his will. He did not want to fashion a
song from Susana's tragedy. But the words stormed within him
and would not be denied. They marched into place to musical
notes only heard by Felipe's inner ear. Don Angel's sibilant
voice was in the song, and Susana's soft protest. Susana the
undefended! Susana *almita! Almita perdida!*

Yes, that was its name and her song. *Almita perdida*, the
lament of a young wife who had lost her soul.

Lost? By whose edict? Don Angel's? Certainly not Felipe's.
He could not regard Susana as lost. The lament throbbed in
his mind, beautiful and secret. Felipe knew it for the saddest
and best of all his songs. It added to his sadness that this sad
little song, throbbing with heartbreak, must never be heard.

[4]

The next morning, which was the thirteenth of February, found Don Angel in one of his rare amiable moods. The poisons of his rage had been exhausted in the scene of the preceding night. He noticed at once the vacant space between Susana's cot and the wall.

"What has become of your dog?"

It was a polite inquiry, and she answered with weary courtesy. She told him briefly of the rising of the rattlesnakes at the rock, and Vengador's effort to protect her, and the way he had run off howling into the oaks. Don Angel listened with interest.

"He ran away to die," he told her, not unkindly. "Dogs do that when poisoned by snakes. He would hunt a hole in the ground or a hollow tree and lie there tearing the flesh from his own bones in his attempt to rid himself of the poison. Believe me, he has been dead for hours."

She put her head in her hands.

"You shed tears?" Don Angel was curious. "Why? He was only a dog, not a Christian. No Masses will be said for him, for he had no soul."

He added with surprising gentleness, "Yes, we will miss Vengador. A finer watchdog I have never owned."

Don Angel's changes in mood always mystified Susana. As they left the tent, he spoke in the friendliest way to the Perea family, congratulating the muleteer again upon his safe return from San Diego. Nicolás answered civilly enough, his wife with an aloofness strange to her, while Felipe only nodded. The musician glanced briefly at Susana, and her eyes, dark with exhaustion, recalled too poignantly his eavesdropping of the night, and his song of the young woman who had lost her soul. He decided to avoid Susana for some time.

There was much else to distract Felipe. The little group was soon caught up in the excitement that swept the camp. Anza's promise to start them off for Monterey as soon as he heard from Moraga had renewed the hopes of the women, and again there was much rushing about for misplaced articles and packing and nervous preparation. The only unhappy ones were those whose men had left with Moraga or were still held at San Diego by Governor Rivera.

Anza warned the colonists to hoard the provisions he had brought from San Diego, for now only St. Francis knew when the San Franciscans would again get under way and there would be no more supplies until they reached Monterey.

In their tents the families discussed anxiously the change in their captain. The truth was, Anza had a personal reason for remaining at San Gabriel. He was accustomed to great hardship. But the long trek in command of an endangered expedition, his many problems with Rivera, the recent bloody Indian campaign, and lastly, the nonstop one-hundred-mile ride from San Diego to San Gabriel had stretched Anza's physical powers beyond endurance.

The San Franciscans needed a strong second-in-command. Only Moraga could fill that place on the final trek to Monterey. There were moments when Anza yielded to the pain that clutched his bowels and doubled his long body over like a reed. His followers never saw him in such moments, and must not. At such times Moraga would be needed to give leadership and courage to the trusting people who had followed Anza to California.

The troubled days went by.

Then, late one night, in pounding rain, two mud-drenched soldiers, on foot, led their exhausted horses over the valley floor and into the camp. They brought the first report from Moraga.

As had been expected, the thieves, on their superior stolen horses, had outdistanced Moraga and his posse. But Moraga was still hot on their trail, and he would overtake them, he sent word to Anza, if he had to track them all the way to the Colorado.

Anza had expected no less from Moraga.

He announced again, "We will wait for him."

February moved along drearily. The rain continued to drum on the canvas roofs at San Gabriel. The San Franciscans were mired in mud and gloom. Their food supply was nearing the vanishing point, and once more they were always hungry and damp and cold.

Susana had thought she would never be able to discuss with anyone Vengador's disappearance. But now she found herself telling a sympathetic Tía María and her son the way of Vengador's death, leaving out all mention of Gil José. Felipe, who knew what had happened between Gil José and Susana at the rock, but not of the rattlesnakes, was fascinated by her description.

He spoke gently. "A hundred of our valuable animals have died on this journey, and of them all only Vengador will be remembered. Rightly, I named him the Avenger. A dog of great valiance. One not to be forgotten."

I will remember Vengador always, Susana was thinking. And Felipe, he, too, will remember.

[5]

On February twentieth, Anza studied the empty southern horizon with Father Font, and both knew their watch for Moraga was hopeless.

Anza said, "He may be following the thieves all the way to Mexico. You are right, Father, I can't keep the colonists here any longer. We will have to move before hunger puts an end to all our energies, or even our lives."

Anza called a mass meeting in the rain. The colonists crept from their tents, shielding themselves with *tilmas* and *rebozos*. But before Anza completed a sentence, they burst into cheers, and their faces brightened with the courage they could show when given the faintest degree of hope.

"We start tomorrow for Monterey," Anza told them. "Lieutenant Moraga, when he reaches here, can follow us."

"You know we are short of food and of horses. Some among us will have to walk. All of us will be hungry. But this time, we know there will be an ending! You have always been brave, and I expect you to be courageous now. Therefore, we set out early tomorrow, and may God grant we find ourselves more welcome at Monterey."

This was not strictly fair to Father Paterno, who had done his best for the pilgrims under the most trying circumstances, and who now agreed the expeditionary cattle might remain on

San Gabriel's grazing land while the cavalcade went on unimpeded. Father Paterno would also advise Moraga of Anza's move when he returned to San Gabriel so that Moraga, his men, and the cattle herd would follow Anza to Monterey.

Once more, Anza split the company. Remaining at San Gabriel to help guard the mission and the colonist's cattle, while waiting for Moraga, were Sergeant Grijalva and four other members of Anza's guard. It mattered little to Susana that Gil José would be left behind at San Gabriel. Not once since the scene at the rock had they looked one another's way.

With Anza would go the seventeen soldiers and their families, who were destined to become the founders of San Francisco. Also with him would go six of his elite guard. With him would go the mule train and some of the scant remaining supplies and a few of the cattle.

At eleven in the morning of this twenty-first of February, the San Franciscans called cheerful good-bys to the occupants of San Gabriel, who were relieved to see the last of them. Still smiling, they turned their faces to the west.

They knew all the hazards ahead. They were leaving a place of comparative safety for the unknown. Figured in miles, the way to Monterey was short, as Father Font assured them, but it was long in discomfort and in danger. The rain was again falling heavily, and the road was a channel of mud. Rivera had told Anza the route would be impassable even for men with strong horses.

There was a greater hazard. The coastal region was densely populated by Indians. Some resented white invasion. Those in several villages above the Santa Barbara Channel had attacked the Anza First Expedition. He had defeated them, which would not ensure their tolerance toward this second group. Only this menace had won Rivera's reluctant consent to Anza's conducting his people to Monterey.

Anza started them coastward, not by the "regular road" that had been followed since the days of the first Spanish explorers, but by a more southerly route.

The horses slid in mud that reached their bellies. Riders fell, crawled to their saddles again, and with grim determination rode on. Felipe rode with Susana's secret heavy upon him, holding his mule close to her Seda. The little mare, that had returned from her flight with Fuego with all passion spent, trudged as sure-footedly as the mule.

Felipe's mule was still beside Susana's Seda early that afternoon when the emigrant train forded the Río de Porciuncula (later the Los Angeles River).

Felipe was in the merriest of moods and was able to make Susana laugh for the first time since the afternoon of the snakes.

Camp was made that night at a place Anza named El Porte-zuelo (west of Glendale), and the second night in the mountains at Aqua Escondida.

Felipe was again riding close to Susana when, on February twenty-third, the procession struggled over the low sierra and down a slope so steep and deep in mud that none dared ride for fear of falling. Even the women left the saddles and led their horses down the mud cascade. The stout little Seda waded downhill with her head lower than her rump. The horse Major took several bad falls and struggled to his feet, snorting and wild-eyed, to the frantic cursing of Don Angel.

And still, on this arduous day, the San Franciscans traveled nearly forty miles, and laid their tired bodies to rest that night on the banks of the Santa Clara River.

They were on the road early the next morning, moving directly westward toward the coast. (Along the southerly rim of the San Fernando Valley.) They were cheered by finding that the road was not growing worse, as Rivera had said it would, but drier and more clearly defined with every mile. Now they were travel-ing the coastal region, midway between the mountains and the shore, and it was unlike any country they had seen before. They met with pine trees and red-limbed madrone and manzanita, and everywhere their horses breasted patches of the spicy wild roses.

Then one morning there were flashes of white overhead, and a raucous screaming, and Tía María pointed upward into the gray sky and pronounced, "These are gulls that fly inland, and tell us we are nearing the sea."

Felipe rode, looking up at the birds with delight on his face, for his brain was already churning with the great anthem he was planning to compose as soon as they reached the Pacific.

[6]

On the twenty-fourth of February, they left their tents to find themselves blanketed in a damp mist like soft, gray wool, and so thick one campfire could hardly be seen from the next. "*La niebla*," explained those who had lived near the sea. Fog was a phenomenon the San Franciscans were to suffer the rest of their lives.

Felipe drank in its dampness, because it came from the sea, but the women set out into it with reluctance, claiming they could not see where their horses were going. One might ride over a cliff, complained Tía María. But the gray threat of the fog lifted as they rode, and rolled off in tremendous cloud masses, and a strong scent reached their nostrils that quickened all hearts. Felipe gave heel to his mule and rode ahead of the others. So he was the first to see the clear, high, cobalt wall, and hear, like the booming of cannon, the voice of the sea. He drank in the savor and sound of it, and his face was that of the acolyte before the altar.

Day after day they would follow westward the white curve of the channel and everywhere on this series of most beautiful *jornadas* they were welcomed by friendly Indians.

That afternoon they reached the first of the many Indian villages of the Santa Barbara region. (La Carpintería, near the river, later known as Buenaventura.) The smiling Indians came out to meet them, and the smiling colonists dismounted. In another moment the sun cloth Anza kept tied to his saddle was stolen. Anza, without rancor, for no less could be expected from these coastal innocents, ordered his men to flourish their muskets. The cloth was returned at once.

Apart from this incident, the welcome was ardent, and made memorable for the travelers by fish which was offered them in tremendous quantities, for all the Santa Barbara Indians were fisherfolk. Their deep red canoes, inlaid with shell pearl, carried ten men and could be manipulated through the roughest seas. They fished in the deep sea and near the shore with shell hooks and lines, and nets and traps woven of tules.

As the cavalcade progressed northward along the channel, the villages increased, the fish became more plentiful, and the Indians friendlier.

The dreamlike advance from the southern to the northern end of the channel was most of the time over dunes rimming a thundering sea. The camps were set near friendly villages.

On their travels the San Franciscans had never met with Indians like those of the Santa Barbara region. They were content, well-nourished, handsome, and happy people. They were notable for their cleanliness, and were lighter skinned than most Indians.

Their tule huts were shaped like igloos. Woven reed mats curtained the windows, and the doors were barred by the great white ribs of whales. In some villages where Indian women had previously been molested by Spanish soldiers the women stayed in the huts while their men stood guard at the doors. Father Font approved this, and kept an equally stern watch over the Anza soldiers.

The channel women were attractive. They wore their long black hair flowing free, with bangs cut over their foreheads, and earrings and many necklaces carved from shells (wampum) that were their dowries. Their capes and skirts of deerskin were very short, and their smiles shy and charming. They walked with grace.

The men were athletic and handsome. Their ears were also pierced to hold the shell earrings, or feathers, or even rolled tubes of tobacco. Some wore nose rings. Their weapons were bows and arrows. They were fond of jokes and games. One field favorite played with sticks resembled hockey.

The channel Indians were a creative people. They wove patterned basketry of reeds and carved articles of wood and stone. They were California's first artists.

[7]

On a late afternoon when the tents were set overlooking the Pacific, Susana met with Tía María, who was annoyed because she had need for her son, who had disappeared.

"That one! He has gone down to the water again." The herb woman lost all patience. "That a man should be so bewitched by the sea! He must compose a hymn for it, he is saying. Tell him, if you meet with him, Susana, he is to spread his smelling pelts outside. I will not have him making shoes in our tent." She added, still in temper, "What other mother has a son who will say, 'I am on my way to devour the sunset'?"

Susana smiled. The sun was indeed on its way into the sea. She crossed dunes to the water and came upon Felipe, who was seated on a patch of sea verbena holding a guitar that was as mute as its owner. He had said very little on this trek along the white curve of the channel. His thoughts were always of the sea, as now, when he sat facing the bright expanse listening to a voice before which his own was mute.

He was not aware of Susana until she dropped lightly with skirts rustling a few feet away on the dunes. They watched in silence as the great flaming ball edged lightly onto the far-off rim of the sea.

Felipe spoke first. "I may have a song for this sunset. There is this great dancer in the west whose skirts are on fire, and the sun is her flaming tambourine."

Susana spoke into his dream. "If the sun is made of fire, why does it not go out when it sinks into the sea?"

"Ah, but it does!" Felipe spoke with assurance. "It warms itself again in the night and blazes up every morning."

"Where does it hide during the night?"

"Why do we care where the sun hides? We know it is certain to come back."

At this wise observation from Felipe, they laughed at the same moment as happily as children.

They watched together before the mighty altar that was the rim of the world. The surging music of the waters did not end—it was the powerful sermon of the universe, and they heard it together, seated a few feet apart in perfect communion.

The fog came rolling in over waves capped with phosphorus. One star showed.

"*Estrella del Norte!*" she said softly. "Even here."

"Yes, but here," said Felipe, "the California Indians call it Runi."

When, at last they walked up the dunes to a sleeping camp, Felipe felt a special gratitude to Susana. He knew she would never ask why he had not composed his song to the sea.

With regret, and still with anticipation, the San Franciscans left the Pacific and, turning inland in a southerly direction, met with the road that would lead them to Monterey.

They entered now a land of many rivers, swollen by heavy rain, and in many places mud made the road almost impassable. Many times the entire cavalcade was mired in mud and unable to move forward. Then the women had to walk and the pack animals were unloaded that men might carry their burdens until a drier stretch of land was reached.

Fog and rain and mud did not discourage the San Franciscans. They were traveling rapidly, and even the sick ones were cheerful, for they were well on their way to Monterey.

They left the channel's last Indian village on the twenty-eighth. Now their route led overland from Point Conception to the Mission of San Luis Obispo, which would be their first non-Indian settlement since San Gabriel. Traveling northwest, they reached the Santa Rosa River at four that afternoon, and found the salt-water river so high in tide their animals could not cross. They did not make camp, but waited until midnight, when the tide lowered, and then made a deep and dangerous fording in the dark.

The next morning they camped at the pleasant inland lake La Graciosa.

The month had been one of many changes, and many hardships, and a renewal of hope. Tomorrow they would start for San Luis Obispo. From there they knew it was only a short distance to Monterey.

March

CHAPTER EIGHT

[1]

On the second of March the San Franciscans left the Indian village of El Buchón. The road led through a canyon and past the base of a hill where there were pits filled with an ill-smelling black substance. "Springs of tar," Father Font described these. The beautiful Santa Lucía Mountains rose on their left, bulwarking them from the sea.

The women had donned what finery was theirs that they might look their best upon arriving at the San Luis Obispo Mission.

They crossed the rich, uncultivated Cañada de los Osos to a beautiful natural setting under the Santa Lucía Mountains, about three leagues from the Pacific. And there, a little before noon, they reached a thriving and successful California mission where a dozen representatives of Spain, priests and soldiers, gave an enthusiastic welcome to these newcomers who had come to colonize the Spanish frontier.

Bells rang and muskets roared, and Father Cavaller stood smiling and holding a smoking censor in the doorway as the mud-stained, ragged San Franciscans, chanting the *Te Deum*, entered the little church to receive the blessings of San Luis Obispo.

The settlement had been founded less than four years before, but it gave an impression of solidity and permanence. It was the last completed California mission, as the work on San Juan Capistrano had been halted by the San Diego uprising. The buildings were of rock and wood, and the church of adobe, and it was here the pilgrims first noticed that the California adobe bricks were of a darker brown than those of Mexico.

The San Franciscans were surprised to learn that the San Luis inhabitants had been dreading their arrival. An exaggerated account of the San Diego uprising had reached the north, and because it had taken place just as Anza and his colonists arrived in California, the northern establishments feared trouble would arrive with them. But the San Luis Obispo people had only to meet Anza to be reassured, and they befriended at once his ragged and eager followers, who were, after all, people from "back home."

There were good conversation and good food, and the San Franciscans were interested to know that much of this mission's meat supply came from the bears that gave their name to the valley. The pilgrims felt more strongly than ever the nearing presence of Father Serra, who considered San Luis Obispo one of the most successful of his "rosary of missions."

Friendships were readily made with the Nochi Indians, who lived in tule-hut villages in and around the valley. Father Font described them as "having better features, and more comely than any other tribe I have seen." The San Franciscans agreed that their women were the prettiest Indian women they had met.

The Nochis' complexions were fair. They may have had European blood. Among their legends was one of Spanish soldiers cast ashore from a galleon wrecked on this coast years before. The survivors had settled here in Bear Valley.

Anza was amazed at the improvements made at the settlement since his first visit. Olive trees and the vineyard of wild vines grafted with European grape cuttings were promising a healthy yield. Many new buildings had been raised, and the grain harvest had been notable. The cattle herd had increased by more than a hundred head.

"What we have done here, you can do," the San Franciscans were assured on every side.

San Luis Obispo was an inspiration to the San Franciscans. In this restful and prosperous setting they were permitted to spend the next day, which was Sunday, in idleness. Anza always tried to provide them with one day of rest after strenuous effort.

[2]

Refreshed in bodies and minds, the San Franciscans left San Luis Obispo the next morning and rode up another steep pass, then down to the Río de Santa Margarita.

They went through valleys threaded with rivers that had to be forded, one after another. Fortunately all were shallow, despite the recent rains. The Monterey River pointed northward to Monterey. The San Franciscans met it after leaving the Margarita and rode straight up it, spending the night on its banks and crossing it the next day to ride the day after to the Nacimiento. They camped the next night on the San Antonio.

Each night their tents were hidden under piled masses of fog that rolled down over the coastal mountains, coming in from the sea.

The third day found them following the San Antonio River through bottom land where there were many oak trees festooned with gray moss. At four that afternoon they reached another beautiful valley in the Santa Lucías. Here the rich bottom land was under cultivation. There were many of the large oaks that gave the valley its name—Valle de los Robles.

In this Edenic setting rose the finest pearl in Serra's rosary of missions, that of San Antonio de Padua, founded five years before by Serra in honor of the gentle Franciscan whose sermons had been so eloquent they even moved the cold hearts of fish.

Here they were lovingly welcomed. Father Sitjar and his fellow priests had readied barbecue pits for two fat dressed hogs, and, even more relished by the San Franciscans, the lard had been saved for them. This was a royal gift for people who had lived for months on the stringy, fatless meat of their cattle and an occasional deer. Many, including Father Font, had scurvy sores around their mouths.

Here, as at San Luis Obispo, they saw a mission as it could be, and dreamed larger dreams of their own.

Actually, while St. Anthony's was one of the successful California missions, it had no surplus supplies, and the feast for the San Franciscans was a sacrifice given joyously. In fact, so very poor was this mission that bear meat was its staple diet, as at San Luis Obispo, and the friars often sent Indian neophytes to the ocean for fish, although the Pacific was a one-and-one-half-day journey away.

[3]

The next day, since all had gone so well and time was no longer a sword at their hearts, Anza decreed a day of rest. It was spent in friendly meetings between the visitors and the people of the mission. The holiday was justified when, at one o'clock that afternoon, a shout rang through the valley and a party of horsemen came riding under the oaks. It was the surprise arrival of Moraga and his men! Anza's second-in-command and the posse had caught up with the expedition with a report that would be a major topic of conversation for the San Franciscans for many years.

Susana, staring with the other startled pilgrims at the new arrivals, saw that Gil José was riding beside Moraga. His uniform was mudstained, his face unshaven and lined with exhaustion and dust.

As Anza had suspected, Moraga and his soldiers had chased the horse thieves from San Gabriel back over the way the pilgrims had come, over the mountains, through the desert, and all the way to the Colorado River. At one place they had been attacked by strange Indians, who they learned had taken part in the massacre at San Diego. The posse escaped injury, but several of their horses were wounded.

They rode on after this skirmish in the tracks of the renegades, and after five days of hard riding caught up with the thieves at the Laguna de Santa Olalla. At mention of this lake the pilgrims nodded; they remembered the place of the watermelons!

The thieves were sighted around a campfire surrounded by the good horses stolen from San Gabriel. They yielded after a show of musketry. Moraga placed them under arrest and roped them to their saddles. They were now occupying the pioneer *juzgado* at Mission San Gabriel.

Seven of the expedition's stolen horses were missing, but the best had been recovered and the posse had also recovered some of the cattle that had stampeded as far back as San Gregorio. So Moraga had returned with glory to San Gabriel, only to find that Anza and many of the colonists were gone. Grijalva and the families left at San Gabriel were still there.

Susana found herself sharing the evening meal, as she had so many times before, with the Pereas and Don Angel and Gil José. Outwardly all was serene, but whirlpools moved under the surface. Gil José was trying not to look at Susana, but when he did his glance smoldered. I have much of importance to tell you, his look said. Eyes downcast, in silence, she answered, You have said everything!

But the resurgence of longing left her weak, and she could not eat the good meal Tía María had fashioned of leftover portions of pork.

Don Angel surprisingly was in one of his rare charming moods. He held the small group breathless as he described certain famous matadors he had seen in action in the Plaza de Toros in Mexico City. Even Gil José was spellbound as Don Angel told of the sensitive movements of the hair-breadth withdrawal, the dalliance with death, the thrust of victory. Tía María forgot her dislike of Don Angel and asked eager questions, and he responded with the grave courtesy he would award a great *doña*.

Later that evening Gil José examined Felipe.

"You have kept close guard on the little *señora*? Against Indians and lustful soldiers and other dangers?"

His friend answered softly. "As promised, I have watched her well."

[4]

On March eighth they started the three-day march from San Antonio to Monterey.

As they wound along the base of the Santa Lucías, under skies that continued to threaten rain, their imaginations soared with the knowledge that they were nearing the fortress that guarded Serra's mission.

"Think of the welcome we will be given there!" Tía María gloated over and over. "When the poor missions we have visited were able to provide feasts for us of such magnitude, only think what is waiting for us at Monterey!"

They met the Salinas River again the first day, and followed it due north. They rode the next day over a wide, rich plain made brilliant by wild flowers in the colors of Spain: the red Indian warrior and the golden poppies.

In places they passed Indian villages, but the inhabitants were shy like the mountain Indians they had met in the San Carlos Pass. They were naked save for short skirts of rabbit or antelope skin, and, like most California Indians, bore no weapons.

There was no threat in this land. The pilgrims rode safely, looking ahead to mountains blurred with mist that marked the end of the Lucía range. Beyond these, they knew, waited the bay of Monterey.

They slept well their last night by the Salinas River and on the memorable Sunday morning of March tenth dressed in the remains of their ragged finery, for this day would see them in Monterey. They left the river at eight-thirty and turned southwest along a road that was the future highway to Monterey.

At eleven the mist turned to a drenching rain, and as so many times before, "not a dry thread was left among them." This did not dampen the San Franciscans' spirits; they rode chattering like excited birds in anticipation of meeting Father Serra and seeing his mission. Susana rode in silence.

She was oppressed by Don Angel, who had lapsed into gloom again, and by Gil José's determination to speak with her for reasons she did not know. He rode ahead with Anza, but she felt his demand as if his eyes were turned her way. Felipe trotted alongside her on his mule with his rain-shedding *tilma* over his head and shoulders, and talked cheerfully without requiring an answer. She was grateful for his companionship that gave so much and did not question; still there was a growing despair upon her as she thought of Monterey and the nearing mission, and the saintly presence waiting. . . .

During the last three days she had not permitted Gil José to find her alone for a moment. She had remained close to Tía María and her son, and even to Don Angel. Felipe was making small talk because he could see Susana was unhappy.

The San Franciscans had traveled three days without rest. On this day they rode ten leagues in little more than eight hours, in increasing rain. At four that afternoon they neared the looming pine-dark mountain that gave its name to the bay (El Mounte Rey) and sighted through the pines and the rain the underlying bay, a dark gray slate ruffled with storm but beautiful. Before it flew the red and gold flags on the palisaded barracks. The pilgrims were drenched but jubilant!

What did it matter to these San Franciscans that the vaunted fortress was little stronger than the desert barricades they had built against the Apaches! Over it flew the defiant colors of Spain, and in this moment no prouder or happier people were to be found on the face of the world.

As they neared Monterey they heard the voice of the tides again, and over it a stronger booming from the presidio guns that told them this was journey's end. Cannon roared from enclosures at the four corners of the stockade. Lined up in military formation before the palisade, the small garrison was firing its muskets again and again in thunderous ovation. The San Franciscans were too involved in the excitement of their welcome to notice at first that Monterey was far from being the establishment they had pictured. Later they would take a discerning look and say dubiously to one another, "So this is Monterey!"

It was not the pueblo they expected, but a rough military outpost. The barracks was of pine logs roofed with mud. The small chapel, the commandant's house (where Rivera lived when in residence), and the jail were also of adobe.

There was a crudely outlined plaza and a corral where the army horses were neighing in frenzy at the long procession of strange people and animals dragging their way through the rain.

Monterey was a fortress, set to guard the Mission of San Carlos de Borromeo (or San Carlos del Carmelo) five miles west on the water, where another military force was also stationed. Neither of these defenses was there by the wish of Father Serra, for Carmel, as his mission would be popularly known, needed no guardians, so friendly were the Indians in this region, and so universally beloved was Father Serra.

Still, Monterey to the San Franciscans was one more haven

where they would rest before their final adventure—the last march to their own bay.

They pitched their tents in the embryonic plaza before the palisade and faced their first disappointment. The receptions given them at San Luis Obispo and San Antonio missions had led them to hope for a feast of welcome in this place that was the nucleus of California's Spanish dominion.

No food was given them. The supplies that were to have been waiting for them at Monterey had not arrived.

The women had looked forward to sleeping under roofs again. Here there was not even room in the barracks for Anza and Father Font. The two leaders had to pitch their tents as the pilgrims did, near the stockade in the rain that continued to fall with a violence that increased as evening painted into darkness the bay and mountain of Monterey.

As so many times before, wet clothing steamed over crackling pitch pine fires in the tents. But nothing could rob the San Franciscans of their triumph in having at last reached Monterey.

To Anza alone in his tent, there was no evading the fact that Governor Rivera, in command of this remote land, was the declared enemy of the San Francisco Expedition. Anza, in good faith, had brought two hundred trusting people on a long and dangerous march, and had tried to prepare ahead for their safe and comfortable arrival. The viceroy had charged Rivera to provide the expedition with food and with good and proper housing when they reached Monterey so that he, Anza, could continue on to San Francisco Bay and explore it and make plans for the new settlement. Rivera had ignored the order. How could Anza leave his charges without provisions, where no houses, no matter how temporary, had been readied for them? Even Father Font was being forced to sleep, like Anza himself, under canvas, and both were ill. Anza bowed over his writing table as pain wrenched his bowels again.

Then he remembered the rapturous faces of his San Franciscans as they had ridden into Monterey that afternoon under a curtain of rain.

Those recruited in Culiacán had traveled sixteen hundred dangerous miles and the few from Mexico City—two thousand miles. And he, Anza, had brought them safely through!

A smile gentled the iron mouth. How patient they had been,

and how brave! How willing to carry out his harshest orders, most of which must have been incomprehensible to them! He hoped now they would understand.

[5]

It was Sunday, and their first morning at Monterey.

The colonists came from their tents, exclaiming over the beauty of the scene. The rain had lightened to fog and they were awed by the majesty of the mountain and the expanse of empty bay with its long white shores.

In the Galván tent Don Angel still slept. His mouth, surrounded by great sores aggravated by the salt meat diet, pulsated like a wound with each difficult breath. How very ill he looked, Susana thought without emotion. His cheeks were sunken, the face a death mask. Despite the heavy rain, the night had been too warm for the many blankets he insisted upon, and he had flung them partly off his long, emaciated frame. She saw the angry sores were repeated on his legs and upper arms.

The sight disgusted her, and she rose abruptly and left the tent to come face to face with a red-faced Tía María.

"Susana! I call to you! The Padre Benito has been sighted coming over the sands! You must not miss the arrival of the blessed little saint!"

In her excitement she peered past Susana into the tent.

"You sleep, man? On this morning you must not. No breakfasts are to be eaten that we may meet the blessed Padre Junípero!"

"Father Serra?" Don Angel opened his bleared eyes. "After yesterday's ride I would not rise to meet all the archangels."

Tía María would not be repressed, although her quick eye had taken in the sores on Don Angel's arms.

"To think we are really to look on the face of the blessed little saint who brought us here. Hurry with me, Susana. The others are already waiting on the beach."

She swept from the tent in a hurricane of skirts.

Don Angel smiled at her going, but it was not a good smile. He struggled to sit up. The frilled nightshirt was rumpled by many nights of sweat and uneasy sleep. He tried to shape the hand of his numbed arm into a fist, and could not.

"Help me to my feet," he ordered Susana. "Your noisy friend is right and we must not miss the arrival of our saintly patron, Father Serra. Is not this what you and I have ridden two thousand miles to see?"

They left the tent together and joined the crowd gathering under the fog on the gray beach. Anza and Moraga and Father Font stood with the colonists watching west down the curve of dunes. It was strange to see them all together and on foot, which they so seldom were. The Anza soldiers and those of the presidio were lined up with muskets in readiness to salute the president of missions.

Don Angel took Susana's arm and forced their way through the crowd to the Pereas. She felt Don Angel's mocking eye upon her and wondered what he was thinking and his reason for wanting her here, pressed to the front of the crowd beside the Pereas, who were her closest friends.

Felipe pointed, "There!"

The fog parted, and a wraithlike procession moved toward them over the sand, at its head a limping figure, well remembered by Susana. In the mist Father Serra and the other Carmel Franciscans appeared like unearthly beings, and only at close range did Serra resolve into a small and smiling monk, smaller than she remembered, in a ragged gray robe, belted with a rope from which a crucifix swung. He did not resemble the terrifying figure she had glimpsed so briefly in Mexico City. She saw a round and friendly countenance, although the monk himself was small and thin, and the eyes, magnified by spectacles, were kind.

Then the crowd surged between them. Guns of the presidio and of the expedition shot off salvo after salvo. Even strong men were weeping, but these were joyous tears.

Susana, trapped between awe and terror, saw the wonder of this meeting that meant so much to California. Father Font's usually pale countenance burned with joy at meeting his revered spiritual leader. The meeting between Serra and Anza was poignant. The look on Serra's boyish face was pure light as he limped forward to meet the tall, stern soldier. For, deeply as Serra resented the presence of the military in California, and regretted that the way to the faith bristled with bayonets, as deep was his affection for their soldier chief.

These two, the war lord and the man vowed to poverty, shared a dream. Together they had conjured up a vision called San Francisco. Anza was not a demonstrative man, but his love and respect for Serra were enormous.

With the president were Father Francisco Palou and three other friars from Carmel. One, Father Palou was to play an important role in the future of the San Franciscans.

Serra and Palou had been boyhood friends in Majorca. They had taken their vows to St. Francis together, and to Serra's great joy, Palou had been chosen to aid his missionary work in Mexico and California. The two friends would be parted only by death.

Father Serra led the way to the presidio chapel to celebrate the safe arrival of the colonists with a thanksgiving Mass. "He will speak to us from the altar," the whisper went through the crowd. Susana wanted to flee, but Don Angel's hand was an iron vise on her arm.

"The Mass we will hear together, my wife." His words probed like hot wires. "It has been my desire to hear this priest who has brought such a change in our lives. He will see us together and know you—for he must know you! You and I know you have not changed!"

But he could not force their way forward into the crowded church, and because the Pereas did not try, but took their places meekly in the rear under a station of the cross painted by Indian converts, Don Angel and his wife were obliged to kneel where they were not likely to be seen from the altar. Susana saw Gil José in the front of the church near Anza, and, shrouding her face in the mantilla, she prayed for oblivion.

It was Father Font's great privilege to sing the Mass of thanksgiving. Afterward Father Junípero Serra stepped forward on the altar and held his hands out in blessing and in welcome to his San Franciscans.

The hands of Serra were a peasant's hands, dark and stained by many years of manual labor, for in building the missions he had served as farm hand, mechanic, and laborer, as well as priest.

Still the hands were beautiful, and the hand Susana remembered as having pointed at her like a sword moved now in the gentle gesture of benediction. The eyes behind the glasses, too, that she had seen as pits of flame, held only gentleness.

How could she have seen this man as an archangel of vengeance? Here stood a man small and poor and lame, wearing a robe patched with his own hands. A small, frail man of tremendous power. . . .

She stood breathless, between the tall, spare figure of Don Angel and the sturdy Perea father, waiting the denunciation and the thunder from the pale, gentle mouth.

Then Serra smiled and spoke his love softly for these, who were his children.

He loved them. He loved them for what they were, like himself, ragged and poor, but bravely dedicated to their cause in this new world. In their hands he saw the unseen banners of the California defense against Russia. He loved them for their purpose, their courage, their faults, and simplicity, and their devotion to one another.

He told his pride in their long and dangerous way, in having reached this alien coast as bearers of the dream, so far from Mexico, so far from the protection of Spain.

With grave tenderness he described their new brothers, the Indians they would meet in this region and later around the bay of San Francisco. He begged their kindness to the aborigines.

Susana heard the whisper at her ear, "He does not see you now. But he will!"

After services, the friars mingled with the people outside the church. The crowd moved slowly. The standing and kneeling tired Don Angel, and he left, his face twitching with exhaustion, but Susana lingered, watching from a safe distance as Father Serra saluted the newcomers, with his joyous, "Let us love God!" She saw the way the children ran to him as if to one familiar and loved, and the respect the men showed him, and his way of meeting women, retreating before them in shyness unless they were Indian. His shyness surprised her. It did not seem in keeping with the dynamic personality she remembered.

When Serra crossed the presidio yard, the crowd moved with him, and it was the way it had been in Mexico City when he had been followed in the streets by ragged beggars and men glittering with diamonds, all willing to kneel in the dust to receive his blessing. To Susana, he was still the symbol of doom. To the others, he was a saint who walked ragged and limping in the effulgence of God.

The talk over the belated breakfast fires was all of Junípero Serra, for seeing him was one of the great experiences of these people's lives. It was a relief to Susana that Don Angel had returned to his tent. She could listen with absorption to the discussion of Serra.

He had been born, as had most of the pilgrims, of farm people at Petra, on the island of Majorca. Although of peasant stock, he had been delicate and small and different in every way from his sturdier brothers. He learned to work on the farm, and became skilled in the care of animals and plants and trees. Then it was discovered that the frail boy had a brilliant mind. He was sent to the university. During the years in which he held with distinction the chair of philosophy at Palma, he had ceaselessly prayed and petitioned the church authorities to be permitted to go as a missionary to the New World. Upon taking the vow of poverty, he who had been born Miguel José Serra took the name of Junípero, for the earlier disciple and saint, St. Francis's friend.

Serra arrived in Mexico City in 1749. At that time, the evangelist had been thirty-six years old, a man of spare frame with great luminous eyes that expressed all his thoughts, and already incurably lame from having been bitten by a snake or scorpion on his walk from Vera Cruz to the capital.

He had walked, after a sea voyage made dangerous by storms, carrying the wooden cross he had brought from Palma. For the next seven years he preached in the Mexican capital and in towns, villages, valleys, mountains, and jungles.

He was appalled by Mexico City, its great luxury and greater poverty, corruption among the rich, godlessness among the poor. He looked with horror on the wealthy worshipers in the cathedral, whose extravagant clothing rivaled the garments on the gold and silver images, whose jewels outglittered the myriad candles, while their dissolute faces mocked the serene faces of the saints.

He chose his flocks in the most isolated sections of Mexico. From then on, the Indians held his heart.

He worked with them in their poor fields and taught them the farming wisdom he had learned as a boy on Majorca. Then, limping back into the capital, the Franciscan would excoriate its rich citizens for their profligacy and their heartlessness toward the neglected ones of earth. He flayed the city with his violence. And because he showed it no mercy, but promised it hell-fire and eternal damnation, the city fell to him. He became its great spiritual leader.

Eventually Serra had left old Mexico with Don Gaspar de Portolá and founded the first of the California missions. After that came his meeting with Anza and the formation of a powerful team that planned and fought together for the founding of a future city for St. Francis.

On this March day at Monterey when the San Franciscans heard Serra preach for the first time, he was sixty-three years old, and so fired by the San Francisco dream that he felt that his life's work was only beginning. He was feeble as well as lame. He was a man burning out his life with love and hope, and he retained the humor, the sweetness, and the simplicity of a child.

The San Franciscans continued to speak of Serra, but they became uneasy. The Carmel priests and Moraga and Anza had been closeted in the priest's room in the presidio since Mass was ended. The suspicion grew that something had gone wrong.

Father Serra had heard from Rivera, who was still questioning Indians at San Diego. Not only was food for the starving emigrants being withheld, but it was suspected that Rivera had no intention of returning to Monterey to aid the San Francisco project!

Serra and Anza were bitterly unhappy. It was a sad experience to the two friends who had united their formidable resources for the formation and advancement of San Francisco. Anza had told the viceroy in Mexico City that it was due to Father Serra that California had been saved from Russia. He had added his own warning in behalf of their colonization plan:

"Until Spanish children are born in this part of New Spain, it will never be free of the fear of Russia."

Now children were here, playing under the presidio walls, building sand castles on the Monterey beach, waiting to grow up to be San Franciscans. And in the bodies of women colonists waited other children, and these people in utter trust had followed Anza.

That afternoon Anza and Font and several others accepted Father Serra's warm invitation to visit his Mission Carmelo. Anza and Father Font looked ill. Father Serra begged them to return with his group to the mission. "You will sleep under a roof and have healthy food at the mission," he urged them.

So late that afternoon the worried San Franciscans had the additional anxiety of watching Anza and Father Font ride away over the pine-crested hill road toward Carmel, while Father Serra and his group left on foot by the shore. Several members of Anza's guard went with them, including Gil José, who had been summoned from Tía María's fire for that reason. The colonists watched until both parties vanished in the mist.

Now once more the colonists were left in charge of Moraga, not knowing what was happening to them, but certain that something had gone wrong.

Toward evening the fog lifted, but not the spirits of the San Franciscans. And when a mounted messenger arrived with despatches from Rivera to Anza, they sent him on to Carmel with the certainty that, whatever news he carried, it would be bad.

They guessed rightly. The message made final all the governor had been threatening. It contained definite orders. Anza was not to take his group on to San Francisco Bay. He was not to go there himself to carry out the exploration as planned. He was to remain inactive at Monterey with the colonists "until further notified."

The San Francisco project was ended.

[6]

Fog, rain, and gloom settled heavily over the children of the sun stranded at Monterey. They knew little beyond the fact that red tape had snarled the last chance for St. Francis's city. Then more shocking news reached them from Carmel.

Anza, he who walked like a lion, had broken.

The long struggle to bring the pilgrims to California, the recurrent bouts of dysentery and ague, the many setbacks, and now the final betrayal by Rivera—any and all of these may be blamed.

On March thirteenth he wakened in high fever. Pain like hot wires drew through knee and thigh. His joints locked with pain. He could not move, and the modern medicines from Mexico City did not help.

Word reached his San Franciscans at Carmel. "Our captain may never walk again."

They had faced their many problems with courage, always in the belief that Anza would find a way to extricate them. Now he was helpless, and they were hopelessly trapped at Monterey.

Meanwhile the San Franciscans' supply of corn and wheat was lessening day by day, and what would happen to them when it was gone, and what was happening to Anza, no one knew. But fervent prayers were said, and candles burned in the little Monterey chapel.

Fortunately for the always-hungry San Franciscans, this was the season of Lent and a time for fasting and prayer. Neither was ever more earnestly observed than during this March at Monterey.

Susana prayed with the others for Anza's recovery, and that the hard heart of Rivera might melt. Her private prayers were even more fervent. She asked desperately that the San Franciscans might be permitted to leave Monterey, and that she would not see Father Junípero Serra again.

For in Don Angel a wish was growing to an obsession. He wanted to hear Serra preach one of his violent sermons and he wanted to hear it with Susana.

She knew now Don Angel would never recover from the night of exposure to the ice storm at San Gabriel. The pain ebbed from his arm, leaving it withered and useless, and went into his shoulder. He nursed the arm in the sling Susana fashioned from one of her *rebozos*. But where he had once continually complained of the pain in his arm, or teeth, or bowels, now he was often silent.

In a rare moment of understanding, Susana knew that Don Angel was afraid to die. It shocked her to learn that a man who had been merciless toward all living, human or animals, should be afraid of death.

Most of the time, there was between them the truce of silence. Days went by when he did not leave his cot. She prepared his meals. She washed night clothing stained yellow with the sweats of fever in a cold freshet running from the mountain to the plaza. The weaker Don Angel became, the more his mind seemed to wander. Sometimes he seemed to be staring fixedly at something, real only to him. To herself, Susana wondered. Could Don Angel be considered sane?

The other San Franciscans were openly asking the same question of their absent enemy, Rivera. Now word came from him, not to the stricken Anza at Carmel, but to the authorities at the Monterey presidio.

"Since the San Francisco colonists are to remain at Monterey, they must put all thought of founding another settlement from their minds. Houses shall be built for their occupancy outside the presidio walls, starting at once."

The San Franciscans' last hope of escape died with this order. Now not even Serra's prayers could save their San Francisco project. But they were an obedient people. The men meekly assisted the Monterey soldiers in the felling of pines and shaping of logs. There began to rise around the roughly outlined plaza small one-room log cabins—the first houses of Monterey!

[7]

The women watched the construction work, and with little else to do, either for their families or St. Francis, they awaited what promised to be the saddest Easter of their lives. Among them some looked forward to the completion of the huts and expressed their willingness to settle down beside this bay for the rest of their lives. (Some would do so when the time of decision came.)

Susana was not among these. She was the most anxious to leave the vicinity of Carmel. Still there were pleasant interims in her care of Don Angel when she joined Tía María in exploring the mountain and the shore. Sometimes Felipe went with them when not engaged in work on the cabins.

On such forays Tía María and her son could forget the frustrating ending of their journey, and Susana, for an hour or two, might forget Don Angel.

To the herb woman land and shore were well-stocked open markets. At Monterey, as at Carmel, were many varieties of shellfish, principally black mussels and clams, and the muscular abalone, whose shells could be made into dishes or jewelry. The waters teemed with many kinds of fish.

Only the fact that their supply of corn was running out kept the San Franciscans in a perpetual state of apprehension. Corn was their mainstay. And Tía María, on a day when Felipe was with them and they tired of the shore and turned to the forest, remarked uneasily to her companions, "Perhaps it is time that we start planting Brother Corn in this place, since who knows how long we shall be here?"

They climbed the pine-clad slope over the settlement, up the side of the mountain of the king, chattering like jays as they scuffed through the thick carpet of pine needles, gathering glossy pine cones for the piñon nuts, and keeping a sharp watch for tree and ground fungi and herbs, and such edible plants as the curled fronds of mountain fern.

The three scrambled up a slope laced with silvery winter freshets and tangled with wild grape to a clearing in the forest where the pines met overhead. Tía María came to rest, panting, on a fallen log cushioned with moss, and the others joined her on either side. They sat companionably until able to breathe normally again, and Tía María launched at once into conversation.

"Your man, Susana? He is no better?"

"He is no better. The sores you have seen are spreading. And the pain from his arm has gone to his shoulder and torments him there . . . he does not sleep."

"The sores can be cured." Tía María spoke with conviction. "I have seen such sores on the faces of sailors in Sinaloa who are home from long voyages at sea. It is cured with lemons, but we have no lemons, and the fruits of the roses will serve."

Tía María had removed her shoes upon leaving the settlement and stowed them in her plant basket. But her feet were prehensile as hands and had seemingly grasped an exposed root of their own volition. It was a familiar plant, and a feared one, and she had been astonished to find it growing in this place so

far from its native Sonora, where the sinful had known its uses
for centuries. It disturbed Tía María to find this particular plant
just as they were discussing a situation all knew was hopeless.

Could the root be a sign?

"Clearly, in this moment," she said gently, "I hear the voice
of my mother, saying, 'Little María, this is a root of great evil.
Its power is one of the old secrets entrusted to me, and I to
you, my Daughter. Powdered and laid on the tongue, it can
bring instant death. It is not to be touched save by women
skilled in the ancient teachings. But still, used in smaller ways,
it can cure pain, and empty lungs filled with water, and even
clear madness from the brain!'"

Tía María breathed deeply. She leaned over to pick up the
root her foot had dislodged. Her son and Susana knew that
she took in her hands a stronger medicine than any brought by
their leader, Anza.

"You tell me the pain in your husband's arm has gone into
his shoulder, Susana. That pain is known to me. When it touches
his heart, he will die. Now this root can be used for evil, but
also it is the only medicine I know that can relieve such pain.
I will not make a brew of it, but a hot poultice for you to apply
to his shoulder, and you will see, Don Angel will be relieved of
much that tortures him. I will make this poultice now."

She stood up, still clutching the root, and started down the
hill. The others followed, and she turned her head to say, "Ay,
if only our good Captain Anza would consent to make use of
such a poultice. If two are made, could you carry such an offering
to Carmel, my Son?"

[8]

Captain Anza was relieved of much of his pain by the root
poultice. He was lying under the first roof that had sheltered
him since leaving his presidio at Tubac. He was enjoying the
fresh vegetables from Father Palou's garden and the atmosphere
of peace and love than emanated from this mission of Carmel.
But he was still unable to move his hitherto-obedient body, and
his humiliation was hard to bear.

He had been lying helpless when the word came from Monterey

that Rivera had forbidden the colonists to leave and ordered houses to be built for them. He was finding it more difficult than Father Serra and Father Font to forgive Rivera. The commandant knew exactly what he was doing, but no one else knew why he was nipping the San Francisco project in the bud. It may be that not even Rivera knew.

For six days Anza lay helpless after having been carried to his bed by his soldiers. Then Rivera delivered a final blow, to Anza, this time a personal one. Mexico's greatest hero was being ordered out of California!

The commandant sent word to Anza's second-in-command at Monterey. He, Moraga, was to be in charge of the San Franciscans "after Anza leaves."

Fathers Serra, Font, and Palou met in conference at Anza's bedside. They pondered the grim facts of the impasse. Was it jealousy or insanity that had moved the governor of Upper California to drive Anza out of his terrain? Why was Rivera halting the San Francisco project on the very moment of its victory?

In ordering Anza out of California, they concluded Rivera must have relied upon an authority higher than his own. They did not believe he would take so drastic an action without strong backing. In all the San Francisco planning nothing had ever been said about Anza's leaving the San Franciscans until their mission was accomplished.

The dismissal, they decided, could only have come from the viceroy.

But, as Father Palou told Anza, "It was the Viceroy Bucareli himself who gave you the orders to explore San Francisco Bay."

They would learn later that Rivera's excuse would be this: back in January the viceroy had given Rivera permission to delay the exploration of San Francisco Bay, but only until Anza arrived with his colonists at Monterey. Rivera had used this previous order and the fact that the news of the San Diego uprising had not reached Bucareli in Mexico City at the time it was written. Rivera had sent a report to Bucareli, stating flatly that there were "no suitable sites" for a mission or a presidio near San Francisco Bay.

Anza knew nothing of this exchange, but he reached a decision and, on March eighteenth, still bedfast, he acted. He sent a letter to Rivera at San Diego. He begged the commandant either to come to Monterey and personally take charge of the long-planned San Francisco exploration, as Rivera had promised, or to permit Anza himself, or Moraga, to go. Anza added that, although he had not been asked, he was willing to remain in California, to conduct his colonists to the bay, and oversee the establishment of San Francisco.

In writing this, Anza was offering a sacrifice above and beyond duty. He wrote in physical pain, and with a heart nostalgic for his homeland. He wanted to return to his wife in Sonora. But he had been given an assignment that was still unfilled.

His letter to Rivera was a challenge. Anza sent it in charge of eight soldiers from Monterey who were to reinforce Rivera's defense of San Diego.

It was written to a man whose actions could not be explained in normal terms. No answer came back.

Anza, Serra, Font, and Palou conferred long and earnestly. Anza could not go against the viceroy's orders, if such orders had been given, by taking the San Franciscans on to their destination. He knew, and the others knew, how the families left at Monterey longed to move on. But there was a rift in Rivera's ban, for nothing in the viceroy's purported orders actually forbade Anza's going ahead with the exploring of San Francisco Bay! And Anza had personal knowledge of the viceroy's great interest in the founding of San Francisco. They had discussed it together in Mexico City, when Bucareli had ordered Anza to investigate the northern bay and clear away the mystery of it once and for all.

True, that order had been given prior to the troubles at San Diego, but it had never been rescinded!

Anza discussed this fine point with the friars. They agreed with Anza's decision. "My allegiance is not to Rivera, but to the viceroy!"

Anza decided to carry out Rivera's first order in part. He would leave the women and children of the expedition at Monterey. Then, with their soldier-husbands, he would set out to explore San Francisco Bay. He would start at once before Rivera thought up new tricks for paralyzing the San Francisco project.

Anza had made up his mind to fight fire with fire.

Easter would come on March twenty-fourth that year. Three

days before that, Anza forced himself to his feet, only to fall back helpless. He could not leave his bed. The Carmel surgeon was summoned. He warned Anza, "You are not well enough to attempt the ride to the northern bay."

Don Angel had lost all interest in the San Francisco project and in almost all else that once had mattered to him. By day he was lucid enough and increasingly unpleasant. He spoke but little, and then only to complain of one thing or another. He had no appetite, and the *atole* fed to him by Susana spilled in his beard, which had turned to the color of frost.

"Corn soup is not what I ask for . . . why must it always be that! A fowl, perhaps, in a sauce *mole* . . ."

But there were no fowl to be spared. At times Tía María came with quail or a young rabbit trapped by Felipe. Susana tried to keep Tía María from entering the tent. She feared that the alert herb woman might learn much Susana did not want her to know. For as lucid as Don Angel might be by day, toward evening, as the sun ceased to warm the cool, damp air of Monterey, a fever rose in his body to offset the cold, and with it his thoughts rose and wandered into strange places. Each evening after sunset Don Angel lapsed into a feverish monologue that at first had no meaning for Susana. Then she began to understand what he was trying to say, and his mutterings appalled her. No one else, she determined, must ever hear Don Angel at such times.

And still, during these ravings, Don Angel did not mention Susana. His mind had turned back to a time before he had known her. He lost all awareness of her presence, and spoke to persons and of events of which she knew nothing. She looked aghast into the guilt-ridden vistas of another soul. She heard of cruelties and corruptions she did not understand, and the names of women cast off by Don Angel in his years of callous conquest.

Then one night he spoke in a loud, harsh voice: "How long has that woman been standing there?"

By the light of the candle, Susana saw that the blank, protruding eyes were fixed, not on her, but at a place before the canvas wall.

The skin tightened on her scalp. Whoever Don Angel saw

was very real to him. She said gently, "There is no woman. We are alone."

His response chilled her. It was not made to her.

"You think I cannot see you, spying on me? Would you speak ill of me and have me beaten? Why do you never forgive me?"

And suddenly, the arrogant voice broke and the long, narrow face was distorted with tears. "Why do you turn away, Maurita?"

After that this one woman's name was spoken over and over. In Don Angel's imagination, sick with fever, Maurita came each night and stood in silence by his bed. Sometimes he spoke to her with panic, cajoling, pleading for attention, understanding, and forgiveness, even pity.

Who was Maurita? Susana wondered.

All around her in the camp there were sound and cheerfulness. She missed the gay companionship that had made bearable the months of hunger and exposure over mountains and deserts and streams. She dared not leave the tent. She sat listening to Don Angel's conversation, directed mostly now to the phantom that watched with them through the nights. At times it seemed to her that his speech was that of a frightened child.

Aberration came only with the nights. Each morning Don Angel woke in a rational state, but with no interest in what went on outside the Galván tent. Day after day, while the others waited anxiously for word of the ailing Anza, he lay supine on his bed, refusing food and refusing to answer Susana when she spoke to him.

But his eyes followed her about the tent, and she feared him more in his rational moods than when his mind wandered. She did not know what he was thinking.

There were times when a false energy raised him from his bed. "Why do you let me sleep, woman, with so much to be done?" But the energy was short-lived. His shriveling arm prevented Don Angel's helping with the building of the cabins, nor could he take his musket and hunt deer in the woods like other men. He would be on his cot again, staring into space in a way that terrified Susana. Then he might speak to her in tones of menace.

"I must hear this great preacher, Padre Serra, at Carmel.

You and I—together. When the sun is full and the pain in my bones is gone . . . we go!"

It was the idea that obsessed his days. Only lack of strength prevented his putting it into action.

Having frightened her, Don Angel might spend an hour or so in the sleep neither he nor Susana had known in the night, and she could escape out of doors. Felipe met her on one of these mornings when she had carried her mending to a pine stump and was sitting there in the watery sunlight. It was one of the rare mornings when the fog had lifted and sunlight was scudding over the bay in flashings of dull silver.

"Come with me," he offered. "I have that of much interest to show you."

"And your mother, Felipe?"

"My mother has work to do, and also she has seen this marvel early this morning."

"I should not leave my husband. He is not well, as you know."

"He sleeps all the time. My mother tells me. And what I would show you you are not likely to see again."

Susana left her sewing on the stump and went with Felipe. None of their neighbors would think ill of any woman leaving the camp with the musician, so well known and liked by everyone. Susana had developed much of the curiosity of the Pereas. During their travels she had learned to observe and enjoy what was seen. So she followed as Felipe led shoreward and westward over the gray curve of beach between hills and bay that led toward Carmel.

"Do we go to the mission?" she asked with sudden panic, but Felipe laughed and assured her they would not go that far.

She gave way to enjoyment then. The fog had lifted, revealing the magnificent stretch of sea and sand, rimmed by trees twisted into strange shapes by the wind. The waves brought treasures to their feet. She stooped to pick up a starfish, and walked on carrying it in her hand.

Dark rocks jutted from the water, from which sounded a steady barking. Could these be dogs, Susana wondered? She did not have to ask, for Felipe saw her puzzlement.

"They are seals. They have the faces of dogs," he explained.

She looked hard at the dark, wet bodies cavorting on the rocks, and saw they did have dog faces that reminded her of

Vengador. She felt her heart twist with sadness, thinking how greatly that joyous dog would have enjoyed racing over these Monterey sands. And Felipe, noting her sadness, pointed farther out over the waves where fountains played against the gray sky, and explained these were flung up by whales, which were sea beasts larger than could be imagined.

The two paused on the rim of a chimneylike aperture set deep in rock. At the bottom sea tides roared and swirled and cast up showers of spume. Susana drew back, afraid.

"A whirlpool," explained Felipe.

They were out of sight of the presidio when Felipe put his finger to his lips and led the way in silence up the dunes to a grove of the twisted trees. One tree stood apart. They stood facing it, and Susana was bewildered. Surely this was a cypress, but alive!

It was a tree shape of shimmering movement. Each twig twinkled and quivered in the pale sunlight. The entire tree was flashing bronze and gold.

Felipe spoke in a whisper. *"Mariposas del Rey!"*

Clouds of the magnificent monarch butterflies covered all trees around them—oak and cypress and pine.

"Old Indians have told us they come each year," Felipe continued to whisper as if too loud a sound might drive the beautiful creatures away. "From where they come, the Indians do not know, or where they go when they leave. They come in late fall, in November, they say, and now it is March. They are late this year because the winter has been cold."

Looking more closely, Susana saw that the clusters of winged creatures vibrated with the fluttering of the wings that were of dark velvet inlaid with silver gilt. The wind veered, and the sheets of wings shifted to gold.

"They make love," said Felipe softly. "All things do in different ways."

He saw color rise in her pale cheeks, and for reasons he did not understand the usually gentle Felipe felt angry.

A long time they stood watching, reluctant to leave the grove. Suddenly a tree throbbed with more active life and seemed to rise in the air. Then the monarchs rose by the millions and, swarming together in glittering clouds, flew eastward over the bay. The dance of the lovely gossamer creatures against the dark sky was an exquisite ending to the strange drama.

Felipe and Susana did not speak as they walked back to Monterey. They were too impressed by having been present in that rare moment of the annual departure of the monarch butterflies from Monterey.

[9]

The next day was the Saturday preceding Easter Sunday. Easter was the time of renewed birth and promise, and a new awareness of life. The women and children began the gathering of wild flowers and wild fruits to decorate the Easter altars. And, at Carmel, Anza, in a renaissance of determination, had his men help him from his sickbed, assist him in dressing, and lift him to his saddle. Moraga had brought word of the colonists' unhappiness from Monterey.

Clinging to the pommel, Anza led the way under a fog-dark sky over the pine-dark hill road, and with him rode Father Font and Moraga, a corporal, two members of the Monterey guard, and eight members of his own elite guard, including Gil José.

The adamant will that had conquered the Southwest had been revived by the need of Anza's San Franciscans at Monterey.

Susana saw the procession ride down the misted road through the pines. She saw Anza, pale as a specter in his saddle, and beside him Gil José. She did not answer Tía María's jubilant cry and the shouts of the colonists as they recognized their leader. She hurried away from the tents, past the stockade, and to the water's edge. There in the damp fog she wandered like one lost.

Gil José's mind did not move as swiftly as did Gil José the man. It had taken him many weeks to sort out his thoughts concerning Susana. Since the last time they had spoken together and parted in unforgiving anger, he had been tormented more by what might have been said than by what had.

He had tried to live up to his promise and forget her existence. That had been impossible. His surliness had worsened as they approached what all had considered journey's end. Orders from the madman Rivera had held him captive. Now, it seemed, the San Franciscans were to remain indefinitely at Monterey, where there were many single soldiers. And where, he had heard while at Carmel, Susana had been seen with his friend Felipe—on some errand involving butterflies? The more Gil José had tried to tell himself he did not care, the more Gil José knew he was lying. His mind turned black with the old jealousy, and he knew he cared and would always care what happened to Susana.

So, catching up with her on the fog-burdened beach, he wanted to make Susana understand all he had been enduring at Carmel.

"I must speak. There is so little time. I leave tomorrow with our captain. Did you know we are to explore San Francisco Bay no matter what has been said by El Diablo? ("The Devil" had become the accepted name for Rivera among the Anza soldiers.) You have avoided me, Susana, but now I must have an answer to my question—one question only—which I beg of you now with all my soul."

And, having said this, Gil José could not remember what he wished to say. He stood with his proud head lowered, a man anguished and abject.

Susana was bewildered. Could this be the Gil José who had cursed her at their last meeting?

"What is it you ask?"

He stammered.

"On the grave of your mother you must answer truthfully. This I must know; was he who hanged himself your one love? Were there others?"

She took time to answer. Gil José was too overwrought to recognize the resentment in her voice.

"There were no others."

One question only, Gil José had said? Now the subject was open Gil José had a hundred to ask. He had brooded over these during the time pride had kept him from Susana. Now he must know all that had led up to the death on the Calle de Tacuba. Questions were fired like musketry.

"Then it was your husband who brought him to the house? Your husband who left you together?"

"That is how it began."

"That you, a woman, should have been so tempted! Tell me of your first meeting!"

She answered his questions simply. He summed them up to his own satisfaction.

"So you were betrothed at five years of age and married at fifteen. To a man who then was old. And until then you are certain you were touched by no man?"

She shook her head. She was infinitely weary, she had no idea why.

"And after that—no man? Until the lad?"

"None."

"Had you no thought of the disgrace, the shame to your name, and your husband?"

Again she shook her head.

"One question more," demanded Gil José, who had already asked many. "Is it true that when you married Don Angel he was impotent with his years?"

"True."

Then Gil José looked down as if, for the first time, seeing, instead of the pale sprig of womanhood he remembered, a Susana enriched by months of sun and rain and outdoor living. The clear and lustrous eyes were saddened again in the way he remembered, but her face washed by the fog was lovely and clear-skinned, and her lips full and provocative. A branch of womanhood was before him in full bloom, promising fruition.

In that moment Gil José was in love as never before. He trembled with the triumph of understanding.

"Do you not know, Susana, that a married woman has the right to one man? Rejoice that you had but one! Because Don Angel was no husband to you, there was no sin in the choice you made."

And still, as she did not speak, "He who hanged himself was your only love. So you had but one husband after all. And the old man whose name you wear is so close to death that you are as much a widow as the Feliciana who married at San Gabriel."

The thought was new to Susana. Gil José's face burned over hers. Once more, hell yawned at their feet. His arms were around her.

"Now nothing is between us. Susana, little dove . . . do you not understand? I forgive you! Heart and soul, I forgive you!"

She screamed at him then, "You question? As he has questioned, all these years?"

Gil José was too content with his own logic to become angry. He stroked her hair with a gentle hand.

"Now, are you not happy to know yourself forgiven? You are mine again! I must leave tomorrow, but while I am gone, do not for one moment forget that you are mine, Susana! And forgiven!"

When he left her, his walk and the way his head was held were bold again. By whose right? she asked fiercely of his back, fading into the fog. Have I not been forgiven by all the saints in heaven? Only Don Angel, one of the most earthly of beings, did not forgive. And now, Gil José, who had condemned her, had yielded.

She stood with her lower lip pushed out like a thoughtful child.

She had not forgotten that Gil José had called her whore.

[10]

The next morning Easter Mass was sung in the Monterey chapel. Following services, the San Franciscans gathered outside the presidio palisade to see Captain Anza assisted onto his horse. It was nine-thirty in the morning when he led his exploration group away from Monterey and toward the Salinas Valley. With him rode Father Font, Lieutenant Moraga, eight soldiers of Anza's original guard from Tubac, including Gil José, Corporal Robles, and twenty other soldiers of the Monterey Presidio. They took with them a band of free horses and the mule pack that had served the expedition so long and well.

The San Franciscans were disappointed because none of the Carmel fathers rode with the party. Father Palou had wished to go. But Father Serra had thought it best that no representative of his mission rode with Anza. Rivera would learn of it, and might complain to Bucareli that the exploring of San Francisco Bay was a missionary venture. Serra believed in avoiding trouble when possible with Rivera, which was difficult under any circumstances.

The colonists knew this move was Anza's last cast for the future of San Francisco. If he could succeed in exploring the mysterious port and find there sites suitable for "a foundation," which Rivera had persisted in denying existed to Bucareli, then permission might be given for the founding of their dream city.

Since leaving Mexico, Anza had taken many chances. This was his last. The future of San Francisco rested upon it. His charges looked after him with love in their eyes and prayers for his success.

Susana would remember Gil José's looking back as he rode off northward with the others. The burning look of love and possession was in his eyes again. She did not lift her hand in farewell.

March dragged to its misty end at Monterey, leaving the San Franciscans more anxious than ever before, and with Susana spending much of her hours in loneliness with a man who was demented and dying.

April

CHAPTER NINE

[1]

April opened with new promises. It was springtime at last in California.

The colonists' vaqueros drove their cattle and horses deep into the Carmel Valley, where the rich pasture soon erased memories and scars of the pilgrimage from the animals. Each time Susana saw Seda, the little mare was fatter—a veritable butter ball of a horse.

At Monterey the cabins were finished. They were mere shells of raw pine, one-room affairs scented with resin, but they were the first roofs the wanderers had slept under since leaving their homes, and they were shelter against the clammy mists and rains of April. The San Franciscans appreciated them, while hoping they were to be temporary.

To Susana the cabin was as confining as the tent. Don Angel had been carried into it by Felipe, like a great baby, and once in his cot remained there, sunk in lethargy. When he gave voice, it was with discontent leveled at Susana, and had nothing to do with the general disappointment the other colonists felt at having been brought so far only to be stopped short of their objective.

Don Angel had one interest only, which was his intention to attend Mass at Carmel, where, in a way she did not as yet understand, Susana would be face to face with the person she most dreaded on earth. And still, during the dreadful nights, he could arouse her compassion. She had learned the phantom Maurita was a nurse Don Angel had loved and feared as a child.

She could forget the burden of caring for Don Angel only during the excursions made with Tía María into the pine

forests or along the beach. In both places they found succulent
tidbits to supplement their meager allowances of corn. One day
Susana found Tía María outside the Perea cabin on her knees.
Surely this was a garden she was planting in this place where
they had only expected to remain overnight!

"Why not, when we may stay here forever?" Tía María argued.
"It is never wasteful to plant a garden. It takes my thoughts from
all we hoped for and may never see. . . . I am too old to be unhappy, and when I put seeds into the earth I have something
to look for, something I know will happen, no matter what happens to me."

Around Tía María were stacked the bundles of twigs and
seedlings and roots and packages of seeds she had brought from
Sinaloa or gleaned along the way. The perspiration on her
dark face did not dim her look of pure joy as her fingers set
roots and twigs and tamped them in the earth. Felipe sat nearby
on a severed stump, plucking idly at his guitar. Gardening was
women's work. He smiled as Tía María pushed black and shiny
seeds into the rich, sandy loam.

Tía María scowled at her son. "Ha, you recognize the water-
melon seeds Susana and I gathered after the Indian feast at
Yuma! You laughed at us then, my Son. You will not laugh when
melons ripen in the sands of Monterey."

Felipe spoke lazily. "By that time we will have long been gone
from Monterey."

But Tía María would not be discouraged. "By the kindness
of the saints, we will be gone. Then others will enjoy what I
have planted. Does it matter who eats the harvest? It is the
planting that is of importance."

So Felipe sang to them while Susana helped the herb woman
carry water from the rivulet to nourish the plantings.

[2]

Then, on April eighth, Gil José was back. On that day the
explorers returned to Monterey, and with them the San Francisco
dream returned in full force.

Anza was looking better, as did Father Font, and all the party
wore a trimphant air. No one had ever seen Gil José in such a

jubilant state. Their exploration of San Francisco Bay had been more rewarding than anyone had dreamed.

But Anza was still suffering the agonizing pain in his thigh, and he did not even dismount at Monterey but rode on directly to Carmel, where he could have proper medical attention and rest while giving Father Serra his personal account of San Francisco Bay.

Father Font and several soldiers went with Anza. The other explorers were left at Monterey to recover from their arduous journey and to fire the colonists with descriptions of the place that had for so long been the loadstone of all their lives. What they had to relate fired the San Franciscans with longing to see for themselves the magic port.

Each of the adventurers drew a circle of eager listeners, and Susana joined the largest, around Gil José. His eyes went at once to Susana, and from that moment, he spoke for her. She felt no compunction at being there. Don Angel slept, making up for a disturbing night.

Gil José was a not a man of words. His color and his voice rose as he struggled to describe the wonders he had seen with Anza.

"Surely our San Francisco is the most beautiful bay in this world! It stretches in every direction, between mountains and hills, bluer than any waters we have seen." He struggled but could not find words.

"I cannot wait to live with you in this place that is so beautiful!"

"You?" This was Felipe, for Susana could not have spoken. "But you will not be one of us there. You will be returning to Horcasitas with our captain."

"No!" Gil José shouted denial. "I am not going back! When I saw that bay I knew I belonged there! Then I asked my captain, and he said yes, I could stay here in California. I can go with you. I am to be a San Franciscan. You know a presidio is to be built there, as well as the mission for St. Francis, and these sites Captain Anza chose and quickly decided upon. There are many Indians around the bay, and soldiers will be needed. So I am to be one of the soldiers of San Francisco, and I will be there to protect you."

His fierce look went to Susana. She realized that Gil José was sacrificing his career with his adored Captain Anza to be with her. His other listeners knew too, but they accepted the situation, being practical people. After all, Don Angel could not live much longer. This may have been why Anza had been willing to part with a favorite guardsman, for he too was a soldier who understood devotion as well as he did the artifices of war.

Tía María broke into the silence.

"How soon can we leave for this wonderful place?"

But Gil José could only shrug eloquent shoulders. "Our captain has not heard from that man Rivera, who is still at San Diego. Until he gives consent, San Francisco cannot be built. We do not know what harm he will do my captain when he learns we explored the bay without his permission."

Susana returned to Don Angel. In the general excitement, no one noticed her departure but Gil José.

[3]

"What is the noise out there?" asked Don Angel.

Susana explained. "Captain Anza and his party returned. The captain goes on to Carmel. He is not well."

Don Angel blinked bulging eyes. A sly smile of malice bowed the thin lips. He was not the same man who had whimpered like a child in the night.

"I, too, would see Carmel," he said arrogantly. "This Sunday, when everyone will be there, you and I will be in the mission to hear the little Padre Junípero deliver one of his sermons made of fire. Then I shall see what powers this preacher has that are so great they have taken one life known to us, and been the ruin of mine. We shall see who among these friends will still be yours, when that sermon ends."

She knew at last what his intentions were. Nothing would satisfy Don Angel but her complete humiliation. Her only hope was that Don Angel might overlook Sunday, since he took so little interest in the passing of time. But he did not forget.

On that morning his first words were, on waking, "Is this Sunday?"

Neither had slept. Don Angel's pleading with the phantom Maurita had kept both awake. He was pale from illness and having been long indoors, and his whole body trembled as Susana helped him to his feet and into the travel-stained clothing that was his best.

He stood, wavering and tall, with head outthrust as if to balance a body attenuated by sickness. His cheeks were so sunken the nose seemed more beaklike, and the gaunt head seemed more than ever like that of some predatory bird.

Felipe had brought the Galván horses from pasture. It took him and his father's combined efforts to get Don Angel into the saddle. On other Sundays the Perea family would have walked to Carmel, as did many of the colonists, but today they rode their mules with Don Angel, six miles by the hill road under the dark shafts of pines. Felipe rode close to Don Angel, ready to protect him if he fell. At times he stole glances at Susana that were warm with understanding and pity. He may have known, as Susana did, what Don Angel had in mind.

Susana saw nothing of the trip, nor had she spoken a word that morning. Nor would she recall her first sight of Carmel, that settlement between river and bay all the San Franciscans had looked forward to seeing since leaving Mexico.

Only Tía María was chattering in a pleased way. "At last, Susana, we are to hear our blessed little saint. Ay, the sermons he is famous for—strong men shed tears! But do not be afraid, for even as he scolds he tells us how to be good and escape the punishment he talks about. . . ."

They left their mounts to graze beside the river, and walked past the neophytes' huts into the barricade.

Bells hanging from a wooden frame outside the mission were ringing as Don Angel's little group entered the church. The two Perea men walked on either side of Don Angel to support him.

The interior of the church was longer and larger than the size of the mission would suggest. It was dim and roughly finished, but there were areas brightened by candles and crude paintings by Indian neophytes. Worshipers were standing closely together. There were the colonist families and presidio soldiers that had walked from Monterey, and the Carmel soldiers, and many families of Indian converts. Susana saw Gil José, standing among other members of the elite guard surrounding Anza. He might have been the only person there. Although the space of the church was between them, they seemed to meet face to face.

Don Angel forced his small party to a place directly under a carved wooden pulpit that hung on the whitewashed wall like an oriole's nest on a tree.

Narrow steps led from the floor up to the empty pulpit.

The Franciscan fathers, Serra, Font, Palou, Cambón, and several others, were on the altar with their Indian acolytes. They wore the embroidered robes of ritual brought at such cost from Mexico City.

Incense and chanted words rose in the dim church. The congregation kneeled and rose many times from the earth floor, and each time Susana felt that Don Angel, crowded against her, had greater difficulty in rising. But he held Susana to his side with amazing strength, and not once, even in prayer, did he take his eyes from the moving figure of Father Junípero Serra.

Mass ended.

The congregation stirred, and a murmur of apprehension filled the church as Father Serra left the altar. When he reappeared on the stairs leading to the wall pulpit, he had discarded the rich vestments, and his frail body wore the patched gray robe with which all were familiar. There was a breathless wait while he climbed, with steps made slow and painful by the lame leg. When he appeared, at last, over their heads in the pulpit, he seemed again the small, friendly monk they knew and loved, with the candlelight casting a glow, like a halo, over the tonsured head, and the large, eloquent eyes made more enormous by the spectacles he always wore. Somehow he appeared more spiritual and awe-inspiring than he had in the gorgeous accouterments of the Mass.

For a moment he stood looking down on the uplifted heads of the people he considered his children, but to each person his look gave a separate message, and Susana felt that his glance brushed by her. All eyes were on the small robed figure as, with gentle, toil-darkened hands, Serra began the adjusting of certain articles lying before him on the pulpit's ledge.

One by one, in silence, he displayed them. At each movement a groan rose, for although not everyone had seen these articles in use, all knew their significance. So there was horror as Father Serra showed, in turn, the heavy wooden cross, the human skull, the lighted candle, a stone stained ominously dark, and the cruel, many-thonged scourge, the flagellum, with its many whips tipped with metal.

He showed them, lastly, a heavy iron chain, and at sight of this there were outbursts of whimpering and protesting wailings of "No!" mainly from the women.

For at intervals, when Father Serra felt his flock was lapsing into sinful ways, usually when the Spanish soldiers became too free with the Indian girls, he punished himself in atonement for their sins. He had gained the respect of the Indians with these demonstrations, for to them the ability to bear pain was the highest human attribute, and their own tests during puberty rites were so agonizing the boys often died. Still, Indian converts and Spanish soldiers dreaded these exhibitions, for although morals might weaken, their love for Serra remained strong.

Then, as they watched, some quietly weeping, the small figure in the pulpit seemed to grow taller and more commanding, as if Serra filled the church with flame. His eyes flashed, his words thundered, each soul before him was a sounding board, and its secrets were known to him. This was the Serra of judgment that had so terrified Susana in Mexico City. She quailed before him now, but Don Angel's iron grip on her arm held her upright and kept her facing the pulpit.

The priest held the skull in his hands.

"Behold this skull, sons and daughters of sin! Do not ask whose thoughts were once in this cage of bone. Whose eyes looked through these bony sockets, who spoke through these toothless jaws! Listen, and do not weep, for tears will not help you. Touch your own head with your hand!—and know, this is your skull that I hold! This you will be, a few years, or perhaps hours, from now! A husk of bone, falling apart in the earth. Ah, if that would be all that remained of you! If only the evil in your lives could be buried and forgotten! But you will not be given the blessing of obliteration. No, even after death you must go on to the unending punishment, to hell, to the death that never dies!

"You must face judgment before the King of Kings!

"Oh, erring Daughter, sinful Son, what evils born in you, burning in you, are threatening your eternal souls? What wrongs are you committing that will condemn you to hell eternal? What punishments await you there, unless you confess your sins? Unless you repent. Repent!"

It was the shouted summons of doom Susana remembered. She had fled from it before in terror.

"Ah!" The syllable burst from the lips of Don Angel.

Serra's voice rose again.

"You do not repent? Behold what punishments await. . . ."

He replaced the skull. Groaning came from those who knew what would follow as Serra loosed the Franciscan robe so that it hung by the white rope around his narrow hips. Then everywhere rose gasps of horror and of protest. The ribs stood out like a cage, and between them, all saw the beating of Serra's heart in a body that was welted and crisscrossed, torso, shoulders, breast, and arms, with the healed or still open and suppurating wounds.

Serra lifted the burning candle and held its flame against his wounded breast.

"The fire, dear children! This is but one small touch of the fire! Think of it lasting forever, in flames larger than our world, that you must suffer screaming forever and ever. . . . Think that for all eternity you must bear the fire unless you repent—repent!"

The smell of scorching flesh annihilated the fragrance of incense. Women screamed and children sickened. Men turned away faces working with grief. Cries of lamentation rose and every woman was in tears.

Serra's features contorted and were drenched in perspiration. The mouth that could smile with such sweetness was clenched in agony. Blisters rose on the tortured chest. Still there was ecstasy in his anguish.

"Weep, dear ones, weep!" he shouted. "I suffer for your sins, that you may understand, and repent!"

Susana felt Don Angel's hand on her shoulder pressing her down, heard his voice in her ear. "Heed him, woman! Repent! Cry out your sins to him—confess you are what you are—repent, as he bids you repent!"

The priest did not seem to hear the lamentations and sobbing as he put the candle down and lifted the heavy iron chain. He flailed his body, lashing the chain from side to side. Blood spurted from unhealed wounds on his shoulders and back. Every face reflected his agony, every back felt the weight of the iron, and cries of grief echoed every blow.

Then the words, so terribly remembered, thundered in Susana's ears.

"I suffer for your sins! Oh, my beloved children, pity yourselves, not me! Save yourselves from greater suffering than this. Shed tears for your own salvation, not for me! Repent! Repent . . ."

Susana sat frozen with pity and terror. Don Angel, dropping her arm, lunged forward. He staggered to the pulpit and stood under Serra, lifting hands like claws.

"Not you the sinner, Father! *Mea culpa!* Give me the scourge!"

His words were lost in incoherence. Spittle foamed on his lips. But his hands pulled down the bloodied chain. Groveling, sobbing, penitent for sins that would never be known, Don Angel flailed his crouched body again and again until a heavy weight seemed to force him down. He pitched forward full length on the adobe floor.

Susana looked down at the long frame locking in paralysis. She saw the strongly featured face slowly drain to gray. Only the eyes bulging from their bony sockets hinted that Don Angel lived.

Hundreds watched outside the church, crossing their breasts and murmuring prayers, as Gil José and Felipe Perea placed the stricken man in a canvas litter slung between two of the Perea mules. Gil José had been the first to reach Don Angel after he fell. The two men led the mules over the hill road to Monterey. Tía María and her husband and Susana followed, leading their mounts, and a goodly share of the colonist families walked behind them.

Later Susana would remember the flash of gloating on Gil José's face as he had helped Felipe carry Don Angel out of the church. It was the triumphant expression Gil José had worn when he rode off the field after defeating Don Angel in the roping of the wild bulls.

She suspected that, while every muscle of Don Angel's was locked in helplessness, he was still aware of the actions and

words of those who tended him. So she was grateful when Gil
José made no attempt to speak to her after they reached Monterey
and it was Felipe who carried Don Angel into the cabin.

[4]

The joyous mood that had marked Anza's return from the
San Francisco exploration deserted the San Franciscans. No word
came from the south. Rivera was still in San Diego, "keeping
his distance between us," as Anza wrote angrily in his diary.

After a few more days Anza reached the reluctant conclusion
that, if he left California, Rivera might co-operate with Lieutenant
Moraga in behalf of the San Francisco project. Moraga had not
roused Rivera's jealousy, nor his enmity.

Anza sent Sergeant Góngora, with two members of his own
guard and two soldiers from Monterey, with letters to the eva-
sive Rivera. In them he told the commandant that he was
leaving California. He asked Rivera to meet him on his way
south, later in the month, at Mission San Gabriel.

"We can consult there," he wrote.

This was his only hope of winning Rivera over to the idea
of building San Francisco. For Anza knew, and wrote in bitter
comment, that it was not the founding of San Francisco that
Rivera opposed, but Anza's share in its founding.

On the following day, a weak and pallid Anza, still showing
the ravages of illness, rode with Father Font and his staff to
Monterey, and in formal dedication turned over to Lieutenant
Moraga the San Franciscans and their destiny, and "all the
affairs of the expedition which had come under my command."
It was a tragic ceremony. The colonists went with heavy hearts
to their cabins.

Susana spent her days and nights now with a man who could
neither move nor speak.

She saw only Tía María, who came with offerings of *atole*
or herb tea. She did not ask the herb woman into the sickroom.
She knew that Don Angel would not want her there. To Susana
the most dreadful part of Don Angel's affliction was his awareness.
His eyes spoke his horror of the herb woman when he heard

her voice outside. Susana closed the door against those who came out of curiosity to see if life still flickered in Don Angel.

Susana saw nothing of Gil José. He had not come near her since bringing Don Angel home. But she heard his voice often and knew that he was always close at hand and waiting. She fixed her attention on the needs of the stricken man.

The mission surgeon came from Carmel, sent by Serra. He prodded, probed, and flexed dead muscles. He held a candle before the bulging eyes and looked deep and long. Pressed by the frightened Susana, he said to Don Angel's hearing, "Nothing can be done for this man."

"How long . . ." She could not go on.

The surgeon's brief glance pitied Susana. "He may die to-morrow. He may live a year or many years. One sees he was once a powerful man."

Tía María saw the medico depart and her curiosity could not be contained. She entered the cabin over Susana's protests and stood with arms akimbo staring down at the body on the canvas cot. She spoke with contempt to Don Angel.

"You! Why do you not die?"

Susana made a frantic gesture. "Be silent!" she pleaded. "He hears!"

The herb woman turned angrily to Susana.

"He has made you suffer! I do not forgive his treatment of you!"

Tía María spat her disgust at the bed.

"You must not—" Susana was not allowed to finish.

"You fear this monster, Susana? Do not, for he will never harm you again. God has seen to that. Now only a breath of life remains in him, and think with what ease it can be blown away!"

Tía María warmed to her subject. "The root I showed you in the forest! The mushrooms you have seen with rose tintings! A hundred such things are ready at your hand. One mouthful of the mushroom soup and this man would be out of his misery, for he undergoes such misery as no animal can know. Look into those eyes! Can you not see his longing to be set free?"

Susana looked and shuddered. The protruding eyes certainly pleaded. But could she be certain that look asked for release?

Tía María took Susana's hand and her voice gentled.

"Where, when you are widowed, will you find another man like Gil José? He will not wait forever. Two lives, Susana, are held by the thread of life on this bed. One must think of life, not of death, Susana. Think of Gil José! Not of a man who cannot be said to be alive."

"But he is alive," Susana answered with difficulty. "While he lives I must care for him. Why, I do not know, but it must be. So do not tell me what could be done to harm him, but what I can do for him."

Tía María saw that Susana's mind was made up. She shrugged her plump shoulders.

"There is a manipulation of the muscles I can teach you," she said sullenly, "and a brew—but perhaps it would be better to get advice that is more respected than mine. You say the mission surgeon says nothing can be done? Then I will consult with the veterinarian at the presidio. He knows ways a surgeon would despise, as my cures are despised, but which may be of help after all."

"The man who attends to the army mules?"

"And why not! Even the blessed little father Serra asked help from such a man for his wounded leg!" The herb woman left and Susana returned to the motionless man. She tended Don Angel as one would a newborn babe. She sponged the frozen body and spooned *atole* between the locked gums, wiping away that which ran from the gaping mouth. It seemed to her the staring eyes still held anxiety.

Tía María was gone a long time. She returned carrying a water jug in which small, dark objects were swimming.

"These are leeches," she explained. "My son Felipe found them for you in the Carmel River. This is on the advice of the veterinarian, who believes as I do, that if we could look into the brain of this Don Angel we would see in it some sort of animal that is devouring his blood. How else can we explain what has happened to him?

"This beast," Tía María continued, stripping bedding and nightshirt from the helpless Don Angel until he was bared to the waist, "is feeding on the veins of your husband. It will live while he lives. If we permit the leeches to drink a certain amount of this man's blood, the serpent coiled in his brain will starve and die. But if we take too much blood, the man will die. Bloodletting is an art. Watch now!"

As she spoke she was lifting the hideous creatures from the jar and placing them one by one on Don Angel's temples, throat, chest, knees, wrists, and abdomen. Don Angel watched her helplessly. The dark, flat shapes fastened sucking mouths on his veins and began to swell. Tía María straightened up her thick body and drew Susana to the door.

"Now listen well, Susana, for I know you do not want this man to die. If the worms are left on his body longer than a half hour he cannot live. See, the sun is out." Tía María pointed to the crest of the mountain. "It stands now over that pine. When it touches that other pine," she pointed again, "then, do do not delay for one moment! Remove the leeches. Twist them, that their mouths will open. Leave them on longer, and your man will die."

And she gave Susana a long, level look that might have meant anything.

Then Tía María was gone, and Susana sat watching with aversion as the ugly shapes continued to swell. She looked forward with physical revulsion to touching them when the moment of removal came. She kept careful watch of the pine that would signal the passing of the half hour.

Suddenly Gil José appeared in the doorway.

"We must speak!" His simple command brought immediate happiness.

"But I cannot leave him."

He said stoutly, "Tía María has told me of the leeches. There is time to talk. We can watch the pine from the water's edge."

She went with him, and what harm was there in going, with all the life of Monterey around them and the children building sand castles on the rim of the bay? They left the dunes to be hidden by cypress and then they were melted into one another, holding, whispering the same incoherent words.

There was no one else in the world. They did not notice the afternoon fog that swept in ruthlessly over the water, graying the sky over the cypress tops and hiding the sun.

Words whispered, mouth to mouth.

"I must go back."

"You must not go."

"The sun moves."

"There is no sun. Look up, Susana. See, it is hidden! This is a sign from heaven that this man is not to live!"

She struggled against his arms, weakly.

"But he is still alive!"

"He is the man of our hatred. Confess that you hate him, Susana!"

She acknowledged by silence. Yes, she hated and had always hated Don Angel.

Gil José pressed argument with lips and hands. "Most loved one, what happened to him in the church was done for you and me by God. The miracle was left for us to complete. Leaving him will not be like killing. He will go to sleep, without knowing. He will be free, then, of the curse he has carried. And you and I, Susana, we will be like this, together, forever. . . ! Susana, I am staying here in California only to be with you. . . ."

She remembered the sucking mouths on the long body lying helpless while being drained of its life's liquid. She struggled to put into words all she wanted Gil José to understand. She lacked the ability to explain that no man could estimate the value of another's life.

He felt her indecision and held her more closely.

"I could have killed him many times, Susana. Often I have longed to place my knife in his heart. I held my hand from him, not to bring shame on you.

"Now God shows me the way! Not your guilt, Susana, and not mine, but that of the worms from the river. Let them drain what is left of this miserable life. No one will be able to say how he died, and truthfully, all at Monterey and Carmel now speak of Don Angel as if he were already dead."

She wavered.

"No, I must go to him." But she spoke faintly, unwilling to go.

"Let him die calling you," said Gil José brutally.

That was the revelation, the remembering that Don Angel could not call! Could Gil José be right in willing that Don Angel should meet death now instead of years from now?

What had been the meaning of Serra's flagellation? Susana

had wondered at the time—was there then a sacrament of suffering?

Gil José was certain he had won.

"I take his death on my soul, Susana. See, I hold you and will not let you go to him. I will plead the justice of my act before God and all the saints. It is right that this man dies now. Only," and Gil José's body stiffened in sudden rage, "I could wish him a less gentle death! Had I my way, I would end him in a way he would remember through all his eternities in hell!"

It was then her nostrils contracted from an odor long familiar. She had scented it many times emanating from the skin of Don Angel. Now it came from the strong and healthy Gil José. This was not the miasma of frustration and old age, but the heavily scented odor of his hatred for Don Angel.

She screamed, "No!" With a violence that startled them both, Susana flung herself away from the soldier. Weeping and stumbling, she ran from the grove, and past groups of wondering neighbors who stared after her until she reached her own door.

Don Angel lay as she had left him, but his eyes had closed. The lids were sunken and shriveled, and the leeches on his body were swollen with dark blood. With shaking hands she tore them away, remembering to twist them as Tía María had warned. She flung them with loathing through the open door. She spoke through her tears to Don Angel.

"See, this is Susana who tends you! You are not dying. You will not die. No harm will come to you. No one will be permitted to harm you while I am with you. And I will not leave you— never, Don Angel!"

But she did leave him. An hour later, when by the uneasy fluttering of the eyelids she knew Don Angel was sunk again in that lethargy that served as sleep, she left the cabin quietly and went to the presidio. Anza was there, she knew, and was using the priest's room as a temporary office. She did not hear the murmurs of the soldiers clustered about his door, and even if Gil José had been one of them she would have pursued her errand. She was admitted to a room where Captain Anza rose from a desk on which maps were spread. He had been routing his return trip to Mexico. He received her with the courtesy he gave all women.

She spoke bravely.

"Your Excellency. The soldier, Gil José Terrez . . ."

"Yes, señora?" Anza spoke with great kindness. Here was a situation that had cost him much thought. He knew, as all knew, that Don Angel, while close to death, might live many years.

"He has asked your permission to remain here at Monterey."

"And been given that permission." Anza studied Susana, wondering if the decision he had made had been wrong. He had never heard the young woman speak before, and he could see that this meeting was taking the last of her courage.

"You are returning to Mexico, Captain Anza." It was a statement. All knew that the hated Rivera had ordered his return.

"We leave tomorrow."

Her eyes lifted to his. "When you go, Captain Anza, take Gil José with you?"

No further explanation was needed. Anza's expression did not change. His heart melted, but his voice remained cold.

"Be assured, señora, the soldier Terrez returns to Horcasitas with me."

[5]

The San Franciscans watched dim-eyed until the Anza company vanished between the foothills on its way to the Salinas River. Father Serra and his group returned to Carmel to pray for their deliverance, as Moses had once prayed for the deliverance of his people from the despotism of Egypt.

According to a roll called by Father Font before leaving, one hundred and ninety-three men, women, and children of the San Francisco Expedition were left at Monterey.

They listened patiently, since they were polite people, while their new leader gave them a brief address. Moraga tried to cheer them, but his heart was as heavy as theirs. They took no encouragement from his speech. They liked Moraga, but he was not Anza.

As they turned back to their rough new settlement, the shadow of the king's mountain lay over it.

Now they knew themselves to be completely fatherless and deserted, and what of St. Francis's city now, and what would become of them?

What more could happen to brave people, with their leader gone? They would remember Anza as Cortez was remembered—Cortez, who burned his ships on American shores that his men might have no way to return to Spain amd just remain in the strange new world "with only God's help and our own stout hearts." To those of Indian heritage the name of Cortez would remain accursed, but he did bring many human values to America. He destroyed, but he also built. He saw to the construction of good ships and new buildings, and future Americans would owe to Cortez the introduction of silk culture, and trees and seeds and plants, and sheep and cattle and horses brought from Spain. Cortez killed, but he could be just. Once he hanged one of his own soldiers for stealing chickens from an Indian.

The Indian people of Mexico did not know of these merits. They remembered the bloodshed and pillage, and the desecration and ruin of their ancient temples, and the man's physical ugliness.

Cortez, the conquistador, dies neglected and bitter, and unvalued by his king, for whom, in a moment of revelation, he had laid claim to California.

Anza would not suffer such indignity. He left California defeated, but he sat his horse like a conqueror.

The San Franciscans were to experience many more changes, but they would remember Anza with a deep personal love. Susana would remember Anza, but the face of Gil José, who rode with him, and turned back to her one last tragic and reproachful glance, would never be erased from her mind.

Felipe was at her side. He said softly, "You have sent my friend from you?"

"He told you that? Then it is so."

"He may never forgive you," said Felipe, but gently, for he could see into the depths of her loneliness.

His round and luminous eyes held secrets. She wondered, then, how much Felipe knew.

She recounted to Don Angel in carefully expressed words the departure of Anza and Father Font and the Anza soldiers. She listed the soldiers that had gone, including Gil José. She did not hesitate to pronounce Gil José's name. She did not know if Don Angel understood what she was saying, nor did it seem to matter any more.

[6]

Anza's departure from Monterey began the most absurd chapter in California's early history. It was far more tragic than comic to the San Franciscans, who would take some time to piece together the tangled events and see them as drama, and even then would find the leading character, villain or lunatic, impossible to understand.

For Anza and his party were less than twenty miles from Monterey when they met with Sergeant Góngora, whom Anza had sent from Carmel with the message to Rivera.

Góngora was on his way back to Monterey with letters to Anza from Rivera. He said that Rivera had left San Diego and was close behind him, also heading for Monterey. He drew Anza aside. "Governor Rivera is behaving very strangely," he confided. "I am positive he has lost his mind."

Rivera, the sergeant continued, had refused to accept or read letters Góngora had brought him from Anza. He had written Anza in reply without knowing their contents. As Anza expected, the messages were insulting repetitions of Rivera's demands: All thoughts of a future San Francisco were to be forgotten and the San Franciscans were ordered point blank not to leave Monterey.

Anza told Góngora to continue on to Monterey and report the unhappy news to Father Serra and the San Franciscans. He continued on his way with greater anxiety than before.

A few miles more and he met Rivera on the trail.

Anza noted that Rivera did indeed look mad. The Commandant of California was mounted on a mule and wrapped from head to boot in a thick blue woolen serape. Even his head was hidden by the blanket. His beard jutted from its folds like a shrub. Anza and Rivera were so angry with one another they at first gave no signs of recognition. Rivera had just ridden five hundred miles to meet Anza, seething with rage against Anza. Anza, riding to meet Rivera, did not even rein in his horse. As the two mounts passed he asked Rivera sarcastically, "And how is *your* health?"

Rivera muttered peevishly, "My left leg troubles me."

"A pity. *Adios.*" Anza did not stop. Neither did Rivera, who rode past Father Font and the soldiers as if they were invisible. Anza's party gaped after him. Rivera turned in his saddle and shouted angrily after Anza:

"Your reply to my letter may be sent to Mexico City or wherever you like!"

"Good!" Anza replied calmly, not caring whether Rivera heard or not, and rode on. He would never forgive Rivera.

Góngora reached Monterey and the San Franciscans learned that their worst suspicions of Rivera were justified. Then, on the nineteenth of April, who should appear at Monterey but the Monster himself! Bearded, booted, and plumed, Rivera swaggered through the presidio followed by looks of open hatred from the colonists. He ignored them. They were hungry? Let them starve.

His contempt for them was extended to their new leader, Moraga, who defied him. A noisy quarrel between the two men was heard by many, ending in Rivera's final, hysterial shout, "And I say San Francisco shall not be founded!"

Moraga would be frank in stating that he considered Rivera insane.

The shocked San Franciscans saw the Rivera arrogance shown even to the revered Father Serra. Rivera brought with him letters to the president of missions from the mission fathers at San Diego. It would have seemed natural for Rivera to have sent the letters on to Carmel by a presidio soldier or servant, but Rivera was not one to miss an opportunity to humiliate. He sent word to Serra, "Come to Monterey and collect your letters, since my left leg pains me and I cannot go to you."

And Serra, who did not believe Rivera's claim to injury, did go on foot for his letters, limping over the beach from Carmel to Monterey.

Serra found that the seals of the letters had been broken. "By accident," Rivera explained to Serra, adding, "I did not read them!"

This Serra would never believe, for the letters written by the San Diego priests to their president at Carmel contained a shocking charge against Rivera. The commandant had committed an unforgivable sin at San Diego and the priests had excommunicated him.

Rivera, swaggering around Monterey, did not behave like a man who had been outlawed by his church. He resented the ban, and by some strange transition of that resentment, blamed the San Franciscans and their project. They had nothing to do with the episode at San Diego, but they suffered for it, more, certainly, than did the arrogant Rivera. His sin shocked them profoundly.

Rivera had been excommunicated by the San Diego priests for having violated the ancient right to sanctuary.

He had been carrying on his endless campaign of reprisal against the Indians there when one of the leaders of the Indian attack, a former neophyte named Carlos, took refuge from Rivera's soldiers in the church. It was believed that he did this on the advice of the San Diego fathers, who were as sickened as Anza had been by Rivera's insatiable demand for bloodshed. Rivera ordered the Indian out of the church. Carlos was afraid to leave. The priests defended him, protesting that he was penitent and had the protection of sanctuary. Rivera drew his sword and, followed by a squad of soldiers, pushed the fathers aside and dragged the Indian out of the church.

Now the true purpose of Rivera's return to Monterey was revealed. He had come back to demand that Serra annul the edict passed on him by the San Diego church authorities.

This crime against a terrified Indian placed a powerful weapon in Father Serra's hands. The penitent Carlos had been mercilessly dealt with. Rivera rode to Carmel and quarreled with Serra, who wrote out a full report of the commandant's strange actions for the viceroy. Rivera's offense was not his first against the Church in California. Nor was it the first time Rivera had committed the serious offense of tampering with a priest's mail.

Serra withheld the lifting of the ban.

Rivera lost his temper and demanded absolution from Serra.

Father Serra had the final word. "I refuse to grant absolution until you return the Indian Carlos to sanctuary."

And at this, as suddenly as Rivera had appeared in Monterey, Rivera was gone. He took with him nearly all of the Monterey soldiers and most of the saddle animals from the presidio "that they might not go to the establishment of the port of San Francisco to which he was violently opposed."

And so April, which had promised so much, perished in hopelessness for the San Franciscans at Monterey.

These events, or as much as were known to her, Susana reported in detail to a man she was not certain understood. Talking relieved the loneliness of the sickroom. She hoped some of her conversation reached into the unimaginable aloneness that imprisoned what life remained to Don Angel.

May

CHAPTER TEN

[1]

When May began some of the San Franciscans gave up and settled down for life at Monterey. They planted gardens like Tía María, but hers was a temporary measure to fill time before moving on, as she, and the majority, believed they would in time. All were certain that a curse would fall on Rivera.

Susana seldom left Don Angel. There were no more walks in the forest with Tía María, or along the bay's edge with Felipe. Whenever she passed her door, left open to the misted sun and the glittering water, she was overcome by an almost irresistible urge to flee from the fetid cabin and the dying man. But she could not leave him; she was not certain why.

Because she rebuffed visitors, and she was nearly always alone with Don Angel in the dark threat filling the cabin, she had begun the habit of speaking aloud, as much to herself as to him. Seated beside him, busy with food or mending, she might tell him of any small events in the colony, and then find herself telling him of her life with him, of which he had known and cared so little.

"He has left now," she told Don Angel mournfully. "Gil José, one you hated, will never come back. He is gone like the first one. . . ."

She continued to speak while manipulating sagged muscles and clotted veins in the Indian method of massage taught her by Tía María, which eased the patient so that he usually fell asleep during the treatment. Often it seemed that what life remained to Don Angel flowed from Susana's hands. Still nothing moved but the stone-gray eyes that had seen so much and understood the first unbroken night of sleep in many years. Drenched in sleep, she seemed to hear a voice she knew, soft with pity: "Pray for his soul, my Daughter!" She would remember that when she woke to find it was midmorning.

Don Angel's burial service in the presidio chapel was quietly carried out, and the colonists and all others were encouraged to forget his memory.

Susana returned to her cabin to find it swept and fragrant with field flowers and herbs. The second army cot had been folded and put away. She had never before slept completely alone in a room. Night followed night in which she slept well.

"This one," Tía María said of Susana to her son, "her face becomes again that of a young girl! And still, there is on her that shadow of deep sorrow. I wish I knew . . ."

Felipe had no intention of sharing his own knowledge with his mother, who concluded the conversation by saying, "A pity, that with the old one gone, Gil José should now be far away."

The Pereas were not alone in realizing that Susana was like one who had lived in a dark tunnel and was released into the fullness of the sun. She was now an attractive young widow in a womanless army outpost. Don Angel had not been long in his hillside grave before she wakened one night to singing. Felipe? she wondered, disbelieving. But no, the music outside her window lacked musicianship, and the impassioned whispering that followed was not Felipe's. Others heard the serenade. Tía María teased and then scolded her.

"It is not right for a young woman to live alone, and your man was for a long time living while not alive. No one will blame you for marrying almost at once. The man Tiburcio, who serenaded you, is known to me, a sober soldier and originally from Sinaloa, and what better can be said of a man? Then you would have your own establishment, and we could leave knowing you were well cared for here at this beautiful Monterey. You would have a home, when for the rest of us, who knows where we will be going?"

And Monterey was beautiful this Maytime.

Susana was stubborn. "I will go where you are going."

She did not say what she truly wanted, which was to see for herself the magnificent port of San Francisco that had moved the usually inarticulate Gil José to such raptures of description.

She took no interest in the shy soldier who watched at a distance by day and became bold by night.

Felipe spoke to her. "You mourn this husband who is dead when widows who have lost better men do not." He was strumming his guitar in her doorway, an image of contented idleness, but she knew he had been felling logs all morning in the forest.

She could not explain to Felipe that her mourning for Don Angel was not for his death but for the years of his life that he had tossed away like a man who flings gold on a gambling table. And I, she thought sadly, I have half a life remaining and perhaps more, and shall I waste it as did Don Angel? What can be done with it now?

"I do not grieve," she said staunchly.

"But you are not happy."

She regarded Felipe curiously. His sombrero was pushed back, and his eyes were clear as a child's.

"Felipe," she asked sadly, "does nothing ever hurt you?"

"But certainly! Many things. I do not like being held here at Monterey like a wing-clipped cockerel. But in certain matters one must make up one's mind. Do the corners of the mouth turn up, or down? It is a matter of choice. I have learned it is as easy to laugh as to cry, and afterward one feels better."

He thought this over, well pleased with himself, and finished in triumph, "And also, it is more pleasant for those who know me."

"Yes!" Susana was astonished. "That is certainly true."

Felipe spoke then with a seriousness he had never before shown Susana.

"When I saw you that first time, you walked like a doll moved with strings. You spoke like one who dreams. Now you are released from an intolerable burden, and still there is this sadness upon you. What weighs on your heart, Susana?"

She wanted to speak and could not. He went on gently, "Little friend, among all else, is it the earthquake that shook Mexico City that night? Do you believe God terrified a million innocent people to punish you? I am from the country, Susana, but I would never believe that."

She was staring at him. "You know? How . . . ?"

Felipe smiled. "I? I am a listener at canvas walls. But it is not to my advantage nor yours that I know what happened in

Mexico City. You have lived in blindness, believing what Don
Angel forced you to believe. I would help you if I could, but
I cannot. If I were a priest, certainly, you could say to me,
Father Felipe, absolve me! And I would do that, and you would
be at peace. But I am not a monk, as you may have noticed.
Still there is one who can return life to your smile. Your heart
needs opening, Susana, and think, the holder of the key is only
five miles away!

"The greatest of all living saints is our neighbor—*ay*, I know
you fear Father Serra more than anyone in this world. But it is
best to walk forward into fear, Susana—then it retreats before
you. Go to him, Susana! Carmel is only a short way along the
water. I will walk with you."

Felipe was no longer the laughing troubadour, but a most
serious young man.

She went with him.

They walked without speaking over the dunes to Carmel. Felipe
had not brought his guitar; this was a serious mission. Susana
did not know of the music drumming in his heart that he would
never sing to anyone, his most beautiful *Almita Perdida*. It was
a short distance, as he had said, but the way was long to Susana.
Many times she halted, longing to turn back, but did not.
As they entered the valley of the Carmel River her shoes dragged
in the sand.

At the same moment they saw the robed figure like a gray
shadow in the entrance of the mission. He might have been
waiting for them. His salutation was grave and sweet. "*Amar a
Dios, niños.*"

They murmured in unison, "Love unto God," and Susana
followed the Franciscan into the dark interior.

Felipe, left to his own devices, wandered aimlessly about the
settlement. He peered into Serra's cabin, next to the church, the
door of which stood open. A moment he stood, sombrero in
hand, like one facing a shrine. It was a one-room cabin, built
of logs and thatched with tule like the mission—in fact, a monk's
cell, less than twelve feet square. The president's many cats
wandered in and out freely, for, like St. Francis, Serra was a
lover of animals. Felipe studied with respect the almost bare
room. The walls were empty of all but the crucifix and the

flagellum. The only furnishings were the rough pine table on which lay Serra's Latin Bible, a stool, and a narrow plank bed laced with rawhide.

Felipe crossed himself piously and wandered on. He found a dune comfortably cushioned with sea lavender and settled down to heal his anxiety for Susana in the surge of the water. His thoughts began rocking in rhythm with the waves, song crowded his throat, and presently words rose in the metrical rhythm of the sea. It was a forlorn little song Felipe sang while waiting for Susana, not at all like most of Felipe's making, but there it was, leaving his lips to meet the musical surge of the Pacific:

> "You of the city,
> Tenderly gracious,
> Why have you come
> To torment and absorb me?
> I who was simple,
> A countryman only,
> Who knew quiet fields
> And the silence of evenings,
> Now tremble with longing
> For streets you have traveled,
> For crowds and high buildings. . . ."

Felipe broke off, abashed. Susana was coming down the sloping beach from the mission. He stood up, marveling to see her so strong and at peace, and with an incandescence about her as of lighted candles. Whatever she had asked in the confessional, out of the depths of her being, had been answered.

He knew then the shadow that had been her second self was gone.

They had nothing to say as they walked back over the beach to Monterey. Without words they passed the tree where they had watched the departure of the butterflies, and the rocks where the seals still barked with the faces of Vengador. They walked on, each deep in thought.

Susana's mind churned with the never-to-be-forgotten meeting in the mission.

She had sickened with terror at that first glimpse of Serra in the shadowy entrance to the church. Felipe's presence steadied her.

Seemingly, Serra had been waiting; he had always known! What he had to say to Susana in that pioneer mission enfolded her for life in a compassion stronger than the world.

She would remember the sounds of her own weeping. "I wanted his death!"

"But you did not let him die. You forgave!"

And she would remember his gentleness. "Little Daughter, did you know our beloved leader St. Francis died blind, having lost his sight weeping tears of pity?"

Words were like torches, lighting the years ahead.

She would remember thinking, Only a saint's voice could hold such tenderness. She learned she had been right in believing pain to be as sacred as death. She had lacked the skill to explain this to Tía María. But to this humble monk with the unearthly power she could reveal that it was a child in a dying man to whom she had given her protection and even her love. Serra's last words solaced. "One who forgives is forgiven." And when he made the sign of blessing over her head, tears fell on her hands. Black places that had long been closed in her heart, opened, and the Susana who met Felipe outside the mission at Carmel was indeed Susana María de la Luz—Susana of the Light.

[3]

It took time to realize she was free. Her life had the stillness that follows tempest. The days at Monterey followed one after another, and no duties claimed her to time or the house. It was empty and soundless and clean.

Don Angel's hillside grave began showing the first jade-pale fronds of California poppies. Spring was almost over. Still the mornings were drizzling and cold, and not at all as the people from Mexico believed May should be.

On one of these unpleasant mornings a small figure in a patched gray robe limped across the roughly outlined square.

The straggling settlement of Monterey with its rows of flat-roofed cabins was not unlike the Petra where Serra had played as a child. Now he walked slowly, yielding to the pain in the always-open wound in his leg, but smiling his joyous smile at all he met. He carried great bundles under either arm, but lifted a hand to make the sign of the cross over a small boy playing in the sand.

"Can you direct me to the Widow Galván?"

The title sounded strange to Susana. The neighbors, who watched in silence as the Franciscan entered her cabin, saw him standing apart from her, for when not inside a church Serra was shy with women.

But his smile was friendly and his determination apparent. The customary, "Let us love God," was followed by a firm, "I am told you are a seamstress of merit."

He had brought a bolt of blue cloth and one of red. These he unrolled on the pine table Felipe had made for Susana. They were cut into small shirts and dresses.

"These are for my little naked angels at Carmel." The blue eyes behind the glasses twinkled. "The Indian children there dress as they might in Eden until we provide clothing. These I have cut out myself, and as you can see, the teachings of my order do not include dress design." He smiled drolly. "Also, I am not at ease with a needle."

Susana lifted the coarse garments, estimating the time required.

"They will be ready within the week, little Father."

"Good. I will come for them. And bring more, if I may!"

She found herself smiling.

After he left she wondered, Is his assignment intended to leave me no time in which to grieve for the death of Don Angel? No, for he knew she did not. To keep empty hands from mischief? Perhaps! She took up the work with a stirring of amusement, for he had even brought an iron needle and matching thread!

How practical he was, she thought, this wise, kind saint. She sat down to the sewing, and the first contingent of curious women arrived, with Tía María foremost in excited wonder. Tía María offered her services at once. Others volunteered, and the last days of May were given over to the project. Several Indian mothers came shyly to the cabin and learned the simple stitches under Susana's direction. So the first sewing group began in Monterey. Maguey needles flew and conversation flourished. Small children, colonial and native, were brought in to serve as models, for Serra's patterns were of his own making and cut in a way a small girl might for a doll. As he had said, and Susana re-

peated laughingly to her fellow-workers, the Franciscan teachings
did not include modern design. Susana fitted the first garments
and others brought her in time from Carmel by the pleased president to more graceful lines, and added small pockets and belts
and collars, and even small patches of the embroidery taught to
her in childhood by the convent nuns.

[4]

On the twenty-first of May, the beautiful empty harbor of
Monterey was graced by the miracle of sails. The appearance on
the bay of a ship seemed as unreal to the colonists as the
mirages that had startled them on the desert. It was the little
transport vessel *San Antonio*, first of three such ships to arrive
on their yearly voyage up the coast from San Blas, having left
there two months before, on March ninth. It brought badly
needed supplies for the Monterey Presidio, and would carry pine
lumber back to San Diego, where rebuilding was going on under
the direction of Governor Rivera.

The *San Antonio* brought nothing for the hungry and worried
San Franciscans. But it did bring word that a second ship, the
Príncipe, was on its way with more goods for Monterey, while
the third packet, the *San Carlos*, which had started at the same
time, would bring supplies for the San Franciscans!

This was great news, and the colonists were encouraged by
the almost immediate arrival of the *Príncipe* on the heels of the
San Antonio. But their own ship the *San Carlos*, where was
she? The three transports had left San Blas on the same day.

Captain Choquet of the *San Antonio* tried to reassure them.
"The *San Carlos* is a slower ship than mine."

They would not be comforted. The failure of St. Francis's
own vessel to arrive was just one more of the many tricks fate
was playing.

On May twenty-eighth, like a dazzling bolt out of the heavens,
an event raised their hopes to the heights again. Riding into
Monterey came a ragged and smiling caravan, and the stranded
ones gave frantic welcome to the San Francisco families Rivera
had ordered to remain at San Gabriel in the care of Sergeant

Grijalva. Now Grijalva proudly led the twelve soldiers with their families into the raw new colony at Monterey.

It was a tearful reunion, for the two divisions, left stranded at separate missions, had endured much. No one could stop talking. The new arrivals had been the last to see Anza and had waved him off in tears from San Gabriel. There were glowing reports of the former Widow Feliciana and her husband. But the greatest news was brought by Grijalva to Lieutenant Moraga. It was a letter from Anza, and Moraga read it with a grin he could not control to the reunited San Franciscans. At every sentence their cries of jubilation rent the foggy air, for the letter put an end to their long isolation.

Governor Rivera, that ogre, had relented!

It was not a gracious yielding. The man who was responsible for Anza's humiliation and many of Serra's woes, who had divided and delayed the San Franciscans and left them impoverished and helpless, had been forced to yield at last. He was consenting to the founding of San Francisco.

No one would ever know what brought about his change of policy, but then, no one ever understood Rivera. Had he waited until he was certain that his envied rival, Anza, had left California? Robbing the national hero of his greatest dream was Rivera's meanest triumph.

On the other hand, fear may have moved Rivera. Serra had been adamant in refusing to lift the edict of excommunication. The governor had suffered under the ban. He was being eyed askance as a moral outcast.

There was the added worry as to what might happen to his reputation in Mexico City, now that Anza was on his way there. What the country's leading hero had to say regarding Rivera would be heard with respect. Rivera recalled uneasily the many vicious letters he had written to the viceroy, attacking Anza and his colonists. Rivera may have cast a long look to his future.

He had been pondering this dilemma in his resentful mind when an order reached him at San Diego that even he dared not ignore. It came directly from the viceroy in Mexico City. It was a sharp command regarding the new establishment: "Get on with it."

Rivera's hand was forced. It was then he sent Sergeant Góngora to San Gabriel with orders that Sergeant Grijalva, in charge there of the deserted families, was to take them to rejoin those at Monterey. Grijalva rushed them off to Monterey before Rivera could change his mind.

Grijalva also brought explicit orders from Anza to Moraga. It was an underwriting of Rivera's order. Moraga was to take twenty of the soldiers and their families who had left Sonora with Anza, and the nonmilitary San Franciscans and their families. This reunited version of the San Francisco Expedition was to leave Monterey "at once" and proceed to the northern bay and found there the San Francisco Presidio on the site Anza had chosen.

Rivera had added one serious qualification. In one last spiteful gesture against Father Serra, Anza, and the San Francisco project, he had agreed to the founding of the fortress and no more.

Rivera's edict was final.

"The mission will have to wait."

The San Franciscans were ravaged by joy and dismay. How disappointed their beloved Anza would be when he learned their shared dream was being halved by Rivera! On the day of Grijalva's arrival Moraga told them that he was not taking the chance of Rivera's fickle mind changing again. As soon as they could get ready, he promised, he would lead them on to San Francisco.

The next day Moraga rode over the pine-crowned ridge to Carmel to give the report to Father Serra.

The president of missions rejoiced at the good news and was not dismayed by the bad. He had developed a certain skill in evading the wiles of Governor Rivera.

"So St. Francis has to wait for his mission?" he commented. "But he is a strong saint, and will not wait long. You will see, my son Moraga!"

And the two, planning, considering, decided that two of the friars from the Carmel Mission, Fra Francisco Palou and Fra Pedro Cambón, would accompany the San Franciscans, attend to their spiritual needs on the way, and remain with them while the founding of the military establishment was building.

"Then," Father Serra explained gently, "if and when the mission is built, they will be there!"

Moraga rode back contentedly to Monterey. He summoned the colonists.

"We start for San Francisco in mid-June. You have two weeks to get ready."

The order roused the colonists like a bugle summons. Monterey and Carmel fell into a frenzy of preparation. Tents were unrolled and aired and long-stored camping equipment unpacked. Everyone was at work. Susana was busily completing her sewing tasks assigned by Serra, turning over Don Angel's worn clothing to Indians she had made her friends, sorting over what poor goods remained to her. The army tent she had shared with Don Angel was needed elsewhere, for families had grown to greater size during the stay at Monterey. "You will travel with us," Tía María said firmly. "Now, you are of my children."

June

CHAPTER ELEVEN

[1]

The *San Carlos*, also known as the *Golden Fleece*, was a small three-masted frigate made formidable by swivel guns mounted on her deck. These bristled in defiance of any foreign captains who might be sailing along the California coast.

She had been running packet duty from San Blas to Monterey. Often she had fought her way north only to be driven back again and again by winds. Once she was forced back almost to Panama. And now, although this June weather seemed equable at Monterey, the pilgrims knew fierce storms and heavy winds out at sea, and in these, it was apparent, the little *San Carlos* was lost, perhaps forever.

There was nothing to be done but watch and pray for her arrival, for she carried the provisions for the settlement at San Francisco.

Then on June third a square of white showed on the bay, flanked by other, triangular sails, and she was there! The little *San Carlos* moved across the water in a slow and dignified advance, for she was heavily burdened with supplies for the San Franciscans who were gathered cheering on the shore, by none other than the Viceroy Bucareli. She also carried supplies for the Monterey Presidio. In a breath-taking moment she halted her stately progress to drop anchor. Captain Don Fernando Quiros and two chaplains came ashore in a small boat to be greeted formally and gratefully by Lieutenant Moraga in behalf of the excited San Franciscans.

For the next week the group was wildly busy, preparing to leave. Moraga oversaw the activities of the colonists while directing the unloading of the presidio goods from the *San Carlos* and replacing the space with supplies belonging to the San Franciscans. Moraga was shipping most of the San Franciscans' heavier properties by sea to save mule power. Included among these were churchly properties that had been brought by Father Font for the future mission. These were taken aboard because everyone believed with Father Serra that eventually a mission would be built for St. Francis.

Other of the emigrant supplies consisted of provisions, and farm and household material, such as blankets and iron tools, and great iron bean pots—the pilgrims could enjoy frijoles again—and the gifts Anza had chosen for the San Francisco Indians, who would hopefully be converted to Christianity and would assist in building the new settlement. Also aboard were bells to hang in the tower of the future mission, and bunting and Spanish flags to add color to the dedication ceremonies, and several cannons to roar out the triumph of a new Spanish settlement in the far west.

The little packet was soon loaded and ready to sail to meet the colonists, who were to march overland to their port of San Francisco.

But again, delay! The last-minute snag was due to the cannons that had been taken from the presidio at Monterey and were to serve the presidio at San Francisco. But the guns were military property and could not be released by anyone but the commandant of the Monterey Presidio, who of course was Governor Rivera. Early in June a letter had been rushed to Rivera from Moraga, but no answer came.

The *San Carlos* could not sail without his permission. The dread grew that Rivera would not only refuse the departure of the ship but also find some way of keeping the San Franciscans at Monterey.

Moraga decided to take no chances. He gave a final order to the San Franciscans.

"With or without the ship, we will set out on the seventeenth as planned!"

The expeditionary horses and cattle that had been grazing in the Carmel Valley were rounded up and brought to Monterey. Among them were the little mare, Seda, and the black gelding that had belonged to Don Angel.

Susana regarded the pair with dismay when they were brought

her by Felipe. Poor Major! His coat had not been touched by a currycomb since leaving Mexico.

As for Seda, the little mare was now as bulging as in the days when she had filled her belly with air to resist the cinch. She had grown astonishingly fat on the green hills of Carmel.

Felipe laughed at her appearance and said: "Now you are truly the toad-horse our friend Gil José named you!" Susana scowled at him.

Felipe's smile was as clear as the morning.

"Susana, do you not see your little mare is with foal?"

No, Susana had not known, nor did Seda, with head hanging and sides swollen, remember her hour in the sun with that fiery prince of steeds, Gil José's army stallion, Fuego! The desert elopement would bear fruit at San Francisco in a colt that would be Susana's last link with the soldier Gil José.

Felipe tactfully turned her attention to Major. "A good horse walks under this dusty rug." He fashioned a brush of chaparral twigs and began vigorously grooming the matted coat. The sensitive horse stood quivering but without moving, as if appreciative of the care being given. It was more than an hour before the tender sides shone and the long black mane and tail were freed of tangles and cockleburs.

Felipe stood back, brushing his dusty hands. "Anza himself would be proud to own this horse. He is worth a great deal. If you sell him you will be a rich woman."

Never! thought Susana quickly. She would not sell Major, who had been the only creature Don Angel had cared for, and who in turn had been faithful to the limit of his strength to Don Angel. She couldn't explain that or express her gratitude to Felipe, to his parents, and all they had meant to her on the long pilgrimage.

"Major is for you," she managed to say.

And when Felipe protested, Susana almost wept in her insistence that no one but Felipe must be permitted to ride Major.

[2]

They did not make the dramatic and colorful appearance they had upon leaving Mexico. The members of the Anza Second Expedition assembled for departure before the Monterey Presidio were fewer in number, both human and animal, and the uniforms of the soldiers and the clothing of the families were scant and travel-stained. And still, Lieutenant Moraga could survey his San Franciscans with pride, for they were the brave survivors of a tremendous undertaking.

In all, there were now only one hundred and fifty of the two hundred and forty men, women, and children who had set out from Tubac with Captain Anza.

With them went the mule train, free horses, and two hundred head of cattle. Among these were the eighty-six cows from Carmel that, as Father Serra and Moraga had planned, were "incorporated into those for the San Francisco presidio." For, as Serra had commented, blue eyes twinkling behind his glasses, a San Francisco mission would certainly be built in time, and when that happened mission cattle should be there!

"It was three in the afternoon when I set them in motion," Moraga would write in his diary. He led the line as the San Franciscans set off on their final march "from the presidio of Monterey to the port of San Francisco."

They were watched by those who were to remain at Monterey. They did not look back. They rode after Moraga, who had taken the place of their beloved Anza, singing the "*Olabado*" with Fathers Palou and Cambón, who had taken over their spiritual leadership from Father Font.

Felipe sat Don Angel's former gelding with a dignity worthy of his mount. Even his mother gave grudging admiration. "You are not as handsome as Captain Anza, my Son." It was the closest her caustic tongue could come to a compliment.

Major had been polished with a rubbing cloth. His head was high, and his well-brushed mane and tail swung free. The heavy Spanish saddle and bridle had been oiled and rubbed by Felipe, and the silver *conchos* shone. Major was once more a cherished mount. He paid hovering attention to his unwieldy companion Seda, so broad now in body that Susana rode as comfortably as in a palanquin. There would be times when the little mare had difficulty in breathing, and then Susana would walk with Tía María, chattering beside her and leading her mule.

The two friends would remember later how many miles, now

and previously, they had walked beside the procession, enjoying the scenery and their conversation more when on foot than in the saddle.

The advance was leisurely. There were more pregnant women than before, and months of nonriding had left thighs tender to the saddle. Why hurry? Time was no longer of importance. The San Francisco port would wait for them, and on this journey up the coast they would meet with no Indian ambush, no dearth of water or forage for the beasts.

Moraga and the officers rode with the caravan all that first day, turning back at the Salinas River, to complete the loading of the *San Carlos*. Afterward Moraga would rejoin the company.

The San Franciscans raised their tents for the night on the banks of the river as they had on so many rivers along the way. The next morning they forded the Salinas and headed in a straggling line over the Salinas Valley.

It took them ten days to ride from Monterey to San Francisco. They threaded arroyos and valleys and crossed rivers. The coast range (the Santa Cruz Mountains) marched with them as a western protection against the sea.

They were following in the footsteps of Anza. This was the route he had taken on his way to explore the bay of San Francisco. They knew now, as he had learned, that California wore many faces. They rode through dry and green places, through desertlike patches, past groves of great limbed oaks and sycamores. They marched across valleys, penetrated arroyos, crossed shallow rivers, and the gravel beds of creeks dry with summer. California was unwinding for them like a pictorial scroll, livened with the dark faces of Indians who left their brush huts in the valleys to watch the procession ride by. There people showed astonishment at the cows, which they had never seen. They were gentle Indians, unfriendly, unused to effort.

On the second day the San Franciscans camped at Las Llagas, where these people who had once been children of the sun suffered in a heat more intense than any they had experienced since leaving the desert. There Moraga caught up with them. He reported that he had left the *San Carlos* fully laded and ready to sail on Monterey Bay, but up to the minute of his leaving no word had come from Governor Rivera.

He started them early the next morning. After crossing the Pájaro River they came upon a large herd of elk with great branching antlers. Roasted meat revived palates dulled by a steady diet of boiled corn and beans.

It was good to escape the heat, to ride on in the shadow of foothills, past the site of San Juan Bautista, past the Arroyo de San José Cupertino, under the tall redwood that had been measured by Father Font and named the Palo Alto, along the Río de San Francisquito and through the Arroyo de San Mateo, where there were bear and more elk. Then it was an easy ride to the Arroyo de San Francisco, and from there, the next morning, over hills lapping a bay so magnificent it left them mute, to the site Anza had chosen.

They reached it at eleven in the morning of June twenty-seventh, 1776. Journey's end, the place they would not leave again, was the iris-fringed lagoon Anza had chosen for them and named Laguna Dolores.

[3]

The lagoon was rimmed with tules and blue iris, and its waters were roiled by flocks of wild ducks. The hills in the morning light were purple and gold and blue with summer bloom. There were many trees, oak and red-limbed manzanita and pine. The hungry San Franciscans glimpsed antelope and deer grazing under the trees. Scattered over the endless hills were Indian brush huts that clung like limpets against the powerful wind sweeping in from the sea.

The San Franciscans' dazzled eyes followed the far reaches of the bay below them. A bay? This port of St. Francis's set with islands was more like an inland sea! As far as they could see, the southeastern expanse of water pushed blue fingers between golden hills. The bay was a great jewel carved in the shape of a hand that left its imprint deep in the hills.

This was their world, untouched and new! No fence marred the lands. No sail disturbed the splendid stretches of water.

There was the sharp, salt fragrance of the sea, and the scents of mint and wild roses and strawberries.

Susana looked over the blue lagoon to a matchless world. She felt a stab of pity for Gil José, who had seen and loved this land and been banished from all hope of seeing it again by her will.

She wondered then, as she had before, if her appeal to Anza had been wrong. But the pang of remembering was not as deep as before. The gallant figure of Gil José was diminishing, riding farther away from this place of miraculous beauty.

The San Franciscans would understand the reason their bay had managed to remain a mystery for centuries when they learned of the way the fog could blanket its narrow entry (the Golden Gate) hiding it from any vessel sailing past, like a blanket hung over a door.

Back in 1595 a Spanish galleon commanded by Sebastián Rodrigues Cermeno had been wrecked on the California coast. He and other survivors returned to civilization with tantalizing reports of a magnificent bay. So the legend began.

Drake and Shelvocke, for England, and Spanish galleon commanders ranged the Pacific coast hunting the mysterious party. It was not seen again until 1769, the year Serra arrived in California and the missions began. Then Sergeant José Francisco de Ortega, stationed at newly founded San Diego but hunting in the north, crossed a series of hills and found himself staring down at an expanse of water so tremendous that he brought back confusing reports. Had it been a bay, an inlet, a small sea? He could not be sure. He could find no words to describe its beauty, nor did any of the others who had glimpsed it. And like the others, he could not point out the place where it lay.

It was then that Anza and Serra knew the mystery bay was no legend but existed, and although still uncertain as to what it was, or where it was, they planned a mission to be built on its shores.

Five years after Ortega's discovery, in 1774, the San Franciscans' own ship, the little packet *San Carlos*, had set out to find the legendary port. For nine days the little ship cruised the fog-shrouded California coast, buffeted to and fro by heavy winds, while captain and crew prayed to St. Francis to lift the fog and reveal the long-hidden secret of his lost bay.

And on the ninth day, miracle within miracle, the fog wall fell before the golden portals, and the San Franciscans' *San Carlos* had been the first ship to sail into the legendary harbor of St. Francis.

Moraga, a worthy inheritor of Anza's dream, gave the colonists no time in which to admire their new setting.

No sooner were the tents set up around the lagoon than he had the men cutting trees for their future permanent homes, and this on the very day of their arrival! The women unpacked household wares and began the preparation of their first San Francisco supper. It was their usual poor fare of corn meal and beans, but a delightful surprise came from their new neighbors, the Indians, who came swarming over the hills to greet the new-comers, wearing broad smiles and very little else. They were not a handsome people, but they were very friendly. The San Franciscans could not have had better neighbors. While the tents were raised the Indians made their friendliness apparent with gifts of edible seeds, and black mussels and other delicious shellfish from the bay.

The Indian men rushed whooping to the lagoon, where the pilgrims had noticed rafts made of tules floating on the water. Manning these, they pushed off over the lake, while releasing clouds of arrows into the flocks of wild duck. They brought back dozens of birds, and the San Franciscans, who so often had gone to bed hungry, spent their first night beside their lagoon with stomachs filled with roast duck.

The canvas village on the Laguna Dolores was exactly like all the others the San Franciscans had raised along the past many hundred miles. Here they would await the arrival of the *San Carlos*, for only then could the actual work of the founding of San Francisco begin. They settled down on that day of arrival as they had in so many other strange, new places, only this place was their own.

Susana felt this strongly on the afternoon of that day as she carried an armful of the crisp blue iris into the tent of the Perea family, of which she had become a member. Many families had been compelled to share tents on the pilgrimage, and did so with a scrupulous propriety, for these passionate and outspoken people were notable for their modesty. She arranged the flowers in ollas. They brightened the stained canvas walls.

Felipe carried her portmanteau into the tent and laid it on the wall of saddlebags and Tía María's packages of seeds and saplings with which, each night, he gave privacy to Susana's corner. She lifted the lid and looked down on the trunk's contents with a whimsical look.

"You are smiling," Felipe accused. He was weary, having spent the afternoon hewing logs to Moraga's orders, but his tone was one of amusement. "What secrets do you keep from me, Susana?"

"I am thinking." She spoke thoughtfully. "What we unpack now in these tents we will carry into our homes when we build them. We will never again pack our saddlebags and portmanteaus."

"That is true." And, surprisingly, each spoke with regret for the long adventure ended. Permanency was sweet, but there was a shared excitement in starting anew on each morning, never knowing how far they would ride or where they would be when night fell.

Their eyes met, luminous with understanding.

[4]

Only a few days were left of this momentous June, and the San Franciscans filled each day with activity.

Since their provisions were dangerously low, and there was no sign of the *San Carlos*, Moraga sent hunting parties out after elk. The huge beasts had been made wary by Indian arrows, and skillfully evaded the musket-bearing soldiers. Moraga did what he had been forced to do during the delays at San Gabriel and Monterey. Once more, he put his hungry families on half rations.

He worried about his charges in other ways. The soldiers' uniforms were worn out and all other clothing was in rags. The emigrants were almost as naked as the Indians. The savage San Francisco winds slashed like knives through fog that rolled in each morning over the many hills. Moraga sent a pack train of fifteen mules back to Monterey with a letter begging for food and clothing for his people.

Three times Moraga would be forced to send the pack train to Monterey begging for supplies to keep the founders of San Francisco alive. Each time Nicolás Perea rode with the train, but none of these trips brought anxiety to Tía María, who had ridden the distance herself and knew the way was safe.

Still there was anxiety in the tent village of Dolores, for the question became more demanding day by day: What had happened to the *San Carlos?* Until it came, with the goods needed to begin the new settlement, no actual building could begin.

Moraga disliked delays and refused to accept defeat. The day after their arrival, June twenty-eighth, was packed with action. He led a party on a brief trip of exploration to a "white cliff" over the bay (Fort Point) overlooking the narrow opening into the Pacific. It was sealed in on either side by the hills that came down in slanted lines of purple and blue, but when the sun flashed through the fog their smooth slopes turned to gold.

This promontory was the site for the future presidio that had been chosen by Anza and Father Font. It met with equal approval from Moraga and Father Palou.

Riding back to Dolores, Moraga pondered the situation. Rivera's orders had been explicit. "The presidio is to be built at once. A mission must not be built."

But, Moraga argued, the mission had been authorized by the viceroy! And Rivera was far away, at San Diego. Also, a presidio was not an immediate necessity in this place where all the Indians were friendly.

Moraga not only disliked Governor Rivera; he thought him insane. His loyalty was to Anza and Father Serra. The lieutenant reached the lagoon, and, with the enthusiastic agreement of Fathers Cambón and Palou, he set every man and woman in the colony to work cutting boughs, saplings, and tule. The altar was set up in the open, and over it willing hands raised a brushwood *enramada.* Such rustic booths served as many of the first California missions.

It was only an open shed, but it was St. Francis's chapel and the first building constructed on the site of the future San Francisco.

Moraga, tongue in cheek, excused its building: "This is not a permanent structure."

His pilgrims were a religious group, he argued, and entitled to hold services in the open air!

On the next day, which was June twenty-ninth and the feast day of Sts. Peter and Paul, a congregation of thin and shivering worshipers heard Father Palou sing the first Mass in the rustic shrine dedicated to Nuestra Señora de Los Dolores (Our Lady of the Sorrows), which was the seedling Mission of St. Francis of Assisi, and, in time, be known to us as Mission Dolores.

In this way, San Francisco began.

July

CHAPTER TWELVE

[1]

The foggy month of July was spent by the San Franciscans in their tents on the Laguna de los Dolores. The men continued to cut logs for the construction work that would start when the *San Carlos* came. Stacks of logs mounted around the lake, and the concern of the colonists grew. Where was their missing transport?

Moraga made another of his masterly decisions. They would not wait to begin work on the presidio! He and some of the soldiers moved to the point, threw up tule huts as shelter against the fog and wind, and began building. The families stayed in the lake camp in charge of Fathers Palou and Cambón.

At both sites anxious watch was kept for the *San Carlos*. A small chapel rose at the presidio site where the soldiers prayed each day for the safety of the ship. At Dolores, Mass was sung daily before the altar under the rustic shed. St. Francis was petitioned daily at both places. Still the suspicion grew that the little ship with all the colonists' fortunes aboard was lying somewhere out on the floor of the Pacific.

Meantime the log piles continued to mount and the workers at both places were as busy as ants preparing for winter.

Moraga would not permit discouragement. "As soon as the *San Carlos* arrives we will start the mission, with or without the permission of Governor Rivera."

Fathers Palou and Cambón began drawing plans for the mission-to-be.

Everyone felt better now that a decision had been made. Everyone had work to do. Even the children helped cut tules around the lagoon. Susana and Tía María and the other women bound the reeds into thatch for future roofs. They stripped manzanita of its thin reddish bark and wove strips into altar cloths for the rustic altar, suspecting that all the churchly paraphernalia from Mexico had gone down somewhere in the Pacific.

There was no shortage of labor. The Indians were eager to learn white man's ways and be of service. Indians served as enthusiastic guides on the trips of exploration Moraga made in the vicinity of the bay. The wild game the natives were delighted to exchange for small supplies of beads was a welcome supplement to the colony's diminishing supply of corn and beans.

Tía María and Susana found time to indulge in the exploring trips they had enjoyed since their friendship began.

They climbed hills and probed valleys near the mission, gathering the sweet, powdery berries of the manzanita and the tiny fragrant strawberries that jeweled the dunes. They gathered armfuls of the pungent mint they had noted on the day of arrival. This trailing vine was the *yerba buena* (good herb) that, steeped into a medicinal tea, helped many a colonist over late summer colds.

Many other useful herbs and plants grew on San Francisco's still uncounted hills. Tía María taught Susana these, by name, taste, touch, or smell. She told Susana the individual values, qualities, and dangers of these dried herbs, pods, leaves, roots, and strips of bark.

If, at such times, Felipe chanced to wander into the tent, Tía María would stop speaking and glare at her son until he left.

Susana knew that she was being paid a singular honor. She protested.

"All this you are teaching me, Tía María, are they things I should know? You have said such knowledge is handed down among your people from mother to daughter. What right have I to know such things?"

Tía María's look was unfathomable.

"I have taught these to my first-born daughter in Sinaloa. She holds secrets that will be held by her first-born daughter and her daughter's first-born. That has always been our way. But here in this new California only I know of such matters, and here they should be known. I have no daughter with me, and such things must not be spoken to men, not even to one's only remaining son. And now certain signs have been given me—"

"No!" Susana cried out. In a flash of revelation she glimpsed the emptiness of a world without Tía María. Now she saw with panic the way the smooth, dark cheeks were thinned by months of privation, and the flashes of silver in the short black hair. "Nothing must ever happen to you, Tía María. You are good and strong. . . ."

The inscrutable black eyes warmed. "My goodness will be judged in paradise, my little friend. As for my strength, you may notice I puff on these hills as noisily as your mare Seda, who is about to present you with a colt. But what I know," the dark eyes searched for understanding, "cannot go with me. Still they are of importance and must be remembered. So all that is good and all that is bad in these things I must teach you, that you may know what to use and what to avoid, and you must hold to yourself these secrets that are centuries old, and in time, when you are old, hand them over to another."

Susana could not speak.

Tía María concluded in simple words, "You, I have had reason to trust."

Those who loved Tía María could not blind their eyes to the fact that she was aging rapidly, as Indian women often age. She who had been able to impress Captain Anza and Father Font with her medical wisdom had the respect of all her fellow colonists. The time would come when, if there was illness or accident or a child to be born on the Laguna de los Dolores, a day or night call would be sent for Susana.

But this was in the future.

The present was filled with activity and anxiety, and July was ending, and the *San Carlos* was still missing. Then, with the end of the month, Moraga's patience ended.

[2]

"There is no use in waiting any longer for the ship," Moraga decided. "We will start work on the mission."

On the first of August the colonists began to build a permanent mission at Dolores. The available materials were mud and wood and willing hearts. Men and women worked side by side, raising the log walls and plastering them with clay patted into place with their hands.

The mission was no modest affair as the Franciscan fathers planned it. St. Francis's church would be fifty-four feet long! Father Serra and Anza had pictured this mission as the supreme pearl in California's rosary of missions, and those who worked on its building kept their dream in mind.

It was as well that Moraga had decided not to wait for the arrival of the *San Carlos*. The packet had left Monterey in July. It did not arrive in the port of San Francisco until August eighteenth, and then what a tale those on board had to tell!

The brave little ship had sailed from Monterey Bay out into the open Pacific, where, although it was the height of summer, it was assailed by savage winds slashing down out of the north. The *San Carlos* was driven farther out to sea, then pushed south, below Monterey Bay, and almost to San Diego. It struggled up the coast again only to meet again with storms that drove it past the San Francisco entrance and northward on to Point Reyes.

For weeks the *San Carlos* fought for survival. It reached the fog-locked entrance to San Francisco Bay again and again only to be driven past by heavy winds. One morning the captain and crew prayed together to St. Francis that they be permitted to enter his port.

And again, as before, the winds sank and the fog banks parted, and the *San Carlos* was able to drop anchor by night before the entrance. Early in the next afternoon, on the eighteenth of August, it struggled into the bay and like a gull with tired gray wings came to rest against the island, notable for its pelicans (and hence named Alcatraz).

The ship had sailed two thousand miles in making the brief run between Monterey and San Francisco Bay!

Jubilant shouts of "*Viva!*" hailed the small boat from the *San Carlos* as it came ashore under the white cliff.

The San Franciscans gave an emotional welcome to friends they had seen last at Monterey, Captain Quiros and his two pilots and the ship's chaplain, Father José Nocedal. The newcomers might have expected to rest after their ordeal by sea. But no, they were rushed off at once to inspect the site of the presidio and then to Dolores to survey conditions there. When they had approved both spots First Pilot Don José Canizares was set to work drawing up plans for the presidio, which would include a warehouse, guardhouse, and homes for the soldiers' families.

Captain Quiros gave full support to the exuberant Moraga. He detailed the two carpenters from the *San Carlos* to work with the San Franciscans. A storm of activity started at both sites, and two villages sprang up like mushrooms after rain.

To the colonists, who had suffered so many delays and frustrations, the rapidity with which their plans were now racing to conclusion seemed incredible. In another month the mission's foundations were laid and its walls were rising, while at the presidio there were the chapel and a warehouse. St. Francis's fortress, which would guard his mission, was now in existence. Moraga and the priests began laying plans for the formal dedication of both presidio and mission.

September seventeenth is the feast day of the stigmata of St. Francis and the date chosen for the dedication of the presidio. One year before in September, the San Francisco Expedition had wound its way out of Horcasitas and headed for an unknown world.

On this day all remaining of this original expedition, the one hundred and fifty San Franciscans, their priests, and Lieutenant Moraga, together with Captain Quiros and all the crew from the *San Carlos* (save for a few left on deck to man the guns), and a large assemblage of naked Indians, convened before the new chapel on the white cliff for the formal dedication of the Presidio of San Francisco.

The ceremony of formal possession was followed by the solemn Mass of dedication. The little church filled with worshipers. Then bells pealed and muskets roared, echoed by the thunder of the swivel guns from the little ship anchored on the bay, so terrifying the poor Indians that they fled and were not seen again "for many days." Some did not return until December.

They realized then that if everyone worked, and to the limit of his strength, the mission might be finished in time for the celebration of St. Francis's own feast day, which was the fourth of October!

They knew that it was an impossible undertaking. But also, they knew, it would be done.

The day after the presidio celebration everyone was back at work and more industriously than before. Now that the warehouse was finished, the unloading of the *San Carlos* began.

All the rest of that summer, soldiers, sailors, and civilians worked together at the two settlements. Paths deepened between the point and lagoon. The men worked in teams, with the women helping to handle the tule thatches and to fill the log crevices with wet adobe. A sense of joyous haste drove everyone.

October came, searing the tule blades and bringing notes of yellow and bronze to the hills. The two frontier villages were finished, and most of the big buildings. All were of the same materials and the same plan, of logs plastered with mud, and with flat roofs, Spanish style, thatched with tule. The four largest structures were the commandant's house and the warehouse at the presidio, and the two churches. Of these Dolores was the largest and handsomest.

St. Francis's day was nearing and his mission was still unfinished. All hands turned to work on the large building rising over the manzanita. The people worked with a dedication that would have brought tears to the eyes of the Franciscan Junípero Serra.

Felipe and Susana worked as a team in the interior of the mission. Felipe brought baskets of mud from the lagoon and helped Susana spread the mixture over the log walls. The empty church was damp and very cold, and their hands stiffened. Susana shook the dripping ooze from her fingers and stood back to survey the firm imprint of her hand on the wall.

Felipe smiled. "You leave your mark! Your handprint will be there forever, and all who come to this church will remember Susana."

"They will not know my name," she said thoughtfully.

"What difference! As my mother says, and too often, it is the planting that matters, and not the planter."

And with everyone working together in this companionable and cheerful fashion the mission was completed by the eve of the feast day of St. Francis.

Moraga was away on one of his many exploring trips around the bay, so the actual celebration was postponed until his return. Father Palou blessed the mission on St. Francis's eve, but on the day itself only a Mass was sung.

Then Moraga was back, jubilant with accounts of rivers and lakes and bays branching out of the "harbor of harbors." He reported to the colonists, and later to the viceroy, "There is no end to this California!"

The ceremony of taking formal possession of the mission took place on October ninth.

The San Franciscans looked with awe on the mission. Their own hands had built this edifice that seemed to them more majestic than any of the remembered churches of Mexico, and more splendid to Susana than the great cathedral in Mexico City. It and the houses were draped with bright-colored bunting. Over the tule roofs the royal colors of Spain snapped in the fierce wind.

The dedication Mass was sung by four priests. Strong men lifted the framed image of the saint to their shoulders and carried it slowly into the church, followed by a solemn, chanting procession of colonists, soldiers, and sailors, with even the small children chanting or attempting to follow the words of the "Te Deum Laudamus."

Then Father Serra's sweet-toned bells began sounding the news that all this land and its new settlements belonged to God and King Carlos Three.

The hearts of the worshipers pounded to cannon fire. A fierce pride crept into the reverent words of thanksgiving. The thunder of the guns was the voice of their newly born San Francisco.

Now let the English prowl this coast! Let Russia dare try to colonize California! Spanish power will answer through our fine new guns!

As the worshipers filed slowly out of the church, Susana drew her *rebozo* over her face to hide the joyous tears. She saw that many of the San Franciscans were weeping. Even the eyes of Nicolás Perea were damp. Susana wondered briefly who felt most deeply, one who concealed, like the quiet man Perea, or Tía María, whose dark round face revealed every passing emotion, or Felipe, who translated every experience into song. The thought passed briefly. She looked around at the others leaving the mission, all grown familiar, and each for one reason or another dear to Susana. As Tía María had said at the beginning of the pilgrimage, the San Franciscans were as one family.

The scent of barbecue met nostrils still scenting the sweetness of incense. Two beeves that had roasted through the preceding night were being lifted from their smoking pits by the lagoon. Tears and reverence gave way before the pots of chile-seasoned beans and corn cooked in many ways that supplemented the fiesta.

The celebrants did not notice the growing dark or the way the fog moved in like a bannered army from the sea. It rose like a parchment scroll, concealing the bay, the hills, the tips of oaks and pines.

Susana sat with her plate balanced on her knees, transfixed by a vision and a voice. She heard again Father Font, saying: "We will build another city as beautiful as Mexico!"

In that moment, she saw in her mind a city antique and splendid, laced by waterways, and in the future another, equally beautiful, lying on these many hills over the branching expanses of dark water.

The frontier mission over the lagoon would grow into one of the leading mission settlements in the West, then into a village known as Yerba Buena for the good herb cherished by Tía María, and lastly into the city that would be known as San Francisco.

For a moment, Susana was as certain of this as Tía María had been the many times she had glimpsed incidents in the future.

"Your eyes! They stare into the fog!" This was Felipe, who chanced to be seated beside Susana. "What are you seeing, Susana?"

She could share the rapture of the dream with Felipe.

"I was thinking of Father Font. . . ."

[3]

Through the end of that summer of 1776, and into the fall, the *San Carlos* remained at rest on the bay. It did not leave until October twenty-first, and during that time the sailors continued to help the busy San Franciscans. The mission settlement continued to grow, unknown (it was hoped) to the villainous Rivera.

Everyone had work of his or her own. There was plowing to be done in preparation for the spring planting, and the breeding of cattle to be attended. The women made clothing from the bales of cloth brought by the *San Carlos*. Susana, with Tía María's aid, began the planting of a garden and assisted the other women with their sewing.

As the demand for lumber subsided, Felipe Perea laid down his ax and unpacked his shoemaker's tools. His bundles of raw hides were unwelcome in the home of his mother, and Felipe presently occupied a small shop near the mission. Here he cut leather and stitched, and was always willing to put down his awl in favor of his guitar. The shop became a popular meeting place.

Life ran evenly enough after the *San Carlos* left, but it could never be humdrum for these people. Late in November they had a surprise visit from Governor Rivera.

The bearded politician was suddenly in their midst, swaggering about with his customary arrogance, and peering with his bird's-eye look about the new village. The mission drew his attention. The San Franciscans watched with anxious hearts. They had dreaded his wrath when he learned the mission had been built in defiance of his orders. Now he confused them more than ever. The unpredictable commandant wagged his head. "I'm glad of it," was all he had to say about the founding of the Mission Dolores.

Then, as suddenly as he had appeared, he was gone. The colonists breathed normally again.

"Who knows what to think of this Rivera?" demanded Tía María. "Has anyone ever known of such a man?"

The San Franciscans would never forget those who had first led them in their great adventure. They heard reports from time to time of Father Font, living out his long and serviceable life in Sonora as an honored member of the Mexican priesthood. They never wholly lost touch with Anza. These who had wept when their captain had been forced to leave them took pride as one honor after another was given him. Rivera had not been able to dim the luster of their captain's fame.

The colonists would learn, much later, that on the first day of June, the very day they had obeyed their banished leader's final order and set out on their last march from Monterey to San Francisco, Anza had at last reached his Horcasitas home. They rejoiced in retrospect for that gala return, the meeting with his beloved Doña Ana, the fiesta he and she gave their friends, and the formal dinner given in his honor by Governor Crespi. They pictured the way his worn but handsome features, ravaged by his charges' many problems and sufferings, would be relaxing under the love shown him in Sonora.

They heard that the king in Spain knew the importance of Anza. In recognition of his achievement as explorer, peacemaker, and conqueror, and his successful leading of the San Francisco Expedition, Anza was made governor of the entire Southwest. His long life was lived out in distinction and glory.

And his enemy, Governor Rivera?

The San Franciscans would learn in time of his ending. It was as strange and violent as his life. Returning to Mexico in 1781, he reached the Colorado, where the once friendly Yumas promptly massacred him.

Father Serra was unable to pay his first visit to the northern mission until a year after its founding. Despite his increasing lameness he walked all the way from Carmel. Word of his arrival raced between the lagoon and the point, and all the colonists hurried to welcome him to the mission village. Susana was among those who ran to meet him. She was shocked by the change in the evangelist.

At this time Father Serra was sixty-four years old, but suffering had aged and attenuated the body of the priest. Only the wraith of the man remained. The blue eyes were faded and sunken under the spectacles, but they still blazed with happiness as Serra held out his arms in blessing to these people who were the children of his beloved St. Francis.

They too had changed. They looked bronzed and healthy and assured. None of them knew the pangs of hunger now. None went in rags. They wore cotton dresses or shirts and trousers made by the women, and many walked in shoes made for them by Felipe Perea.

The gentle blue gaze met the eyes of Susana. Serra was smiling.

She went to him without fear. How many lives had she lived since their first meeting before the church of San Fernando? The blue eyes missed nothing. The Franciscan noticed the radiance of Susana. He noticed that the broad gold Galván ring on her hand had been replaced by a simple ring such as most of the women wore, one beaten by hand from Mexican silver. He saw the strong, dark hand that closed protectively over Susana's in a gesture that promised safety against all that had threatened or would ever threaten her.

The eyes that met his were limpid. A woman who stands beside the man she loves does not question.

The Franciscan had only to look at the silver ring to understand. To the young woman who faced him, glowing with life, it seemed that the priest had always understood all that had happened to Susana.

There was a twinkle in the dimming blue eyes as Serra turned to the proud young man beside Susana.

"And you, my son Felipe?" he asked, kindly.